Fanie Fourie's Lobola

Nape 'a Motana

UNIVERSITY OF KWAZULU-NATAL PRESS

Published in 2007 by University of KwaZulu-Natal Press
Private Bag X01
Scottsville 3209
South Africa
Email: books@ukzn.ac.za
Website: www.ukznpress.co.za

© Nape 'a Motana 2007

ISBN 13: 978-1-86914-103-5

All rights reserved. No part of this publication may be reproduced or transmitted in any form or by any means, electronic or mechanical, including photocopying, recording or any information storage and retrieval system, without prior permission in writing from University of KwaZulu-Natal Press.

Editor: Elana Bregin
Layout and design: Rock Bottom Design
Cover design: Flying Ant Designs
             Sebastien Quevauvilliers

Printed and bound by Pinetown Printers.

Acknowledgements

Thank you to Maureen Gxoyiya and Johan Heyns for contributing some useful suggestions when the story was still in the form of a feature-film script, generously sponsored by the then Department of Arts, Culture, Science and Technology, whose 'hands, legs and face' were in the person of Lindi Ndebele.

Thank you to the readers of my earlier novel draft, Natalie Mnisi, Ingrid Zinde and Reboile Motswasele, whose comments and corrections were so useful.

I cannot forget to thank you, my niece, my brother's daughter, Mmamoraka Motana, for teaching me the wedding song, *Mmamosetsana* ('The girl's [bride's] mother').

Thanks too, African composers, for blessing generations with these classic celebratory folklore songs, some of which I have adapted slightly.

To a few publishers who shall remain unnamed, for giving me some rejection letters, which became a blessing when I was compelled to dig harder and deeper in search of the literary silver, gold and diamonds!

To my family who had to bear with me when the pressure of working on the project made me less than a prize-winning husband and father. My grown-up daughters, Mmasello and Thabang have consistently been appreciative and supportive of my talent. *Ke a leboga makgarebe* – thank you girls!

I am purposefully thanking my publisher and editor last because *Mojamorago ke kgoši* – 'He who eats last is a king'! Let thanks that can fill a 40-litre *mmadisepe* – three-legged cast-iron pot – be directed to UKZN Press for agreeing to be my midwife, enthusiastic that my story deserved to see the literary light of day.

To my editor, Elana Bregin, I say *ngiyabonga dadewethu* – thank you sister, for your industriousness, warmth, respect and sensitivity, which have always stretched me towards perfection. Thank you for being a no-nonsense quality controller, determined to see a better product hitting the market!

Last, but significantly not least, I should like to thank *Ramatlaohle-Makgonatšohle*, my Creator, who has been my source of health, strength and wisdom! Hallelujah!

♥ To my wife, Sibongile and my sons, Ramaswaile and Bafana-Bafana, who will, through this product of the sweat of my brow, understand why I had to spend many hours pecking away at the computer keyboard; who will, as a result, appreciate that their sacrifice has been worthwhile! ♥

Pronunciation Guide

Sepedi can be a tricky language to pronounce for those who are not familiar with it. The following guide may be helpful, using a few sample words from the glossary on page 321. Some isiZulu and Afrikaans words have also been included:

Agee	ah-gay (guttural 'g', stress on 'gay')
Aowaa	ah-oh-wah (syllables run together; stress on 'ah' and 'wah')
Buti	bootee (stress on 'boo')
Chisa	chee-sah (stress on 'chee')
Dankie	dung-key (stress on 'dung')
Die volk	dee falk (Afrikaans)
Dumela	doo-meh-lah (stress on 'meh')
Hao	how-ooh
Hee-banna	hay-bah-nn-ah (stress on 'hay' and 'nn')
Iu-iu-iu	ee-oo-ee-oo (stress on 'ee')
Ja	yaa (Afrikaans)
Kgoromente	goh-roh-men-tay (guttural 'g' stress on 'men')
Kgoši	go-shee (stress on guttural 'g')
Kudu	koo-doo (stress on 'doo')
Meisie	may-see (stress on 'may') (Afrikaans)
Muti	moo-tee (stress on 'tee') (isiZulu)
Nê	neh ('e' as in 'egg') (Afrikaans)
Ngwetši	'ngway-tjee (evenly stressed, 'ng' is soft as in 'sing')
Palakata	pah-lah-ka-ta (evenly stressed)
Ruri	roo-ree (stress on 'roo')
Sangoma	sung-gor-mah (stress on 'sung') (isiZulu)
Šatee	shah-tay (stress on 'shah')

1

The man stepped into the doctor's surgery, puffing on a cigarette. The sign on the door said, '*Ngaka*' – 'Surgery'. A young woman in nurse's uniform stood behind the counter and surveyed him quizzically. She appeared somewhat confused by the sight of him. He pretended not to notice her astonishment. Recovering, she pointed smilingly to a large black-and-red 'NO SMOKING' sign on the wall. Apologising, the man put out the smouldering end of his cigarette between his moistened index finger and thumb and threw the butt into a bin.

'Just a minute please,' the nurse said, fixing her gaze on the open appointment diary in front of her; aided by a pencil in her right hand she ticked at something on the page. She guessed, rightly, that he was the one who had called previously to enquire about an appointment. She had assumed at the time that he was enquiring on someone else's behalf. Catching him in the act of eyeing her with frank interest, the nurse smiled.

'You are very early. Dr Makgabo will only be in at 9.30.'

'That's okay. I'll wait,' the man replied.

The open admiration of his stare was making her uncomfortable. But what could she, child of Bakone do? To be feasted on by desiring male eyes had become the shadow on her work.

The nurse asked the man if he was coming to the surgery for the first time; he answered in the affirmative. As he spoke, she unconsciously craned her neck backwards a little, clearly repelled by the tobacco smell of his breath. He apologised for the second time. With a nod and a smile, she handed him a new patient's form to fill out. She was about to explain something when a whistling sound interrupted her.

'Excuse me a moment.' The nurse flashed a polite smile and hurried into a room at the back to switch off the boiling kettle. It was one of the old kind that did not have an automatic shut-off mechanism.

The man watched her go and then return, his interest in her patently revealed. A thought crossed his mind: *Oh my, what a lovely chick!* A beauty she was indeed!

She showed him which parts of the form to complete and he began to fill in the details required. Handing the completed form back to her, he asked what her name was.

'Dimakatjo,' she told him; the word rang like music in his ears.

'And you are Fanie Fourie?'

'Yes.'

He strolled over to the row of plastic chairs against the wall, sat down on the first one and picked up a glossy magazine, featuring beautiful and successful black women, from the pile on the small table beside him. As the nurse checked through his form his hungry eyes had an opportunity to feast on her coffee-coloured face; this beauty whom the gods of Afrika had undoubtedly blessed with splendid dimples, cheeks smooth enough to compete with a day-old infant's skin, large eyes skilfully made up to enhance the deep brown of the irises, and a charming hairstyle of extended plaits that were divided by several neat, tight 'ant paths', starting from the front just above her forehead and stretching to the back of her head.

She looked up briefly to tell him that the form was 'all okay', and his ears savoured the warm treasure of her vocal chords. His sideways glance swept over her face as she transferred some of the information from the form onto a new patient's card. When she raised her gaze again, Fanie smiled and winked at her, but she did not reward him with a smile in return. *Aowaa!* Instead, she became even more visibly busy with her paperwork for the next few minutes. She then paused in her activity and twisted her neck around to look behind her.

There was no one behind her, she knew there was no one. Her colleague had gone out to buy some *vetkoek* for their breakfast.

When the nurse scratched her ear with her left hand her admirer observed that her ring finger was free of a wedding band. Good news for him! Modest Dimakatjo wondered what was so special about her to attract this intense scrutiny. She was used to admiration from black patients; but to be looked at with such interest by a white guy was something new to her. She was intrigued to know what he was doing there in a black doctor's surgery.

Peeping up from underneath her lashes at the man sitting across the way, she saw a round, bearded face with a ruddy complexion and a pair of slightly bulging, wise-looking brown eyes. He looked, to her, like a typical *boer*, except that his hair was too long. Her critical gaze noted disapprovingly that his build was on the chubby side, while the nicotine stains on his fingers spoke of a heavy smoker.

Fanie was not aware of her observation, for his gaze at that moment was downcast. His attention, however, was not on the magazine through which he was paging but on the object of his troubled thoughts, behind the counter. His eye had no choice but to follow where his thoughts went. He again tried to catch the nurse's eye and smile at her, but she wouldn't give him the chance.

He was feeling a little out of place here, perhaps because this was his first time at this surgery, which served black patients in the industrial area of Pretoria West. He had been persuaded by his black colleague, George Maunatlala, to try this doctor's practice, since it was close to the Jacaranda Welding Company where they both worked. Fanie's usual doctor, an Afrikaans-speaking general practitioner at the Louis Pasteur Medical Centre in the heart of Pretoria, had recently moved away.

The door opened and two black patients came ambling in. They greeted Dimakatjo with familiarity, then sat down next to Fanie, greeting him in Afrikaans. He mumbled something in reply. He could see that they were surprised to see a white guy at 'their' surgery. It was more than a decade into 'new' South Africa, but their eyes had never yet landed on a sight like this. It was still as rare as seeing a white chap queueing at a taxi rank, or packed into a taxi bound for Mamelodi or one of the other black residential areas.

Dimakatjo was writing in a notebook now, her pen vomiting words, words, words. She put it down at last and turned to a new task, sticking labels onto small glass bottles containing medicinal mixtures. She paused in her labour to steal a quick look at the white guy; but this time it was his eyes that avoided colliding with hers and swiftly glued themselves back to the magazine.

Dimakatjo's colleague, Nthabiseng, entered the surgery holding a plastic shopping bag containing *vetkoek* – the delicious cakes that were also known as *magwinya* – and a litre of milk. Dimakatjo took the bag from her and hurried away from the counter.

'Kwae-kwae-kwae' was the chopping sound made by Dimakatjo's medium-heeled black patent shoes, known in this part of the country as *dikwae-kwae*, after the sound they made. She was strutting briskly towards the little kitchenette to make tea for herself and Nthabiseng.

He who had been bitten by the louse and bedbug of love could not keep his eyes off her disappearing rear-end. His heart was pounding and his mouth felt dry. He was surprised by his own reactions, for he was not usually given to such quick attractions.

His heart told him that she was 'The One!' but his head said: *But I had no idea that it would be somebody black . . . !*

He switched off his thoughts and tried to concentrate on the article he was reading, wishing the doctor would hurry up and come. His symptoms felt like they were getting worse. Adrenalin was rushing through him, making his palms sweaty and his stomach full of mad butterflies. He longed for a cigarette, but he was afraid of incurring the nurse's displeasure.

Dimakatjo duly reappeared, carrying two mugs of tea and a plate piled with eight light-brown, tender cakes for her and Nthabiseng's breakfast. Health-conscious Dimakatjo spoiled herself with *magwinya* once a week. On other days she brought fruit salad to work, or toasted cheese-and-tomato health bread, or egg-and-tomato sandwiches in her plastic lunch container.

In the mornings before coming to work, Dimakatjo routinely drank half a litre of black honeybush tea, which she believed helped her to stay trim. In the evenings she ate a light supper of steamed vegetables with white meat such as chicken or fish. Thanks to living according to such healthy principles, 25-year-old Dimakatjo looked in perfect shape. She was glad she had not inherited her mother's huge frame, that would routinely draw wolf whistles and appreciative cries of '*dudlu!*' from lustful labourers, whose favourite pastime seemed to be to tease and exchange banter with passing African women: '*Sheep, we buy tail; cow, we choose a flabby thigh!*' Remarks such as these, they regarded as culturally acceptable.

The two nurses ate their breakfast behind the counter, chatting in low tones. More patients arrived and took their places on the chairs. Several pairs of curious eyes were cast in the white guy's direction. The other patients sat discussing Fanie in Sepedi, not realising that he could understand them.

'When I look at this *ngamola* sitting here then I am convinced that we truly live in new South Africa,' said one black patient to his neighbour.

'No, that's still not good enough,' she responded. 'What will impress me is to see a black farmer driving his small *bakkie* that is crammed with white labourers huddled together like sheep at the back!'

Dimakatjo and Nthabiseng finished their breakfast and took the dirty cups and plates through to the kitchenette. At that moment, a nattily dressed, sweep-you-off-your-feet kind of guy entered the reception area. The eyes of black patients and the white one fixed themselves in fascination on this eye-catching beau, who stepped confidently behind the counter and walked towards the kitchenette, clutching a bouquet of flowers. Fanie's heart sank low and his shoulders slumped visibly, for he immediately suspected that the smart guy must be Dimakatjo's man.

A few minutes later his spirits lifted again, as the dashing Romeo emerged from the kitchenette, walking hand in hand not with Dimakatjo but Nthabiseng. Fanie heaved a heartfelt sigh of relief.

It was the 10th of February – four days before the much anticipated February 14th Valentine's Day. Nthabiseng's beau-in-her-life, known as Jack Mabotja, had decided to bestow an early gift of flowers and giant-sized Valentine card on his love, since he was soon to leave town on one of his frequent trips away as a travelling sales rep. This meant that he would be out of town for the all-important Lovers' Day itself.

'Nthabi, you two are meant for each other,' remarked Dimakatjo, following behind the lovebirds. 'I wish you could simply walk straight into the Home Affairs office right now!'

'To do what?' asked Nthabiseng, clearly tickled by the idea.

'Get married, of course!'

Nthabiseng and Jack burst into loud, appreciative laughter.

While Nthabiseng accompanied Jack out, Dimakatjo found a moment to read her colleague's Valentine's Day card. There, for anyone's eyes to feast on, was a picture of carefree lovers in swimsuits, clearly having a wonderful time on a tropical island surrounded by canoes, palm trees and plentiful banana and pineapple trees. It invoked in Dimakatjo's mind an image of the Garden of Eden, where Adam and Eve, as it was told in the Bible, had a hell of a good time until God chased them out of Paradise.

While she was still dwelling on the card, Dimakatjo caught a glimpse through the window of Jack and Nthabiseng kissing passionately on the steps outside the surgery, oblivious to the people around them. Pain gnawed at Dimakatjo's heart and tears welled up in her big brown eyes as she thought about the sorry state of her own love-life.

Dimakatjo was going out with Tau Mabitsela, an attorney by profession and owner of a nice-looking German-made convertible, known colloquially as '*Selahla*'. This, in the eyes of the township, meant that he had 'arrived'; for the BMW was seen as the car to aspire to in black culture – the ultimate status symbol of the upwardly mobile.

Viewed from a distance, the relationship between Tau and Dimakatjo appeared perfectly harmonious. But from Dimakatjo's point of view, the path of love was strewn with thorns and stones. Dimakatjo was convinced that Tau cared more about liquor than her, and as a result they had umpteen quarrels. She hated the smell of liquor, especially brandy, and loathed even more the behaviour that went with its consumption. She had pleaded with Tau time after time to limit his intake or stop drinking completely. But her earnest requests landed on indifferent ears. Tau's dedicated chain-smoking was another source of great irritation to her and only aggravated the situation.

Bloodshot-eyed Tau, with untrimmed beard and liquor-laden breath, was fond of visiting Dimakatjo when he was at his drunkest and most raucous worst. He would arrive bellowing shebeen songs in a loud and off-key voice: '*Mmasehlana wa bjalwa mpolae, nka bolawa ke wena, nka rata!*' ('Beautiful brown sorghum beer, I would be pleased to be killed by you!') And: '*Ke mang a boditšeng . . . Sweetie lovie gore nna ke nwa bjalwa?*' ('Who told my lover that I take liquor, that I take liquor, and sleep at parties?')

Dimakatjo frequently complained to Tau that liquor-and-tobacco- flavoured kisses made her bilious; to placate her, Tau would suck mint-flavoured sweets or chew musk-flavoured bubblegum. These strategies, however, had as little effect as heavy perfume used to disguise body odour.

Notwithstanding these difficulties, Dimakatjo was reluctant to end things with Tau. If she jilted him, she would elicit disapproving tongue-clicks and hisses from among her people, who didn't believe in short-lived romantic adventures. Perhaps Tau did not take her seriously as a lover since they had grown up together in the same village. Tau was the son of the village chief. Dimakatjo could only hope that, as she was often advised by other women who had experienced similar problems, Tau would one day give up his excessive drinking.

One of the village elders, Tau's maternal aunt Dikeledi, had once advised Dimakatjo: 'If you throw this man away, the next woman is going to say "thank you!" with open palms.'

'Why do you say that, aunt?' asked Dimakatjo.

'Because people change. If you jilt Tau the next girl will scrub him. He will become clean – "*twaa*-white!" Just like a sheet soaked in a champion washing powder!' She vibrated the back of her hand, sinewy and weather-beaten, to emphasise the words '*twaa*-white'.

'A woman's hands are meant to clean her man and his mess; it is this same man of whom you will speak proudly to your children, telling them how far you have come with him. But you young women, your hands are there only to receive what the man has to give!'

And so, despite some stones among the mung beans on the path of love, Dimakatjo did not think seriously of jilting Tau. After all, in her community it was considered 'normal' for women to have such problems. Who didn't?

Dimakatjo and Nthabiseng continued with their tasks of sticking labels onto bottles of medicinal mixture and small plastic bags of tablets, and answering the busy phone. The waiting room was now looking crowded, with more than half of the plastic chairs filled.

'What are you doing on Valentine's Day?' Dimakatjo asked her friend with a knowing smile.

'Nothing, Maki.'

'You are lying, Nthabi!'

'No, I'm not lying. Jack is away on Valentine's Day so I'm doing nothing. But the day afterwards, Jack is taking me to Sun City!' boasted Nthabiseng. She spoke the words 'Sun City' somewhat musically, with a ring of excitement.

'I wish I were you, Nthabi!'

'I wish I were *you*, Maki . . . '

'*Why?*'

'Because. You have everything. You are pretty, you have a nice figure . . . you look like a Miss Mamelodi beauty queen!'

'Come on, Nthabi!'

'I'm serious Maki! Most of the men who walk in here just want to shower you with love. And . . . the man that you are going out with is the son of a chief!'

'*Ja*, well, Tau is a nice guy . . . when he is sober. But he is very conservative. He doesn't believe in things like Valentine's Day. He says it is the white man's clever way of making money out of blacks.'

'Well life doesn't begin and end with Valentine's Day. Tau is a lawyer, he drives a BM – what more do you want, Maki?'

'You are right, Nthabi. But the problem with sons of chiefs, you know, is that they marry several wives. Just like their fathers and grandfathers.'

'Why let that bother you? You will be Wife Number One. Chief Wife!'

Dimakatjo shook her head emphatically. 'I am very jealous, Nthabi. I can't share my man!'

2

At 9.30 exactly Dr Lesiba Makgabo entered the waiting room of the surgery, his trademark stethoscope dangling around his neck. Fifteen patients were now waiting and the waiting room was full of the sounds of coughing, snuffling, sneezing and the odd groan or two.

The doctor greeted Dimakatjo and Nthabiseng cheerfully and disappeared into his consulting room two doors down from the kitchenette. Dimakatjo called the name of the first patient on her list: 'Mr Fanie Fourie!' and Fanie sprang to his feet and entered the doctor's consulting room.

Fanie put his buttocks down on the chair indicated and greeted the doctor, who seemed somewhat surprised to be attending to the first white patient in his five years of practising as a general practitioner.

He listened to Fanie's symptoms, thoroughly examined him and diagnosed high blood pressure. After writing on Fanie's file in the indecipherable cursive script so typical of doctors, the physician advised his patient to cut down on salt, stay off fatty foods and try to lose some weight. Fanie was 29 years old but he looked older because of his big frame, which he had inherited from his mother. The doctor also told him that he needed to give up smoking. He wrote out a prescription and then referred the patient back to Dimakatjo, who handed him a packet of tablets and some mixture in a small bottle, saying: 'Shake the bottle before you drink. One spoonful, three times a day. Two tablets, three times a day. With food. Thank you. Goodbye!'

Fanie astonished Dimakatjo when he spoke in Sepedi and enquired about the meaning of her name.

'It means "Surprise",' she told him.

He then asked her what her surname was and was told: 'Machabaphala.'

'Pleased to know you, Dimakatjo Machabaphala,' he smiled, stumbling a little over the long surname.

'Pleased to know you, Mr Fourie!' she smiled back.

'I have to thank you. The way you have been so good to me, I'm healed even before I take my prescription. You can have your medicines back!'

They laughed together.

'It's my pleasure to serve you, Mr Fourie!'

'Please, call me Fanie.'

Fanie told Dimakatjo that he had learned to speak Sepedi as a boy growing up at Potgietersrus (now Ga-Mokopane in the Limpopo Province), while Dimakatjo told him that she was born and raised not far from there at a village near Pietersburg, now known as Polokwane. Fanie then asked for Dimakatjo's telephone number. She hesitated, pretending she had not heard him properly.

'Give him Maki, give him!' hissed Nthabiseng from behind her. She had been listening avidly to the exchange.

Dimakatjo obediently wrote her work telephone number down on a piece of paper and handed it to smiling Fanie, who took hold of her hand and lightly squeezed it. She blushed and quickly pulled her hand out of his. Still beaming, Fanie stepped towards the door. Turning back, he kissed his hand and blew the kiss towards Dimakatjo who waved at him shyly. Fanie walked out into the street, all smiles, so busy looking back at Dimakatjo that he bumped into an old woman who was entering the waiting room.

'Sorry *baas*!' the old woman apologised.

'Sorry auntie,' he said back to her in Sepedi, grinning at her amazed look.

Watching Fanie through the window as he went off, Nthabiseng smiled at Dimakatjo and said: 'I told you that you are the darling of the male patients!'

Dimakatjo simply chuckled, and called the next patient.

Fanie, bursting with life and vitality, drove cheerfully all the way to his place of work, the Jacaranda Welding Company. Indeed, his symptoms had disappeared like magic. The most amazing thing had happened to him: he had fallen in love at first sight! He was now more convinced than ever that Dimakatjo was 'The One!'

He entered his office in the Personnel Section, puffing absent-mindedly on a cigarette, still smiling to himself. Just in time, he remembered that smoking in the building was not permitted. His colleague, George Maunatlala, recently become his boss, told him that his girlfriend, Gerda, had phoned. Fanie heard the news in silence. He sat down on his chair and dialled a number. George thought Fanie was phoning Gerda back but, in fact, his colleague was phoning someone else.

'Hello?' Fanie said into the phone. 'This is Fanie. Fanie Fourie. Your patient from this morning . . . '

Before he could get further, he was interrupted by his ringing cellphone. Fanie looked at the name on the message window and handed the implement over to George, gesturing to him to go out of the office to take the call. While George obligingly did so, Fanie invited Dimakatjo to meet him for lunch the next day.

George came back in and handed him the cellphone with an inscrutable expression. Fanie coolly finished his conversation with Dimakatjo before he took it: 'Okay. You think about it and I'll phone you again tomorrow,' he said.

He put down the receiver and reluctantly reached for his cell to take Gerda's call. As soon as she heard his voice, suspicious Gerda demanded to know why he had put her on hold and who he had been speaking to. Fanie lied and said that he had been talking to someone at the Department of Labour. Gerda then told him that she had booked a table at their favourite restaurant for Valentine's Day, where they would have dinner by candlelight.

Fanie responded without enthusiasm. When he put the phone down, George flashed him a knowing smile.

'What's happening, Fanie?'

'Why?'

'I can tell that something is brewing . . .'

'What do you mean?'

'You are in love, aren't you? And it's not with Gerda.'

Fanie said nothing. But his smile gave it all away.

'Let me tell you something, Fanie. A woman is like a *sangoma*. If you are in love with someone else she can smell it!'

Fanie laughed dismissively.

'I'm serious,' said George, whose smiling face contradicted his words. 'Now tell me Fanie . . . *are* you in love with somebody new? Did you meet someone at the doctor's surgery today?'

'Why do you say that?'

'I told you . . . I can smell something.'

'Are you also a *sangoma*?' Fanie laughed. 'It's none of your business anyway!'

There followed a thoughtful pause.

'Indeed, men are problematic. They are never satisfied,' George philosophised. 'They are like elephants that keep on nibbling, nibbling at green and tender plants.' He pointed a finger at Fanie. 'Men can be so irresponsible. They set fire to a woman and then, when the poor woman is in flames, they run away crying, "Fire, get away from me!"'

'What are you trying to tell me, George?'

'You have heard me, Fanie!'

It was almost ten years ago that Fanie had first started going out with Gerda Moerdyk-van-Schalkwyk, a 26-year-old Afrikaans *meisie* who worked as a hairdresser at one of the salons in the Pretoria city centre. When they first met, Fanie's hormones had persuaded him that he was 'in love' with her. Gerda was dark-haired and striking-looking, almost as tall as Fanie. Like many 'liberated' young white women, she had taken up smoking and now saw it as a necessary evil to keep her weight down.

Fanie and Gerda had met one December at the bank where they both had holiday jobs, helping with the festive season rush. Fanie's mother, who worked for the bank, had helped him to get a job there as a temporary teller, while Gerda was taken on as a receptionist in the enquiries section.

When Fanie was first introduced to Gerda, a black man in his early forties who had worked at the same bank for many years but, because of the colour of his skin, had never been promoted above messenger status, remarked in Sepedi to Gloria, 'the tea-girl': '*Agaa!* Today the cat and the mouse have met! We will see what the cat will do with this mouse!'

In fact, it did not take longer than a week for the cat to 'paw' the mouse, and before Fanie and Gerda knew it they were boyfriend and girlfriend. Since it was the first time for both of them, it was easy for them to imagine themselves in love with each other.

Under ordinary circumstances, it would have been unlikely for their paths to have crossed at all. Gerda came from a struggling family of eight children, living in the Daanville suburb of 'poor whites' in the west of Pretoria. After she had passed her Standard Eight, there was no way that her parents, with seven other children to put through school, could manage to take her education further. Once her holiday job at the bank came to an end, she had no choice but to look for some sort of trade and start to earn her living. Fortunately, the Department of Labour came to her rescue with a three-month basic training course in hairdressing, a qualification that subsequently helped her to get employment as an apprentice at a hair salon in the city centre.

Fanie meanwhile, having completed his Matric at D.F. Malan Hoërskool in Potgietersrus, went on to study for a two-year diploma in Personnel Management at Pretoria West Technical College.

As the saying goes: '*Thoka ya kgole ga e bolae mmutla*' – 'The club thrown by a hunter from a long distance doesn't kill a rabbit.' Given the distance between them, it was perhaps not surprising that Fanie and Gerda's relationship was soon in trouble; their love did not so much grow sour, as cooled. Since neither of them had the nerve to pronounce their relationship dead, they did not put a formal end to their liaison but simply stopped seeing and phoning each other.

During this period Gerda fell in love with a car mechanic, but that relationship didn't last long. When it crashed, she went running back to Fanie. Since he himself was not involved with anybody else, and since they had never formally broken up, he felt he had no option but to resume where they had left off.

It was a far from perfect union. They were not well suited to each other in temperament or outlook. Punctilious Gerda was irritated by easy-going Fanie's lack of punctuality, while Fanie had to bear with Gerda's impatience, fussiness and temperamental outbursts. More than once he attempted to end the relationship, but each time Gerda's distress made him weaken and relent. Gerda's desperation to keep clinging to such an imperfect union could, perhaps, be attributed to the fact that, although still in her twenties, she felt she had long waited for wedding bells to chime.

Fanie had, in his way, remained faithful to her, neglecting to venture out in search of greener pastures; until that fateful day when he, the first white patient ever to set foot in Dr Makgabo's surgery, fell head-over-heels for Dimakatjo, the beautiful black nurse.

3

It was 7.00 a.m. on the 11th of February. Fanie kicked off his blankets sleepily. The rumbling of municipal buses and heavy-duty trucks outside his window had served as a belated alarm clock. As usual, he had overslept and had to give himself a quick 'cat-style' wash and forgo breakfast. He swallowed his blood-pressure medicines, thinking of Dimakatjo, and dashed out the door to his car.

His white BMW, second-hand but still in good condition, ploughed through the heavy traffic, managing to make it to Fanie's place of work by just past eight o'clock; he was 30 minutes late. George, Fanie's boss, glanced meaningfully at the clock as Fanie skidded in.

'Late again,' he said. 'We'll have to dock your pay.' Then his grin broke through. 'You have overslept because of an overdose of love!' he winked.

'*Moenie nonsens praat jong!*' ('Don't talk nonsense man!') retorted Fanie with a smile.

George looked Fanie in the eye and laughed.

'What's funny?' Fanie demanded.

'How are you going to cope with two women? You can hardly manage one!'

'Who told you there's another woman?'

George's response was more laughter.

The two-litre kettle that George had put on to boil switched itself off. From the supply cupboard Fanie brought out two mugs, in which he put coffee granules, milk and sugar; he poured hot water into both mugs, stirred, and gave one to George. They sipped in silence as they checked their diaries and planned their schedules for the day. Since the Jacaranda Welding Company had joined the computer age only a few months previously, their priority task was to computerise the files of all the workers, transferring the information from hard copy to disk. Time galloped and before they knew it they heard the *Ngweee!* of the siren, announcing it was lunchtime. Fanie took his car keys, slipped his wallet into his pocket and prepared to exit.

'Where are you off to, Fanie?' curious George enquired.

'None of your business!' replied Fanie, clutching his keys with one hand and a pair of sunglasses with the other.

Amused, George sang: '*Rotwane e lebile lapeng la'bo kgarebe!*' ('The suitor's walking-stick is pointing towards the girl's home!')

Fanie laughed to himself as he unlocked the door of his car. George assumed that Fanie was off to see a new white lover; it never occurred to him that the prize his colleague was panting after was somebody black.

Fanie parked his car in front of an Italian café and takeaway in Rebecca Street that was a popular lunchtime haunt for workers in the area. Its main advantage was that it was within walking distance of Dr Makgabo's rooms, since Dimakatjo had refused to let Fanie pick her up from the surgery.

Fanie looked carefully around him for any sign of a woman resembling Dimakatjo. She was nowhere to be found by his hungry eyes. His heart was gnawed by sudden anxiety: *What if she fails to pitch up?* But he was confident that she would not disappoint him.

To while away the time until she appeared, he listened to a CD on his car CD-player. For once in his life he had been punctual. He felt he could not afford to jeopardise this crucially important date in his life. It had taken some persuading to get Dimakatjo to agree to meet him in the first place. Each time he phoned, he was met by the same response: that she would 'think about it'. It was only when he threatened to come and sit in the waiting room and not leave until she said 'yes', that she had finally agreed.

Seven minutes went by that felt like seventy. At last Dimakatjo appeared, ambling across from the park opposite the café. Fanie's face lit up with a relieved smile. He almost leapt out of the car, such was his hurry to greet the flower of his heart. She was even more beautiful than he remembered, with her enchanting dimples and radiant smile. He escorted her into the café and they joined the queue at the counter.

'What will you have, Dimakatjo?' enquired Fanie.

'Please call me Maki!'

'Okay, Maki!'

Fanie and Dimakatjo were watched with utmost curiosity by the other customers as they stood at the counter to place their order, for this was not a venue where white faces were often seen.

'I will have an apple,' Dimakatjo said.

'Come on Maki, don't be shy!' said Fanie. 'Can't I get you a hamburger, or a cheeseburger or something?'

'I don't eat red meat. I will have a vegetarian burger.'

Fanie bought two burgers, vegetarian for Maki and steak for himself, and two fruit juices. He had first ordered a Coke for himself but changed his mind when he heard her insisting on a hundred per cent fruit juice. He wanted to buy her a chocolate for dessert but she stood firm in her desire for a large, luscious red apple instead.

They sauntered towards the well-tended park that was full of fish ponds, rose-filled rockeries and an array of trees and shrubs, with ample lawns of neatly cut green grass dotted with benches. Fanie dared to take Dimakatjo's hand as they walked and, to her own surprise, she allowed it. Every so often she would lift their joined hands and gaze at their entwined fingers, as if fascinated by the sight of Fanie's white flesh against the smooth coffee-brown of her own.

They chose a secluded spot at the far corner of the park and perched themselves on one of the benches there.

'So you don't eat red meat?' Fanie enquired, after swallowing the mouthful that he was absent-mindedly chewing.

'That's right.'

'*Blerry* health fanatic, *eh?*'

Dimakatjo laughed, exposing her tongue and teeth in a way that was just too irresistible to Fanie. Her laughter was the sweetest, most symphonic sound he had ever heard. It was the kind of laughter that stirred all his male senses . . . seductive, overpowering and yet so invigorating to his libido that he could happily have made love to her right there and then.

Fanie was tempted to tickle her armpits so that she would keep on titillating his ears. He imagined the two of them locked in the arms of love, with her churning out that rich laughter, her chin ploughing deep into his shoulder, his fingertips tiptoeing over her ribcage as if she were a concertina.

'Maybe you can help me to be as health-conscious as you are. Dr Makgabo said I must lose some weight. But I am a *boer*, you know; I grew up munching *pap*, *boerewors* and *potjiekos*,' he said.

'You people have a lot in common with us blacks,' was Dimakatjo's reply.

'*Ja!*' Fanie spoke with his mouth full of food, nodding vigorously to emphasise his agreement with Dimakatjo's statement.

Dimakatjo hadn't started on her burger yet. Fanie tried to coax her, breaking off a piece and trying to insert it into her mouth, but she turned her face away and assured him that she had her own hands. Presently, they finished their meal and turned to their juices. Fanie then instructed Dimakatjo to eat her apple but she insisted that she was already full and that she would rather save it for supper.

Fanie took out his cigarettes, lit one and puffed away with enjoyment, while his eyes unrestrainedly explored the living landscape known as Dimakatjo. As the curls of cigarette smoke spiralled upwards, she could not pretend that it did not bother her. She fanned at the smoke with her open palm, trying to beat it away. Remorseful at having once again offended her, Fanie apologised and quickly extinguished his cigarette on the bench.

'It's a bad habit, I know,' he said. 'I started smoking when I was only sixteen. My mother taught me smoking. She is a chain-smoker,' he told her.

Fanie's smoking habit reminded Dimakatjo of Tau. Guilt lanced through her at the thought of him. Even though she told herself that she and Fanie were doing nothing wrong, she knew that if Tau knew that she was sitting here having lunch and holding hands with another man, he wouldn't agree.

At that point Fanie moved closer to Dimakatjo, who quickly shifted away. Fanie followed until Dimakatjo was sitting balanced on only one buttock at the very edge of the bench.

'Nowhere to go now,' Fanie teased her.

'I will sit down on the lawn!' she teased back.

'I will follow you!'

'Then I will run away.'

'I will chase and overtake you!'

'And then what?'

'Kiss you!'

They laughed together with relish. As before, Fanie was totally charmed and seduced by Dimakatjo's manner of laughing. He desired nothing more than to embrace her. And kiss her extremely irresistible juicy and sensual African lips.

He pulled Dimakatjo towards him and gently patted her shoulder, exploring her biceps, elbows, arms, hands and, finally, her fingers, concentrating on her unadorned ring finger. At this juncture she looked him straight in the eye. She was tempted to tell him about Tau, but couldn't bring herself to do it at that moment. She found his big brown eyes very romantic; but she pretended she was not one bit affected.

Fanie, for his part, wanted nothing so much as to pinch her plump and lustrous thigh, but restrained himself. He bent towards her and tried to plant a kiss; but she swung her head away from him and the missile consequently failed dismally to hit its target. He was not offended, however, remembering belatedly that she was repelled by the smell of tobacco. She drew a few more centimetres away from him, and this time Fanie did not move closer.

'You don't dislike me?' he asked her.

'No! Why?' A pause; then: 'I'm not used to kissing in public; I don't enjoy being a bioscope!'

'Then would you be prepared to be a bioscope at my place?'

Dimakatjo quivered with the laughter that so titillated Fanie.

'Answer my question, Maki . . .'

A considering pause. Then: 'Where is your place?' she asked.

'Strijdomhuis.'

'I don't know what that is. It sounds like a prison – or army barracks!' she laughed.

'It's a block of flats. At the corner of Van der Walt and Scheiding streets in Berea.'

The desire to caress and kiss her was painfully difficult to contain; but he could not kiss her here, for she did not want to be a public 'bioscope'.

'Will you come to my flat, Maki?'

'When?'

'Tomorrow. I'll come and fetch you from work. At 4.30,' replied Fanie promptly, scarcely able to believe that she had asked, 'when?'

Dimakatjo was silent.

'Please come, Maki!'

'I'll think about it.'

With that Fanie had to be content.

Five minutes before the lunch hour expired, Fanie dropped Dimakatjo off in front of Dr Makgabo's surgery. They bid each other an undramatic farewell, without so much as a kiss or hug. Nthabiseng was full of curiosity to hear about Dimakatjo's lunchtime *tête-à-tête*, but there was no time for idle chat since there were patients waiting to be served. A steady stream arrived throughout the afternoon as there was a virulent flu outbreak in the region, and Dr Makgabo's surgery was the only one that served the whole industrial area.

To Fanie, back at Jacaranda Welding, time seemed to crawl, and he wished it were within his power to make the sun gallop faster. Fortunately, the repeated replay of that memorable lunchtime with Dimakatjo broke the monotony of the work tasks and added spice to the slow hours. George, though he looked thoughtfully at Fanie's dreamy eyes, did not bother asking about his lunchtime date since he expected to be told it was none of his business. George could never have guessed that the time would come when Fanie's love-life would be very much his business!

The 12th of February dawned in a flush of rosy light. As the saying goes, '*the dawn never begrudges anyone*'; it simply dawns, and soon the sun shines on everyone's faces, whether good or bad. There were only two days left until the much anticipated Valentine's Day, and dedicated lovers everywhere continued with their countdown in happy expectation.

For Dimakatjo, there was nothing to look forward to since her man, Tau, did not attach any importance to 'the white man's day'. Dimakatjo pondered over the fact that she had now become the romantic target of 'a white man'. Romantic overtures were nothing new to her. Over the years, she had had umpteen approaches by men promising her the moon and stars, but she had always found it easy to decline such offers. Strangely, despite her dissatisfaction with her relationship with Tau, she had resigned herself to being with him always. Perhaps she had become trapped without realising it in a romantic comfort zone.

Whenever her heart urged her to open herself to another man, she would remember her aunt's advice: '*A woman's hands are meant to clean her man and his mess, until he is clean and* twaa-*white, like a sheet dipped in a champion washing powder!*'

Dimakatjo was a well-brought-up girl from the hands of the Ga-Mabitsela villagers near Polokwane. '*You young women of today, your hands are there only to receive what the man gives.*' She was determined that this accusation would not be applicable to her. She could not afford to be a disappointment to her people. *Aowaa!*

When she was a young girl growing up in the conservative rural community, her people had inculcated a sense of high morality into her. If she had slipped in the city mud and become a bad girl, her people would soon know it from *pudi-ya-tsela*, the busy village grapevine. The villagers would endlessly wag their index fingers at her homestead, mouthing exclamations and click sounds of utter disgust.

She had never imagined that she would receive romantic overtures from a white man – or that she could feel attracted to him in return. Like so many people in the community, she had always considered that black women who took up with white guys were women of questionable morals. *Tiekie-lines* – brazen tarts! Gold-diggers! She had despised them passionately.

The pace of things, since she had met Fanie, made her uncomfortable. It was all happening too fast for her liking. And there was, of course, the question of her involvement with Tau. But Fanie's romantic overtures, coming as they did during the Valentine season of flowers, gifts and physical expressions of love, caught her at a time when she was especially vulnerable.

That morning during her tea-break, she had browsed through Nthabiseng's copy of *Top Chicks*, a popular 'glossy' aimed at trendy young black women. This one was a 'Valentine Special' edition, bursting with pictures of trendsetting couples and icons – the famous, bold and beautiful ones – dressed in their sparkling best, dining out at the classiest restaurants. The magazine pages were filled with a variety of merchandise such as wines, candles, toiletry, perfumes, music CDs, chocolates, clothing and even furniture, all marketed through the colourful label of this hearts-and-flowers day.

Dimakatjo's wistful eyes landed on a picture of a stunning red lacquer vase containing twelve blood-red roses, one for each month of the year. The picture was captioned: 'The colour of love', and the accompanying article proclaimed: 'Love is in the air! Valentine's Day is the perfect opportunity to impress your loved one with your cooking skills.'

Dimakatjo smiled forlornly. She knew that all these lovers' messages were written for the lucky ones such as Nthabiseng. Definitely not for Dimakatjo! Because Valentine-insensitive Tau would no doubt arrive at her place on Lovers' Day drunk as usual, with not a gift in hand nor sweet word on his lips, but only brandy and cigarette stink on his breath.

It was for these reasons that she found Fanie's passionate overtures so hard to resist. In just a few hours he would be arriving to collect her and take her to his flat. The voice of her upbringing warned her that this was not the right way to behave. A well-brought-up girl did not do such things, did not spend an evening alone in the flat of a man she hardly knew and had only just met – even if she wasn't already going out with someone else! But in her present mood, the voice of her emotion was stronger. Just two days ago Dimakatjo had told Nthabiseng that she was not prepared to share a man; would she herself be prepared to be shared by two men?

She flipped through more pages until she came to the 'Stars Foretell' section. Her horoscope prediction for Valentine's week read: *'Your best chances of love are right at your doorstep, and the journey is promising; but watch out for a few thorns on the stems below the roses.'*

Nthabiseng's star-sign prediction, when Dimakatjo read it to her later, drew loud peals of laughter from the two avid horoscope followers, for it said: *'Open that huge compassionate heart of yours. Get out of your normal routine and dream big, love big!'*

4

It was just before 4.30 p.m., Dimakatjo's *tshaile* – knock-off time. Fanie's car was already waiting in front of Dr Makgabo's surgery. He was sitting inside the car, smoking somewhat pensively, soft romantic music resonating from the CD in the player.

His heart leapt as Dimakatjo appeared. She had changed out of her uniform into a tight-fitting summer dress that outlined her delectable curves and exposed flesh in just the right places. Today, the braided hairstyle was split into two bunches divided by a centre parting. Fanie leapt out of the car and stood looking breathlessly at this vision of beauty walking towards him.

As she drew level with him, he swept her into a bear-hug, then walked round to open the passenger door for her. She got in, her face radiating a smile; this quickly faded, however, as the trapped smoke in the car suffused her nostrils, making her eyes water and sending her into a coughing fit. Fanie took the cue and quickly extinguished the cigarette he had been smoking. He rolled the window down and started up the car, silently cursing whoever it was who had first loosed this poison called tobacco on the world.

In a surprisingly short space of time, the white BMW had cleaved through the traffic and was entering the gates of Strijdomhuis, the small four-storey block that stood at the intersection of one-way Van Der Walt and Scheiding Street in Pretoria's dense Berea flatland.

Fanie had been resident here for three months now. Before he moved to Strijdomhuis he used to stay with his widowed mother and his sister at Koedoespoort – formerly a low-income suburb for white railway workers and tradesmen in the east of Pretoria. His flat was on the third floor of the small block that only housed 50 people in total, compared to buildings such as the twenty-storey Toria Gardens, which boasted about 2 000 residents.

What was surprising about Strijdomhuis was that, notwithstanding 'new' South Africa, it still serviced whites only. There was not a single black face to be seen in its corridors, excepting the labourer, Nicholas Molwantwa. The managing trustees did not see any reason to compromise their right-wing values – which they called 'standards'; *aowaa!* They were, in fact, proud of them. Whenever a flat was vacated by a white individual or family, they made certain that it was occupied by other whites.

What bonded the residents of this building together was not only the colour of their prejudices but also their seniority and the fact that most of them had lived here together for numerous years. Fanie was one of the few exceptions who belonged to the 'younger generation' – that is, under 30 years of age.

Fanie and Nicholas, the flat-cleaner, had a good relationship which had started when Fanie had first moved into Strijdomhuis; Nicholas's was one of the pairs of hands that had helped carry furniture and belongings from the hired truck into Fanie's flat. Fanie later found out that Nicholas was a member of the Zion Christian Church, or ZCC. Every Sunday, he would proudly put on the two-piece khaki uniform and silver star-badge of the Zionist *Mokhukhu* dancers. The uniform was worn with *manyanyatha* – hand-stitched white leather shoes with soles made of truck-tyre rubber. These were also colloquially known as *di-voetsek!* Nicholas invariably addressed Fanie as '*baas* Fanie', despite Fanie's numerous protests at being addressed in such a fashion.

When the lovebirds arrived at Strijdomhuis, Fanie parked the BMW in his allotted parking bay and jumped out to open the door for Dimakatjo, well aware that they were being watched with curiosity – if not hostility – by some of his conservative neighbours, a group of *tannies* standing on the first-floor communal balcony. These Afrikaans-speaking sexa- and septuagenarians, after adding one and one which gave them five, instantly reverted to their role of *skinderbekke* – 'gossip-mongers'.

To these old folks, it was inconceivable that any decent young white man from their own block of flats could be genuinely attracted to a black woman. To them, interracial relationships only flourished in parts of the country that they regarded as 'Sodom and Gomorrah'.

On the ground floor, Fanie and Dimakatjo joined a young white couple and an elderly white pair in waiting for the lift. Although Fanie and Dimakatjo were standing well apart, their mere presence together as white man and black woman produced a shockwave and drew disapproving reactions from these Strijdomhuis residents. The young white couple's faces froze into masks, while the old man and woman looked at each other and cast their eyes heavenwards, giving clear signal of their disapproval. Their expressions were those of people who smelled a bad odour but were too polite to say so.

To everyone's relief, the lift arrived at last. They all stepped in and the tension-filled contraption groaned its slow way upwards, opening and closing its doors obediently and finally ejecting Fanie and Dimakatjo on the third floor. Fanie unlocked the door of number 31, sensing that he was still being watched by several pairs of disapproving eyes from behind the doors to his left and right. He stood back to let Dimakatjo enter; she did so cautiously, her quick, observant eyes glancing all over the flat, taking in everything. It was a modest two-bedroom with a lounge-cum-dining-room and a small kitchen and bathroom. Fanie guided her into the lounge, his right hand gently holding her waist, the other gesturing to her to be seated on the three-seater sofa. He waited for Dimakatjo to sit down before seating himself on the one-seater opposite. Then he leapt to his feet again and dashed to the kitchen to fetch some drinks.

Dimakatjo took the opportunity to look around some more. Her feminine eyes quickly assessed the décor: the furniture consisted of rich and heavy blue-gum wood; the grey carpets contrasted beautifully with the burgundy colour of the sofas; four huge pot-plants were strategically placed at the cardinal points of the lounge, and on the shelving of the room-divider a range of African artifacts was displayed. Dimakatjo's face lit up as her wandering gaze landed on two rag-and-bead dolls.

'Where did you get these?' she enquired, as Fanie came back into the room carrying two tall glasses filled with fruit juice, balanced on saucers.

'I bought them at the Pretoria Zoo. Do you like them?' He approached her sofa and carefully put down one of the glasses and a saucer on a side table next to her.

'Yes! They are dressed like the Bapedi of Moletji, where I come from.'

Fanie beamed at her. 'Isn't it a coincidence!'

He sat down again on his chair and took a small sip of his juice, while Dimakatjo took a deep gulp of hers. They gazed at each other, momentarily at a loss for words, then both began talking together. Their laughter thawed the ice and after that the conversation flowed more naturally. They talked about their jobs, and Fanie mentioned his colleague George, with whom he had worked for many years and who had become his friend and was now his boss. Dimakatjo reminded Fanie of their first meeting, when Fanie had entered the surgery smoking, and her shock at seeing him. Although she had previously spoken to him on the phone and could tell from his voice that he was white, she had assumed at the time that he was booking the appointment for one of his workers; she had never expected that it was for Fanie himself! They had a good laugh about that.

Time slipped by unnoticed; the juices were sipped to the last drop. Again the conversation faltered and in the silence, Fanie's eyes scrutinised Dimakatjo from her feet to her head. Becoming suddenly bashful, she looked away, tugging at the hem of her short, thigh-revealing dress that was dotted with large, red roses whose stems had no thorns. She recalled her horoscope prediction for the week: *'Your best chances of love are right at your doorstep, and the journey is promising; but watch out for a few thorns on the stems below the roses.'* As she stood up to take the empty glasses through to the small kitchen, she wondered what – or who – the thorns would prove to be.

When she came back to the lounge, she found that Fanie had moved his chair closer to the sofa she was sitting on. She wanted to move it away again, as it had intruded into her personal space, but she thought it would be lack of courtesy to do so. In the stretching moments of silence she stared at the carpet, feeling the brown eyes of Fanie avidly examining her. She dared to lift her gaze and look back at him; they exchanged smiles. Fanie stood up and went to insert a romantic CD into the player. He took out a cigarette and lit it without thinking, then recalled how much she disliked tobacco and quickly extinguished it. They caught each other's glances and laughed again. Dimakatjo excused herself to go to the bathroom, while Fanie went back to the kitchen and returned with a bowl full of pears, apples, prunes and apricots. They nibbled for a while in silence, exposing their palates to the delicious flavours of the fruit.

Fanie's bold gaze travelled from Dimakatjo's face to her waist and from there to her breasts with their firm nipples. His hungry eyes remained on her while he slowly bit into a plump and juicy pear. She helped herself to some apricots, savouring them sensuously, and then slowly reached for a delicious green apple. She was very aware of constantly being under his close and searching scrutiny; it made her self-conscious and unable to do justice to the apple in her hand. There was, in both of them, a feeling of suspense, an awareness that there was unfinished business between them that must be finished. But each hesitated to make the first move for fear of rebuff. Dimakatjo longed to be able to say: 'Fanie, why have you invited me to your flat?' But modesty would not permit her to be so open. She felt like a foolish mouse that had been invited to supper by the cat and accepted, even though it fully suspected that it was to be the meal! While Fanie, for his part, felt like a cat that needed no motivational speaker to whet its appetite for the mouse nestling between its paws.

This time the CD playing was Hugh Masekela's romantic 'Ooh, baby, baby!' Dimakatjo was amazed that a white guy like Fanie should enjoy playing 'black music'; she guessed that his colleague, George, had influenced him to cultivate such a taste. Fanie, however, had an ulterior motive for choosing this particular CD. He had put it on in the hope that it would help psyche Dimakatjo into a love-making mood. All at once, Fanie sprang up from his chair and made a beeline for Dimakatjo's sofa, seating himself very close to her. She responded, as she had in the park, by perching herself on the extreme edge of her seat. Indefatigable Fanie pulled her back towards him and then deftly slipped off her shoes, as well as his own.

Feigning irritation, Dimakatjo looked into Fanie's deep brown irises; he responded with dismissive laughter. Dimakatjo realised the folly of having placed herself in a situation that gave this man a golden opportunity to pounce on her *somaar thuu-tšea!* – just getting it easily, without any hassle.

Fanie embraced her, leaning his bearded face against hers. His pleasure was short-lived, however, for she placed her palms on his shoulders and gently but firmly pushed him away. Seeing his dejected look, she flashed him a shy smile. Fanie's rueful grin seemed to concede to her maidenly modesty; but only for a moment. With infinite tenderness, inch by careful inch, his love-hungry hand began to explore her hands, arms, biceps, shoulders, neck and, finally, her breasts.

Dimakatjo removed Fanie's naughty hand; Fanie once more responded with dismissive laughter and renewed his assault, his behaviour typical of men in pursuit of a conquest. When she again removed his hand, he paused momentarily, then brushed her soft, smooth cheek with the back of his hand; at this, her resistance melted and she smiled. Unexpectedly, Fanie stood up; Dimakatjo felt a pang of disappointment, wondering if his interest in her had suddenly waned. But he was only going as far as the CD-player. He pressed the repeat button for the 'Ooh, baby, baby!' track and then returned to her.

His hands and arms itching to do what they could do very well, he descended to embrace her again. She smiled seductively up at him; but that smile quickly vanished from her face as she regretted behaving in a way that he might construe as 'cheap'. Fanie picked up her shift in mood and enquired if anything was the matter.

'Nothing,' was Dimakatjo's reply.

Because she was not a stone but a woman of flesh and blood, she could not deny her deep-seated need to love and be loved – to touch and be touched. Her body responded to Fanie's naughty hands, and she had no choice but to smile at his stratagems. Her sweet smile, accentuated by sensuous and luscious African lips, was just too irresistible to Fanie; he drew her down to the sofa, cradling her across his legs, while his kisses explored her throat and neck. When his face approached hers, she twisted her head from side to side in a futile attempt to avoid being kissed on the mouth. Fanie, however, managed to throw in a few very quality kisses. He was satisfied that he had infiltrated her defenses; he was pleased with the progress thus far.

Dimakatjo was conscious of nothing but his fierce, warm lips with which he surely but steadily broke down her resistance. Each kiss, like an incoming tide, was a slight advance on its predecessor, each touch just a little more intimate and, therefore, devastating to her diminishing resistance. Lust-fired Fanie began to unbutton the rose-flowered dress of seemingly love-drugged Dimakatjo. The fire in his blood increased with every button that he managed to snap loose.

When his lustful eyes landed on her tight bra with its moderately sized contents, his loud-pounding heart seemed to say: *I-want-it-now! I want-it-now! Now-now-now!*

Fanie fired off another Molotov-cocktail kiss, pressing her breast to his hairy chest. By this time, Dimakatjo's dress was hanging on her biceps; there was no time to be neat in the face of Fanie's crude and urgent desire. Dimakatjo found herself torn between resistance and submission, as if she were two girls in one body. But, as lustful Fanie became more and more determined to slake his desire, the resistance side of her unexpectedly took command.

'Stop, Fanie, stop!' Dimakatjo's urgent cry surprised Fanie, who had assumed she was as ready for his long-awaited penetration as he was. She struggled up from underneath his weight.

'Come on, take it easy, Maki!'

'*Êh-êh*, Fanie! No!'

'Why not? If we are both ready why can't we do it NOW?'

With her last ounce of willpower Dimakatjo wrenched herself free, sprang up, hoisted her dress back onto her shoulders and began buttoning herself up.

'What are you doing, Maki? Don't be afraid of me.'

'I'm not afraid of you!'

'Is it because I'm white and you're black?'

'No!'

'What then?' Fanie reached towards her with the intention of rubbing her shoulder soothingly.

'No, don't touch me!' protested Dimakatjo.

'Don't be so difficult, baby! This is new South Africa!'

'So what?'

'A white guy can lay a black chick!'

'Fanie, what do you take me for? A prostitute?'

'*Ag nee wat . . . !*' At that, Fanie unexpectedly covered his face with the palms of his hands. He gave up the fight to satisfy his desire, coming back to his senses as his temperature began to stabilise, wondering what was happening to his sanity.

'I'm sorry, madam!'

'I'm not your madam!' Fire-spitting Dimakatjo hurriedly put on her shoes, grabbed her handbag and stormed out of the flat. Fanie had left the keys dangling in the door. It flashed through his mind that he had blundered; if a man lures a woman to his place, he should, after locking the door put the keys in his pocket. Then his innate decency surfaced and he was ashamed for even thinking such a thing.

'No, Maki, please don't run away!'

But he was talking to an empty room.

5

Stunned, Fanie realised that he had '*pinched the tail of a black mamba*'. He faced the bitter truth that he had taken her compliance for granted, presumptuously assuming that she wouldn't refuse him – perhaps taking advantage of the fact that he was white and she was black. But something in him protested: *Come on Fanie, this is not true! We are in new South Africa, where the colour of one's skin is no longer relevant!*

Fanie waited for a while, still clinging to the minuscule hope that Dimakatjo might change her mind and return to his flat. When that didn't happen, he hurried out, thinking that he would catch her at the lift. But there was no one to be seen there. He pressed the button to summon the lift, entered and pressed 'Ground'. Dimakatjo was not to be found in the foyer either; so Fanie rushed out into the street, where he saw her marching briskly about a block away, clearly still in a huff, looking neither backwards nor sideways.

The emotional part of him told him to run after her, while the rational part said: *No, what will people think of you, a white man chasing after a black woman? What if she screams 'Help! Rape!'?* Fanie returned to his flat with the aim of gulping down an entire bottle of wine in order to get drunk and drown his woes. Once there, however, he changed his mind, snatched up his car keys and headed out again, with the intention of overtaking Dimakatjo and persuading her back to his flat.

Heading towards the Mamelodi taxi rank in his swift car, Fanie scanned both sides of Van der Walt Street. He crossed three sets of robots without spotting any sign of Dimakatjo. The fact that she was a health fanatic and member of a fitness club enabled her to walk very briskly indeed, even breaking into a run at one point, causing people to turn and look behind her in the assumption that a mugger must be hot on her heels. Dimakatjo did not want to be overtaken by Fanie and be part of the spectacle of a crazy white guy trying to persuade her to get into his car. She had almost reached the taxi rank when Fanie spotted her. He was about to press down hard on the accelerator and shoot across the intersection, but at that moment the amber robot turned red. Cursing, he hooted, and several people stared towards his car; not Dimakatjo, however!

To Fanie's great chagrin, the woman he was panting after boarded one of the taxis and banged the door closed behind her; the taxi drove away. Fanie felt like screaming. He drove back to his flat a greatly disappointed man.

The 13th of February dawned: a day of fresh opportunity for those with unfinished business to finish and new endeavours to begin. For Fanie, it was time to rethink his feelings for Dimakatjo. The question of whether to pursue or forget about her begged an immediate answer.

Fanie had 'two hearts', clashing within him like belligerent elephants. The first heart said: *Just throw in the towel broer; for you have lost with a technical knock-out!* Whereas the second heart encouraged him to persevere on the perilous path of love, promising that in the end, amidst cheers and applause, a winner's garland would be placed around his sweat-streaked neck.

When Dimakatjo awoke that morning she could think of nothing except what had happened the previous day at Fanie's flat. She wondered if she would lose him, or whether he would still chase after her. According to the precepts that she had been brought up with, a young man must not be given a heart of love just '*thuu-tšea!*' – 'on a platter!' No; a young man on the trail of love must be as patient and persistent as a salesperson. Dimakatjo had also learned from the experiences of other Mamelodi women that men attach little value to easy-to-get 'tarts'.

She thought back to the time when she was just a barefoot thirteen year old, wearing the uniform of black dungarees with white shirt; how, when a boy proposed love to her, she would shyly speak with a soft voice, her bashful eyes flitting in all directions; how, during a tense moment, she would begin to draw a pumpkin or the map of Afrika with her big toe, while biting her small fingernail; how the boy would be looking at her like a hawk hungry for meat; and how she would finally say in a tender, romantic voice: 'I'm still going to think it over.'

While she lay musing about this time-consuming business called love and the accident of falling into it, time moved on and when she glanced at the bedside clock she saw it was already past 8.00. She had decided not to go in to work this morning, for she did not want to see or talk to Fanie.

Discovering that her cellphone was out of airtime, she dashed out to the *spaza* shop opposite her home, where she stocked up on a pre-paid voucher and a few other items. She called the surgery and when Nthabiseng answered, asked her to tell Dr Makgabo that she wasn't feeling well and wouldn't be in that day.

Back inside her *mokhukhu*, the decent shack that she called home, Dimakatjo wondered if she had not blundered by running out of Fanie's flat the previous night; she asked herself why she had behaved in that emotional way. She wished that she had been able to act more rationally and assertively, so that Fanie would respect her for who she was – a well-brought-up village girl who was not in the city to mess up her life with the 'taste-and-pass' type of wolves. Remembering how her Sunday School teacher used to quote the 'wolves in sheepskins' verse from the Bible, she felt comforted and vindicated in her behaviour; yes, she had done the right thing by being tough on Fanie! Had he made love to her there and then as he had wanted to, she would now be feeling very cheated. She would be angry with herself. And probably cry. But it would be too late for tears.

Fanie went off to work that morning with a black and heavy heart. Even George could detect that something was amiss with him. The only sure way of shedding light on anything would be for Fanie to speak to Dimakatjo – the medicine of his bruised heart. He tried calling her at her place of work but Nthabiseng told him that Dimakatjo had not reported for work that morning.

'Why? What's the problem?' Fanie demanded, suddenly feeling guilt-stricken.

'She is sick,' responded Nthabiseng.

'Sick? But she was fine yesterday! What's the matter with her?'

'I don't know. Please call tomorrow. Maybe she will be back at work then.'

6

February the 14th had dawned at last – a cause for celebration for those who cherished any expectations about this Lovers' Day. Light and sunrays chased the darkness out of Mandela Village, a sprawling ten-kilometre stretch of shantytown in the East Section of Mamelodi. On the main street, primarily used by taxis and buses stood, among other structures, a neatly constructed four-roomed *mokhukhu*; this shack consisted of walls made of planks and roofed with corrugated plastic. In an attempt to make the walls more presentable and durable, the planks were covered with zinc sheeting firmly fastened with nails. The two rooms facing the street were fitted with large windows framed by curtains, giving clear indication that the owner had a special taste for good things. This particular shack belonged to Dimakatjo, child of Bakone.

The green *stoep* in front added a touch of glamour. The tiny patch of lawn in the yard was neatly cut and well looked after by hard-working Dimakatjo. In summer, flowers of diverse colours, heights and shapes made the place even more attractive. Opposite her shack was the *spaza* shop, where sweets, fruit, vegetables, cigarettes, cooldrinks and a variety of groceries were sold. Denneboom train station was a convenient five-kilometre ride away.

Waking with the daybreak, Dimakatjo lay in bed and thought about the day ahead of her. Today, she felt ready to tackle work. The previous night she had rested, although more in body than soul. She would have liked to be able to switch her mind off from bothering and fussing about what she could not change; a shattered earthenware pot that could not be reconstructed. She thought back sadly to her horoscope prediction that had proven to be so accurate: *'Your best chances of love are right at your doorstep, and the journey is promising; but watch out for a few thorns on the stems below the roses.'*

The journey – the drive to Fanie's flat – had, indeed, been promising; life had seemed all roses. Now, the thorns were out with all the vengeance they could muster to sour what she had thought was an exciting new chapter of her life. She wondered if she would still be able to believe in 'Stars Foretell' predictions after this.

Switching on the radio she found herself listening to a Valentine's Day special. Most of the listeners appeared to be teenage girls or young women, phoning in to send romantic greetings to their lovers. Dimakatjo wished she were one of these fortunate ones, bold enough to tell the whole world that they were on fire with love. With a sigh she rose and began to get ready for the day.

By 7.30 she was ready to leave, inspecting herself in the full-length mirror for the last time. *Aowaa, ruri!* Despite her low spirits, she couldn't help being cheered by the vision she presented. She was dressed in a calf-length African-print dress of black, green and purple. The tailoring, texture and colour of the garment was unmistakably Nigerian, and it came with matching *doek* and handbag. She had made herself up carefully and her eyeshadow blended exceptionally well with the purple tones of the material. Her open-toed sandals exposed the bronze-painted nails of a pair of size six feet. From her ears dangled wood-and-bead earrings of about five centimetres long, and her arms were adorned with bronze bangles the exact shade of her nailpolish.

Dimakatjo smiled at herself, lightly touching her fingers to her smooth, dusky-pink cheeks, wetting her fingertip to smooth her eyebrows and mock-kissing with her pink-lipsticked mouth. Her radiant image proclaimed that today she was perhaps the most beautiful woman in Mandela Village – if not in the whole of Mamelodi, and even Pretoria! Despite the state of her love-life, she had decided to dress up for Valentine's Day; if only there were a Romeo who appreciated her enough to make this special day memorable for her!

She felt a brief moment of envy for Nthabiseng, whose boyfriend would be taking her to Sun City for a post-Valentine's Day celebration. Yet, at the same time, she felt satisfied with being

Dimakatjo. She recalled the days when she was training as a nurse at Kalafong Nursing College, when some of the nursing sisters who had no boyfriends used to buy themselves flowers and gifts during the Valentine craze. She made up her mind that she would do the same for herself today.

Grabbing her handbag, she strutted out of her *mokhukhu*, locking the door behind her. She thumbed down a taxi which took her to Denneboom station, where she boarded a train. Alighting in Pretoria West, she walked for ten minutes as usual and reached Dr Makgabo's surgery at 8.30 on the dot. Nthabiseng had not yet arrived, so she put on water to boil in the old electric kettle and made herself a cup of herbal tea without milk, which she drank somewhat pensively. When Nthabiseng arrived, her eyes couldn't miss the excellence of Dimakatjo's appearance.

'Maki – *tsena ka mo!*' exclaimed Nthabiseng, whose words literally meant, 'have my congratulatory handshake!' Dimakatjo laughed as Nthabiseng continued to lavish praises on her. 'Maki, I like your *s'kwerekwere* style. It's terrific! You really look like a queen from West Afrika!' Nthabiseng raised up her hands and brought them down to slap Dimakatjo's open palms; the process was then swiftly repeated, with Nthabiseng's palms now bashed by Dimakatjo's hands.

'What a pity you have to put on your uniform. Why don't you just stay like that today and be the Valentine Queen?' Nthabiseng laughingly suggested.

When Fanie awoke that morning there was still warfare in his heart, with his 'two hearts' not agreeing. Standing in front of his bathroom mirror, he stared moodily at his new beardless image. It was the first time that he had put a razor blade to his chin in over two years. His chin now looked like well-shaved pork. He had simply felt, when he awoke, an irrepressible urge to do something new; to start this fresh day looking different. While the first heart was busy giving him reasons why he should throw in the towel with Dimakatjo, the second heart kept interrupting, cautioning: *Wag 'n bietjie, boetie!* ('Wait a bit, little brother!') *Just be patient and you will be rewarded.* Fanie recalled the Boy Scout motto in Afrikaans: '*Hou moed, hou koers!*' – 'Don't lose courage, stay on course!'

Fanie listened to the second heart. Absolutely convinced that he must now become a different Fanie, he combed his hair backwards from his forehead, took an elastic band and tied his hair back, making a ponytail style that surprised him; he had never tried that style in his life before. He was tempted to add an earring, which would certainly transform him – into one of those 'arty-farty' types, the kind who worked in advertising or recording studios.

It crossed his mind to wonder what Gerda would think of his new image; but his focus and energy were channelled more towards Dimakatjo, the Black Pearl. The last thing he did before he walked out of the flat was to take the remaining cigarettes from his packet, grimly break them into pieces and flush them down the toilet. He was surprised at his strong motivation to defeat the stubborn tobacco habit; he believed he had just achieved it without spending one cent on remedies, doctors or psychologists!

At ten o'clock, just as Dimakatjo and Nthabiseng were sitting down to their morning break of tea with health biscuits, they heard the desk phone crying: *Trrring-trrring!*

Dimakatjo, who picked up the receiver, was gripped by anxiety. She waited with bated breath for the caller to speak, then quickly put the phone down. As she had both feared and hoped, the caller was Fanie. She felt very confused; one part of her wanted to speak to him, while the other heart told her she was not yet ready for that.

'Who was that?' enquired Nthabiseng curiously.

'It was . . . just a wrong number,' lied Dimakatjo uncomfortably. A few minutes later the phone rang again and this time Nthabiseng took the call. She listened attentively, then said, 'Please hold' and held the receiver out to Dimakatjo with a smile: 'It's yours, Maki.'

Dimakatjo pulled twice at her chin with her thumb and index finger, a non-verbal way of asking whether the caller was male.

Shrewd Nthabiseng put her two fists on her chest, indicating that the caller was female. Despite this, Dimakatjo's heart began to thump erratically: *Gooh-gooh-gooohh!*

As she suspected the caller was, indeed, Fanie. Without wasting any time, he apologised for his behaviour that had caused her to walk out of his flat on their last meeting.

Dimakatjo graciously accepted his apology, adding that she was also sorry that she had so angrily walked out. At that, he vaguely said that he would keep in touch and hung up.

With mixed feelings Dimakatjo slowly replaced the receiver. She was relieved to have so easily resolved what had felt like nightmarish unfinished business. But she was disappointed, too, that Fanie seemed to be in such a hurry to finish the conversation. She had expected him to say more, to ask when they could meet again, eyeball to eyeball, in order to mend what was broken. She had no way of guessing what was in Fanie's heart.

A few hours later, when the lunchtime siren sounded at Jacaranda Welding Company, Fanie did not join George in heading for the staff canteen as usual. He told his friend that he was rushing out to the stationery shop. George watched thoughtfully from the courtyard as 'new look' Fanie got hurriedly into his car and sped off. He was convinced that Fanie was hiding something from him, but he was confident that the time would come when all would be revealed. The truth would be like the moon, emerging naked out of the napkins of clouds.

Fanie drove three blocks to the Kwagga shopping centre in Pretoria West. As he was parking, his cellphone rang. It was Gerda. She wanted to confirm the time for their Valentine's supper that evening. Coolly, Fanie replied that something important had come up and he was going to have to cancel their plans for dinner. They would have to postpone it until the following evening instead.

'I can't talk now,' he said. And cut the call before surprised Gerda could find her voice to protest.

Furious, Gerda tried to phone back. But all she got was his voicemail message telling her that Fanie was not available.

Fanie disappeared into the shopping mall and emerged 30 minutes later with a gift-wrapped parcel under his arm.

At Dr Makgabo's surgery, Dimakatjo, still dressed in her Valentine finery, was busy dispensing tablets and bottles while Nthabiseng ticked off patients' names in the diary. When Dimakatjo raised her head, her eyes landed on clean-shaven Fanie, with unfamiliar ponytail hairstyle, standing on the other side of the counter. He wore tight, pitch-black pants with an arty, deep-blue shirt decorated with dancing stick figures that looked like they were from a Khoisan cave painting. She found him menacingly handsome. His brown eyes were vivacious with excitement and his smile, devastatingly charming.

Child of Bakone felt short of breath. Before she could recover from the shock of seeing him there, Fanie dropped something on the desk in front of her: a bouquet of twelve red roses and a gift-wrapped parcel. This was a pleasant bombshell that she had never expected! Excitedly Dimakatjo grabbed the gift, kissed it and pressed it to her chest; in front of everyone, she leapt around the counter to kiss Fanie on his pink, clean-shaven cheek. Conscious of the watching eyes, Fanie also kissed her on the cheek, though he would have much preferred a genuine mouth-to-mouth kiss.

'I don't know how to thank you, Mr Fourie!' cooed Dimakatjo, for the benefit of the listening ears.

'You are very welcome, Maki!'

'But what are you doing here, Fanie? Please don't neglect your job or you will be fired!'

'I'm on lunch. And I am fired . . . with love!' beamed Fanie wittily.

They said their goodbyes and Fanie went on his way, watched by several pairs of inquisitive eyes. The gazes of patients, nurses and doctor alike followed the ponytailed Romeo as he left the surgery and walked to his car in the parking lot outside.

'And he also drives a BM! You have indeed hit the jackpot, my friend!' hissed Nthabiseng excitedly, with just a tinge of envy in her voice, as she thumped Dimakatjo's shoulder. Dimakatjo chuckled softly and carried her roses through to the kitchen to put them in water.

There, she took a private moment to investigate her gift. She first carefully removed the card that was stuck to the parcel, then tore off the wrapping paper, revealing contents that made her gasp: a meticulously crafted copper bangle, and a necklace as thick as a finger, formed of bright, multicoloured Ndebele beads. Dimakatjo read the printed message on the card:

In you my life's
Sure to thrive
And sprout!
You are more precious
More priceless than
Mountain-heaps of gold and diamonds.

At the bottom of the card Fanie had written: 'With tons of love, from me.' He had signed his name and also added his telephone numbers.

Dimakatjo kissed the card tearfully. Putting on the copper bangle, she was struck by how well it went with the outfit she was wearing. She spent a long time admiring the necklace, turning it over and over in her hands; this was not the kind of thing to be worn from Monday to Friday. *Aowaa!* She decided she would wear this necklace only on a very special occasion.

Extremely touched by her gifts, she wanted to run after Fanie, to thank him again, hug him and kiss his clean-shaven cheek.

7

At Fanie's place of work, George walked towards Fanie's desk, commenting that he hadn't seen Fanie take a smoke break all day.

'I've given up,' Fanie told him.

George was impressed. 'Does your new girlfriend have anything to do with this new non-smoking Fanie?' he teased.

'*Ja*, she hates smoking. She is very health-conscious. No more junk-food for me either.' Fanie prodded his stomach and added: 'Beer-belly, your days are numbered!'

The two men laughed with relish. George had not the faintest idea that Fanie was counting the chickens before they had even hatched.

'What's her name?' enquired George.

'None of your *blerry* business!'

George shook his head and smiled indulgently at his love-bugged colleague.

'Gerda called you. She said please phone her. She said your cellphone was switched off.'

'I have already spoken to her,' Fanie said disinterestedly.

George shrugged his shoulders. Fanie remembered what his colleague had once said to him: '*A woman is like a* sangoma. *If you are in love with someone she can smell it.*'

The telephone rang at Fanie's desk.

'It's probably Gerda again,' said George.

'I don't want to speak to her. Please answer and tell her I'm still out of the office.'

George obligingly picked up the receiver.

'It's not Gerda,' he assured Fanie, blocking the mouthpiece with his hand.

Smiling, Fanie took the phone from George.

Dimakatjo's voice exploded excitedly in his ear: 'What a surprise! Thank you very much, Fanie!'

'Your pleasure is my pleasure, Maki!'

Fanie was extremely delighted that his strategy had achieved its aim of making a good impression on the woman of his dreams.

'Maki, what are you doing after *tshaile* today?'

'Nothing special, Fanie.'

Dimakatjo had conferred thoroughly with her heart and had decided that – Tau or no Tau – this was an opportune moment to take the plunge into an unknown pool of romance.

'Can you come to my place, Maki? I promise I will behave myself this time . . . ' Fanie held his breath until he heard her say: 'Okay.'

'Can I collect you after work . . . ?'

'No, don't worry Fanie. I'll need to go home first. This time I will come to your place by myself. What's the number of your flat again?'

'Number 31. Take the lift to the third floor.'

'Fine. I'll be there at about 6.30.'

George laughed aloud as a beaming Fanie put the phone down.

'Tell me Fanie, is your new lover a black woman?'

'What makes you say that?'

'You mean it's none of my *blerry* business?' responded George.

'That's right!'

For a while they didn't speak, busy with their various tasks. But Fanie could feel George's probing eyes on him, his mind busy doing the arithmetic of Fanie's love-life. Fanie left him to draw his own conclusions; he felt that it was not the right time to share the secrets of his heart with anyone.

Knock-off time came at last. Fanie sped home and spent the next hour getting things ready for his guest of honour.

At exactly 6.30 he heard a knock at his door. When he looked through the peephole he saw Dimakatjo – the flower of his desert, the woman *more priceless than mountain-heaps of gold and diamonds*, as the Valentine card had put it.

Fanie opened the door with a dancing heart, flames in his eyes and fire in his bones. He wanted to give her a hell of a hug and a kiss to end all kisses. But he restrained himself, deciding rather to shake her hand; once he had her hand in his, however, he found himself raising it to his mouth and kissing the knuckles, holding them to his lips a good deal longer than was necessary. This drew rapturous peals of laughter from Dimakatjo.

That evening Dimakatjo and Fanie had a whale of a time, celebrating Valentine's Day together at Fanie's flat. Seated together on one sofa they tickled their palates with fruit juices, snacks, and dried fruit. Music was additional food for their romance. They held hands and Fanie caressed her waist, sliding his hand up to her armpit, but without going 'too far'. She, had he but known it, was very ready tonight for his torrid kisses, and even more of his heart and body; but he was the one who held back now, for he didn't want to take the chance of scaring her off again. On this occasion, the mouse had visited a tame and harmless vegetarian cat!

As always, Dimakatjo's laughter was indescribably enticing to love-struck Fanie. She exuded magnetic charm through her eyes, hands, fingers, lips, tongue and even the tone of her voice. He was consumed by the desire to kiss her, his hands aching to do what they could do best. Her alluring scent filled his nostrils, and self-control was forgotten. In an instant he had embraced her tightly, with the aim of teaching her an unforgettable kissing lesson; but she restrained him. To give herself time to gather her thoughts, she nibbled and swallowed a delicious dried peach; then she looked him straight in his brown and bubbling eyes and said: 'Do you love me, Fanie?'

'*Natuurlik, my skattebol!*' ('Of course, my sweetheart!')

'But you haven't told me, have you? Last time you just wanted my *kuku*!'

'What is *kuku*?'

Dimakatjo playfully slapped her hand against Fanie's cheek, and they both roared with mirth. Fanie interrupted Dimakatjo's laughter with a tender kiss; this stimulated hunger for more kisses. Dimakatjo felt the heat of Fanie's devouring gaze. As he moved his face towards her again she caught her breath expectantly, anticipating another terrific kiss; but instead, he softly patted her cheek and stood up to go and insert a romantic CD in the player. He stretched his arms out sideways, as if to embrace someone, and began dancing a waltz; then he halted and smiled at Dimakatjo.

'Come on, join me!' he invited.

She hesitated, and then roared again with rich laughter as Fanie came to uproot her physically from her seat. He planted her firmly on her feet and held her close, her breast pressed to his chest. It was a golden opportunity for a romantic cheek-to-cheek dance. But Fanie repeatedly trod on Dimakatjo's toes, causing her to scream in her mother's language: '*Joo-mma-wee!*' She then revenged herself on him, and '*Eina!*' Fanie groaned in Afrikaans. After that track they sat down to replenish their energy with more fruit juice.

'Maki, do you have a boyfriend?' Fanie asked her unexpectedly.

She hesitated in her response, then guiltily said: 'No, why?'

'No, it can't be true! Are you telling me that such a beautiful girl like you has no man in her life?' persisted Fanie incredulously.

Dimakatjo responded with evasive laughter.

'You must tell me the truth, Maki!'

'I will tell you the truth when you tell *me* the truth. Have *you* got a girlfriend, Fanie?'

'Answer my question first, Maki!'

Dimakatjo quivered with more laughter. 'No, you tell me!'

'Okay,' said Fanie, 'Yes, I have!'

Dimakatjo's laughter stopped abruptly.

'What's her name?'

'Gerda Moerdyk-van-Schalkwyk,' said Fanie very reluctantly.

'Oh, a real *boer eh*! Do you love her?'

'Yes,' said Fanie without thinking.

'What? You love her? Are you telling me you LOVE HER?' Dimakatjo leapt to her feet, grabbed her handbag and marched towards the door.

'No, no, Maki – I was only joking! Of course I don't love her – I love *you*! She is just running after me, that's all!' exclaimed Fanie.

'I am not convinced, Fanie!'

'Maki, you are my sweetie-pie, my jam-and-peanut-butter, my paradise-walking-on-two-legs . . . !' pleaded Fanie, kneeling contritely.

'If you tell me that you love me,' he added, 'I will break it off with her right now. I will tell her that I am in love with a beautiful black chick! She will be very jealous, but I won't care a damn! It's the first time that I have fallen really in love. I truly love you Maki! With all my heart and . . . my *veldskoene*!' he finished, his voice breaking.

Dimakatjo looked at him in silence. 'I don't believe you, Fanie! Why are you telling me all that rubbish?'

'Please . . . madam!'

'I'm not your madam!' objected Dimakatjo, stabbing her finger at Fanie.

At that, they both burst out laughing, then held hands, embraced and finally kissed. Fanie was so energised that he lifted her up to his navel, swung her around and then kissed her again before planting her down in front of him.

The rest of the evening passed in a trice. What the lovers wished would flare and flourish unceasingly had to come to an end. For, as the saying goes, *'that which doesn't come to an end foreshadows omen'*. The Valentine's party ended at 9.30. Dimakatjo would have been happy to be dropped off at the Bloed Street taxi rank, from where she would take a taxi to Mamelodi. But Fanie insisted on driving her back to the shack she called her house and home.

8

A brief half hour later, the headlamps of Fanie's BMW swept up the pockmarked main street of Mandela Village and illuminated the front facade of Dimakatjo's neat shack. They kissed lingeringly while the passenger door of the car was open, heedless of the fact that they might be seen by somebody's eyes somewhere in the darkness. *For the one who tiptoes and crawls is seen by the one who lies down.*

Bigboy, the owner of the *spaza* shop opposite Dimakatjo's shack, was busy counting the takings for the day when something within him said: *Watch out!* Bigboy was one of Tau's lackeys. He hero-worshipped Tau, from whom he sought bits of legal advice and whom he reverently addressed as 'Bra T'.

He saw with his own two eyes a white *ngamola* – a prosperous-looking person – kissing Dimakatjo, Tau's woman. Bigboy watched, wide-eyed, as the German-made car reversed in front of Dimakatjo's shack; she smiled and waved at the driver who hooted before revving the engine and speeding off. Bigboy reflected that when he reported back to Tau, it wouldn't be necessary for him to say 'I was told that this and this happened', or 'I heard from the goat by the roadside that your Maki did xyz'. *Aowaa!* In this case, he had seen it all with his own two eyes.

Unlocking the door to her shack, Dimakatjo entered and stepped quickly to the window of her lounge, where she watched the tail-lights of Fanie's car bobbing away down the dark, uneven street of the shantytown.

That night she slept peacefully, smiling in her dreams, assured that the journey of love was, indeed, promising, and that whatever thorns there were on the stems of the roses were too trivial to bother about.

Back at his flat Fanie, still fired up with desire, reflected with surprise on his self-control in the presence of the sensuous and provocative Dimakatjo. He felt a great sense of achievement concerning his ability to tame his inner beast. He had no doubt that she would respect him the more for it. *A man will earn respect for being interested more in what is between a woman's ears than what is between her tender thighs*, thought Fanie, impressed by his own maturity in entertaining such a notion. He felt very satisfied with himself; but then confidence waned, beset by a barrage of questions from his 'other heart': *Are you certain you love this black woman? Is it love, or simply lust? Just curiosity to 'taste and pass'? What if you lose interest in her after having her* kuku?

He laughed aloud as he thought of how Dimakatjo had said to him a few hours earlier: 'All you wanted was to have my *kuku*!' He tried to make his mind veer off this erotic track, but in vain. Then he thought about his mother, whose racial hang-ups could fill volumes. *How will the old lady react when she comes to hear that I, her lily-white boy, am in love with a black woman?* The answer was obvious: his mother's resistance would be as formidable as a mountain. She would, no doubt, accuse him of having lost his sanity. *What's wrong with you?* he could hear her saying. *Are you mad, Fanie? How can you dump a decent Afrikaans* meisie *like Gerda, with whom you have been in love for many years, for a black* hoermeid *you hardly know? You don't even know if the tart has AIDS or not!*

He decided then and there that, however daunting the challenges ahead, Dimakatjo was worth the gamble; if this backfired, he would bear the blame and be the wiser for it. He comforted himself that at least he would be able to count on his sister, Anna-Marie, for support. He was positive that she would be fully in favour of his adventurous new relationship. She had always been something of a rebel, refusing to toe the conservative line – a fact that had been the cause of many bitter family arguments between her and their mother.

As for Gerda . . . he would cross that river when he came to it. He intended to phone her in the morning and arrange for them to meet that evening for dinner. There, he would break the news to her that their relationship was over.

Fanie was still thinking about this and the umpteen other concerns milling around in his head when, miraculously, he fell asleep.

He dreamt he was walking hand in hand with Dimakatjo. They were strolling through the right-wing suburb of Daanville that was notorious for its palpable poverty and rabid neo-Nazi Afrikaners. Suddenly, from both sides of the street appeared white men, women and children who vented their hatred, hurling all sorts of insults at Fanie and Dimakatjo. Dimakatjo, though unfamiliar with some of the hate-words that poured out like diarrhoea in Afrikaans, could hear clearly the words 'Kaffer! Kaffer!' repeated with unflagging vocal energy.

The next instant, rotten eggs and over-ripe tomatoes rained down on the lovers and ferocious dogs were set on them. Since they both wore *takkies* they had no problem in running for their lives, racing towards the taxi route that was about a block away. In the taxi, Fanie and Dimakatjo were enthusiastically welcomed by the black passengers on board, some of them proffering their hands to Fanie, exclaiming: '*Sebara, sebara!*' – 'brother-in-law, brother-in-law!' The next thing, they were in Fanie's flat, where Fanie insisted on making love to Dimakatjo. And she didn't hesitate to respond. They undressed and engaged in foreplay. Dimakatjo insisted on a condom, but Fanie said, 'No ways! I want it flesh-to-flesh!' Irritated, Dimakatjo said: 'Fanie, you are not going to have my *kuku* then!' And she began to put her clothes back on; but in the dream Fanie overpowered her and made wonderful love to her . . .

Shortly afterwards, Fanie woke up. The dream was so vivid that he was sure Dimakatjo was in the bed with him; only to find that he was embracing his pillow.

That evening, Fanie drove to Willow Trees Restaurant in Pretoria East, where he had arranged to meet Gerda. Willow Trees was part of a franchise of popular restaurants with a unique design. It comprised little thatched-roof rondavels or circular huts, each one able to accommodate parties of up to six people.

When Fanie arrived he found Gerda seated in the smoking section, cigarette in hand. These rondavels reminded Fanie of the huts in the villages in Ga-Mokopane (Potgietersrus), where he had lived until he was thirteen years old. He wished he had invited Dimakatjo to this restaurant; the two of them would have reminisced about rural life.

Gerda was well-dressed in a smart burgundy two-piece suit, topped with a neckerchief. Her dark hair had been freshly styled into soft curls and her careful make-up, perfume and newly polished nails all indicated that she had made a calculated effort to impress Fanie.

When Gerda's eyes landed on the 'new look' Fanie, clean-shaven and sporting the unfamiliar ponytail, she scarcely recognised him at first. Her spirits plummeted, for she was convinced from the bottom of her unhappy heart that Fanie was in love with another woman.

They exchanged greetings and dutiful kisses. Fanie had no sooner sat down than he beckoned the waiter over.

'What will you have?' Fanie asked Gerda, as the waiter handed them menus. He didn't wait for her answer but gave in his own order without delay.

Gerda raised her eyebrows when he asked for pure fruit juice instead of his usual favourite – an unhealthy soot-black softdrink. She was further surprised when he ordered grilled fish with salad, instead of his customary large, well-done T-bone steak with egg and chips on the side.

'Since when have you stopped eating red meat?' Gerda couldn't suppress her curiosity, that was brewing into irritation.

'Since last week.'

'Why? What happened?'

'Nothing dramatic. I just decided to eat more healthily. The doctor said I have high blood pressure and I should watch my diet.'

Gerda also noted that he asked for fresh fruit salad instead of ice-cream for dessert. With a hint of defiance, she gave in her own order of a medium-rare rump steak with chips and salad.

The waiter went away and Gerda and Fanie sat in silence. Gerda lit up another cigarette and offered one to Fanie, who shook his head and fanned away her smoke in an irritated way.

'What's the matter?' Gerda said. 'Oh, don't tell me you've given up smoking, too!'

'That's right,' said Fanie.

Savagely she crushed out her hardly smoked cigarette into the ashtray.

'You were the one who taught me to smoke! Remember, Mr Perfect Guy?'

'Yes, but now I've quit. And I don't like the smell any more.'

'When did you quit?'

'Last week.'

'Last week, last week!' said Gerda in a temper. 'And I suppose you also changed your hairstyle last week? What was happening with you last week, Fanie?'

There was a brief pause. Fanie hesitated to venture a word. 'I just decided to change, that's all,' he responded weakly. 'I wanted to try a different look for a change. And to stop smoking. You can also stop . . . '

'I can't!'

'Yes, you can Gerda!'

'No I can't. Smoking helps to make me slim . . . '

Fanie grunted with disbelief.

'*Ek is ernstig*, Fanie!' ('I'm serious, Fanie!') insisted Gerda. 'And it also soothes my nerves.'

Fanie chose not to respond to what sounded to him like a teenager's cliché. His face, however, spelt out to Gerda that he was not impressed with her justifications.

The waiter brought their drinks: fruit cocktail for Fanie, and a diet cooldrink for Gerda. Fanie took two strong sips of his iced fruit juice. He was relieved to have the opportunity to concentrate on the refreshing coldness of ice cubes and the sweetness of the juice. Gerda took the opportunity to scrutinise him anew. She saw that he wore black; all black, from his shoes to his shoulders. She was curious to know why he had chosen to put on such sombre attire, but she felt reluctant to ask him for fear of his answer. She shrank from hearing that he had dressed himself in black for a reason – like a priest who had come to conduct the funeral rites for the love she was so stubbornly hanging onto; the sickly and failing relationship that would, almost certainly, be pronounced dead-on-arrival at the love hospital. *Rest in peace dead love! Dust to dust, ashes to ashes. Amen!*

Fanie, for his part, thought that it must be immediately obvious to any observer from their lack of conversation and their stiff body language that this meeting would be their last. Even the act of eating the food on their plates seemed, to him, a joyless exercise, mere drudgery for tongue and teeth.

Looking up, he found Gerda's baffled gaze on him.

'What's happening with you, Fanie?'

'What do you mean?'

'You are a changed person! Your clothes . . . your eating habits . . . your . . . everything about you says . . . '

'What?'

'That something big has happened. Tell me Fanie . . . are you in love with someone else?'

Fanie feigned deafness for a moment. He tried to buy time by concentrating on his fruit juice, gulping it down without even tasting what he was drinking. '*A woman is like a* sangoma. *If you are in love with someone she can smell it,*' he thought.

'Answer me, Fanie!'

The seconds multiplied into a minute.

'I'm asking you a question, Fanie. Please have the decency to give me an honest answer!'

'All right then,' responded Fanie curtly.

'All right what?'

'Yes, I'm in love with another woman!'

Gerda lit up a cigarette with a shaking hand. 'Who is she? I'm waiting Fanie!'

It was on the tip of Fanie's tongue to tell her. But he shrank from the scene that would ensue. He feared that if Gerda heard the truth about her rival in love an ambulance would have to be called for her.

So all he said was: 'What does it matter who she is? The point is that you and I are finished!'

The look on Gerda's face as he said it made him feel a pang of guilt. But his heart had no space in it for sympathy for Gerda; it was too full up with feeling for his new love.

It wasn't a pleasant journey back to Gerda's place. Fanie was forced to give her a lift home since there were no buses into town at that time of night. All the way in the car, Gerda chain-smoked until he felt choked to death. She alternated between accusing him shrilly of two-timing her, and pleading with him not to throw her over.

When they at last arrived at her flat he could hardly wait for her to get out, his impatient foot already revving the accelerator before she had even opened the door.

Gerda had no option but to alight. With a bleeding heart she entered her flat, her mind still reeling from the shock of Fanie's revelation. She was compelled to face the hard and bitter truth: that Fanie had had the gall to invite her to dinner not to celebrate a romantic evening with her, but to show her beyond a shadow of doubt that he belonged to someone else – another woman, with whom he had almost certainly celebrated Valentine's Day.

Poor Gerda cried bucketfuls of bitter tears.

On Monday Fanie arrived at work with his face beaming as if he had netted the '*Tata ma-millions*' lottery. On this occasion, he did not hesitate to disclose to George that he was insanely in love with Dimakatjo. George shook Fanie's hand in the extended African handshake, grinning from ear to ear.

'Well done, boy!' he enthused, patting Fanie's shoulder. 'Love has finally snared you!'

'Thank you George.'

'It's great to be truly in love, isn't it Fanie?'

'Absolutely!'

'So you are now a relative of us blacks!'

'Well, you can say so . . . if our relationship will end in marriage.'

George laughed and squeezed Fanie's arm.

'*Hei sebara*, we want *lobola*; you mustn't just *jol* around with this woman, okay?'

'*Ja baas!*'

'Listen, you owe me a drink!'

'Why?' asked Fanie.

'Because you are now my brother-in-law! The way to the girl's place should be dotted with gifts!'

The two friends laughed heartily together.

At Dr Makgabo's surgery Dimakatjo and Nthabiseng were busy with the post-mortems of how they had spent their various romantic weekends.

'Please tell me the truth, Maki. Did he . . . *er* . . . make love to you?'

'No!'

'You are lying, Maki!'

'*Mnci' strue!*' ('I'm telling nothing but truth!')

'Really?'

'I swear by your mother!'

'Just don't be too difficult, Maki,' Nthabiseng warned.

'Fanie guesses that there is another guy in my life.'

'Who? Tau? Don't be a fool *wena*! You should tell him you are free as a bird!'

'I didn't want to be an easy bird, that will not be treasured by the fowler.'

'Be careful Maki, don't be too hard to get. If you take too long the man will be gone! Remember, if a billy-goat licks a bit of salt he will come back tomorrow.'

Dimakatjo nodded her head thoughtfully. 'You know, I am not very much impressed with Tau,' she said. 'I don't know why I have endured the relationship so long.'

'Choose Fanie!' her friend urged her. 'White men, when they are in love, have tender care: they spoil their women with nice presents, breakfast in bed . . . they help to cook, and change the baby's nappies, and . . . '

Dimakatjo interrupted with loud peals of amusement.

'But black men!' Nthabiseng continued. 'They read newspapers when there's work to be done, and they are quick to "panelbeat" their women!'

The waiting room was still filled with Dimakatjo and Nthabiseng's excited chatter when Dr Makgabo entered, unnoticed by the two women.

'You girls are having a good time!' remarked the doctor who, for once, found not a single patient waiting for his attention. As a result, he took a moment to socialise with the two nurses.

'So, ladies, how was your Valentine's weekend?' he enquired.

'*She* had a super time with her man in Sun City!' Dimakatjo grabbed the first opportunity, pointing at Nthabiseng.

'Yes, but Doctor, Maki had a very romantic evening with our first white patient!' Nthabiseng enthused.

'Did she now?' smiled Dr Makgabo. 'What was the guy's name again?'

'Fanie Fourie,' said Nthabiseng and Dimakatjo simultaneously.

'*Ja*, that's right. No wonder Mr Fourie no longer visits our surgery! Love has cured him of his troubles, and his heart is beating as strong as a galloping horse: *Maki-Maki-Maki!*'

They all laughed, savouring the doctor's sense of humour.

That afternoon Fanie called Dimakatjo and invited her to go on a picnic with him the following weekend. To this she sweetly replied: 'Yes Fanie, I'd love to!'

Nthabiseng's warning that she must not play too hard to get was already beginning to pay dividends.

For Fanie, the remaining days of the week seemed to crawl by. On Friday he arrived early at work, put the kettle on and laid out the cups, tea-bags, milk and other paraphernalia. When George arrived he stared in astonishment at Fanie's unusually organised efforts. There were even health muffins to go with the tea.

Fanie wasted no time in telling George that he was taking Dimakatjo out on a picnic the following day. George stared thoughtfully at his glowing face.

'You are absurdly in love, *eh?* The black girl has indeed bewitched you!'

'I don't mind being bewitched. All I care about is that tomorrow she will be in my two arms and hands!'

George laughed quietly to himself.

Fanie gave George a cup of coffee while he helped himself to black herbal tea. He was still trying to acquire the taste and he couldn't help making a face after the first few swallows. Conversation halted for a time as the two men checked their diaries, read their emails and prioritised their tasks for the day.

'How's your mother going to react to your choice of woman?' asked George presently, having had some experience of Fanie's mother on the occasions when she had phoned her son at work.

'I don't expect that she is going to say "Hallelujah!" Not right off, anyway. She is old-fashioned in her thinking, you know. That's how she was brought up. But I have my own life to live and she will just have to get to like the idea.'

'So tell me Fanie, what do you find so interesting about a black woman?'

'Love knows no colour,' retorted Fanie.

Then he flashed a naughty smile: 'A black woman is quality. She is a Mercedes Benz!'

'And what is a white woman? A Volkswagen?' George retorted.

They were still laughing at their joke when Fanie's desk phone rang. They both stared at it without moving.

'Will you answer?' Fanie asked George. 'If it's Gerda, then I am not here, okay?'

'And if she is not Gerda? Should I still say you are out?'

Grinning, George picked up the receiver: 'Hello? Who is that speaking? Oh, Gerda . . . No, I'm sorry, he is out. No, I don't know when he will be back . . . Yes, I'll give him your message.'

George put the receiver down thoughtfully.

'Shame. The Volkswagen sounds upset,' he said.

9

Saturday morning came at last. Fanie had spent a restless night, sleeping the 'stop-and-go' type of sleep known as *sepatikana*. When the first amber rays came filtering into his flat, he was already out of bed and busily preparing for the event to come. It was the finest of summer mornings. The golden sun shone down as though bestowing its blessing on the world and everything seemed to sparkle with happy expectancy. In a very short time, everything was ready and securely stored in the roomy boot of Fanie's car.

Dimakatjo, by contrast, had slept the 'sleep of a bull', like an infant whose tummy was tight with *matutu* – 'mother's milk'. The first thought in her mind when she awoke at 6.00 a.m. was that this was the day of the picnic; the day when she and Fanie would see their new-found love come to bloom.

Rising without delay, she heated water for her 'bath'; using a gas bottle she boiled a potful, which she then mixed with cold water in a large plastic basin. This was the routine ablution of women in her situation, who did not have properly equipped bathrooms because they lived in so-called 'informal settlements'. Dimakatjo dressed herself with care and by seven o'clock, according to her wristwatch, she was dressed and ready to go.

She wore a purple shirt tucked into a pair of tight-fitting Bermuda shorts fitted with loops at the waist, through which a wide black belt was slotted. Her shirt was of transparent nylon, and through it one could see the lacy black bra that contained her voluptuous medium sized breasts. A matching black ribbon tied the braided strands of her hair together. Her face looked radiant, thanks to its careful application of rich bronze make-up base and dusky blusher, and her arresting eyes appeared even larger than usual, their natural beauty enhanced by perfectly applied eyeshadow, black kohl eyeliner and mascara.

She stood for a moment critically viewing herself in the full-length mirror, trying to see herself through Fanie's eyes. She was not unsatisfied with what she saw. To complete the picture, she added big, trendy sunglasses, which she thought made her look mysteriously alluring. Her full African lips were coloured with a luscious apricot lipstick. *Mmalo!* Child of Bakone was, indeed, ready for the picnic. And Fanie!

She was so consumed by her preparations that she had forgotten to prepare herself some breakfast. She chewed an energy bar and gulped down a glass of fruit juice. No one could blame her for forgoing a proper breakfast today. She was already full of the picnic that she had not yet touched with her tongue.

By that time Fanie, too, was already fully dressed, in blue Bermuda shorts and a big, multicoloured shirt adorned with pictures of huge butterflies and flowers. He wore camping sandals on his feet and his chin was freshly shaven. He had even remembered to add a slap or two of French aftershave lotion, that he was certain would stir an amorous response from deep in the guts of Dimakatjo. He also took out a pouch containing sunglasses and inserted it into the top pocket of his shirt. At last he was ready for the picnic. And Dimakatjo!

At that moment Fanie's landline rang. He was sure that the caller must be Dimakatjo, but he felt a moment of doubt as he picked up the receiver. He therefore did not hurry to say, 'Hello?' but instead waited for the caller to speak first.

As he had feared, it was Gerda. *The bitch is still chasing after me!* was Fanie's unkind thought. Without saying a word he gently set the receiver down, then immediately removed it from the handset.

A short while later when Dimakatjo phoned Fanie's cellphone, the voicemail message came on: 'Hi, I'm not available to answer your call. Please leave your name and telephone number and I will call you back.' Fanie had switched off his cell before he went to sleep and had forgotten to switch it back on again.

Dimakatjo left a message: 'It's Maki. How far are you? Hurry up, Fanie! I'm impatiently waiting. Bye!'

She then decided to try him on his landline but, much to her disappointment, it was engaged. Frustrated, Dimakatjo phoned again a short while later and found that Fanie's phone was still engaged. She wondered jealously who he could be having such a long conversation with so early on a Saturday morning.

Fanie, meanwhile, had already left the flat. He drove out of the gate and joined the Saturday morning traffic stream in Van der Walt Street. Instead of driving straight to Mamelodi to fetch Dimakatjo he decided to pass by his mother's house in Koedoespoort to collect his post.

Seeing a pharmacy up ahead, the thought occurred to him to stop and buy a packet of condoms. But something reckless in him said: *Hey, don't worry about the condoms, why don't you just have it flesh-to-flesh?*

He drove on past the pharmacy; but at the next robots, he turned around and went back again to buy the condoms. As he was paying for them, he remembered to turn on his cellphone. It rang almost immediately.

'Where are you, Fanie?' Dimakatjo's voice asked impatiently.
'At the pharmacy.'
'What are you doing there? Are you sick?'
'No! I'm buying . . . some mint sweets for you.'
'Why was your home phone engaged all the time?'
'I was speaking to Mariekie.'
'Who's Mariekie?'
'She is my sis . . . !'
'What? I can't hear you!'

The reception on Dimakatjo's end began to break up. Fanie's voice became muffled and unclear.

'Mariekie is my sis . . . ' tried Fanie again, but this time Dimakatjo's cellphone cut out completely and he was forced to hang up.

She is my what? My sweetheart? Dimakatjo asked herself, with more than a tinge of anxiety. Could Fanie dare to speak of someone as his sweetheart, when she knew herself to be the only queen? No one but Fanie could answer that question.

Doubt began to gnaw at Dimakatjo's heart. She cursed the cellphone for its unreliability and for leaving her hanging in this merciless fashion.

Fanie, meanwhile, finished his purchases, not forgetting the mint sweets for Dimakatjo, lest he be exposed for lying. He couldn't tell her that he was buying condoms; but he knew that when the time came she would insist on them, the way that it had happened in his dream. And he, too, did not want to be reckless with his new love.

A short while later Fanie's BMW drew up at 33 Moreletta Straat in the suburb of Koedoespoort. Formerly reserved exclusively for white railway workers and their families, Koedoespoort was now becoming more mixed. This was where Fanie had been raised from the age of thirteen when his parents had relocated from Potgietersrus to Pretoria.

Number 33 was an old house with a sloping roof and a veranda in the front. It was surrounded with wire-fencing and had a tidily kept lawn.

When Fanie entered, using his key, he found the family's loyal and long-serving domestic worker, Selina Mamabolo, preparing breakfast in the kitchen. As he greeted the jovial and slightly obese Selina, his sister Anna-Marie entered; they kissed affectionately in greeting. It was easy to see they were brother and sister, for they looked alike, although Anna-Marie was of a more petite build than her brother.

'This is a nice surprise! How are you *boetie*? We haven't seen you for a while.'

'I'm good, thank you. And you Riekie?'

'*Ja*, also good. What are you doing here so early in the morning?'

'I just came to get my post.'

'*Ma* will be glad to see you. I'll go tell her you're here.'

Anna-Marie walked out of the kitchen and Fanie strolled through the familiar rooms, glancing around to see what was new. Nothing had changed here in the three months since he had moved out. On the lounge and dining-room walls were several framed family photographs, among them an old wedding portrait of his parents. His eyes drifted from there to his high-school photograph nearby: he wore a rugby jersey and his blond hair was cut very short at the back and sides. There was also an old photo of all the family members together, he and Anna-Marie aged five and three years respectively. His nostalgic gaze then moved across to the photo of his father, wearing the military uniform of a now defunct right-wing Afrikaner resistance movement. Although he and his father hadn't agreed politically, Fanie still felt heartsore about him and regretted his early death.

Anna-Marie joined him in the dining-room and invited him to stay for breakfast. But Fanie told his sister that he was in a hurry as he was on his way to a picnic.

'Who are you going to picnic with? Is Gerda with you?' enquired Anna-Marie, walking to the window to peer out at Fanie's empty car.

'No, not Gerda,' Fanie said. 'We've broken up.'

Anna-Marie nodded without surprise. 'I never thought you two suited each other,' she said. 'So who's the lucky date for today?'

'Her name is Dimakatjo . . . Maki.'

'That sounds like a black name!'

'Yes, it is.'

Anna-Marie's eyes filled with amazed laughter.

'Really? You are seeing a black woman, Fanie?'

'That's right. But we are just friends . . . so far,' Fanie told her smilingly.

At that point their mother, Louise, entered the kitchen, wearing a morning-gown and slippers, the inevitable cigarette in her hands. She was a large, grey-haired woman in her late fifties, who bore a strong resemblance to her son.

As Fanie leaned forward to kiss her, the smoke from her cigarette got up his nose and he broke into a coughing fit. Louise looked at him in surprise as he waved the smoke away.

'What's the matter? All of a sudden you don't like smoke?'

'That's right,' said Fanie, 'I've given up smoking.'

'Since when?'

'Last week.'

'Why?'

'No reason,' said Fanie. 'I just want to be healthy.'

His mother's eyes scrutinised him closely. 'And the hairstyle?'

'I needed a change,' Fanie said uncomfortably.

His mother's interrogation reminded him of Gerda. She looked like she had more to say on the subject. But all she said was: 'Tell Selina what you want for breakfast.'

'He's not staying,' said Anna-Marie. 'I've already asked him. He's on his way to . . . '

'To do some fishing,' said Fanie hastily. 'At Hartebeespoort Dam.'

Louise's eyes looked shrewdly from Anna-Marie's grinning face to Fanie's flushed and uncomfortable one. It wasn't hard to guess that something was up between the siblings – something that Louise wasn't being told. But she decided to hold her peace for the moment.

After that, the conversation turned to other things. Louise told Fanie that his Uncle Pieter wasn't well and that he had a bad dose of flu. Fanie voiced his sympathy, promising that he would call 'the old man' to see how he was getting on.

Selina brought Fanie's post and soon afterwards the son bid his mother goodbye.

Anna-Marie walked her brother out of the house. From the window, Louise watched them, admiring the picture the siblings made, walking hand in hand to Fanie's car. Selina handed her a mugful of well-brewed *moerkoffie*, the kind of pitch-black, aromatic coffee especially preferred by farm-raised Afrikaners. Louise stood with her mug in one hand and a cigarette in the other, wishing she could hear the conversation between her offspring. For her mother's nose told her that '*daar is iets wat hulle wegsteek*' ('There is something that they are hiding').

'So, *boetie*, you are head-over-heels in the new South Africa now?' teased Anna-Marie, as she brushed the hairy arm of her brother affectionately.

Fanie chuckled at her comment, then grew suddenly serious: 'But please Riekie, don't breathe a word of this to *ma*. You know what she's like about these things.'

'I won't, I promise. But don't be too hard on her,' Anna-Marie said. 'Remember that people of her generation were brought up in the 1950s when a black man was just a *kaffer* . . .'

'And a black woman was a *kaffermeid* . . .'

'*Ja*, and all white men were *baas* and white women were *miesies*. You can't expect people with that upbringing to suddenly rejoice at your relationship,' concluded Anna-Marie.

Fanie nodded in agreement.

'What did you say your woman's name is?' Anna-Marie asked after a moment.

'Maki.'

'A nice short name!'

Fanie grinned. 'She's a really nice chick. And good for me, you know. Very health conscious.'

'So that's why you stopped smoking? Because of her influence?'

'Yes.'

'Wonderful! I like her already! When can I meet her?'

'Soon,' Fanie promised.

Suddenly Anna-Marie turned her face towards the house. Fanie did likewise. Brother and sister saw their mother gazing out at them, very intently, as if her heart was burning to know what they were talking about. It was as if she had somehow managed to eavesdrop on what she was not supposed to hear.

Fanie quickly hugged and kissed his sister and bid her goodbye. He got into the car and turned the ignition key. The engine rumbled smoothly to life and with a final wave, he sped away from Moreletta Straat.

Fanie's departure left a very thoughtful silence in the house.

After breakfast Louise sat outside on the *stoep* – the cool and spacious veranda that adjoined the lounge – from where she summoned her daughter. Anna-Marie came and Louise commanded her to sit down next to her. Anna-Marie could tell from her mother's stern tone that something was up.

Louise launched without delay into her attack: '*Ja, julle skinderbekke!*' ('Yes, you gossip-mongers!') she said. 'What were you and that brother of yours so busy whispering about out there?'

'*Nee ma*, don't worry; we were not talking about you!' Anna-Marie said, laughing uneasily.

'*Luister* Mariekie. I was not born yesterday! Fanie is not going fishing, is he? Is he? *Ja of nee?*' ('Yes or no?')

Anna-Marie didn't know what to say. Fanie's pleading words still rang in her ears: '*But please Riekie, don't breathe a word to ma!*'

'So what's going on, Mariekie? You might as well tell me; I already know.'

Anna-Marie looked at her mother in dismay. 'You know?' she said. 'How could you know!'

So there is something! Louise thought triumphantly.

'I overheard a few words out of Fanie's mouth,' she lied, 'when you were talking together in the kitchen.'

'About Fanie's new girlfriend, you mean? Then you know that she is bl . . . ' Just in time, Anna-Marie caught the words back.

'His new girlfriend! You mean he's broken up with Gerda and he didn't tell me? So that's what you two were so busy whispering about!'

'We weren't whispering, *ma!*'

'Yes you were! And that's why Fanie lowered his voice in the kitchen! He didn't want me to find out . . . '

'So how did you hear him if he lowered his voice?' asked Anna-Marie, realising too late that she had been tricked.

Louise did not take up her daughter's challenge.

'Is there something else you are not telling me, Mariekie?' she demanded.

Mother and daughter spoke within earshot of Selina who was bustling about, shifting the furniture as she prepared to vacuum the carpets. Selina had overheard Fanie telling Anna-Marie about Dimakatjo. For even though whites often spoke in the presence of their domestic workers as if they were lifeless statues, *an ear has no lid,* as the saying goes. Selina had added one and one and got the answer right. She was very intrigued by what she had overheard; but now she kept her mouth firmly shut. For Selina did not want to be the bearer of bad news – *aowaa!* She suspected that it would not go down at all well with the *miesies,* and she did not want to be the one in the firing line.

Cold tension descended on the comfortable old house. Louise had heard Anna-Marie's earlier slip of the tongue, but she could not believe that what she thought she had heard could be true. She wanted her suspicions confirmed there and then; again she demanded an immediate answer to her question. When she herself was Anna-Marie's age, she would not have dared to defy and disrespect her own mother in such a way. But Anna-Marie would not budge; she would not breach the trust invested in her by her adored brother.

Louise was so annoyed that she stood up and walked to her bedroom without saying another word. Anna-Marie could not guess if her mother was going there to pray, or cry.

10

Dimakatjo waited impatiently for Fanie to arrive. She had long since spruced herself up again and had put on an apron to avoid being dirtied by even the most minute speck of dust that her critical eye might fail to detect. She whiled away the time by browsing through the latest copy of *Top Chicks* – her favourite magazine. From the table of contents she identified the horoscopes page. This week's star-sign prediction read: '*Plan to be more adventurous and energetic with regard to sexual intimacy.*' She was exceedingly tickled by the advice and burst out laughing, surprised by the tremendous leap of pleasure that her heart gave her.

She was still lost in her pleasant forest of romantic thoughts when Fanie's car materialised – *palakata!* – in front of her eyes. Within seconds his gentle knock came at the door of Dimakatjo's shack. Hastily she stripped off the apron.

'*Kom binne!*' ('Come in!') she responded, her voice resonant with charm. Fanie needed no second invitation. He strode in and swept her up into a tight bear-hug, before throwing a hot kiss her way. The fragrance of her skin stirred his blood and sent it roaring lustily around his body.

'*Magtig* but you look sexy, Maki!'

'Thank you, Fanie!' she smiled.

As she collected her things, Fanie glanced around her neat lounge. The inside of her house was done out so well that it was hard to believe it was a shack. He was full of admiration for the way she had transformed it into a warm and cheerful home.

His gaze landed on the glossy magazine that she had been reading and he was reminded strongly of the copy he had browsed through in the doctor's waiting room on that fateful morning almost two weeks previously, when his eyes had first landed on the woman who, in such a short time, had come to be *more precious than mountain-heaps of gold and diamonds!*

The eyes of curious onlookers to the north, east, south and west of Dimakatjo's *mokhukhu* were firmly fixed on Fanie and Dimakatjo as they got into the car. From the *spaza* shop opposite, one pair of eyes watched with particular interest: the hawk-eyes belonging to Bigboy, Tau's lackey and *mpimpi* – 'informer'. Fortunately, Tau himself was out of town for an extended period, involved in a court case elsewhere in the country. Dimakatjo was, anyway, beyond caring. Who could spare precious moments for such insignificant details when love cooed so enticingly from up ahead?

Fanie put on his seat belt and leaned across to fasten Dimakatjo's – an action that exposed his nostrils once again to her seductive perfume. He could not resist the temptation to pinch her smooth thigh. They both laughed, and as always Fanie was greatly tickled by her manner of laughing.

As they drove off, the onlookers continued to feast their eyes until Fanie's white car was out of sight. Bigboy would no doubt have many pages to update in his hot gossip diary.

Once out of Mamelodi, Fanie speeded up and the next few kilometres sped by on carefree wings of laughter and lovers' chatter. They arrived at an intersection, where Fanie chose the road that led to Thomlinson Camp nature resort. For a while they were quiet as the powerful engine whispered up and down the hills and valleys of Mpumalanga province. Fanie's gaze, fixed on the winding road, would every now and then divert itself to the flower of his love-hungry heart. He rested his left hand on her thigh, and she let it rest there, since it was behaving itself.

Fanie wished he weren't driving; he wished he were seated with her on the back seat of the car where he would have ample chance to admire, touch and fondle this bundle of ecstacy called Dimakatjo. He looked at her stealthily and she surveyed him in turn, her eyes glinting with naughtiness, as if she could read what was going through his mind; they both burst into laughter.

Again they fell quiet. Fanie was picturing in his mind a scene at the picnic spot, when she would be in his two arms. Dimakatjo's mind, however, was busy with something entirely different.

Her thoughts had backtracked to the conversation she had had with Fanie on his cellphone an hour or so earlier, when she had asked him why his landline was engaged. He had told her that he was speaking to someone called Mariekie. She had asked: *'Who's Mariekie?'* And he had replied: *'She is my s . . .'* At that point Dimakatjo's cellphone had cut out, leaving her totally frustrated. *She's my what?* Dimakatjo asked herself now. Her mind struggled to complete the sentence. *My sweetheart?* She wanted to ask him again but she was afraid to do so, for fear of his answer.

'What's wrong, Maki? Why are you so quiet?' Fanie asked.

'Nothing's wrong,' replied Dimakatjo.

Fanie, changing gear in preparation for the steep slope ahead, shot her a quick glance. He could see that she was not in the same high spirits in which she had been a few minutes ago.

So you are a cheat, Fanie, secretly in love with another woman . . . ? was on the tip of her tongue to say; but she bit back the acid in her mouth. Fanie pinched her thigh playfully, but she did not react. Worry began to gnaw at his heart. He put on his indicator and stopped the car at the side of the road, then undid his seat belt and turned to face her.

'Tell me what's wrong,' he said to her quietly.

The moment of truth had arrived and since she could not evade it, she ventured to grab the buffalo by the horns: 'Tell me Fanie, who were you speaking to this morning when your telephone was engaged for such a long time?'

Fanie made no reply but frowned as though mystified.

'You had the nerve to tell me that you were speaking to someone you called your *sweetheart . . .* !' continued child of Bakone who, not so long ago, had confided to Nthabiseng: *'I am very jealous, Nthabi. I can't share a man!'*

Fanie seemed relieved rather than dismayed by her words.

'Let me tell you the truth . . .'

'So you were lying to me?'

'Sometimes that kind of lying is unavoidable, so as not to harm your loved one's feelings. I told you I was speaking to Mariekie my sister, but I lied . . . '

'Did you not say, "*my sweetheart*"?'

'No! But I wasn't speaking to Mariekie. I had left the phone off the hook because Gerda . . . '

'Are you still speaking to your old flame? Why am I here then?'

With that, Dimakatjo opened the car door, grabbed her handbag, and strode away briskly.

Fanie jumped out, too and hurriedly overtook her; he wanted to speak but the words jammed on his tongue. He could only gesture desperately with his open palm.

'Listen Fanie, I'm taking a taxi back to Mamelodi.'

'Wait, Maki! Give me a chance to explain!' Fanie grabbed her by the hand and led her over to a tree, where he made her lean against the trunk. He faced her, eyelashes to eyelashes and held her hands firmly in his.

'Please do not worry any more about Gerda, my sweetie-pie. When you tried to speak to me this morning the phone was engaged because I did not want to speak to her.'

She was still stern-faced as he finished.

'She had phoned me a few moments before, but I put the phone down when I realised it was her and left it off the hook.'

Dimakatjo's face gradually began to soften into a tentative smile. Fanie hurried on: 'That's why, when you tried to call me . . . '

'I understand. I understand. Listen Fanie . . . '

Fanie listened.

'I do not,' pronounced Dimakatjo, mimicking a judge's demeanour, 'find the accused guilty! Discharged and dismissed!'

They laughed in unison and hugged and kissed each other in relief. Fanie led his beloved back to the car and the journey resumed without incident.

Shortly afterwards, they saw a signboard on which was written 'Thomlinson Camp' and Fanie turned off onto the gravel road.

They were now at the top of a gentle hill and there below them, about half a kilometre further on, lay the Tomlinson dam, one of the favourite fishing and picnicking spots in the region.

Since the road was narrow and winding and the surface full of potholes they were forced to travel slowly, which afforded the lovers an opportunity to admire the scenery and identify a good spot where they could park and relax. The grass was still magnificently green after the summer rains and small animals such as veld rats and *meerkatte* could be seen darting here and there, playing hide-and-seek with their lovers. The air was fresh and unpolluted, filled with the musical twitter of birds. The time was now 11.30 and the morning sun was at full strength.

Fanie drove closer to the dam and parked his car in the shade between two drooping willow trees that looked like a couple engaged in a pre-mating dance. Climbing out of the car, he inspected the spot, then asked Dimakatjo if she was satisfied, to which she replied in the affirmative.

Dimakatjo took out a rug from the boot and spread it on the green and tender grass while Fanie unloaded plastic shopping bags full of picnic goodies. Dimakatjo then brought out the cooler bag, in which packets of ice-blocks gently rattled against fruit juice bottles. Fanie chivalrously grabbed the cooler bag out of her hands, protesting that she must not strain herself with such a heavy load. What he didn't say was that the heavy load that she would soon be carrying would be himself, and that she should be saving her strength for that! Dimakatjo smilingly reminded him that in the rural areas black women frequently hoed the maize fields, held the ox-driven plough, herded cattle and did multiple other so-called 'masculine' chores.

The lovers sat down and marvelled at the peace and tranquility around them. Strangely, there were no fishermen to be seen and the picnic spot was deserted, save for one lone white couple at the far corner. An amazing variety of bird calls could be heard from the trees and bushes around them: '*Tswiiyoo-Tswiiyoo! Tswerrr-Tswerrr! Koweee-Koweee!*'

Presently, the white couple packed up their belongings and left.

'They are leaving because they don't like looking at a black and white couple maybe,' Fanie joked.

'That's their problem then,' smiled Dimakatjo.

'Okay, then let's mind our own business,' he smiled back at her.

He handed her a glass, kept one for himself, then opened the cooler bag and took out a litre of chilled fruit-cocktail juice, which he poured for her and for himself. They said toasts for the strength of their love and sipped with enjoyment. Close by, a cricket produced a chirping sound that fascinated Fanie; he stood up and surveyed the grass as if it would be a simple task to find the small insect. Then he saw wild flowers and squatted down to admire them. Dimakatjo got to her feet and advanced stealthily towards him; unexpectedly, she leapt up and landed on Fanie's back, her weight knocking them both over. They fell in a heap and exploded into loud, joyous peals of laughter.

Fanie grabbed Dimakatjo's willing hand and drew her forward along the shore of the dam. As they continued to explore the area, he insisted on carrying her to avoid any risk of her stepping on a scorpion or centipede with her bare feet. Before she even had time to agree, she found herself airborne, held securely in Fanie's strong arms. She made no protest, fully aware that this was an excuse to be romantic.

With her arms around his neck, one of his arms under her knees and the other supporting her back, Fanie plodded on, staggering a little under her weight and using her body as a shield against the branches of trees – something that drew more peals of laughter from Dimakatjo. Her exposed tongue and teeth were, as always, just too irresistible for him. Before putting her down – her considerable weight almost causing him to throw her down – he planted a juicy kiss on her wide-open lips. She savoured it with closed eyes.

Fanie made a fire with the charcoal he had thought to bring and they roasted their meal on skewers of wood over the coals: a bit of *boerewors* for him, a piece of fish for Dimakatjo, and huge, tasty brown mushrooms for both of them. The lovers ate and were full, although what filled them most was love for each other. A female dove cooed: '*Kung-kurrruu! Kung-kurrruu!*' while the deeper-voiced male seemed to warble richly: '*Aku-kuthu-kuthuuu-motho! Aku-kuthu-kuthuuu-motho!*'

With no one else about, Fanie and Dimakatjo felt as free as if they were in their own bedroom. The lovers gazed amorously into each other's eyes, hugged, and pressed their mouths together. But when Fanie tried to deepen the kiss, Dimakatjo pulled back and turned her head away. Fanie was not offended by her hard-to-get tactic, however, for he saw that she was feeling suddenly shy. He saw no reason to have to rush anything in this relaxed and tranquil place.

To buy time, Dimakatjo began to pack away the aftermath of their picnic, scraping the plates clean and storing the rubbish in one of the plastic shopping bags. She brought out some dried fruit and nuts for them to chew and they sat contently nibbling.

Fanie knew that the time had come for him to take the initiative. They had reached the line that they must this day boldly cross over. Fanie knew that there was risk involved, but he was ready for the risk.

Before any new experience, there is always a moment of hesitation at the prospect of entering into the unknown for the first time. But someone must make it happen, must take responsibility for turning expectation into reality. When faced with the first bite of a fleshy fruit that one's mouth has been watering for, no hungry person needs to be told: 'Now plunge your teeth into it!'

A little over a week ago when Fanie had tried to make love to Dimakatjo at his flat, she had stormed out in a huff. The incident had almost ruined their relationship. Now here they were again at those risky crossroads. This was the opportune moment he had to seize. This time if she should run away, he would chase her with all his stamina until he caught her, and woo her with such tenderness and passion that all her resistance would melt away.

Fanie turned her face towards him. And she could see the hot light of desire flare in his brown eyes as they looked deep into her own. As if pulled by a powerful magnet he moved his face closer and closer to hers. Dimakatjo saw him lick his lips in preparation for unleashing a hearty kiss. She averted her face half-heartedly, as the hard-to-get 'village maiden' values made a brief resurgence within her; then she banished them resolutely and yielded to Fanie's determined mouth, eagerly receiving his passionate kiss for as long as he chose to prolong it.

All previous kisses were comparatively light and mild compared to this one. This kiss was a genuine one hundred per cent red-hot lover's kiss that explored and tasted every corner of her luscious mouth.

At last Fanie released her and murmured: 'You taste as good as a pineapple!'

A sound in the bushes behind them made them turn. A *meerkat* was chasing his mate. What clearly seemed to be the male of the species overtook the female and mated matter-of-factly; the session was short but robust. Fanie and Dimakatjo exchanged amorous glances.

'Let's do as they are doing,' Fanie suggested, flashing a salacious smile at Dimakatjo. Playfully she smacked his chin, then stood up and ran away around some shrubs, with him hot on her heels. Fanie overtook her and pinched her buttocks; she pinched him back. He gripped her hands behind her back and kissed her soundly, while Dimakatjo turned her face back and forth, unsuccessfully playing at hard-to-be-kissed. Laughing, they returned to the rug and sat down face to face, with locked arms and ankles. Somewhere at the water's edge a bullfrog croaked: '*Wa-rraa! Wa-rraaa!*' Dimakatjo laughed.

'Why are you laughing?' Fanie stroked her smooth cheek, his brown eyes glittering with ardour.

'The frogs,' she explained. 'They are saying: "*Wa-rraa! Wa-rraaa!*" which in Sepedi means . . . '

'My brother, my brother!' Fanie finished the sentence for her, reminding her that he had not lost his Sepedi language skills.

They had a good laugh at that.

Fanie went to the cooler bag, from where he took out a bunch of delicious-looking thumb-sized green seedless grapes with ice-water dripping from them. Transferring them onto a plate, he made Dimakatjo lie face-up across his thighs, then plucked the grapes in twos and inserted them into her mouth. She chewed and swallowed with relish, then raised herself up and smiled somewhat lecherously at him. He pulled her into his arms and began kissing her again, skilfully unbuttoning the top two buttons of her blouse to free her bust, in order to increase the field for his kisses; she did not demur. He continued his exploring, his kisses growing ever fiercer and more torrid, while she tried impotently to restrain his agile hands.

She was trying very hard to hold back the murmurs of endearment that rose in her throat, the tender words in her own language that welled up inside her. For she was afraid Fanie would think that she was as experienced as *mahlwa-a-di-bona* – a brazen prostitute. But it was increasingly difficult to suppress her enraptured feelings.

She didn't want Fanie to feel that he had conquered her entirely, that he now possessed her, soul, body and bones. But the truth was, she loved this man with all her heart and every vein and blood vessel in her body; with her liver, kidneys and pancreas gland as well. This man did not need her woman's hands to scrub him until he was '*clean and* twaa-*white like a sheet soaked in a champion washing powder*'. He would not come to her stinking of alcohol and cigarette fumes, hardly able to stand on his two feet.

As Fanie's hands continued to do an excellent job of stimulating the erogenous zones of her body, Dimakatjo was no longer even conscious of the different colour of his skin. But the stubborn village-maiden values still vied for possession of her.

'Fanie, don't cause a fire that you can't put out!' she murmured breathlessly.

For a very brief moment Fanie recalled something similar that George had once said to him: '*Men can be so irresponsible. They set fire to a woman and then, when the poor woman is in flames, they run away crying "Fire, get away from me!"*'

Despite her fears, Dimakatjo knew that the time for holding back was over. Now was the moment to release the fire in her. Boldly, she threw more wood into Fanie's fire, uninhibitedly rubbing his temples, ear lobes, the back of his neck, and his chin; highly aroused, Fanie pressed her to him, and they kissed with relish and gusto.

He had no option but to respond proactively to the bombardment of sex hormones she triggered in him; while she, for her part, was completely magnetised by the touch, sight and smell of him. He felt the swelling of her tender breasts against his chest. His burning lust was killing him! He unleashed more kisses and, this time, she surrendered herself completely to their intoxicating fire, yielding up her mouth to kiss after demanding kiss, her body responding to his roving hands. The lover in her had reached a point of no return, and the village-maiden values were, finally, forced into retreat, persuaded to sit on the sidelines and watch.

The rest, as it is said, was history!

Forty-five minutes later Fanie sighed with deep satisfaction. His sexual appetite was satisfied, the animal passion that had waited so long to be released, slaked at last. He was gratified beyond words that their love-making had proved to be so worth waiting for. He had tasted her *kuku* – not flesh-on-flesh but no less blissful for that. What an experience! Inexpressible! Out of this world! That 'first bite', that first taste had exceeded all expectations, for sexual appetite had been fuelled by the feelings of his heart. He could only hope that she, in turn, was not disappointed.

In fact, the impact of that sexual encounter was, for Dimakatjo, equally earth-shattering. She said little on the drive home, lost in recalling how she had lost her virginity when she was in Standard Nine. In her culture, when a man had sex with a woman, he later boasted: 'I have eaten her!' That reduced any woman to a mere object and gave her the status of a victim. She hoped with all her heart that Fanie did not now see her in that way. But at the same time, she was glad that *it* had happened. Elation filled her as she recalled her horoscope's advice: *'Plan to be more adventurous and energetic with regard to sexual intimacy.'*

Many thoughts traversed the maze of Fanie's brain on the drive home. He felt that there was no more going back on this relationship; he resolved that he would not just 'taste and pass' Dimakatjo, in the way of many white men, who treated black girls as mere sex objects.

He thought about the reaction of older, conservative whites like his mother, when they found out that he and Dimakatjo were sexually involved; about the many young whites who had died defending the values of apartheid; and about what older South Africans would remember as the 'Immorality Act' – one of the laws during the heydays of apartheid that forbade sexual contact between blacks and whites.

He wondered what would have happened to him and Dimakatjo during those days of old South Africa; they would probably have been arrested and their underwear used by the investigating police officers as 'Exhibits A & B'. He could imagine the prosecutor pointing ac-cusingly at him during the court hearing:

> *Mr Fourie you, a person of European origin were, on such-and-such a day, found naked from your waist down having illicit sexual relations with accused number two, a Bantu woman in terms of the Bantu Administration Act of 1927. According to this* prima facie *evidence you are being charged in terms of the Immorality Act of 1957, section 16 sub-section 2 item (a) sub-items (i) and (ii) of the Union of South Africa.*

Shivers ran down Fanie's spine as he thought of the many mixed-race couples of the time who had had to undergo humiliation of this kind.

He dropped Dimakatjo off in Mamelodi and drove back slowly to his flat, replaying the scenes of their lovemaking in his mind. A soft smile blossomed on his face; he would never forget until the day of his death how Dimakatjo had softly murmured in her language: *'Joo-mma-weee!'*, as she reached her orgasm.

11

Blue Monday; Fanie, however, was high on *babalase* – a hangover of love-making. He was at work in body only, while his mind rewound endlessly to the unforgettable experience of the picnic.

George could see that his colleague was miles away, but there was no time to pry, for there was a mountain-load of workers' files to plough through and transfer onto the system before the end of February deadline.

Thanks to the love stimulant that acted like caffeine in his veins, Fanie felt wide awake and alert, and despite his distracted mind, he managed to focus on his work until knock-off time.

Dimakatjo, meanwhile, found herself waking very early that morning. She imagined that her body needed less sleep because she was in love; she also observed that she ate less than usual – concluding that her love-swollen heart was interfering with her appetite. She didn't mind too much, however, musing that this would help her to stay trim and beautiful.

She took an earlier train than usual in to work. Because she was short of money that day, she chose to travel third class, where commuters were packed like sardines in the coaches. She sat on a long, hard seat, squashed between two male labourers in overalls. There was hardly a commotion-free moment as the train stopped at umpteen stations and commuters alighted and boarded, shuffled along and pushed their way in and out. Train hawkers shouted their wares, moving through the packed carriages, while the train evangelists read from their threadbare Bibles and preached their fire-

and-brimstone messages to the snoring and chattering commuters: '*Fornicators shall never inherit the Kingdom of God!*'

The converted ones punctuated the sermons with spirited 'Hallelujahs!' and 'Amens!' Dimakatjo was neither listening nor snoring; like Fanie, she was lost in her thoughts, transported back to the picnic spot many kilometres away.

Arriving at work half an hour ahead of time, she made herself a cup of pleasant-smelling herbal tea that she sipped while browsing through her *Top Chicks* magazine, which she was still busy with. When she came to the horoscopes page, she smiled smugly as she reread the advice her star-sign prediction gave, thinking with satisfaction that she had, indeed, been *more adventurous and energetic with regard to sexual intimacy*!

Her daydreaming eyes landed on an article headed: 'When love is over.' This prompted her to think of writing a letter to Tau, with the intention of telling him: *Hit the road, Jack!* She had heard nothing from him since he had unexpectedly left on his business trip ten days previously, and her life felt cleaner and more peaceful without him. But all too soon he would be returning, expecting to pick up where they had left off. Dimakatjo liked the idea of breaking up with him by letter because 'a letter is fearless', as the boys used to say when they proposed love to their chosen sweethearts by writing to them. A letter would make it possible for her to express her feelings without being intimidated by eye contact or interruption.

Dimakatjo knew that word of her comings and goings with Fanie would very soon be hitting Tau's ear via Bigboy, the faithful *mpimpi*. Tau would learn that a certain white *ngamola* who drove a fancy BMW had collected Dimakatjo at such-and-such a time and brought her back at whatever time.

She had decided that now was the perfect time to break things off with Tau, since she had met the man of her dreams. The relationship between Tau and her was over. Dead and cold! No more! She didn't want Tau to have any excuse to keep on bugging her. Therefore, on this very day, her hand would write words on a death certificate. No more would her 'woman's hands' continue to clean Tau's mess, until he was '*twaa*-white' like a newly-washed sheet.

Without further ado, she took up a pen and wrote Tau a 'jilting' letter:

Dear Tau

I don't have good news for you. But I think it is better for both of us that I should have this letter waiting for you on your return. Tau, we have been going out for many years, but the fruit of our relationship never tasted good to me. The fruit constipated me and left me feeling always hungry.

Love should be enjoyed and not endured. As the saying goes, forcing a huge chunk of meat into a small earthenware pot only breaks the pot. The time has arrived for us to part ways, and I will appreciate it if there is no bad feeling.

Please don't phone me. And please don't come to my place and sing 'Ke mang a boditseng . . .' It will be of no use. The path where love used to walk is now filled with thorn bush. Let's just accept it Tau!

I am enclosing your photos, the dress ring you gave me and the wooden bangle that you bought me when you went to Venda. As for the photos of me that you have, please destroy them – tear them up or burn them; I don't want them back.

Thank you for everything. I hope that you will find love soon with someone else.

DM

Before putting the letter into a large khaki envelope she re-read every word, and nodded her head with satisfaction. She enclosed the photos and other articles that Tau had given her, affixed a stamp and put the letter aside, with the intention of dropping it into a postbox at the station on her way home. Then she spent the remaining time until Nthabiseng's arrival daydreaming about Fanie.

She thought how exhilarating it would be to be married to him. He was so much the 'modern man' in his outlook – unlike Tau, son of a chief, whose values were steeped in what she and her more sophisticated peers regarded as 'backward' culture. In this kind of culture when you, a young woman, complained to your in-laws that their child, your husband, did not sleep at home at night, the female elders, whose eyes had seen many, many things, would quickly answer: '*A man is an axe; he is borrowed overnight!*' In other words, you were expected to be accommodating.

Just before 8.30 Nthabiseng walked in. While she prepared some tea for herself in the kitchen, Dimakatjo made the first call of the day . . . to none other than Fanie. His phone was engaged, however, because he was phoning her at the same time. After a few minutes they tried to call each other again but the phones were still engaged, because they had again phoned each other at the same time. At last they managed to hear each other's voices, both of them bursting into laughter on realising that their telephones were engaged because they had phoned each other simultaneously. The quick five-minute phone conversation they shared acted like a breakfast tonic on their spirits.

12

That Friday evening Fanie had invited Dimakatjo for dinner at Roodevallei Holiday Resort, having read in George's copy of *Gauteng Ditaba* that the renowned trombonist, Jonas Gwangwa, would be performing there, together with other musicians.

At *tshaile* time Fanie's car drew up in the parking area in front of Dr Makgabo's surgery. Before long, he heard the familiar sound of Dimakatjo's shoes approaching: '*Kwae-kwae-kwae!*' He was reminded of the first day that he had seen her in the surgery when he, love-bitten, could not keep his eyes off her and she had turned her back on him, strutting off to the kitchenette behind the counter.

Dimakatjo had changed out of her nurse's uniform into casual attire – a pair of well-faded blue denim pants and matching sleeveless shirt that exposed her biceps. Over her shoulder hung a sling bag containing the clothes that she would wear that evening for the Roodevallei outing. Her face lit up when she caught sight of him and she shot a sparkling smile his way.

Fanie leapt out of the car and hurried around to open the door for Princess Dimakatjo. Their kiss was in the language of lovers, and their four eyeballs communicated volumes to each other. Fanie drove straight to his flat, where they would bathe and change into fresh clothes for their evening date. His car cruised into the yard of Strijdomhuis and he guided the vehicle smoothly between the white lines of his parking bay, pulling up the handbrake with a *tjwerrr!* sound before the car had even halted completely. Again he leapt out and rushed round to open the passenger door for Dimakatjo; but this time she had forestalled him and let herself out of the car. As a result, Fanie's chivalrous gesture was wasted effort, a fact that drew laughter from them both.

Fanie and Dimakatjo walked hand in hand towards the entrance of the building. Dimakatjo felt that they were being watched by several pairs of not-too-friendly eyes. She imagined the hissing whispers in their wake: '*Kyk! Daar gaan Fanie en sy swarte!*' ('Look, there goes Fanie and his black!') '*Foie tog* – this white boy has a screw loose!'

She was tempted to say to Fanie, as on their first date: '*I don't enjoy being a bioscope.*'

Her self-conscious feelings were not misplaced for the lovers were, indeed, providing 'a bioscope' for the old *tannies* in the building who had nothing to do but *skinder* all day long. On this particular day they had a strenuous job to do; their eyes having taken in the sight of Fanie and Dimakatjo walking hand in hand together, their aged lips would now gallop the equivalent of kilometres, peddling the delicious *skinder-praatjies* –'gossip'– about the white boy who had crossed the racial red line: *Whose child is he? A loose screw in his head certainly needs to be tinkered with . . . walaa-walaa-walaa-walaaaa!* And so on until sunset.

Nicholas Molwantwa, the handyman of Strijdomhuis was, as usual, busy at his duties, cleaning the outside windows, when his eyes landed on Fanie and Dimakatjo sauntering into the foyer area. Beaming an enormous smile, he whistled, guffawed and leapt up in the energetic *Mokhukhu* dance postures, finally giving Fanie a strong African handshake. What was poison to the *skinderbekke* was honey to Nicholas's mouth.

'Is this black woman your girlfriend?' he asked.

Fanie and Dimakatjo smiled bashfully in answer.

'This one you must marry, *baas* Fanie! And you must send me to part with your *lobola*!' Nicholas enthused, bestowing another handshake and more appreciative guffaws and smiles.

Fanie and Dimakatjo laughed at that and Nicholas laughed with them.

'Whose child are you?' he asked Dimakatjo, addressing her in the traditional Sepedi fashion.

'I'm child of Machabaphala,' she answered in the appropriate way.

The lift arrived and the couple entered, their fingers still entwined. This time round they had it to themselves.

In the flat Dimakatjo had a bath while Fanie prepared some aromatic herbal tea. Nicholas's words: *'Is she your girlfriend? This one you must marry, baas Fanie!'* turned and turned in his mind.

Fanie's nostrils picked up the scent of very pleasant-smelling perfume, and his feet took him to where the fragrance proceeded from. He almost collided with Dimakatjo, coming out of the bathroom wrapped in a peach bath towel. The top half of the towel was wound around her breasts, one end safely tucked under to hold it up; where the towel ended appeared the shapely knees, legs and feet of Dimakatjo. Fanie ogled her hungrily, inspecting this vision of beauty from the top of her head to the tips of her toes.

'Maki, you have lovely feet!'

'Thank you Fanie!'

'And gorgeous legs.'

'Thanks!'

'And . . . ehr . . . fantastic breasts.'

She chuckled.

'And adorable kissable lips and . . . '

Fanie started to pull her towards the bedroom but: 'Not tonight, darling!' Dimakatjo said. Smiling to neutralise the disappointment of her words, she told him: *'Ke bona kgwedi'* – 'I am seeing the moon'. Dimakatjo saw the fierce, lion-like gleam in Fanie's brown eyes and sensed his surging desire. She knew what would have happened had she not told him she was menstruating.

Fanie had a quick shower, while Dimakatjo changed into her evening attire – not the kind of thing that she would wear from Monday to Friday. *Aowaa!* She wore an ankle-length cream-white Xhosa skirt embroidered with golden blocks, and a sleeveless black blouse, low-cut and tantalisingly tight. Fanie was a little disappointed to see that she had not put on the special Ndebele necklace that was his Valentine gift to her; instead, she had hung around her neck a simple string of *mokgalo*-berry beads. He wanted to ask her why she was not wearing his gift but felt a little awkward to do so.

He was glad, however, to see on her right wrist the meticulously crafted copper bangle that was the other part of his Valentine gift.

Fanie was quiet as they drove to Roodevallei. For even though his heart was bursting with exhilaration at the prospect of their evening together, Nicholas's words were still turning over in his mind: '*Is she your girlfriend? This one you must marry*, baas *Fanie!*'

By seven o'clock they had arrived at the appointed venue. They joined the queue at the security boom and were given a visitor's form to fill out. As they drove on towards the parking area, Fanie could see in his rear-view mirror six more cars lined up behind him, all waiting to be let into this popular venue of pleasure.

The lovers walked with their arms around each other towards the entertainment centre. Jonas Gwangwa's piercing trombone could be heard on the night breeze, luring them on. Dimakatjo leaned her shoulder against Fanie's left bicep as they stood at the entrance and looked around for someone to show them to their table. Already, about 200 people were seated in a hall with the capacity of 500. The guests were helping themselves to snacks set out in bowls on their tables, while drinks were ordered. As Fanie and Dimakatjo pulled up their chairs and sat down, several pairs of eyes focused on them, for they made a very striking couple.

Fanie, too, had dressed up for the occasion. He wore a purple evening suit, with black silk shirt and green bow tie, his long hair tied back in its new ponytail style. Child of Machabaphala had draped her shoulders with a soft Indian shawl, and wrapped a Xhosa *doek* around her head.

After a delicious dinner of traditional African dishes, Fanie was ready for the dance floor. As the evening wore on, the mood of the diners grew more mellow and the band toned down its songs. The numbers became more bluesy and romantic; Fanie asked Dimakatjo to join him on the dance floor and she was more than willing. The lovers danced cheek to cheek – an excuse to touch, feel and enjoy each other's closeness. Dimakatjo's perfume added fire to Fanie's fire, and he briefly wished they were back in the privacy of his flat; but then he remembered that she was 'seeing her moon'. Tonight the robot was red, but soon it would be green again and he would be able to put restraint aside.

As they went back to their table, a house photographer hired for the evening made his way over to them and took their photo, writing down their names and contact details in his notebook. After he left, Fanie stood up again and led Dimakatjo over to an empty table right at the back of the hall, where they would have more privacy. Nicholas's words continued to throb in his head like the beat of a kettle drum: *'This one you must marry,* baas *Fanie! And you must send me to part with your* lobola.'

Without wasting any time, Fanie pulled his chair close to Dimakatjo's and bent his head to her ear: 'Maki my honey-pie,' he said softly.

She struggled to hear him over the music. 'What are you saying, Fanie?'

He leaned in closer and took the opportunity to kiss her neck. She pinched his hand as if warning: *This is too much for me!* But Fanie was oblivious to the fact that there were people around them. Absent-mindedly he moved his hand down to stroke her inviting breast, but she intercepted it and captured his fingers in her own. 'Maki, my apple-tart, you know how much I love you . . . ' His voice breaking, he had to stop there for a moment, overwhelmed by his own emotion.

'I hear you, Fanie.'

'If I haven't told you this before, I want to tell you tonight.'

'Tell me then!'

'Haven't I told you?'

'Told me what?'

'That I have never loved a woman this way before; and that I have never been loved by a woman in the way that you are doing.'

Now it was Dimakatjo's turn to be overcome. No man had ever said such things to her, or made her feel the way that he was making her feel now.

'Listen Maki,' continued Fanie, 'I don't want to just *jol* around and waste your time and mine.' There he paused and licked his lips, drawing in his breath in preparation for the most important sentence he had ever uttered: 'I want to marry you, Maki!'

'Really?' she looked at him incredulously, tears glinting like stars in her eyes.

'Will you marry me, Maki?'

Stunned into silence, she buried her face in her palms.

'Yes, of course, Fanie!' she said. And burst into sobs of joy. Fanie took a serviette from the table and tenderly wiped her tears away. He patted her shoulder soothingly, as if rocking a baby to sleep.

Dimakatjo flashed him a grateful smile, one teardrop still lingering at the top of her cheek, just below the eye socket.

For the remainder of the evening they talked, smiled, held hands and caressed each other with their feet, for they had removed their shoes under the table. They looked deep into each other's pupils, seeing reflected there the Fanie and Dimakatjo that they had never seen before.

They were so absorbed in each other's company that they did not even realise that they were among the last few diners remaining in the hall. When Fanie turned his head he was surprised to see two tall glasses filled with grape juice that had been standing there for a while, untouched and unseen, for when the waiter brought their order, neither Fanie nor Dimakatjo had noticed his arrival. The courteous waiter had put the glasses down and gone away again, not wanting to disturb the couple, who were clearly far away and in another world – a realm best known to lovers, lunatics and opium-drugged artists.

13

The following Monday, coming home from work, Gerda alighted from the municipal bus and walked the short distance to her bachelor flat in Daanville. The advantage of living here was that these flats were relatively affordable, since a hairdresser's salary did not allow for high-priced accommodation. But the area was far from ideal. The flats tended to be overcrowded and the buildings were generally not well maintained. Many young people who were just starting out came to live in this area and then moved to Sunnyside or Arcadia as their income improved. Formerly the exclusive preserve of low-income whites, Daanville was slowly opening up to other races. Although there were now brown faces to be seen in some of the buildings, in general the area was still as conservative as ever.

Gerda's living space was not very organised. Yesterday's blouse and trousers lay crumpled on the floor. An unwashed coffee mug, besmeared with red lipstick, sat on the crumb-littered counter along with a mould-filled glass, a half-full mug of cold black coffee, and an ashtray piled high with cigarette ash and butts. If anyone had entered Gerda's room on that day, the first thing they would be met with was clouds of cigarette smoke, followed by a white hand jerkily tapping ash into an ashtray and, finally, the stressed face of a young white woman, her eyes bloodshot from crying.

It was the first week of March. Almost three weeks after Valentine's Day. Gerda would never forget this year's Valentine's disaster – the Lovers' Day that she had not celebrated with Fanie because Fanie had been busy celebrating it with someone else. The evening that followed had been perhaps the blackest day of her life thus far. Fanie had worn black to their meeting, like a priest officiating at funeral rites; for he had come not to celebrate their romantic union but to pronounce *'dust to dust, ashes to ashes, rest in peace'* on their dead love.

Three long, lonely and unhappy weeks had gone by since then. And still Gerda found it difficult to accept that when love was dead, it could not be roused to life again; it could not 'kick open the coffin', as had happened with Lazarus when Jesus said to him: 'Come out!' As Fanie saw it, the relationship had crumbled to pieces like an earthenware pot that could not be reconstructed. But in Gerda's eyes, it had merely cracked a little, like a calabash that could be sewn with twine and would then be as good as new, able to scoop up water again to satisfy the thirst of the heart.

Gerda remembered how she had first met Fanie; how their love had blossomed when they both did holiday work at the bank, and how much Fanie's mother used to like her. Gerda also knew Anna-Marie, although she had not got on so well with her. She had always secretly felt that Anna-Marie did not entirely approve of Gerda's relationship with Fanie. As Gerda's thoughts travelled back and traversed the past sequences of her love-life with Fanie, she suddenly felt as though she were reading her own obituary, and she became scared.

As the week neared its end, she had plucked up her dwindling courage and phoned Fanie who, without mincing his words, asked her to stop wasting both of their time and leave him alone, as he was in love with someone else.

'It's over Gerda. It's been over for a long time. You must forget about me now,' he'd said. 'Go find someone who can make you happy.'

Gerda wept fresh bucketfuls of tears at his words; she gulped down two glasses of white wine, which made her cry even harder. Tears wouldn't retrieve that which was lost nor resuscitate what was dead, but they made her feel better, for they helped to flush the pain of rejection out of her system.

When she awoke the next morning, she felt confused: one part of her was convinced that chasing after Fanie would not do her any good, while another part insisted she must not give up. She told herself that life was, anyway, nothing but a perpetual struggle towards getting or achieving something; something that was achievable only if you were prepared to sacrifice for its attainment, to shed sweat, dignity, tears, and even blood.

Discouraging though Fanie's reaction had been, her stubborn pride would not let her give up. Something inside her urged: *Don't give up, Gerda. People who give up are as good as dead!*

Fanie entered his office confidently, put his briefcase down on the desk, loosened the grip of his tie and put the air-conditioner on; for this March day was stiflingly hot, pending the season's change to the cooler weather of autumn. George was off at a managers' meeting, so Fanie had the office to himself. He sat down on his high-backed chair and opened his diary, staring dutifully at the list of tasks for the day. Then he got up again and went off to make himself his morning cup of aromatic herbal tea.

Pensively sipping, he switched on his computer and began to read his emails. Every now and then a private thought would cross his mind and his face would soften into a tender smile. He was so involved with his own thoughts that it took him a moment to realise that George had entered the office.

George asked him how his weekend had been. Fanie was in the middle of filling him in on the evening at Roodevallei, and how he had proposed marriage to Dimakatjo there, when the phone rang. They both looked at it without enthusiasm.

'It's yours,' George said to Fanie. 'Better answer it.'

'No, you answer for me. If it's Gerda tell her I'm not here.'

George shook his head. 'You must answer, Fanie. I can't go on lying for you,' he said.

The phone stopped ringing. Fanie smiled in relief.

'Fanie, you must finish your business with Gerda,' George told him sternly.

'I've tried,' Fanie said. 'She knows it's finished. I told her I'm in love with someone else. But she is the kind of woman who doesn't take "no" for an answer.'

'Does she know who that "someone else" is?'

'No,' said Fanie. 'What difference would it make? The point is that Gerda and I are over. And if she can't accept that then it's her problem.'

George stayed thoughtfully silent. Then he said: 'You know that if you are in love with a black woman, then you must be prepared to part with *lobola* for her?'

'*Lobola*? You're not serious! Why should I pay *lobola*? It's new South Africa now!'

'New South Africa or not, *lobola* is still a must in our culture, *boetie*!'

'How much is it?'

'That depends.'

'On what?'

'Many things. On the girl's educational standard, her parents' socio-economic level, and even their tribe. It also depends on the attitude of the girl's family and their reasonableness or greed.'

Fanie digested this in silence.

'Are there written guidelines? Is there a government department responsible for *lobola*?'

'No!' laughed George. 'This is free enterprise!'

'How do I know then if I am being exploited?'

'It's part of the game of love, Fanie. No pain, no gain!'

'I will ask Maki to help,' Fanie decided.

'You can't.'

'Why not?'

'Because. It would not be culturally okay to do so.'

'Not culturally okay?'

George nodded smilingly.

That afternoon after lunch, as Fanie and George were coming back from the staff canteen, they heard the desk phone ringing. Since he was first into the office, George picked up the receiver.

'Yes *mevrou*. Yes, he's here. Hold a minute please.' He held the phone out to Fanie. 'It's yours, Fanie. I don't know who it is,' he said, in answer to Fanie's questioning look. 'She says her name is Grace Swanepoel.'

Puzzled, Fanie took the phone from him.

'Hallo Fanie,' said Gerda's broken voice. '*Ek wag nog vir jou!*' ('I'm still waiting for you!') 'Please, let us talk . . . *asseblief* Fanie, *asseblief* . . . !'

'Listen here Gerda, I've told you you are wasting your time! You must leave me alone now,' replied Fanie, before slamming down the receiver.

'She is crazy!' he said to George.

'You have made her crazy. It is you who started the fire, remember?' was George's unsympathetic response.

The phone rang again and Fanie ran out of the office. Laughing, George took the call, then went in search of his friend, whom he found hiding in the archives' storeroom, to tell him he had another caller.

This time it was Dimakatjo. Fanie's face was all smiles as he spoke to her.

They made arrangements for the weekend, agreeing that she would come and visit him.

George eavesdropped on the conversation without embarrassment.

'What?' said Fanie as he put the phone down, seeing his friend's stern expression.

George gave a shrug. 'I just hope you are not going to break this woman's heart like you did the last one,' he said.

14

The following Saturday towards lunchtime, Dimakatjo ambled up to the electronic gate of Strijdomhuis and stretched her hand to the intercom panel beside it. She pressed the button for number 31 and heard Fanie's voice responding cheerfully. The side gate clicked open. And the woman *more precious than mountain-heaps of gold and diamonds* entered. Taking the lift to Fanie's floor, she knocked at his door; Fanie's voice called to her to come in, for the door was unlocked.

Fanie was busy in the kitchen. A good cook who had learnt his skills from his mother, he was at the stove, juggling pots and pans of varying sizes. He wore an apron and held an egg-lifter in his right hand. Hurrying towards Dimakatjo, he lifted her hand to his lips and pressed a playful kiss on her knuckles. Then he swept her into his arms and kissed her ardently.

'*Mmalo! Ruri* you are a good cook, *eh!*' exclaimed Dimakatjo, hungrily sniffing the aromas that rose from the various pots; there was fried fish in one pan, steamed broccoli, mashed potato and spring-onion-and-tomato-gravy simmering in the other pots.

Fanie laughed at her compliment.

'Thank you; I enjoy cooking,' he said.

Not to be outdone, Dimakatjo threw together a delicious salad from the fresh produce she found in the fridge and various additions from the cupboards. Fanie left the pots simmering on low and went to put on a CD.

A short time later the couple sat down at the impeccably laid table and prepared to titillate their tastebuds with the feast. They ate with much enjoyment, talk and laughter competing with food for space in their mouths, clearly relishing each other's company as much as the tasty food on their plates. After they'd finished, Dimakatjo cleared the table. Fanie wanted her to leave the washing up for later, but the perfectionist in her prevailed and she insisted on doing it there and then. She declined his offer of help, insisting he had done enough by cooking the delicious meal. Fanie was forced to acquiesce. But, secretly, all he wanted was to be able to enfold the pearl of his heart in his love-aching *boere* arms.

To pass the moments of waiting, he played the role of disc jockey. Dimakatjo was pleasantly surprised when he put on the love ballads of Ringo Madlingozi, performed in the singer's trademark velvet voice and distinctly enunciated isiXhosa. The washing up went swiftly as magic and Dimakatjo hummed along as she rinsed soap suds from the crockery and transferred the plates and utensils from sink to dish rack.

By the time she joined Fanie in the lounge she was more than ready to snuggle into the eager arms of her man. She was not allowed to put her behind down on the sofa just yet, however, as Fanie insisted they should dance cheek to cheek. Holding each other close, they gently massaged each other's shoulder blades. When Fanie's hands slid down to her bottom, she reached around and removed his naughty fingers that were playing her cheeks with enthusiasm, as if she were a piano. Whenever he trod on her toes with his large feet, she grimaced with a wincing smile that he found completely irresistible. Unable to help himself, he planted umpteen kisses on her cheeks, neck, shoulders and, finally, her willing lips.

The next time he trod on her toes she screamed '*Joo-mma-weee!*' And the exclamation reminded him deliciously of their picnic lovemaking. The CD track ended and she asked for a repeat, but Fanie did not want to disengage his arms in order to comply. *Aowaa!* He just loved to see the black lily of his heart locked in the safety of his hairy white arms!

Suddenly there was a knock at the door. Fanie went, nervously, to look through the peephole.

'Who was that?' asked Dimakatjo, when he came back to her.

'Vegetable hawker. I thought it might be my sister, Anna-Marie,' he lied. In fact, he had been afraid it might be Gerda turning up on his doorstep.

'Tell me about your family,' said Dimakatjo. 'Are your parents still alive?'

'My mother is. My father was killed about fourteen years ago in a railway accident. He worked for South African Railways as a ticket collector.'

'I'm sorry. How many children are you?'

'Two. My sister and myself.'

They danced on in silence for a time.

'If my mother had to come here now, she would faint!' Fanie remarked presently.

'Why?'

'She won't appreciate our relationship. That you are the woman of my dreams. For her, colour is still a big issue. She's very old-fashioned that way.'

Dimakatjo digested this in silence. 'When will I get to meet her?' she asked.

Unexpectedly, Fanie answered her in Sepedi: '*O se tshwenyege, moratiwa!*' ('Don't worry, sweetheart!')

Dimakatjo laughed at this. 'Where did you learn to speak such good Sepedi?'

'I grew up on my grandfather's *plaas* in Potgietersrus. I used to play with the children of the black servants and workers there. I taught them English and my black friends taught me Sepedi. We used to make bulls with clay, and then we would make our bulls fight until they destroyed one another.'

'How old were you when you moved from there?'

'About twelve or thirteen.'

They had stopped dancing now and sat down together on the sofa. The moment had turned serious, as Fanie tried to express the things of his heart. He told Dimakatjo that the boys of his age, as well as older boys and even black adults, used to address him as *kleinbaas*, his sister as *kleinmiesies*, and his grandfather as *oubaas*. At the time he saw nothing wrong with this; but when he thought back to it now it distressed him.

His mind replayed snapshots from that period in his life and he groped for the words to express to Dimakatjo what it had been like. He could picture himself in the school uniform of the Potgietersrus Afrikaans Laerskool: short khaki pants, khaki shirt and cap. He remembered how he wore a pair of school shoes while his black friends went barefoot. The black boys were always proud to associate with *kleinbaas* Fanie.

At that point Fanie broke off his tale to head for the kitchen, from where he returned carrying two tall glasses full of granadilla juice – a flavour he knew to be Dimakatjo's current favourite. They both gulped thirstily before he continued:

'I also used to play with the little black girls. I used to chase them; they were my friends. The girls would tease me . . . I liked that; then I would give chase, and they would run away and then stop, and tease me again. They would slap their buttocks with their hands, in playful imitation of the big girls, and even show me their panties . . . '

Dimakatjo interrupted Fanie with amused laughter: 'Really?'

'Yes! They showed me their panties made of white flour sacks. But then one day, I was chasing the girls when my mother saw me. I won't forget that day! She called me: "Fanie! Fanie!" She was very angry with me. I stood in front of her, wondering what I had done wrong. And she said: "If I see you chasing those *kaffer* girls again, *ek gaan jou nek breek! Verstaan jy?*"' ('I'm going to break your neck! Do you understand?')

'And did you listen to your mother?' Dimakatjo wanted to know.

'*Ja!*' said Fanie. 'I was very afraid of her. She used to whip us like a man.'

'So you had to wait until you grew up to chase black girls again,' said Dimakatjo teasingly.

'That's right,' grinned Fanie, hugging her. 'Soon after that my mother, sister and I came to join my father in Koedoespoort here in

Pretoria, where he'd got a job on the railways. A year later he had his accident and died.'

Fanie glanced at her pensive face: 'Now it's your turn. Tell me about yourself,' he commanded.

Dimakatjo told Fanie that she had grown up not far from him, in Moletji near Pietersburg, now Polokwane. She had two older sisters who were both married and an older brother named Lukas who lived with her mother at the homestead and was recently divorced from his wife. She told him that after 'sucking her mother's breast', as the saying went, she 'handed it' to the last-born sister, who had recently died, leaving a ten-year-old boy to be raised by the family. Dimakatjo's father, like Fanie's, was dead, passing away five years previously of TB. Her mother was now a pensioner, surviving on a small pension supplemented by what her children sent her, and her younger aunt was a domestic who worked in Polokwane.

'My older aunt is a *sangoma*,' Dimakatjo added.

'A *sangoma*? That's interesting. I want to meet her!'

'You will!'

'Tell me Maki,' said Fanie thoughtfully, 'would your people be against our relationship?'

'No! Most of them would support it.'

'Most of them?'

'There might be opposition from the more radical ones. Some of them still think of whites as the enemy . . . especially *boers* like you!' She tweaked his ear playfully.

At that moment the phone rang.

Fanie seemed in no hurry to answer it.

'Aren't you going to answer your phone?' asked Dimakatjo. Before Fanie could stop her she made a dive and snatched up the receiver.

'*Dumela*,' she greeted sweetly in Sepedi.

'Hullo? Hullo?' Fanie could hear Gerda's sharp voice responding in confusion. 'Sorry, I must have the wrong number.'

Gently Dimakatjo put the phone down. She and Fanie sat staring at it as if it were a snake about to strike.

They both jumped when, a few seconds later, it rang again.

Once again it was Dimakatjo who answered: 'Good day,' she said, 'how can I help you?'

This time there was a pause, then Gerda's voice said: 'Is Mr Fourie there?'

'Let me ask him,' mischievous Dimakatjo replied. 'Who should I tell him is calling?'

'It's Gerda,' she said huffily. 'Gerda Moerdyk-van-Schalkwyk.'

'Oh, Gerda. No, I don't think he'll want to talk to you,' Dimakatjo said, reading Fanie's flushed and dismayed face.

'Who is that? Are you the maid?'

'No, I'm his fiancée,' said Dimakatjo.

The room seemed to vibrate with the loud slam of Gerda's receiver going down. Dimakatjo sat waiting with her hand outstretched. But the phone did not ring again.

Very slowly she turned to face Fanie. 'I want to know, Fanie – why is that woman still panting after you? Why have you not told her about me?' she asked, her expression very forbidding.

'I have tried, Maki, but she won't listen. She still keeps phoning and . . . ' stammered Fanie.

'No Fanie, if you had told her she would not still be phoning. She would not be asking if I was the maid. You have not told her, because you like to keep her on a string!'

'No, no Maki! I have told her that we are over but she won't accept it. She's a tough cookie that one. She will not take "no" for an answer.'

'You are going to phone her back,' said Dimakatjo, her eyes flashing with anger, 'and you are going to talk to her right now. You are going to put an end to her phoning once and for all!'

Fanie seemed to wilt before her eyes.

'I don't want to talk to her, Maki!' he said. 'You don't understand what that woman is like. I've told you – she's one tough bitch, she . . . '

But Dimakatjo didn't wait for him to finish. 'I don't care about the kind of woman she is! She can be tough, she can be deadly . . . she can be a karateka, a snake-charmer, a *boer sangoma* – anything!

If she is a woman and you are still in touch with her, then we have a problem . . . listen Fanie, I will be a bitch today! I will show you a side of me that you don't know. Now you speak to her! You tell her to stop!'

Fanie was dumbfounded by this outburst. He did not want to speak to Gerda. And he especially did not want to speak to her in front of Dimakatjo. He dreaded this prospect with all his heart.

'Why so afraid to speak to her, Fanie? Why are you avoiding her? What are you hiding? Am I a prostitute? Are you ashamed of me?' Dimakatjo ranted on.

Fanie was, indeed, facing a different Dimakatjo. This was the tough side that he had never seen before. Her tongue was bitter with *pherefere* – the home-grown hot chili. Jealousy was written in capital letters all over her face. Fanie had grabbed a venomous snake by its tail, and he was in serious danger of being bitten.

'No, no, no! My sweetie-pie – you've got it all wrong!' pleaded Fanie. He tried to take her hand but she would not be placated.

'You see, Maki . . .' justified Fanie, 'it's the first time that this happens to me. And I don't know how to handle it.'

'It's simple, Fanie!'

'Tell me!'

'You can't have both of us. Choose one of us!'

'I have chosen you, Maki!'

'That's not enough! Actions speak louder than words!' said Dimakatjo, still in that chili-hot, no-nonsense tone. She pointed to the telephone.

'Now tell Gerda to stop bitching after you! Phone her! Now!'

With utmost reluctance Fanie dialled under Dimakatjo's watchful eye. They could both hear Gerda's phone ringing, for Dimakatjo had activated the speaker button on Fanie's phone. The ringing went on grimly, like the tolling of the bells of doom. Just as Gerda, at the other end, finally picked up the receiver, Dimakatjo cut the line.

A quiet moment followed. The couple looked into each other's eyes in mutual and substantial relief. Fanie did not want to reflect on what might have happened had Dimakatjo not cut the call. He had no wish to be in the middle of a vicious telephone war between the two women; he was sure that this new Dimakatjo was quite capable of starting one.

As if reading his thoughts, Dimakatjo flashed a gentle smile that reassured Fanie that things would now be back to normal; bygones would be as corpses, buried on the heap of forgiveness.

'I don't want to be mean to you, Fanie.'

'Thank you, Maki,' said Fanie with sincere gratitude.

They hugged and kissed. A pause followed. Then Fanie said: 'I understand how you feel, Maki. If you love me, you must be jealous.'

She nodded, then playfully slapped his cheek. 'All right, I forgive you, too. Just don't be a naughty boy, okay?'

'Dankie miesies!' responded Fanie.

They both laughed.

Fanie stood up and took the empty glasses through to refill them with fruit juice. They drank quietly, lost in their private thoughts.

Fanie took Dimakatjo's hand in his. 'What are you thinking about, Maki?'

'What are *you* thinking about, Fanie?'

'I will tell you. But only if you . . .'

'No, you first!'

'I *won't* tell you, Maki!'

'All right,' laughed Dimakatjo, 'I have made up my mind to tell you, Fanie.'

'Tell me then!'

'Fanie, actions speak louder than words!'

'What?' said Fanie. 'Okay, wait!' Leaping up, he swept her off her feet, held her suspended in the air, and gave her a smacking kiss on the lips.

'Not a bad idea!' she laughed. 'But still not good enough!'

'Not good enough?' asked Fanie. Unexpectedly he unzipped his trousers: 'Let me get at your *kuku* and I will show you what is good enough!'

Dimakatjo roared with laughter, then smacked Fanie on his cheek, hard enough to sting.

'*Eina!*' he roared. 'Okay, okay,' he said in mock defeat. 'I will buy you a helicopter and we will fly to the moon for a honeymoon!'

'That's teenager stuff! I am a black woman, Fanie.'

Fanie pretended to be deep in thought. 'I know something that will make you happy . . . ' Wide-eyed, Fanie snapped his fingers. 'Something that will make your heart dance . . . '

'And what is that?'

'*Lobola!*'

'Now you have hit the bull's horn, Fanie!' Dimakatjo beamed.

They hugged and kissed again, the sweet word '*lobola*' still ringing deliciously in Dimakatjo's ears.

'George has told me a lot about *lobola*,' continued Fanie.

'What did he tell you?'

'A lot of things.'

'Like what?'

'Like . . . I don't know. It is confusing. But I want a straight answer from you, Maki.'

'What do you want to know?'

'Tell me why I have to part with *lobola* in the first place. Can't I just buy you a nice ring? This is new South Africa, isn't it?'

'New South Africa or not, Fanie, *lobola* is still important. It's a must if you want our marriage to have the blessing of the ancestors. And be taken seriously by my family. *Lobola* is our culture. Without it our marriage won't mean much to me or my people; it will be nothing but *vat-en-sit!*'

'*Vat-en-sit?*'

'Yes! *Vat-en-sit* – living together. That will unfortunately reflect how little value you invest in me and our relationship. That's how it will be seen by me and my people. There is no short-cut, Fanie.'

Dimakatjo paused for breath before firing another salvo: 'Tell me, Fanie, if Nelson Mandela parted with *lobola* for Graça Machel, why can't you do likewise for me?'

Fanie had 'no mouth'. There was no point in putting forward further excuses. Who wouldn't wish to do right by his woman, with Mandela as his model? For a while Fanie held his peace, busy 'nibbling at the bones of his head'.

'Another question, Maki . . .'

'What? Ask, Fanie!' she encouraged.

'If a man wants to pay *lobola* for a woman, how will he know how much . . . is her . . . your worth? What price are you? How much *lobola* must I . . . *er* . . . will your people ask for?'

Dimakatjo seemed very amused by the question. She had never thought she would be asked such a thing.

'How much is my worth?' she exclaimed, bursting into loud peals of laughter.

Fanie laughed with her. Then he stopped and asked: 'Why are you laughing?'

'You are also laughing, Fanie!'

'Yes, but I'm serious! I need to know how much you will cost. And will I have to pay for you in cows?'

Dimakatjo laughed even harder at that.

'I am priceless, Fanie! But no, you won't have to pay in cows.'

'Please tell me how much, Maki!'

'I won't tell you!'

'Why?'

'Because it's our culture, Fanie!'

Fanie recalled that George had told him something similar – something about it not being 'culturally okay' to talk about these things in advance. If, indeed, Fanie loved Dimakatjo – and he did – then he would have to respect the culture of her people.

He saw that Dimakatjo was watching him intently.

'So, Fanie, is it settled? Can I go home and inform my people that you are willing to part with *lobola* for me?'

'Yes, my sweetheart, you can!' Fanie said, sweeping her into his arms for an extended kissing session.

15

It was 4.30 on the following Friday afternoon and Fanie's sister Anna-Marie and his mother Louise were both at home, having knocked off from their respective jobs. Louise was one of the long-serving employees at the People's Bank in the heart of Pretoria, while Anna-Marie worked at a pre-school in Silverton in the east of the city.

Shortly before Fanie's arrival, Anna-Marie and Selina were busy preparing supper in the kitchen, while Louise relaxed with a steaming mug of *moerkoffie* in the lounge. Anna-Marie was telling Selina that she had, out of the blue, received a call from Gerda.

'You know Selina, Gerda is very upset that my brother has broken up with her.'

'*Ag shem, ngwana batho!*' ('Oh shame, poor child!') responded Selina with genuine sympathy.

'Ma liked Gerda. She cannot understand why Fanie would throw away a decent Afrikaans *meisie*, as she puts it, for a black woman.'

'*Uuuwii, ou miesies* must just *vostaan*' ('old missus must just understand') 'that young people are young people. *Mmapelo o ja serati.*' ('The one whose heart is full of love chooses the target of his love.')

At this point Louise entered the kitchen to put her mug and teaspoon into the sink. Selina, who was busy peeling a potato, paused to glance at 'the old lady', as Fanie sometimes referred to his mother. Louise could smell that there were secrets brewing in the kitchen. Selina and Anna-Marie had always had a close relationship, despite the differences in their ages and cultural backgrounds. One thing that bonded the two of them together was their elation at Fanie's new love relationship. Louise hated this camaraderie that came into existence as a result of what palpably offended her.

'*Miesies*, I hear you are not happy that Fanie's new girlfriend is black,' teased outspoken Selina, as Anna-Marie briefly left the kitchen.

'Who told you that?' challenged Louise.

'I won't tell you, *miesies*!'

'You are a *skelm*, Selina!'

Selina did not mind being called a *skelm* – 'rascal' – by her adored *miesies*, for whom she had worked faithfully for almost twenty years. She knew just how far to go in the liberties she took, and she would never take sides against Louise. *Aowaa!* For this black woman knew which side of her thick slice of bread was buttered and generously smeared with red jam and crunchy peanut butter!

'Selina, it is true, I am not happy!' Louise bared her heart to her faithful retainer.

'But why, *miesies*?'

'I will tell you!' With that, Louise marched from the kitchen, returning a few minutes later holding a huge Bible covered in worn brown leather that in some places had turned black with age. Louise had inherited this ancient Book of God from her maternal grandmother.

'I will tell you exactly why I am unhappy with Fanie's new relationship,' Louise said. She sat down and thumbed swiftly through the worn pages until she came to the section she was looking for; there she stopped, running her forefinger down the page.

'Here it is!' Louise raised her hand triumphantly heavenwards, as if calling for witness. 'But you won't understand what it says, Selina, because it's in Dutch. In simple words, it tells us that God made boundaries between different countries and races. God did this because God's plan is that people of the same race should fall in love and marry, have children and raise them in the same culture. Is it clear, Selina?'

'Yes, *miesies*.'

'That's what it says right here. That God made boundaries between the races. Only fools cross these boundaries. And Fanie's late father . . .' Louise solemnly pointed to the framed photograph on the kitchen wall, '. . . won't rest well in his grave!'

Louise closed the Bible with a triumphant snap and looked challengingly at her employee, who simply nodded. No matter what her true feelings, Selina wouldn't dream of arguing with her adored *miesies* who had taken her out of the pit of orphanhood and lifted her up to the hilltop of stable employment, thus making her a 'somebody' among her destitute clanspeople.

Anna-Marie, from the next room, heard what her mother had preached to Selina and was exceedingly incensed with what her ear had picked up. She marched into the kitchen and stood facing her mother challengingly with hands on hips, her body language clearly conveying: *If you are a tiger, then I am a leopard!* In other words, 'Challenge me, and I will challenge you back!'

'Ma, please don't abuse the Bible to justify apartheid!' fumed Anna-Marie. 'You make me ashamed to be an Afrikaner! It's bad enough that we have been prostituting the Bible for decades to justify our oppression and exploitation of our fellow countrymen!'

Louise gave her daughter a look of utmost outrage and stormed out of the kitchen.

At that crucial moment the doorbell chimed, signalling Fanie's arrival. He came sweeping in in good spirits, seeming not to notice the tense atmosphere of the house.

'*Hoe gaan dit, boetie?*' ('How are things going, little brother?') Anna-Marie greeted him affectionately. Fanie hugged and kissed his sister, then greeted Selina, whose tongue slipped, with the result that she addressed him as '*baas* Fanie'. Fanie was not offended, however. In this part of the world old habits died very hard. He understood that the legacy of the past, which had endured for more than 300 years, would not just grind to a halt simply because the political leaders of the country had signed apartheid's death certificate! The habit of inferiority and superiority was deeply engrained in the marrow of a whole generation of South Africans, and would remain so for years to come.

Selina brought a mug and saucer on a tray and put it ready on the coffee table in the lounge for Fanie. At the bottom of the white mug was a generous spoonful of pitch-black *moerkoffie*.

Returning to the kitchen she asked Fanie in Sepedi, with a wide grin on her face: 'How is your woman?'

'She is very well thank you,' said Fanie, answering in the same language.

'Where does she stay?'

'Mamelodi.'

'Whose child is she?'

'Machaba . . . '

'Machaba?'

'No, it's a long surname,' frowned Fanie. 'Ag man . . . I will tell you when I think of it.'

Anna-Marie grabbed Fanie by the hand and led him through to the lounge. Fanie could tell by her expression that she had something on her mind. Selina brought some rusks through and then went out again, leaving the siblings to sit together on the *boer*-antique sofas.

'Where's Maki?' asked Anna-Marie. 'I thought you were going to bring her with you today.'

'No, she's going home to her people this weekend. Anyway, I thought I'd better break the news to *ma* first, before I bring her here.'

'*Ma* already knows.'

'Knows what?'

'That you are going out with someone black.'

'You told her?'

'Not exactly. The last time you were here she saw us talking and guessed that something was going on. She demanded to know. I tried to keep your secret. But she got it out of me later.'

'How did she take it?'

'How do you think? She was furious.'

Selina brought in a kettle with boiling water and poured it into Fanie's cup, which was soon black with *moerkoffie*. Fanie apologised for not having told Selina that he no longer took coffee.

'What will you have then, *boetie*?' Anna-Marie asked.

'I don't suppose you have any health teas?'

'Health teas? Is that what your girlfriend Maki drinks?'

Selina and Anna-Marie burst into peals of delighted laughter.

'If you don't have herbal tea then I'll just have hot water and lemon.'

'*Aowaa!*' exclaimed Selina. 'A woman's business is to make her man fat, not lean!'

There was more laughter, and this time Fanie joined in.

'I promise you *boetie*, next time when you visit us a *sakkie* of herbal tea will be all ready for you,' Anna-Marie assured him.

Fanie suddenly snapped his fingers and shouted: 'Ma-chaba-phala! That's her surname! I remember now!'

'Machabaphala?'

'Yes!'

Selina went off to the kitchen for the hot water and lemon 'tea' that Fanie had requested. Fanie proudly took out an envelope from his shirt pocket and handed it to Anna-Marie; inside were two photos.

'Is this Maki?'

'Yes!' beamed Fanie.

'She looks gorgeous! I like her already!'

Selina, re-entering, now wanted to see the photos, but Anna-Marie playfully withheld them from her, allowing her to see only the back. She finally relented and let Selina look.

'*Hai-hai-hai!* Look at her! A slim girl who eats once a week! She is a *sponono* – a real beauty – this one with dimples in her cheeks!'

She walked out of the lounge with a huge smile on her face.

'Where's *ma*? Is she here?' enquired Fanie.

'Yes. She's somewhere around,' said Anna-Marie tersely. 'She's probably in her bedroom. We had a big fight and I am still angry with her.'

'About what, Riekie?' asked Fanie, sipping his lemon-flavoured concoction.

'You can guess, *boetie*. She cannot accept your relationship. She tries to justify apartheid with the Bible. She told Selina that God made boundaries between different races for a reason and that only fools cross the line.'

Fanie nodded sombrely then quietly said: 'I am not bothered by *ma*'s racial hang-ups, Riekie. That's her problem. I have found the woman of my dreams and I'm not letting her go. Colour is not an issue for Maki and me, and what others think doesn't matter.'

He fell silent for a time, then resumed, speaking very intensely: 'I really love Maki, Riekie. I have never loved a woman like this before, and I was never loved this way by any woman.'

'I'm happy for you, *boetie*,' smiled Anna-Marie. 'And don't worry about *ma*. The old lady will come round. She just needs time to get used to the idea that she may soon have a black daughter-in-law; she never imagined that her own son would choose someone from a different race group!'

She squeezed her brother's hand consolingly, and after that they sat in silence for a while.

Selina, walking past to one of the bedrooms to drop off a floor mat that had been hung out to dry, discovered Louise leaning against the wall of the passage, listening intently to Fanie and Anna-Marie's conversation. She was not in the least embarrassed to be caught eavesdropping and merely lifted a forefinger to her lips to indicate that Selina should go about her business and say nothing. Selina obliged.

'Where are Maki's parents from?' enquired Anna-Marie.

'Her mother's family lives in Ga-Mabitsela, which is a village in the Moletji district, not far from where we used to live as kids. Her mother is also a widow, like *ma*. And guess what, one of her aunts is a *sangoma*!'

'A *sangoma*? That sounds interesting! I wonder what *ma* will have to say about that!'

'She will think that the *sangoma* has bewitched me, to make me fall deeply in love with her niece!'

Fanie and Anna-Marie both chuckled at that.

Selina, passing through again on her way back to the kitchen, could not stop herself from bursting into rich peals of laughter: 'Hey you two children, what do you know about *moratišo*, the love-potion?' she asked.

Fanie and Anna-Marie's laughter joined hers. All were abruptly silenced by Louise's unexpected presence looming in their midst.

'*Ja, jou kaffer skoonma het jou getoor!*' ('Yes, your kaffir mother-in-law has bewitched you!') she said viciously, standing with one hand on her hip, cigarette smoke spewing like vitriol out of her acid mouth.

'Ma, you are a such a disappointment! An embarrassment! You are behind the times!' Anna-Marie fired at her. 'You belong in the museum of apartheid! You don't deserve to be in the new *Suid Afrika!*'

'Mariekie . . . ' Louise interrupted her daughter furiously, 'how dare you speak to me like that . . . !'

'How can *you* speak the way you do about the future mother-in-law of your son?' Anna-Marie shot back.

'Mariekie, Mariekie – I said don't talk to me like that! Or I'll take the strap to you the way I used to when you were little – do you hear me?' shouted Louise, pointing a furious finger at her daughter.

This time it was Selina hiding and listening, and now there was no laughter in her; she was praying with the utmost concentration that sanity should prevail.

'It's okay, Riekie, leave her,' Fanie intervened. 'There is no point in fighting over things we cannot change. If *ma* cannot accept that I am in love with Maki then too bad for her!' He paused to swallow his anger down, then continued: 'Ma, I love you, but please don't spoil my love, my life, my future with your ugly racism. You are my mother and I cannot wish you away. But if you make me choose between you and my love, then it is Maki I will choose.'

With that he got up and left the house.

16

Early that Saturday morning child of Machabaphala was seated aboard a whirlwind taxi that took her swiftly to Polokwane, the capital of Limpopo Province. From here she boarded another taxi to her village of Ga-Mabitsela, whose people were the subjects of Kgoši Thakadu Mabitsela.

Shortly before Dimakatjo arrived to set her foot upon the soil of Ga-Mabitsela, her brother Lukas was at his favourite occupation, busy tinkering with an old BMW that he refused to dismiss as the unredeemable wreck it was – good for nothing but to be turned into scrap material for a fowl-run. Lukas had great faith that one day this old automobile would yet scratch the dirt roads of Ga-Mabitsela with its tyres. He planned to use it as a pirate taxi. His young nephew Sefako, who was full of boundless energy and fond of shooting birds with a catapult, was helping his uncle, as he often did. When Sefako's mother Mmapula, the younger sister of Dimakatjo and Lukas, had died about three years previously, her small son had remained at the Machabaphala homestead to be reared by relatives.

Wearing his favourite grey-chequered '*las*' cap and a pair of greasy overalls, Lukas leaned into the car's open bonnet, Sefako acting as his spanner boy. The sound of an approaching taxi made them look up.

'Look Sefako, there's your aunt!' Lukas said.

From inside the slowing vehicle that was now turning into their yard, they could see Dimakatjo waving at them through the open window.

Wearing a huge smile, ten-year-old Sefako sprinted to welcome his aunt, known to him as *Mmamogolo* Dimakatjo. The driver opened the boot of the taxi and Sefako helped to carry in the supplies that

Dimakatjo had brought: two big pockets of vegetables and fruit, and several packets of frozen meat. Lukas, who was following, cautioned Sefako not to kill himself with the heavy load. Wiping his grease-stained hands on his dirty overalls, Lukas gave his sister a firm handshake and a welcoming smile befitting to a *lekarapa* – a city person who returned only infrequently to visit his or her rural home.

Dimakatjo and the rest of her family then exchanged loud and excited greetings, making themselves a spectacle for the neighbours on every side. They were so overjoyed that one could count their teeth when they smiled and tell what they had swallowed for breakfast from their uninhibited laughter.

Mma-Dimakatjo carefully inspected her daughter from head to toe, and prodded and pinched her biceps. The old woman, Lukas and Dimakatjo all laughed loudly at that, for her actions were those of a mother checking her small child over to see if she was eating properly.

According to rural custom a woman never behaves like a guest in her own home, so Dimakatjo wasted no time in putting on her apron and helping to prepare lunch. Not for nothing is it said that 'A *woman is a baboon whose hands are eaten*' – meaning that her hands are as productive as those of baboons, which never stop moving.

Mma-Dimakatjo had already cooked a stiff white maize-meal porridge. To this was added some of the ingredients from the supplies that Dimakatjo had brought.

A short time later, Dimakatjo served lunch: steaming porridge and boiled chicken, with a tomato-and-spring-onion gravy. The family members sat on the *stoep* in front of the main house and had their lunch there, with Lukas seated on a rickety old bench that he had made out of planks.

Dimakatjo had prepared for herself a separate meal of brown rice mixed with split peas and lentils, and a Greek salad with lots of black olives. Mma-Dimakatjo playfully squinted her eyes sideways to inspect Dimakatjo's plate of food, then smiled meaningfully at

Lukas, who got the message and laughed with her. They were both amused by the 'white people's food' on Dimakatjo's plate.

'*Ngwan'a* Bakone is nursing her figure!' joked Lukas.

Dimakatjo nodded and smiled good-humouredly at her brother. She then shared with her family how she had acquired her health-conscious lifestyle, through working at the doctor's surgery and seeing the cost of bad eating and other unhealthy habits.

After their meal Mma-Dimakatjo, Sefako and Lukas moved to the shade of a *morula* tree behind the main house to drink cooldrink, while industrious Dimakatjo did the washing up. She later sent Sefako to buy his uncle two bottles of beer at a shebeen a short distance down the road.

Daughter of Bakone was in a hurry to finish the dishwashing chores so that she could sit with her people and share the good news that was waiting for them. Two weeks earlier she had written a letter to her mother, explaining that the path of love between her and Tau had grown entangled with thorn bushes, and that the earthenware pot of their dreams was now shattered beyond repair. But she had said nothing of Fanie, preferring to relay this important news face to face and eye to eye.

As Dimakatjo stepped out of the kitchen, her nephew entered the yard with two clinking bottles of his uncle's favourite beer in his hands, his beloved catapult dangling, as usual, around his neck. As Lukas downed the first glassful of cold beer, Dimakatjo called to her nephew, whom she then surprised with an unsurpassed wonder-toy: a yellow-and-green battery-operated *matipane,* or 'tipper-truck'. Sefako leapt about excitedly, clutching his prize, which he then ran to show to his grandmother and uncle.

Mma-Dimakatjo was sitting on a grass mat with her legs folded sideways under her, leaning on her right hand. Dimakatjo brought out a second mat that she spread beside her mother's. She sent Sefako to fetch some apples, pears, and grapes for them to nibble on and sat down with a light sigh.

'Dimakatjo,' said Mma-Dimakatjo, 'your cheeks are not as round as the last time when you were here. Are you well, *morwedi'a* Bakone?'

'Yes, I'm well, *mma*,' replied Dimakatjo who, after many months away, was enjoying being someone's child again. As always she felt young, protected and secure in her mother's presence.

'Dimakatjo is healthy, Mma-Dimakatjo,' added Lukas, who consistently addressed his mother in the more formal way as 'Mma-Dimakatjo.'

'*Mma*,' said Dimakatjo, infusing much affection into the word, 'gone are the days when well-padded young women expected men to reward them, exclaiming, "*Nku re reka mosela!*"' ('A sheep is judged by the fatness of its tail!') They all laughed at this.

'Mma-Dimakatjo, these days men prefer slim women. Fat women eat too much; they cause poverty!'

Again they all roared with laughter, enjoying Lukas's sense of humour. Dimakatjo and her mother nibbled at the apples, grapes and pears that Sefako had brought while Lukas, increasingly good-humoured, savoured his third glass of beer.

Dimakatjo waited for an appropriate pause that would afford her the opportunity to break the good news.

'*Mma* and *buti* Lukas, I'm carrying good news for you.'

'We are listening, my child.'

Dimakatjo then disclosed that she had a new man in her life, and that he was a white *boere seuntjie* by the name of Fanie Fourie. She waited a moment for their amazed faces to register the news. 'Moreover,' she went on, 'he intends parting with *lobola* for me!'

'What are you saying? *Lobola* is coming to our family?' asked Mma-Dimakatjo excitedly.

'Well done sister!' said Lukas, slapping his thigh.

'That is full-cream, my child! That is honey! *Liiuu! Liiuu! O šomile, ngwan'a Bakone!*' ('Well done, child of Bakone!') '*Liiuu! Liiuu!*'

Although Mma-Dimakatjo was sitting down, in her heart she was standing up and dancing. She was extremely exhilarated by the news, for Mma-Dimakatjo was not only rejoicing over her daughter's *lobola*; she was also celebrating the end of being an object of scorn among her peers. While almost all the girls in this village had a child or two by the age of seventeen or eighteen, Dimakatjo was, at her age of 25, still without child. Rumours abounded that she was *nyopa* – an unfruitful woman, a barren mule that would never have a young one.

A group of old women snorting home-made snuff would talk in-between inhaling their pinches of stuff, gossiping about how Mma-Dimakatjo was waiting in vain for a grandchild. Mma-Dimakatjo had been mocked repeatedly by some of these gossip-mongers: 'When are you going to have a grandchild?'

She, poor old woman, would put on a brave face and answer that the right time would come, or that the matter was resting in God's competent hands. If Dimakatjo was asked such a question directly, she would simply tell her inquisitors that she preferred to have a child within a secure relationship of marriage, where the child would be brought up by two parents.

That day Mma-Dimakatjo's heart was 'white', as her people would say: full of peace and joy and all good emotions. At last she would have a grandchild to boast about! *'Ruri Modimo o phala baloi!'* she said, over and over again. 'Indeed God is more powerful than witches!' Mma-Dimakatjo was not bothered that her future son-in-law was a white man – and a *boer* to boot. What was of paramount importance to her was that her daughter would, at last, have a child within the security of marriage.

'I am very happy that I will soon be eating the cattle of my sister's *lobola!*' enthused Lukas, smiling as though he were posing for a toothpaste commercial. He finished the last glass of beer while his mother tasted the last drops of her cooldrink. Dimakatjo then asked Sefako to take the empty glasses back to the kitchen. For a short while they were quiet, pondering over the good fortune that had befallen them.

Mma-Dimakatjo felt light as wind, as though she could, in a fit of frenzy, dance the *'Mmantshegele'* – which was a popular African song and dance among rural women, usually engaged in when they had tasted more than their good share of sorghum beer. She visualised herself the envy of her peers, a proud grandmother dandling a coloured baby boy on her lap; she could distinctly hear the grandchild babbling its baby-talk, crooning, among other words: '*Ouma! Ouma!*' while she replied with grandmother's talk of: '*An-du-du-lu-lu-lu-lu-nu!*' Looking at her daughter, Mma-Dimakatjo recalled the Sepedi proverb: '*An orphan who does not die is awaiting riches*', meaning that if one survives the hardships and remains focused, riches will come. She hugged and kissed Dimakatjo ecstatically, feeling drunk with joy.

The ever-curious villagers saw that something was happening at Machabaphala's place. They saw Dimakatjo arriving by taxi, an event in itself since, for most of these villagers who travelled to and from the city by bus, a taxi remained a status symbol. Watching the goings-on from their neighbouring homesteads, they could see that joy of some kind had overtaken the Machabaphala people.

However, those who knew more, who had already heard certain rumours about Dimakatjo, mouthed exclamations and click sounds of disgust. Young women talked about what they had heard as they walked the one-kilometre distance to the communal water-pump; there they continued to gossip about Dimakatjo: *Have you heard this? Have you heard that?*

The old women who did not have much to do with their time saw Dimakatjo and marvelled at the change in her. They remembered child of Machabaphala when she was still a sucking infant, smacking her lips at her mother's breast-milk. They remembered her when she was a crawling toddler, and when she was barely the age of the fingers on one hand, still licking her mucous-laden upper lip. They talked about Dimakatjo in-between their umpteen pinches of home-made snuff. One of them would insert a pinch into her nostrils and then sneeze: *Eethiyaaaa! Have you heard this? Have you heard that?*

Although Lukas was delighted about the good news that his sister brought and not unhappy to be the brother-in-law of a white guy, at this moment he cherished mixed feelings. He had been particularly disappointed to hear that his sister had ditched Tau, the chief's son, whom he had already started addressing as '*molamo*' and '*sebara*' – 'brother-in-law'. He had heartily approved of that connection and the opportunities it would present. Moreover, he was very sceptical about this new relationship and its chances of lasting.

He wanted to keep this concern to himself, however, this thought that would certainly be like *Ntšhi-sewela* – the adventurous fly that drowns in and spoils the milk, according to the folktale. He tried to dismiss this negative thought, but the thought swelled stubbornly in his mind until he could resist it no more.

Lukas at last took the risk of opening his mouth: 'I don't want to spoil the sweet news, Dimakatjo. But can I ask you a question?'

'You are welcome to, *buti* Lukas.'

'What happened to that son of a chief you were seeing until recently?'

'Tau?'

'Yes, Tau. Must we understand that you no longer love him? He was a nice prosperous catch . . . '

'*Buti*, hasn't *mma* shown you the letter I sent her?' Dimakatjo interrupted her brother, 'In which I explained that . . . '

'I have shown him the letter,' interrupted Mma-Dimakatjo.

'Yes, Mma-Dimakatjo showed me the letter. But I didn't take that letter seriously. Because I know that lovers quarrel; they can fight like cat and dog today and tomorrow you see them walking hand in hand, laughing together as if they had just smoked *dagga*.'

Mma-Dimakatjo and Dimakatjo were amused by this.

'In fact, Tau was here last weekend,' continued Lukas, 'and he talked as if you and he were still together and in love.'

'Did he say we are still in love? If he said that then he told you lies!' said Dimakatjo vehemently. She recalled the phone conversation she had had with Tau after his return, when she had told him in no uncertain terms that the wording of her letter had not been a mistake and that the two of them were, indeed, history.

'And he was drunk as usual. *Poepdronk!*' Mma-Dimakatjo added her wood to the fire.

'But he is just jolly and harmless! He's a nice, sweet, harmless, jolly guy!' defended Lukas.

'Nice and sweet, honey or vinegar, the fact remains I no longer want to be with him. Tau knows that, *buti* Lukas. Next time you see him, please tell him to forget about me.'

Lukas was disappointed. But he did not want to give up. 'Don't make a big deal of Tau's drunkenness,' he said, continuing to be Tau's counsel for the defence. 'There is nothing wrong with liquor. Ninety-nine per cent of men are drinking these days. The most important thing is, a man must look after his family. Am I making sense to you?' He fixed his inebriated eyes on Dimakatjo.

'No!'

'Well, anyway, someone told me this week that Tau is no longer a drunk,' Lukas commented. 'I heard he has even become a member of Bishop Lekganyane's ZCC congregation.'

Dimakatjo pictured Tau in a khaki *Mokhukhu* suit with star-shaped badge and white shoes with truck-tyre soles; she found the picture very amusing.

'Well it's good that he is changing; but that still cannot convince me to change my mind,' she responded.

A short pause followed. Lukas thought: *If Dimakatjo married the son of a chief we would receive a huge amount of lobola. We could have enough money to buy furniture . . . and I would be able to buy parts for my BM! It will be wonderful for our family to be related to the royal family. We could have a big wedding that might be attended by VIPs such as Bishop Lekganyane and President Thabo Mbeki, and other big shots . . .*

'Please forget about Tau, *buti* Lukas,' said Dimakatjo, as if she could read her brother's mind. Lukas had no idea that it was now more than a month since the love of Dimakatjo and Tau had died and been buried by the new love of Dimakatjo and Fanie.

'I hope the white man is not just toying with you,' Lukas said, firing a last salvo. 'I hope he isn't only interested in your body, and will not dump you as soon as his curiosity has been satisfied.'

'Lukas, let's respect your sister's choice,' was their mother's decisive comment. 'Remember the proverb: "*Forcing a huge chunk of meat into a small earthenware pot breaks the pot.*"'

Lukas nodded at his mother, but the old woman could see that her son was not fully convinced. She did not want to say anything more, however, deciding that *the fire burns the one closest to it*. She was not surprised when Lukas expelled the wind out of his mouth again.

'Another question, Dimakatjo. Are you sure that the white man will part with *lobola*?'

'Yes, I am very sure that he will do that. Because he loves me.'

'But whites don't believe in *lobola*,' persisted Lukas. '*Die lahnees koop net* expensive rings' ('Whites buy only expensive rings'), he said, flipping into *tsotsi-taal*. 'And they prefer to spend a lot of money on . . . er . . . what do they call it?'

'Honeymoon?'

'Yes, honeymoon!'

'Lukas, have trust and patience,' Mma-Dimakatjo chided. 'Remember, *Modimo o phala baloi!* – God is more powerful than witches!'

The following afternoon a cousin of Dimakatjo and Lukas, known as Matsobane, paid the Machabaphalas a visit. He was glad to find Dimakatjo home, for he was fond of her. Matsobane, a teacher at the local high school, was a popular figure who had earned the nickname 'Mayibuye', because at one time he had strongly espoused Pan-Africanist political ideology. He was fond of chanting the appropriate slogan: '*Mayibuye iAfrika! iAfrika, izwelethu!*' ('Come back Afrika! Afrika our land!')

As a result, his fellow teachers had taken to addressing him as 'Mayibuye', sometimes adding the title, 'Comrade'; while to the students, he was known as 'Teacher Mayibuye'. Lukas and Dimakatjo, however, preferred to address him as *khazi* – a shorter form of the word for 'cousin', while he addressed them both as *khazi* in his turn. Mma-Dimakatjo, he addressed as *rakgadi* – 'father's sister' or 'aunt'.

Mayibuye was such an ardent advocate of Pan-Africanism that he even smoked a crooked pipe, a habit he had observed and adopted from newspaper photos of the founder of the Pan-African Congress of 'Azania', Robert Sobukwe.

Pictures of Kwame Nkrumah and some of the other founders of Pan-Africanism were pasted on the walls of his lounge. But Mayibuye himself was a rank-and-file member who had no ambitions for any top position in politics; he loved fun, and was fond of applying adapted versions of PAC slogans to his somewhat hectic social life of parties and feasts. 'One man, one bottle of beer' was a favourite of his, adapted from the infamous PAC war-cry of the 1980s, 'One settler, one bullet'.

Wasting no time, Mma-Dimakatjo proudly told Mayibuye that a certain white guy, son of Fourie, intended to part with *lobola* for Dimakatjo, child of Bakone. Mayibuye was so ecstatic to hear the good news that he repeatedly chanted, '*Hee-banna!*'; finally adding his aunt's favourite refrain: '*Ruri Modimo o phala baloi!*' – 'God is indeed more powerful than witches.'

Lukas asked for a few more bottles of beer to celebrate the good news. Dimakatjo forked out the money and the fresh bottles duly arrived courtesy of Sefako.

'*Khazi*,' Mayibuye addressed Dimakatjo, 'tell us more about your *boer* boyfriend. What is his name?'

'Fanie.'

'And his surname is Fourie?'

'That's right,' said Lukas on his sister's behalf.

'Fanie Fourie?'

'That's right,' replied Lukas again. He was becoming drunker and his mouth looser with each swallow that he took. 'Tell Fanie Fourie,' he instructed Dimakatjo, 'that he is not *sebara* – brother-in-law – for *fokol*! I want *mullah* – money! He must part with more *lobola* than that son of a chief that you threw away!'

'Is our brother-in-law rich? What kind of car does he drive?' asked Mayibuye.

'Yes, *khazi*, I wanted to ask that same question!' interrupted Lukas.

'No, he is not rich!' said Dimakatjo quickly.

Lukas and Mayubuye laughed scathingly at that: 'If he is white then he is rich! All whites are rich,' said Mayibuye.

'Tell us what car he has,' demanded Lukas.

Dimakatjo did not want to answer Lukas; she felt that if he knew that Fanie drove a BMW, second-hand or not, her brother would insist on a huge sum of *lobola*. She had witnessed many girls whose relationships with their boyfriends became sour and their hopes of getting married were dashed when their greedy parents and relatives asked for *lobola* amounts that were too high.

'I don't know what car he drives.'

'You know, Dimakatjo!'

'No, *khazi*,' Mayibuye warned Lukas, 'leave her alone.' Mayibuye shifted his attention back to Dimakatjo: '*Khazi*, I don't know your man but I can guess that you have hit a jackpot with him!'

'No, *khazi*, I'm his jackpot!' insisted Dimakatjo.

They all laughed at her wit.

'*Rakgadi*,' Mayibuye addressed Mma-Dimakatjo, 'so you are going to be a white man's mother-in-law!'

'I will say "yes" when I hear cows crying "*moo, moo!*" in the Machabaphala's cattle-pen!'

Mayibuye, Lukas and Dimakatjo laughed heartily at that.

'Let's start preparing for the great day,' suggested Lukas, standing up unsteadily with his over-full glass spilling beer. 'Let's start preparing today! You, *khazi* . . . ' Lukas hiccuped and a strong stench of beer shot from his mouth. 'You will be the Master of Ceremonies . . . ' Again Lukas hiccuped; he sat down heavily and leaned back in his chair.

'Lukas, let's not dance and leap in joy before the drum-beaters pound the drum!' warned Mma-Dimakatjo.

Mayibuye nodded in agreement and gulped down the contents of his tall beer glass.

17

It was the first Thursday in April, just before knock-off time. Fanie was alone in the office since George was attending another of the frequent managers' meetings.

Fanie had just got off the phone to Dimakatjo. They phoned each other daily, saw each other at every opportunity; and the more they had to do with each other, the more he wished that they were already living together. They seemed to have grown even closer, if possible, in the weeks following their *lobola* conversation. This was all the more remarkable to Fanie since they were no longer sexually involved.

Soon after Dimakatjo's return from her weekend at home, when Fanie had tried to make love to her, she had told him: 'If you love me then you must wait. There must be no more sex between us until our *lobola* day.'

Difficult though it was at first, Fanie grew used to the idea and learned to be content with kissing and touching. He was surprised that he could exercise such self-control. Abstinence did not come easily to him. The fire in his blood was never dampened, but for the sake of Dimakatjo and their love, he was willing to make the sacrifice.

Dimakatjo, for her part, was glad to have the excuse to stop having sex with Fanie. It was not that she did not lust for him in return, but she always nursed the anxiety that if she gave herself completely to her man he would soon tire of her. She didn't want to see herself chasing after Fanie like Gerda; neither was she in love with the idea of seeing herself disposed of by Fanie like empty banana peels.

On her last visit home, her mother had said to her: 'Today you are a woman, not a little girl. Now I want to give you an old lady's advice: don't live with a man as if you are his wife. If he wants to marry you, don't just give-give to him *pasela* – for nothing. It will cloy his appetite like too much pork. You know, too, that our church discourages sex before *lobola*.'

Dimakatjo had taken her mother's words to heart. Thanks partly to that hard-to-get strategy, Fanie valued her, if possible, even more highly than before and felt strongly motivated to part with *lobola* for her as soon as possible.

He wanted to talk to George about this *lobola* business and get his advice. They had arranged to head down after knock-off time to the popular Democracy Jazz Café, generally referred to as DJC, in Nelson Mandela Drive.

They went down together in Fanie's car and made their way through the restaurant. A few heads turned as Fanie, sporting his ponytail, and smartly dressed George walked past the veranda towards a corner table in the garden. There were not many other white faces to be seen here, for this was a popular haunt among trendy black patrons, especially of the music-loving kind.

George and Fanie ordered two quart bottles of cold beer. The waiter brought them, and thirsty George took a deep slug of his. He swallowed, licked the foam from his lips and put the glass down on the table with a satisfied thump.

'So what have you got for me, Fanie?' he asked, raising his voice to be heard above the music. A catchy jazz track came through the powerful speakers above their heads.

Fanie hesitated, then said: 'I want to talk to you about the *lobola* for my woman . . .'

'Oh, so you have decided to pay up after all!' grinned George. 'Well done, Fanie! You are doing something manly, wanting to do this properly and not just *jol* around and waste the time of another mother's child!'

Fanie nodded glumly.

'So when do you plan to part with this *lobola*?'

'We have not yet chosen the date. But Maki has already informed her people. She was there the weekend before last.'

'That is good news!' responded George. He glanced at Fanie shrewdly: 'What about your people? Have you told them yet?'

Fanie hesitated: 'About Maki? Yes,' he said.

'Have you taken her to meet them?'

'Not yet. I needed time to prepare them first.'

Fanie downed some of his beer. 'My sister is happy for me,' he said. 'I think she and Maki will like each other.'

'And your mother?'

Fanie shrugged uncomfortably. 'I can't expect her to shout "Hallelujah",' he said.

'Maybe "*voetsek*"?'

They laughed, but to Fanie's ears the laughter had a hollow sound. He took another long swallow of his beer. George watched Fanie's hand raising the glass and putting it down again.

'Fanie, listen to me. *Lobola* is not for boys,' he told his friend seriously.

'What are you trying to tell me, George?'

'What I've just said. Parting with *lobola* is not child's play. It's a serious business between two families . . . '

'I know, I know . . . '

'I just want to be sure that you understand what you are getting into. Most of the time things go smoothly, but I know of *lobola* negotiations that become caught up in a web of difficulties.'

Fanie nodded uncertainly, trying to imagine what difficulties George could be talking about.

'So may your ancestors be with you!'

'I'm white, remember?' said Fanie with a smile.

'That doesn't mean you don't have ancestors. And you'll be marrying into ours, so . . . ' George waved his beer glass in frustration. 'How can I explain ancestors to a white boy?'

'Continue, continue!' Fanie flashed him a disarming smile.

'You must pray,' George said, 'that Maki's people are truthful and fair people, that they should not be people with heads as hard as rocks. If they are a bunch of *tsotsis* full of *mathaithai* – trickery – then the *lobola* negotiations will go along like a limping cow that is forced to walk up a steep mountain. When the girl's relatives are gripped by greed and jealousy then you are faced with problems. Some relatives can also foment a lot of trouble so that the girl should not be married. Jealousy! Witchcraft! These are all snares on the love-road whose destination is *lobola*.'

George could see as he was talking that the mill inside Fanie's head was grinding a lot of hard corn. There was a pause while both men gave serious attention to their beer. Then Fanie nodded gravely and said: 'I can see that *lobola* is, as you have said, no child's play. So how can you help me *ou maat*? What tips can you give me?'

'You must stand on your own two feet, Fanie,' George said sternly. 'Don't expect to be given things on a platter while you are sitting on your buttocks, in the way that you whites used to be pampered during apartheid. *Aowaa!*'

'*Ag* George, *moenie nonsens praat nie!*' warned Fanie; but instantly he flashed a smile, trying to neutralise the unintended sharpness of his words.

George's laughter showed there were no hard feelings.

They hailed the waiter and ordered another round.

'I must repeat, Fanie, that you are doing something manly by deciding to part with *lobola*. Congratulations! Let's have a toast.'

They clinked their bottles together.

'To a successful *lobola!*' George said.

'I'll drink to that!' Fanie replied.

18

Despite her disappointment at Fanie's behaviour and the crushing blow of finding Dimakatjo in his flat on the day she had phoned, Gerda still clung to the hope that his new relationship was just a passing fling. The stubborn voice in her head continued to urge her: *Don't give up Gerda. People who give up are as good as dead!*

One day on impulse she had phoned Fanie's sister Anna-Marie, hoping to find in her an ally and enlist her help in persuading her brother to come to his senses. Anna-Marie, however, did not hesitate to break the news to Gerda that Fanie's new affair was no passing fling but a serious relationship, and that he was madly in love with Dimakatjo.

Crushed by the news Gerda put the phone down, asking herself incredulously: *But a black woman? How can Fanie be seriously in love with someone black? Can it be true that a black woman is more attractive than a white woman?*

A dreadful thought occurred to her: *Maybe it is true! Maybe that's why, during the old South Africa, sexual intercourse between blacks and whites was forbidden!*

Gerda became very bitter. It seemed the ultimate humiliation that her rival in love was black. Never in her life had she imagined that she would be dumped for a woman of another colour.

Early that Thursday morning in April Gerda was already wide awake, lying in bed and smoking her first cigarette of the day. As was often the case these days, she hadn't slept well, tossing and turning all night long as she brooded and schemed over the sorry state of her love-life. Finishing her cigarette, she climbed out of bed and prepared a strong cup of coffee, which she gulped down while she dressed.

By seven o'clock she was at the bus stop, ready to board the bus that would take her into central Pretoria where she worked.

Gerda was employed at Salon Thandi, which had changed its name from the original Salon Marina when it was taken over by Thoko Masilela, a businesswoman from Mamelodi. Thoko had named the salon after her only daughter, Thandi. When Thoko took over, the three other white employees resigned, deciding they would rather look for employment elsewhere than work under a black woman. Apart from the fact that Thoko's skin was the 'wrong' colour, these conservative white women also did not like the fact that Thoko was a Rastafarian; they imagined the respectable salon turning into a den of vice, with blaring reggae music and throngs of '*Jah-man*' *dagga* smokers hanging out there all day long.

Mindful of the fact that jobs were hard to come by Gerda, however, decided to swallow her pride and stay on. Thoko was glad to have her, for she was a good hairdresser and Thoko hoped, through her, to retain some of the original white clientele. Over time, to Gerda's surprise, their relationship had developed an element of genuine affection, for Thoko was an open-hearted woman who treated her employees with kindness and respect.

That morning, soon after Gerda had arrived, she saw Thoko drawing up outside in her snow-white, three-litre BMW. As Thoko reversed into her parking spot, a white hobo turned car washer and parking attendant, who was known only as Japie, stood behind her car, busily making turning motions with his right hand as he helpfully directed Thoko. She had already put on the brake and switched off the engine when he belatedly raised his palm to signal she should stop.

'Morning madam,' said Japie, rubbing his palms together and grinning deferentially, 'can I wash your car today?'

'Okay, Japie,' agreed Thoko with a smile, climbing out of the car and adjusting her outfit – a two-piece African-print in gold and sky-blue, all the way from the Ivory Coast.

Entering the salon Thoko greeted Gerda, then went into the little cubicle that served as her office and stored her handbag safely in the cupboard. Gerda came in, carrying a cupful of the strange-smelling herbal tea that her boss favoured, which Gerda suspected was *ganja* and, for this reason, had never dared to sample, even though Thoko had assured her it was a Chinese tea that kept one energised all day long.

Wearing her work smock Gerda then took the mop and a bucket of water mixed with floor-cleaning liquid and started to mop the floor, while Thoko checked the stocks, looked at her diary, and wrote some cheques. They had the salon to themselves today, for the other hairdressers were off, since it was Monday and likely to be a slow day.

From Thoko's CD-player, set at high volume, boomed the catchy rhythms of Bob Marley, King of Reggae's 'Stand up and fight for your rights'. It had taken Gerda a while to stop being disturbed by this music, but she was used to it now and sometimes even found herself humming along.

Presently, Japie brought in the car keys and handed them to Thoko with the assurance that her car was sparkling clean; she thanked him with a smile and handed him a R20 note. Thoko then told Gerda that she was going to the bank.

For the next hour Gerda sat alone at the reception desk, smoking and brooding, listening to Bob Marley on replay telling her to fight for her rights. The repeat button on the CD-player had stuck and the same track played over and over again. The more that Gerda listened to the song, the more she began to feel the transforming effects of the lyrics; she felt that they were written for her alone.

On impulse, she found herself dialing Fanie's number.

'Can I see you during lunch today?' Gerda said all in a rush as soon as he answered, before he had the chance to put the phone down.

'No, Gerda!'
'Please Fanie! I just want to talk!'
'There's nothing to talk about.'
'I have to see you Fanie! What about tomorrow?'
'I'm busy.'

'Well the next day then.'
'It is the same. I will be busy for the whole week!'
'How about next week . . . ?'
'It's the same Gerda! And next month and next year, too.'

Fanie put the phone down, and the decisive slam of the receiver in her ear was like a sharp nail painfully piercing the flesh of her heart. Gerda cried a few tears, but then was forced to control herself to speak to customers, who telephoned wanting to make appointments for later that day.

Half an hour later, when Thoko returned from the bank, she found Gerda still sitting in the empty salon. Most of the Salon Thandi customers were working women who tended to come in during their lunch hour or towards the end of the working day. Thoko's observant eyes studied Gerda's woebegone face, and she sensed that trouble and pain had happened in her absence.

'Gerda, is there anything bothering you?'
'Nothing, Thoko,' Gerda said.
'You don't look happy . . . why?'
'I'm okay.'
'Are you sure?'

The telephone rang and Thoko turned to answer it. It was another customer wanting to make an appointment. Thoko finished the call, then brought her attention back to Gerda.

'You don't look well, Gerda. You haven't been yourself for weeks. I can see something is upsetting you,' she said kindly. 'Tell me what's wrong and I will see how I can help.'

Gerda remained silent for a few seconds. Then tears came into her eyes and the words gushed out: 'My boyfriend dumped me. He's in love with another woman!'

'I'm sorry. But don't worry, my girl.' Thoko patted Gerda's shoulder comfortingly. 'There are many fish in the sea.'

'All I see are sharks in the sea!'

Thoko laughed: 'Come on, be positive, baby! Just ignore the sharks and think about the fish!'

She asked for more details and Gerda poured out the story to her of Fanie's new relationship with somebody called Dimakatjo.

'Yes, I know the woman,' Thoko said thoughtfully. 'She is a nurse, very beautiful to look at.'

Gerda flushed painfully at Thoko's words.

'There are many white guys who live in Mamelodi and stay in back rooms with their girlfriends. We call these white guys *boMkhonyana-baas* – "son-in-law-bosses". As a result of these liaisons, there are many coloured children in Mamelodi.'

She gave Gerda's shoulder a little shake. 'You white women must wake up! Or we black women are going to grab all your men!'

Gerda was shocked by her blunt words and did not respond.

'The trouble is that you white women are used to having things too easy,' Thoko went on. 'You are not fighters. If a man tries to leave me, I don't take "no" for an answer! I will chase him, overtake him, stand in front of him and force him to come to his senses. I know of many women who have saved their relationships with this approach.'

'That is not going to work for me,' responded Gerda.

'Why not?'

'I've already tried. He won't even speak to me!'

'In that case, there is only one thing to do.'

Gerda looked at Thoko hopefully.

'Forget about the bastard!'

'Forget about him?'

'Yes! Because you feel that fighting is not going to work for you!'

'Maybe you are right,' said Gerda uncertainly. 'Maybe I should just forget about him. As you said, there are many fish in the sea . . . '

'Good girl!'

'If Fanie no longer loves me, then why should I bother about him? Why should I care about him if he doesn't care about me? I'm going to tear up all his photos! And I'm going to . . . ' Here Gerda's words turned into sobs and she burst out crying.

'But I do care about him! I can't just forget about him! I'm not the kind who falls easily out of love . . . !' she wept.

Exasperated, Thoko shook her head.

'You are very confused, my girl. *Ka mmago!*' ('I swear by your mother!')

19

It was Tuesday after knock-off time. Fanie went by his mother's house on his way home from work, for his sister had phoned to say there was something she wanted to show him. Selina let him in and escorted him to the lounge, where he joined Anna-Marie and his mother having their tea.

Louise greeted him stiffly. Fanie looked at her in concern, for her strained face and bloodshot eyes told their own story. Fanie asked if his mother was all right and she replied that she was 'perfectly fine'. It was clear that Louise was not prepared to enter into any post-mortems of their last meeting, when they had confronted each other over his love relationship; she preferred to maintain a chilly distance.

After they had wrung all the life out of the teapot and drunk its contents dry, Selina collected the tea things to take through to the kitchen and wash up. Lifting the tray, she glanced at Fanie naughtily and said: 'How are you progressing with your love?'

Fanie smiled back at her. 'The flames of the fire of love are flying very high, Selina,' he replied.

At this, Selina cackled loudly, in typical African manner: '*Keke-keke-keke-keke . . . hii-hii!*' So overcome with mirth was she that she staggered and almost lost the contents of her tray.

Louise remained deadpan through this exchange, pretending that she had neither heard nor seen anything worth bothering about. She picked up a magazine and became seemingly engrossed in one of the articles.

'When are you parting with *lobola*, *abuti* Fanie?' enquired Selina.

It was the first time that she had addressed Fanie with *abuti*, instead of *baas*; this fact did not go unnoticed by Louise, whose grim face grew even grimmer.

'I don't know the date yet, *ausi* Selina, but I will let you know soon,' answered Fanie. It was also the first time that he had used *ausi* – 'elder sister' – to address Selina. She walked out beaming as if she had swallowed the sun.

'*Lobola?*' Anna-Marie said curiously. 'You must give *lobola* for Maki? How much will you have to pay?'

'I don't know. I am not supposed to know at this stage.'

Fanie could see that his answer did not satisfy his sister.

Louise closed the magazine with a loud slap.

'My boy, you are going to have to sell your car, your flat and the cockroaches to pay this *lobola*. These people make a business out of *lobola*!' she said triumphantly.

'Is it true, *boetie?*' asked Anna-Marie worriedly.

'No!' But Fanie was less certain than he sounded.

Anna-Marie suddenly stood up and walked off to her bedroom, re-emerging with something hidden behind her back. Fanie looked at her curiously, wondering what she had up her sleeve. Bursting with laughter, Anna-Marie produced a traditional oxtail fly-whisk. She waved it back and forth over Fanie's head in the manner of a *ngaka* or medicine-man – much to Louise's bafflement and Fanie's amusement. While Anna-Marie was still doing her dance with the fly-whisk, Selina entered and also had a good laugh.

'*Wat gaan nou aan? Mariekie, is jou kop reg?*' ('What's going on now? Mariekie, is your head okay?') snapped Louise.

'My head is fine. I'm just helping to fan the fires of love!' proclaimed Anna-Marie, handing the fly-whisk to the laughing Fanie.

'*Iu-iu-iuu!*' Selina ululated, '*Šatee! Šatee!*' ('Hooray! Hooray!') She pranced energetically around the room in the style of someone at a traditional wedding celebration.

As Fanie and Anna-Marie burst into more uproarious laughter, Louise stood up and stalked off disgustedly to her bedroom, leaving a subdued silence behind her.

'Is this what you wanted to show me?' Fanie asked Anna-Marie, turning the fly-whisk over in his hands.

Grinning, she nodded.

'It looks very authentic. Where did you get it from?'

'A curio shop!' she laughed. 'I couldn't resist when I saw it.'

Fanie reached across to hug her. 'Thank you, Riekie! I will use it well.'

He glanced at his watch and stood up swiftly: 'I have to go. I have a supper date with Maki. We're going to talk about the *lobola* date. You will come to my *lobola* day, won't you Riekie? Even if *ma* doesn't?'

'Of course!' she assured him. 'Nothing will keep me away. And Selina, too!'

Fanie smiled at her gratefully, then looked suddenly anxious. 'I'm going to need someone from the family to be my representative and negotiate for me on the day,' he said. 'Who am I going to get?'

'I'll do it for you!'

'No, it has to be someone male.'

'Ask Uncle Pieter,' she suggested. 'I'm sure that he would be willing.'

She escorted him to the door.

'Don't worry *boetie. Alles sal regkom!*' ('Everything will be alright') she assured him, as they hugged goodbye. She gave his arm a friendly pinch, then drew back a little to stare intently into his face.

'*En nou?*' ('And now?') Fanie asked her.

'Just taking a last look at my brother. Next time I see you, you may be the son-in-law of Machabaphalas!' she joked.

That evening the lovers dined together at a trendy pizza restaurant in Sandton City, where the carefree buzz made a pleasant background to their conversation. Health fanatic Dimakatjo tended, as a rule, to avoid white-flour products, but on this occasion she had compromised for the sake of love and agreed to eat pizza. After studying the menu, they chose a family-size vegetarian to share.

While waiting for their food to arrive, they sipped cold, refreshing fruit-cocktail juice in lanky glasses, and a short time later an enormous hot and delicious-smelling pizza was put in front of them. The aroma of sizzling olives, green peppers and mushrooms made them salivate and without more ado they plunged their teeth into the generously cut slices.

As they chewed they talked, once again, about how their families had reacted to Fanie's intention to part with *lobola*. Although they had already been over this in detail, the subject could never bore them.

Dimakatjo ate her half of the pizza ravenously while Fanie similarly demolished his portion. Afterwards, they treated their palates to apple-tart and cream for dessert.

Then the conversation took a serious turn as Fanie recalled what George had told him about the fact that *lobola* negotiations could, at times, be difficult.

'I don't know what to expect from your people on *lobola* day,' Fanie told Dimakatjo. 'Will they try to fleece me?'

She considered this for a moment then answered: 'No, my people are okay, Fanie.'

He nodded in relief.

'Except for my brother, Lukas. He can be difficult.'

'Difficult? How?'

Dimakatjo shrugged uneasily: 'Maybe I shouldn't have said that . . .'

'Why? Come on Maki, tell me!'

'I have experience of him from the *lobola* of my two older sisters. He was difficult both times. He made things tough for the families of my sisters' husbands. Their people would plead for a more reasonable amount but he would insist on a high sum and refuse to change his mind.'

Fanie nodded apprehensively. They finished their dessert in silence.

'I have an idea. I hope it's a good one,' Fanie said presently.

'What is it?'

'Let me take your brother out for lunch. Get to know him a little bit.'

'No, you can't do that!' objected Maki.

'Why not?'

'It's our culture! There can't be contact between the families before the day.'

'Culture again? *Ag nee wat*, Maki! I am up to here . . . ' said Fanie, placing his index finger against his throat, 'with all this culture-culture-incorrect business! Come now, we are already long in the new South Africa . . . '

'No, listen Fanie,' Dimakatjo interrupted him, 'this is my culture and you must respect it! If our marriage is to work, it must be done in the right way. We have talked about this in the past . . . '

'I do respect it,' Fanie said. 'But you must also remember that it is not *my* culture, and I don't know how things are done.'

'I know that!' Dimakatjo said. 'But *you* have to realise . . . '

She saw that heads were turning towards them, attracted by their emphatic voices. Lowering her voice, Dimakatjo said in a more conciliatory tone: 'I'm sorry Fanie, I am getting emotional.'

He took her hand and squeezed it.

'It's okay, Maki. I'm sorry, too. It's me who started this problem. Do you think it's pre-*lobola* nerves?'

Dimakatjo laughed at that.

They held hands and kissed across the table, uncaring who might be looking.

Dimakatjo was no longer shy to kiss in public and be a 'bioscope', as she had once put it to Fanie on their first date at the park.

'I don't want things to go wrong, Maki. I don't want my mother to have a reason to celebrate because things have gone wrong. You know what she said to me tonight? "Blacks are making a lot of money out of *lobola*!" And later she told my sister: "*Ek sê vir jou hy gaan kak en betaal!*" ' ('I'm telling you he's going to shit and pay!')

'You must be strong, Fanie! You must pass the test, then my people will respect you as a man.'

The next day at work Fanie informed George of the progress that had been made and the discussion he had had with Dimakatjo. George, when he heard Fanie's worries on the subject, also appealed to Fanie to approach the *lobola* issue as a challenge and not something to be anxious about. But he also inadvertently increased Fanie's anxieties by raising new concerns about witchcraft, which he said could pose a problem. Seeing Fanie's puzzlement George explained that because of jealousy some mischievous people, including some of the relatives, could resort to . . . who knew what? People like that, who were full of ill will, had the potential to unleash their 'black magic cultural weapons' in order to sour and sabotage what should be the great day of *lobola*.

George read from Fanie's smile that he was taking what George said with a large pinch of salt.

'I'm serious, Fanie!' George insisted. Such things can happen. These people can spoil your happiness by creating setbacks – causing tempers and arguments to flare during the negotiations, or infusing the girl's family with greed and stubbornness, or causing the interest of the boy's family to wane, and many other things . . . '

There was a pause while Fanie digested this.

'So what's the solution, George? What can I do to stop them?'

'Leave it to me; I will make a plan,' George promised.

'What kind of a plan?'

'You wait and see! Just trust me,' George grinned, patting him on the shoulder.

Worn out by all the anxieties of the last few days, Fanie asked no more questions, content to leave matters in the capable hands of his friend.

20

That weekend Fanie's uncle, Pieter Claasen, visited his nephew in his Strijdomhuis flat. Sixty-something years old, grey-haired and portly, Oom Pieter truly loved his sister's children. Since he was endowed with a rich smile and a gentle spirit, his nephew and niece found it easy to talk to him like a friend. But he could be tough and shrewd, too, when the situation demanded it.

The old man had already heard from his sister Louise that Fanie 'was running around' with a black woman. Louise had made it clear to her brother that she did not in any way approve of Fanie's love relationship. Oom Pieter had heard his sister out in silence, reserving his own judgement. As a religious man, he had made the crossing into 'new' South Africa a lot more graciously than others of his upbringing and generation. He was determined to hear what his nephew had to say before making up his mind.

At his uncle's request, Fanie explained how he had met Dimakatjo in the doctor's surgery and how their friendship and romantic love had blossomed almost from the first encounter. He told his uncle that in Dimakatjo he had found the love he had been searching for all his life; that she felt the same way about him; and that he had decided to pay *lobola* for her so that their marriage would receive blessing and be considered legitimate in the eyes of her family and community.

Uncle Pieter nodded thoughtfully as Fanie spoke.

'How long have you two been going out?' he asked.

'Since February.'

'February to April. That is only two months,' Uncle Pieter frowned. 'Yet you are satisfied that you love this woman?'

'*Ja oom*,' Fanie said emphatically. 'I have never been more sure of anything.'

A long pause followed. Uncle Pieter's searching eyes remained fixed on his nephew's face, as if he wanted to say more; but he held his tongue.

'I have something to ask you, *oom*,' said Fanie hesitantly.

'Ask,' Oom Pieter encouraged.

Fanie paused for a moment, looking at the carpet as if searching there for inspiration, or courage.

'*Oom*, without an uncle to negotiate for me, the *lobola* discussions will not be easy. It will be as though I am an orphan with no one to speak for me. Please will you help?'

'Fanie, you are my favourite nephew and your happiness means a lot to me. I don't mind helping; but there are two stumbling blocks. One: my sister, your mother, does not give her approval to your intention to marry this woman. According to the Bible, children should respect their parents' wishes . . .'

When Fanie heard 'according to the Bible' he was moved to interrupt his uncle, for he presumed that the old man would try to justify apartheid with the Holy Book, as his mother had done a few weeks previously.

'I hear what you are saying, Oom Pieter. But you can't side with my mother! Parents can be wrong sometimes, and my mother is 50 years behind the times! If she doesn't like my fiancée's black face it's her problem! Maki is the woman of my dreams, and I'm not giving her up for anything!'

Oom Pieter watched Fanie intently as he spoke, letting him have his say.

'*Ma* will have to change with the times,' continued Fanie, 'but I can't sit and wait till she decides to do that. I want to live my full life now. I don't want to be like my father who died while he was still regarding black people as non-people.'

There was silence as he finished. A slow smile began to illuminate the old man's face, like early sunrays prodding the darkness away from the earth's face.

'I hear you, nephew,' Uncle Pieter said. 'I hear you very well. I can hear that you feel strongly about this woman Maki. I needed to be sure of that before I gave my blessing.

'The second problem,' he continued, 'is that I don't know much about the culture of black people. All I know is what I studied in anthropology at Tukkies university a long time ago . . . '

'You mean during apartheid?' exclaimed Fanie. 'With all due respect *oom*, that anthropology was a load of *twak* . . . !'

'*Ja, ja*; I know, I know. But I'm sure some of it must have been true . . . '

'Maybe. But you don't have to worry, *oom*; you will know what to do and say when the time comes.'

Uncle Pieter nodded dubiously.

'Anyway, you won't be alone. I have a black colleague, George Maunatlala, who will also help. He's going to do all the hard work. Your duty is just to be there and . . . '

'Show my white face?'

'No *oom*, your support as an uncle!' Fanie laughed.

Oom Pieter chuckled richly. 'So you have twisted the uncle's tough arm *eh*!'

'Does that mean you'll do it?' asked Fanie in relief.

'*Ja*, you can count on me.'

The old man glanced at his wristwatch and told Fanie that he had to be on his way. He had a meeting of church elders to go to. Fanie saw that it was already past one o'clock. Dimakatjo was due to arrive very shortly. It was on the tip of Fanie's tongue to suggest that his uncle wait and meet her. But then he remembered that it probably wouldn't be 'culturally okay'.

As they were waiting for the lift to arrive Oom Pieter enquired about the date that the *lobola* negotiations were set for.

'We're still deciding,' Fanie said. 'But it will probably be in November. Dimakatjo's family will need time to prepare for the event – and I'll need time to save up my money!' he laughed.

'I'm satisfied with that,' Uncle Pieter smiled. 'It will give you two the chance to know each other better and be sure you're not making a mistake.'

Just before Oom Pieter entered the lift, Fanie asked for his prayers, and the old man assured him of his spiritual support.

Fifteen minutes later Dimakatjo knocked at Fanie's door. He flung it open and she who was *more precious than mountain-heaps of gold and diamonds* came bouncing into his arms, with her radiant smile that lit up her eyes, and her irresistible lips that always seemed to implore: *Kiss me! Kiss me now!* Fanie did just that, very efficiently, since by this time he had had plenty of practice.

Ushering her in, he saw her safely seated on the sofa then hurried to the kitchen to prepare something to drink, while she hummed away to their favourite Ringo Madlingozi love-song that was playing on the CD-player.

Fanie and Dimakatjo had reached the stage where they needed to see or at least talk to each other daily. She preferred to visit him at his place rather than have him visit her – not because she was ashamed of where she lived, but because she had been brought up with the wisdom of the proverb: '*She who eats must always hide what she is eating.*' She had no desire to show Fanie off in Mandela Village, for she felt it was only cheap and vain girls who boasted about their white boyfriends.

In Fanie's view, it would have been perfectly *kosher* for Dimakatjo to live with him in his flat, had she been willing; but she preferred not to do so, heeding her mother's advice not to '*live with a man as if you are his wife and just give-give to him* pasela'.

She had heard similar sayings from others: '*If a man gets milk from a dairy, why should he buy a cow?*' And: '*If you want a young man to marry you do not give him too much of yourself, lest he gets bored and begins to treat you with contempt, as if you were an everyday cooked-cabbage smell!*' All these various bits of counsel buzzed around restlessly in her mind.

Fanie had just served Dimakatjo a glass of fresh orange juice and poured one out for himself when another knock came at the door. This time it was Anna-Marie. Fanie had not wanted to tell Dimakatjo that Anna-Marie would be visiting them that afternoon as he was afraid his sweetheart would tell him it was *culturally what-what*. But when she saw who it was Dimakatjo was overjoyed, for she had been dying to meet Anna-Marie for some time.

Fanie ushered his sister in and introduced the two women. They shook hands shyly, then Anna-Marie hugged and kissed her future sister-in-law on both cheeks.

'I am so pleased to meet you, Maki!' she said warmly.

'I'm also pleased to meet you, Anna-Marie!'

'Just call me Riekie. I've heard a lot about you, Maki. It's wonderful to finally meet you in the flesh!'

'What have you heard, Riekie?'

Anna-Marie responded with laughter.

'What have you told her?' Dimakatjo demanded of Fanie.

They all laughed at her indignation.

They sat and had juice while Fanie kept the conversation going. During the quiet pauses, Anna-Marie and Dimakatjo smiled self-consciously, continually catching each other's eyes while they tried surreptitiously to study each other.

'Can I ask you something, Maki? I'm dying to know how much *lobola* your people are going to ask for you.'

'Riekie! She is not a piece of furniture!' Fanie protested.

'No, it's okay,' Dimakatjo said, 'let her ask.' She turned to Anna-Marie with a smile; 'The truth is, I have no idea! It's something that has to be negotiated on the day.'

With that Anna-Marie had to be satisfied.

To break the ice, Fanie suggested they should all go out for tea somewhere. Dimakatjo and Anna-Marie agreed with alacrity.

A short time later Fanie's car was parked in front of a popular garden tea-house in the east of Pretoria. The Fourie children ambled inside, with Dimakatjo sandwiched between them. Once there, food, as they say, was 'dirt for the teeth', while conversation was 'dirt for the ears'.

Anna-Marie asked Dimakatjo about her work at the surgery and how she became a vegetarian. She, in turn, told Dimakatjo about her job at the pre-school in the city centre.

'It's supposed to be completely integrated,' she said, 'but most of the kids there are from the townships. I'd say it's about 80 per cent black. I hear the same thing from teachers at other pre-schools in Pretoria. No one knows where all the white kids have gone to – it's a big mystery. Maybe their parents are spiriting them away to Orania!' she laughed.

'What's Orania?' Dimakatjo wanted to know.

'Don't you know? It's the right-wing *volkstaat* in the Northern Cape that was founded by Dr Carel Boshoff, Verwoerd's son-in-law. It's supposed to be the *boere droom staat* – the Afrikaner 'dream state'. There's not a single black face to be seen there, or so it's said. Even the petrol attendants and domestics are supposedly white Afrikaners!'

That sparked off a long discussion about people stuck in the time warp of the past, and how they were to be pitied rather than condemned. Suddenly the two women found they had much to talk about. Animated conversation flew back and forth across the table, scarcely leaving time for chewing and swallowing the delicious cakes and desserts they had ordered. By the time they left the gardens, the two women felt like old friends. Fanie and Anna-Marie took Dimakatjo to the Mamelodi taxi rank and dropped her off there at her own insistence. Then they drove back to Fanie's flat, where Anna-Marie had left her car.

The next day at lunchtime George reminded Fanie about his 'anti-witchcraft' assignment. Fanie smiled as he recalled their former discussion. George then searched his pockets and took out a small, round tin, the size of a snuff container, which he handed to Fanie.

'What is it?' asked Fanie suspiciously.

'Black magic ointment,' smiled George.

'*Muti* you mean? You must be joking!'

'I'm serious. This is called *Mafuth'ebhubesi*.'

'Fat of the lion?'

'Very good Fanie!' George beamed. 'Yes, *Mafuth'ebhubesi*. It's a mixture of herbs, fortified with a lion's fat.'

'What's it for?' asked Fanie, turning the tin around in his hands.

'Can't you guess? A lion is the bravest beast. We use its fat to give us courage.'

George took the tin from Fanie's hands, opened it, and held it up to Fanie's nose.

Fanie drew his head back in disgust.

'Phew! It stinks!'

'Come on Fanie, *hema*!' ('breathe in!') 'It won't kill you! It's good for you, white boy.' Again George moved the tin under the resisting nose of Fanie, who finally obliged and took a long sniff.

'*Ahhh*! Potent lion's fat! Source of power and bravery!' George chuckled. 'If you want your *lobola* negotiations to run smoothly, then apply this mixture; it will empower you with poise and dignity and make you impervious to all machinations of the witches and wizards of the village.'

'I didn't know you are a witchdoctor, George!'

'A witch-what? Don't you know that word has been outlawed? Witchdoctor is like *kaffer*. We don't say that any more.'

'What do you say then?'

'Just call me *matwetwe* – the excellent medicine-man!' George joked.

Fanie nodded with wry smile. 'Now, how do I use this *muti*, O excellent medicine-man?' he enquired.

'It's easy. Press your right index finger into the ointment and turn it clockwise and anti-clockwise several times . . . '

Fanie followed the instructions.

'Then you smear the ointment on your forehead and also your eyebrows.'

Fanie obediently lifted his hand.

'No Fanie – not now! Don't put it on yet. You must apply it on the day of *lobola*, not before.'

'What will happen if I put it on now?'

'You will roar like a lion! In fact, you will speak with a lion's voice,' warned George in a serious tone. But his eyes had a twinkle that he couldn't repress.

Fanie could see that George was pulling his leg. Playing along, he breathed in deeply to expand his chest, clenched his fists and flexed his biceps, while emitting loud and fearsome growls.

George laughed at him.

'Can I apply this ointment when I sleep with Maki?' Fanie wanted to know.

'*Ho-ho-hohhh* Fanie! Are you mad? I'm telling you, you won't have a wife!'

'Why?'

'She will run away! No woman can dare to sleep with a lion!'

George and Fanie laughed with loud mirth at his joke.

21

That same evening, stopping by at friends on her way home from work, Thoko *'caught a roadside goat by the tongue'*. She heard the rumour that Dimakatjo's mother was a *sangoma*, and that Dimakatjo had poured a love-potion into Fanie's coffee so that he should dote on her; as a result, he was going around saying ridiculous things such as: '*I have never loved a woman like this before . . .* '

The following day Thoko watched Gerda as she worked, her sympathetic eyes noting all the signs of strain on her employee's face. Gerda was busy with one of the regulars, a black customer who had developed a particular liking for the Afrikaans girl and who would never let anyone but Gerda do her hair. Bob Marley's anthem, 'Stand up and fight for your rights', played loudly in the background, and Gerda was bopping her head to the rhythm without realising it as her busy fingers cut and shaped the client's hair.

Thoko felt considerable sympathy for Gerda. She had developed a soft spot for the white girl. In this, Thoko was reminded of her 70-year-old mother who, despite her great age, had continued to work as a domestic for an equally elderly white woman, about whom she had vowed: 'I won't throw her away!' At the time, Thoko and her siblings had severely criticised their mother for 'worshipping white flesh', as they had put it; now here was Thoko, her own heart filled with pity and compassion for this Afrikaner *meisie*, for whom, initially, she had not imagined she could ever feel any affection.

'How are you feeling today?' she asked Gerda during a quiet moment.

'Better, thank you Thoko. I'm no longer confused.'

'Very good, Gerda my girl! It means you are healed. We all suffer from open wounds that finally heal,' Thoko said.

Gerda nodded thoughtfully but did not comment.

Thoko couldn't resist telling Gerda about the juicy rumour that her ear had tasted concerning Dimakatjo's *sangoma* mother and the alleged love-potion in Fanie's coffee. She soon regretted it, however, for Gerda looked devastated by the news.

'Now listen, white girl; if you love this guy, then do what the Rastaman says: *Stand up and fight for your rights!*'

'I've been trying! But what can I do against *muti*?' Gerda replied.

'Don't fold your arms, girl! Do something! Fight back! Let no one browbeat you, kill you and celebrate on your grave! When Fanie takes one step, you take two. When that daughter of a witch uses black magic, you must double that; *sangoma* for *sangoma*, fire for fire. Because you are white,' continued Thoko, 'you might think you don't believe in these things – what you people call "superstition". But they work! Even the freedom fighters during the struggle used some black magic. White girl, if you don't hear me, then you are a stone!'

Thoko paused to gauge the impact of her speech. At that moment the next appointment entered the salon and Gerda was saved from having to give a response.

During lunchbreak Gerda took a walk, smoking pensively all the way to the small park nearby, where she continued to 'nibble at the bones' of her troubled heart. When she returned, Thoko noticed that she walked with a firmer tread and her carriage seemed lighter.

'Listen Thoko, I have made up my mind,' said Gerda.

'To do what?'

'Fight for my rights, of course!'

'*Buwa sebuwi, buwa!*' ('Speak speaker, speak!') responded Thoko in the traditional way. She was very pleased that the words she had sown had fallen on fertile ground.

Affectionately she patted Gerda's shoulder: 'Yes, fight for your rights, my girl – just as long as your employer is not your target!' she said, to laughter from both of them.

The following Saturday afternoon Thoko's car headed down the tarmac stretch of highway that cut through the expanse of veld to the north-east of Pretoria. Gerda sat beside her, a silent passenger. After travelling for about 50 kilometres, they turned off onto a narrow, unmarked dirt road that wound along between empty fields of grass towards the sprawling settlement of Madibakwena – 'Crocodile's River' – a short distance away. Madibakwena was a village of some thousand households situated on the border of Limpopo and Mpumalanga provinces. Thoko was taking Gerda there to consult *matwetwe* – a traditional healer and diviner well known for his skill in throwing the bones, or '*ditaola*'.

The early winter dusk was just settling in when they reached their destination. As they entered the village, Thoko put her headlights on. The sun had only just disappeared but here it was murky twilight, due to the thick smoke pall from the many evening cooking fires that had been lit; for electricity had not yet reached these parts.

They passed a young couple walking leisurely along the roadside and Thoko stopped the car to confirm directions to the home of the famed medicine-man. The herbalist was well known in the area and much revered by the villagers, who referred to him as '*Vela-ba-hleke*' ('You-appear-and-they-laugh'); they called him this because *Vela-ba-hleke* was the name of one of *matwetwe*'s potent herbal packages that was highly in demand by those who wanted to make a good impression for business or romantic purposes.

The helpful Ndebele-speaking man whom Thoko consulted explained elaborately and with much complicated gesturing exactly where *matwetwe*'s place was, and shortly afterwards they reached the gate of the homestead. On a blackboard affixed to the left of the entrance was written in white chalk: 'Dr Vela-ba-hleke Mnisi – Herbalist', dispelling any doubt that they were at the right place. Relieved, Thoko drove through to the homestead, which comprised three households in a yard the size of two soccer fields.

A young woman who was a trainee herbalist, known as *lethwasana*, was standing in the middle of the *lapa* with her hands politely clasped, palms pressed together and pointing straight ahead. Stepping out of the car, Thoko locked it with the remote and, with Gerda following closely, entered the *lapa*. She called 'Kokoo!' and *lethwasana* came over to them, clearly surprised to see Gerda. White men were a more common sight at the herbalist's place and *lethwasana* saw them regularly. One, a prosperous-looking business man, came to consult *matwetwe* to ask for charms that would make customers flock to his shop. Another wanted a wonder ointment that would aid him to climb up the career ladder in the highly competitive, cut-throat corporate jungle.

The visitors greeted *lethwasana*, who genuflected politely, then led them to the rondavel where *matwetwe* was expectantly waiting. Early that morning when he had thrown the *ditaola* as usual, *matwetwe's* ancestors had shown him through the bones that a special patient would be coming to consult him that day. At *lethwasana's* request, Thoko and Gerda removed their shoes before entering the rondavel.

Inside the gloom of the hut, Gerda's nervous eyes alighted on *matwetwe* – a tiny, bald-headed man with a white goatee and glinting, ruthlessly penetrating eyes. He was seated on the chopped remnants of an aloe trunk, which served as his stool when in consultation. In his right hand was a short white oxtail fly-whisk, the stick of which was decorated with tiny coloured beads, of the kind used by Ndebele craftswomen. The herbalist was bare-chested, and around his neck hung two thick strings of beads that criss-crossed his chest front and back. The beads were interspersed with a few divining bones, porcupine quills, sea shells and underground plant stems, known as *dirokolo*.

Thoko greeted *matwetwe* respectfully, her palms placed together and pointing horizontally outwards; clapping her hands gently twice, she seated herself on a beautifully handcrafted grass mat. Gerda sat down gingerly beside her, copying Thoko's actions like a child observing from a parent.

'I greet you, women of the city,' *matwetwe* said. He nodded at them, his penetrating eyes fixed on Gerda.

Matwetwe's resonant baritone belied his tiny frame. Thoko spoke back to him in Se-Pitoria – a kind of Sepedi spoken in Pretoria, which purists regarded with a degree of contempt. *Matwetwe*, a Swazi by birth, had mastered Sepedi with a perfect accent; his two younger wives, who were also his *mathwasana* – 'initiates' – were instrumental in helping him to excel in this language.

Matwetwe enquired how he could help the visitors. His gaze was now fixed on Thoko who responded without wasting a moment: 'This white girl has problems. Her love-affairs have turned sour; there is nothing that comes right for her. Life is hard and the poor child is sitting on one buttock. She meets men but she never keeps them because they are repelled by *senyama* – the bad luck. We come to see you, Excellent Thrower of Bones and Healer, to ask you to placate the girl's ancestors and wash away her bad luck.'

As Thoko was speaking, *matwetwe*'s eyes were once again fixed on Gerda, who shyly avoided his gaze, her own eyes cast modestly downwards. *Matwetwe* nodded sympathetically at what Thoko was saying. He did not immediately respond but continued to study his patient, who was sitting appropriately the way villagers sat when they were paying attention to someone important: knees folded sideways under her, buttocks resting on heels, and hands clasped demurely in her lap.

Matwetwe took a small bag made from *meerkat* hide from the ground beside him. It contained *ditaola* – the divining bones. With fearful eyes Gerda stared at the bag, as if she anticipated a snake or something equally frightening to emerge from it.

She recalled what Thoko had once said to her: '*You are a white girl, you might not believe in what your people call "superstition". But these things work!*'

Taking her by surprise, the healer spoke directly to Gerda in Sepedi. She glanced at Thoko for guidance, since she had no clue what *matwetwe* was saying to her.

'*Bula diatla mosadi wa lekgowa!*' *matwetwe* commanded the puzzled Gerda.

'He says: "Open your palms, white woman",' Thoko translated. Gerda did as instructed, though somewhat hesitantly, and *matwetwe* poured the bones of different shapes, shades, textures and sizes into her cupped hands.

'Breathe onto the bones!' translated Thoko, and Gerda obliged.

'And throw the bones!' That command, too, was obeyed; Gerda threw *ditaola* as though they were burning her palms. The bones rolled in three directions: left, middle and right. Some of the bones, because of their small size and light weight, rolled faster than the bigger, heavier ones; but all of them were equally important, since they all helped to interpret the patient's life.

'*Vumani-bo!*' ('Agree with me!') chanted the medicine-man.

'*Siyavuma!*' ('We agree!') responded Thoko.

'*Vumani-bo!*'

'*Siyavuma!*' Again Thoko responded, glancing meaningfully at Gerda; but she remained silent.

'Say: "*Si-ya-vu-maa!*"' Thoko instructed in a hiss.

'*Si-yaa-voo-ma!*'

'Faster!'

'*Si-yaa-voo-ma!*' Gerda obliged again, her intonation still distinctly 'white'.

'*Vumani-bo!*'

'*Siyavumaa!*' chanted Gerda, louder and more confidently this time.

Matwetwe took a considered pause, studying the bones intently. His expression became sombre. He waved his fly-whisk vigorously, emitting some incantations and strange guttural sounds.

Thoko, who was no stranger to these rituals, knew that *matwetwe* was consulting his ancestors who had schooled him in the bone-throwing business. Matwetwe belched loudly in the direction of Gerda, who nervously jerked backwards. Matwetwe moved some of the bones into different positions. He tapped lightly on a few of them, as if saying: *Speak, bones of dead animals!*

Matwetwe belched again and this time, Gerda was more prepared for what was coming. Throughout the consultation, the healer continued to speak in Sepedi, addressing Gerda directly while Thoko translated for her. But when Gerda replied to him, Thoko did not need to translate, because *matwetwe* understood English. The healer explained to Thoko that his ancestors forbade him to speak in English when in consultation.

Matwetwe spoke again and Thoko translated: 'He sees a white dog running away with a T-bone steak in its jaws!'

'It must be Fanie! It must be Fanie! Running away with his black girlfriend!' exclaimed Gerda excitedly. 'Tell me doctor, how can we catch the dog?' she asked.

Matwetwe was astonished to find the shy white girl now speaking up so boldly.

Glancing down at the bones for guidance, he shifted his gaze back to Gerda. Then, unexpectedly, he flashed a smile and turned his head towards the door.

'Ngwan'a-Matšhila!' he shouted.

He was calling *lethwasana* who had ushered Thoko and Gerda into his consulting room. Almost instantly, *Ngwan'a-Matšhila*, whose name means 'Child-of-Dirt', entered the hut and stood humbly before her master, with her head bowed, palms pressed together and knees slightly bent, in the traditional posture of subservience. *Matwetwe* instructed his initiate in words that were virtually a code language to Thoko, for she understood nothing of what he said. As soon as *Ngwan'a-Matšhila* had hurried out of the hut again *matwetwe* also walked out.

It was clear that something very important was about to happen. Gerda and Thoko exchanged meaningful looks. Gerda's face was full of questions but Thoko could only shrug in response. *Ngwan'a-Matšhila* and *matwetwe* returned simultaneously, the former holding a smoking, twisted kudu horn, while the latter clutched a bulging bag made from home-tanned animal hide. This bag contained various ground herbs.

Ngwan'a-Matšhila handed *matwetwe* the horn; with his right hand, the medicine-man scooped a measure of ground herbs from the bag, which he sprinkled into the smouldering kudu horn. Smoke wreathed upwards, producing a pungent smell that caused the uninitiated Gerda to cough furiously. *Matwetwe* then circled the smoking horn around Gerda's head. The young woman was visibly nervous, but Thoko leaned across to gently press her breast against Gerda's shoulder blade in support. *Matwetwe* muttered more incantations and strange guttural sounds and gave a loud, growling belch. Gerda was used to this by now, however, and did not feel as threatened as before.

'This is the spear that fights against bad luck,' *matwetwe* said, through Thoko. Thoko then described for Gerda what *matwetwe* was doing above her head with the kudu horn. When he had finished, *Ngwan'a-Matšhila* took the horn and went to put it back in its rightful place. Out of his pocket *matwetwe* now took a small bottle that contained a pitch-black medicinal mixture. He shook the bottle vigorously, examining the contents.

'This is *moratišo*, the love-potion. Pour a teaspoon in your lover's tea and he will love you and lick your hands like a faithful dog,' said *matwetwe*, through Thoko's mouth.

'It's too late for that!' responded Gerda with a tinge of irritation. 'How can I pour it in his tea when he doesn't even want to see me?'

'He doesn't want to see you because of *senyama* – the bad luck . . .' Thoko-*matwetwe* said.

'But the bad luck . . .' Gerda rudely interrupted.

'The bad luck is gone!' Thoko said, as if Gerda hadn't spoken.

'*Ngwan'a-Matšhila!*' *matwetwe* called once more, and the attentive *lethwasana* came hopping in to do her master's bidding before he had even completed the last syllable of her name. *Matwetwe* barked an instruction and Child-of-Dirt leapt out of the consulting room again, re-entering minutes later to kneel before *matwetwe*, dutifully handing him a dry twig. For the second time, *matwetwe* beamed a smile at Gerda. He broke off a small piece from the twig, the size of his little finger.

'He says chew it, it's not bitter; then spit it into your palms and gently rub it on your face, especially above your eyelashes,' Thoko instructed. Gerda chewed the piece of dry twig slowly, her eyes fixed on Thoko, who smiled at her encouragingly. Spitting the chewed pieces into her palms, Gerda smeared them over her face as instructed.

'That is called *vela-ba-hleke*; it means "when you appear, they will laugh like mad people",' Thoko translated.

'Who?' Anxious Gerda fired the question as if she could not believe her ears.

'Men, of course! Don't you have a problem with men? Men will laugh, crazed with desire, when they see you. They will run and pant after you!'

'What?' exclaimed Gerda in dismay. 'Men running after me? Oh no, I don't want that! I don't want to be raped by sex-crazed black men! Please, remove it! I want a shower! Give me a shower! Now!'

Matwetwe and *Ngwan'a-Matšhila* were shocked beyond speech by Gerda's inappropriate behaviour. Even Thoko was taken by surprise.

Ngwan'a-Matšhila grabbed Gerda by the hand and hurried her across to the main house, where she removed the *vela-ba-hleke* prescription with a basinful of water. Within minutes the herb was wiped from Gerda's skin. *Ngwan'a-Matšhila* gave her a towel to dry her face with. Then, with Thoko following closely, Gerda hurried out to the car.

At Thoko's shouted instruction, *Ngwan'a-Matšhila* brought their shoes to them, while *matwetwe* stood watching from the doorway of the hut, hardly able to believe what he had just witnessed. In his more than 50 years as a herbalist, such a thing had never happened before.

'You haven't even paid the bill! Women, I'm warning you . . . !' he shouted at them in English, furiously waving his index finger, known among the villagers as *tšhup'a baloi* – 'the finger that points at witches and wizards'.

'How much is your *blerry* bill?' Gerda shrieked from the safety of the car.

'One hundred rand to open the bag of bones, another hundred to diagnose, and another to . . . !'

'Wait!' Thoko interrupted. 'We'll give you R400!'

She took the money from her pocket and walked back to give *matwetwe* his fee; but the offended diviner of bones of dead animals folded his arms, refusing to receive it from her.

'*Ngwan'a-Matšhila!*' *matwetwe* commanded. He gestured haughtily towards Thoko, and his initiate received the money into her hands instead.

As Thoko's car drove out of the yard at high speed, kicking up dust as it went, *matwetwe* could dimly be seen in the rear-view mirror, still ominously waving *tšhup'a baloi* at the two departing city women.

22

Days passed and gave birth to weeks, which turned into months. Winter walked out and spring walked in and summer said: '*Kokoo!*' and came to visit for a while. For it was late November now, and the warm weather was setting in.

In the hearts of the lovers, too, summer reigned; fed and watered with daily care and tenderness, their love blossomed abundantly, stretching its tendrils in all directions and flourishing like a green and healthy pumpkin plant.

Time was eaten by this thriving love, and before they knew it, there were only ten days to go before the great day of *lobola*. This most important of days was scheduled for the last Saturday in November. So full of joy was Dimakatjo at the prospect of the special day about to dawn that there was room in her thoughts for nothing else. She found herself humming joyful wedding songs as she went about her work at Dr Makgabo's surgery.

Nthabiseng listened, smiling, to the song her friend was singing. She wanted to sing along but it wasn't a tune that was familiar to her. Nthabiseng went off to the toilet, thinking of a suitable wedding song that she could sing for Dimakatjo; she chose a traditional classic, 'A *le a mmona?*' that had been sung by her mother and scores of aunts and uncles for countless years before her *kalana* – the dry placental chord – fell away, and which continued to be sung all through the years that she was growing up.

Returning from the toilets Nthabiseng walked towards Dimakatjo, singing impishly:

A le a mmona?
A le a mmona a itšhela ka meokgo!

Sello sa ma . . .
Sello sa ma-setla-pelo sa maitirelo!

(Do you see her, the bride?
Do you see the one who messes herself with tears?
She's sobbing in a heartrending manner, but only pretending . . .
Because she is really sobbing with joy over her wedding day!)

Dimakatjo, who had just handed a packet of tablets and some bottles of medicinal mixture to a patient, laughed when she heard the song and turned to wag her forefinger at the singer. All the patients in the waiting room joined in their good-humoured laughter, for word had spread that the Jewel of Bakone was soon to be taken off the 'not-yet-married' shelf.

Soon after that the two nurses had their lunchbreak. Dimakatjo had prepared a delicious salad for her and Nthabiseng's lunch, consisting of lettuce, feta cheese, olives, red peppers, onion rings, sprouts and tomatoes; she told Nthabiseng that she had made a resolution to eat no junk food until after her big day.

'You are so lucky, Maki,' Nthabiseng sighed. 'I wish we could change places for a day. So that I could see what true love feels like!'

Dimakatjo looked at her friend in surprise. She had always believed that when it came to love, Nthabiseng was the lucky one, for throughout their friendship it had been Nthabiseng who was spoiled with expensive Valentine's Day gifts; she who was always in someone's love-arms and spared the long seasons of scarcity that love-lorn women termed the 'drought of Egypt'.

'But you have Jack, Nthabi. *He* loves you truly!'

Nthabiseng shook her head mournfully.

'Things are not going so well with us,' she confessed. 'He is playing hide-and-seek with me these days.'

'What do you mean?'

'I haven't seen him in weeks. He is doing a lot of travelling with his salesman job . . . at least that is what he tells me!'

'Maybe it's the truth,' Dimakatjo said.

'It's not the truth, Maki! I know, because someone saw Jack in town on one of the days he was supposed to be out of town. He had his arms around another woman, and he was kissing her in full view of everyone.'

'Are you sure it was him?'

'Very sure. Jack is a heartbreaker,' Nthabiseng said unhappily. 'Everybody warned me when I first started going out with him, but I wouldn't listen. I'm dealing with *legwara-gwara* of Mamelodi!' *Legwara-gwara* was a smooth-talking and heartless trickster. 'Jack is just a playboy who uses and throws girls away like they are disposable toilet paper. I have no doubt that I'm soon going to discover that his sales "work" is, in fact, trading between the thighs of a *skeberesh*!'

'But Jack loves you!' stammered Dimakatjo. 'He's mad about you, Nthabi! He's always bringing you presents and taking you away on weekends and . . . '

Nthabiseng shook her head dolefully. 'Yes, he can be very charming . . . when it suits him. What's worse, he doesn't condomise! Even when you try to insist, he won't have it any other way than flesh-to-flesh; Maki, this man is going to infect me with AIDS, I'm telling you! I love him, but one of these days I'm going to have to tell him: "Hit the road Jack!"'

Dimakatjo could find no words of comfort for her.

After that, their talk turned to other things. Dimakatjo went through to the kitchen to brew some mint tea for the two of them, leaving Nthabiseng alone at the counter. Her eyes fell on the desk calendar and she couldn't help but notice that Dimakatjo had been busy with it. Eleven of the days were circled with blue pen, while the twelfth was circled with red stars and exclamation marks. Grinning, Nthabiseng snatched up the calendar and called to Doctor Makgabo, who was in his office: 'Doctor come and look; see how daughter-in-law of the *boere* is counting the days to her *lobola* day!'

Obligingly Dr Makgabo emerged to witness the ringed calendar, while embarrassed Dimakatjo tried in vain to grab it back from Nthabiseng's teasing hands.

'Who says I'm daughter-in-law of the *boere*? Heh?' Dimakatjo challenged.

That made them all laugh. Nthabiseng again began to sing the wedding song, 'A le a mmona?', while Dimakatjo tried to outdo her by singing her own wedding song. The proceedings became so raucous that the laughing doctor was forced to quieten things down, for the new round of patients was beginning to drift in for their afternoon appointments.

After work that Wednesday Dimakatjo took a taxi to Fanie's office, for they had arranged to meet there and decide on their plans for the evening.

At Jacaranda Welding Company, the *tshaile* siren had long since sounded. George, standing ready to go with his car keys in his right hand and his briefcase in his left, saw that Fanie was, for once, in no hurry to leave.

'Aren't you going home today, Fanie? Are you intending to do overtime?' he joked.

Fanie made no answer, engrossed in turning over the pages of a photo album on his desk. In every photo was Dimakatjo, smiling photogenically into the camera, posing seductively to show off her outfit, or hugging and kissing Fanie. George stepped closer to peer curiously over Fanie's shoulder.

'Could it be that your overtime is Maki?' he teased. Fanie took his nose out of the album and laughed with him. 'Yes, I'm waiting for her to get here,' he smiled.

'What's your programme this evening?' enquired George. 'Are you going out to eat somewhere?'

'We haven't made plans. We'll see when she gets here.'

Fanie knew that when Dimakatjo arrived, they would be in no hurry to go anywhere. They would be content to relax together right there in his office. He had stocked up with plenty of mango juice, Dimakatjo's latest favourite flavour. This month she had been guzzling a lot of it in the hope that mango juice would make her skin smooth and glowing. She also drank a lot of carrot juice, which she believed would make her eyes sparkle like the full moon.

'I'm still anxious about this day of *lobola*, George,' Fanie confessed. 'I don't know what to expect from Maki's people.'

'Take it easy, Fanie. You are going to discover that *lobola* is fun!'

'I'll have to take your word for it.'

'But you must also remember, no pain, no gain!'

Fanie gave him a dismayed look. 'Don't mention pain, man! It makes me nervous!'

George simply smiled serenely.

'Is your mother still so adamant that she doesn't want you to marry Maki?' he asked.

'Yes. I hoped she'd come around by now. But things are getting worse, not better. My sister told me yesterday that our mother is being treated for ulcers.'

'Ulcers?' echoed George incredulously.

'Yes! Mariekie saw it written down on the doctor's prescription note. She said it mentioned treatment for chronic ... acute ... gastric ... *ag*, something or other; you know those big words doctors use.'

'This is serious, Fanie!'

Fanie nodded glumly. 'She's also been seeing a psychiatrist, Riekie says. But she won't talk about any of it.'

'*Hee-banna!* It just shows how difficult it is for people like her to change. They are the kind of people who vow "over my dead body"! Their hearts are like stone.'

Fanie nodded again.

'The only way of changing your mother's heart,' George went on, 'would be children ... '

'Children?'

'Yes, children!'

'What do you mean?'

'If you and Maki could have a nice little boy or girl, and make your mother a grandmother, she might change her mind and accept Maki.'

'Maybe you are right, George,' said Fanie thoughtfully.

'Would you like your first-born to be a baby boy?' asked George.

Before Fanie, still digesting the question, could answer, George rattled on: 'Then put a cap on when you make love!'

The two men laughed loudly at his joke and Fanie pinched George's arm. They had another good laugh; then George glanced at his watch.

'Fanie, I must go. I have to pick up my daughter from school sports.' George lived with his family in Soshanguve township just outside Pretoria.

'Give Maki my love,' he said, as he prepared to walk out of the office.

'I'll do that,' said Fanie. 'Hey,' he called, as George disappeared out the door, 'what must I do if I want to have a baby girl? Put on a bêret or a *doek?*'

George popped his head back in and the two men roared appreciatively, like children never tiring of the same stale old joke.

Just as George was about to go out for the second time, Dimakatjo arrived. She and George greeted each other affectionately, for they knew each other well by now.

'And how is daughter-in-law of the Fouries?' he asked her, shaking hands with a broad smile.

'I'm very fine *abuti* George, and you?'

'Also fine. Are you looking forward to your *lobola* day?' He didn't wait for an answer but went on: 'You must eat well and sleep well. The Fouries must part with *lobola* for a well-built girl. Remember, *nku re reka mosela!* – "a sheep is bought because of the fatness of its tail!"' They all shook with mirth at his joke.

'Oh, that reminds me . . . ' George said.

'What have you forgotten?' enquired Fanie.

'The knife! Fanie, you must remember to buy a pocket-knife. On the day of *lobola* they will ask it from us. To slaughter a sheep for the in-laws.'

'I will attend to that,' promised Fanie.

'And remember to put on your cap when you . . . okay!' George and Fanie once more laughed long and loudly.

'What's funny? Put on the cap for what?' Dimakatjo wanted to know.

But George and Fanie simply chuckled again, like naughty schoolboys.

George finally left. Dimakatjo told Fanie that she intended to visit home that weekend, for her people wanted to consult her about the preparations for *lobola* day, now just over one week away.

'Why can't I drive you to your home?' asked Fanie.

Dimakatjo, predictably, answered that it would be culturally incorrect to do so. This time, however, Fanie dug his heels in, and his word prevailed.

'But,' Dimakatjo warned, 'you will just drop me at the gate, okay?'

Fanie did not ask 'why?' but simply nodded.

'I will signal to you to drive away if there is someone in the house,' continued Dimakatjo. 'If there is no one there, then you can enter. But you will have to disappear as soon as someone arrives. If they meet you at the door, they may not greet you; it's not because they are being rude. And please don't you greet them either.'

Fanie nodded again. In the pause that followed, his brown eyes warmly studied Dimakatjo, the woman *more priceless than mountain-heaps of gold and diamonds*.

She became a little uncomfortable under his amorous gaze. Her reaction surprised her, for she had no reason to feel as if she were 'a bioscope' here. Her shy smile beamed out and Fanie felt the jaws of desire nibbling at his pulsating heart. He grabbed her nape, gently pulling her head towards his and tilting his face to the left in order to smack her lips with his own in a slightly skew kiss.

'I'm looking forward to living with you as my w . . . w . . . ' Fanie seemed to run out of breath suddenly.

'Your wife?' Dimakatjo finished for him.

'Yes!'

They held hands and kissed tenderly.

'I'm positive I have not made a bad bargain,' said Fanie, playing with her fingers.

'What if you are disappointed?'

'I shan't be!'

'And I am certain I have made a good bargain, too!'

The lovers embraced ardently. And for a while, they forgot everything but each other.

At that very moment, had the lovebirds but known it, Gerda was on her way to Fanie's place of work.

In the intervening months following her ill-starred visit to *matwetwe* with Thandi, she had tried her utmost to put Fanie from her thoughts; but the harder she tried, the worse her obsession seemed to grow. The previous night she had had a particularly disturbing dream about him.

She dreamt that she was strolling hand in hand with Fanie along the pavements of Koedoespoort when a speeding car appeared out of nowhere and stopped beside them with a screech of brakes. Out of the car leapt a woman she had never seen before; a beautiful black woman with braided hair who, in an instant, transformed into a horrible witch. Pointing her forefinger threateningly at Gerda, the woman warned her to stay away from Fanie or face torment she would never forget. Gerda replied stubbornly that she would never leave Fanie as he was her first and only boyfriend, the one who had taken her virginity. The witch's eyes glistened with fury and she shook her forefinger at Gerda: *'Jou fokken white bitch!'* she screeched. And with an explosive *'Thwaa! Thwaa!'* sound, she shot Gerda with an AK47.

Gerda woke in shock, convinced that she must be covered in blood. Then she realised that the gunshots had come from outside, infiltrating her sleep from the street below her window. She felt greatly disturbed by the dream, remembering how happy she and Fanie had been, strolling down the street hand in hand before the witch appeared. She was certain that if she could only see Fanie face to face she would be able to break the spell that he was under and bring him to his senses. Since he wouldn't answer her calls, she decided there was only one thing left to try. Desperation had driven her to desperate measures.

Wednesday happened, fortuitously, to be her early finishing day at the salon. She finished up around three o'clock and then headed for the central bus depot several blocks away. By the time she had found the right bus and taken the journey across town to the industrial area where Fanie's work was, *tshaile* time had come and gone at the Welding Company. Gerda could only hope that something had happened to delay his departure and that she would still find Fanie at his office.

Alighting from the bus, she hurried across the street towards the building with the large sign that said, 'Jacaranda Welding Company'. Looking up, she saw that the lights were on in the window of Fanie's office. A small voice said to her: *What if he is not alone?* But she ignored it. Adrenalin was pumping through her blood and Bob Marley's song echoed in her head like a rousing anthem.

Fight for your rights Gerda, don't give up, she told herself. *People who give up are as good as dead!*

Fanie imagined that George, by this time, was already long gone on his way to pick up his daughter from school. But, in fact, he had not yet left the parking lot, for his wife had phoned to tell him that sports had finished early and his daughter now had to be picked up from her friend's house, where she had gone from school. Since there was no longer any rush, George sat on in the car for a few minutes, listening to the news headlines on the radio. He started up the engine and was about to drive out of the gates when he saw, to his surprise, a white woman walking hurriedly towards him; she waved at him agitatedly and he stopped the car and rolled the window down.

The woman enquired if Fanie was still in his office. Before George could reply, she said that she was Fanie's sister and that she had very urgent news to deliver to him.

'Is it about his mother?' asked George in concern, thinking about the conversation he had had with Fanie earlier.

George had never met Fanie's sister, Anna-Marie, so he had no way of knowing that it was not her, but Gerda that he was talking to. Smiling, he held his hand out and said: 'I'm Fanie's friend George, and I'm very pleased to meet you!'

George then got out of the car and took Gerda upstairs.

In Fanie's office, the unsuspecting lovers were still locked in their embrace. Fanie was busy unleashing a series of passionate kisses, his industrious tongue doing a thorough job of exploring Dimakatjo's mouth, when a tap at the door interrupted them.

Fanie disengaged himself reluctantly and went to see who it could be. The door opened and in stepped a beaming George.

'A special visitor for you, Fanie . . . your sister!' he said, ushering Gerda in.

Fanie stared in dismay, rendered speechless for a moment.

'She is not my sister! What are you doing here?' he said to Gerda. 'Why won't you leave me alone?'

'Fanie *my skattebol*,' said Gerda tearfully. 'Don't talk to me like that! Why are you so cruel to me? You won't answer my phone calls, you don't return my messages . . . '

George realised belatedly that he had been tricked by Gerda. 'I'm sorry Fanie! She said she was your sister!'

At the sight of Gerda, Dimakatjo felt anxiety quiver through her. She herself had never yet been confronted by another woman over a man. But she had witnessed umpteen incidents where scorned and humiliated women tackled their husbands' or lovers' new flames in undignified and vulgar public showdowns: '*You are stealing my man . . . !*' '*Tie your dog on your dog-chain!*' '*Feed your dog and it won't bark* hawuu-hawuu! *after me!*' First the ugly words, vicious insults pouring like diarrhoea. Then, gory street-fights erupting, the screeching rivals clawing at each other's flesh and body parts with no holds barred. Dimakatjo had never thought this could happen to her.

She responded instinctively by leaning possessively against Fanie's shoulder, indicating beyond any doubt that he was hers; from the top of his head to the tips of his toes – her sole property. Gerda did not need to be a *sangoma* to smell that Fanie was, indeed, bewitched, trapped in love-arms from which there was no escape.

The memory of Thoko's words entered Gerda's mind: '*You white women must wake up; black women are going to grab your men!*'

The tide of adrenalin in Gerda's blood rose to even higher levels. *Don't give up, Gerda. People who give up are as good as dead!*

'You're making a fool of yourself, Gerda,' said Fanie quietly. 'Stop wasting your time here. You can see for yourself that I am in love with another woman.'

'Love!' snorted Gerda in blistering response. 'No; black magic you mean! But when those herbs of your *sangoma* mother-in-law are *kaput*,' she hissed, 'then you will come crawling back to *me*!' Her eyes sparkled with malicious fury.

'It will never happen! And anyway, who told you that Maki's mother is a *sangoma*? It's her aunt!'

'It's the same thing! You have been bewitched!'

'I don't care!'

'You must care!'

Dimakatjo and George stood silently, unwilling spectators to the screaming match between the former lovers.

George was embarrassed. He wanted to go, since what was happening was none of his business. But Fanie, seeing him sidling towards the door, appealed: 'No, don't go, George!'

George understood that Fanie desired his help in extinguishing this out-of-control fire, but he didn't know what he could say or do that would help.

Dimakatjo was not unaffected by what was happening in front of her. She was not a stone that had no feelings, and Gerda's insulting comments roused her hot anger.

'Who is this woman, Fanie?' she demanded, though of course she knew very well.

Gerda turned to look at her, examining her with the expression of one who has just sucked a lemon.

'I'm sure, by now, you know me! Gerda Moerdyk-van-Schalkwyk! And you, I suppose, are his new flame?'

'My name is not 'His New Flame'! I am Dimakatjo Machabaphala!'

'I am glad to know you at last!' said Gerda sarcastically, thrusting out a battle-ready hand; Dimakatjo ignored it. She faced Gerda squarely, as if to say: *'If you are a tiger then I'm a leopard.'*

'I am not glad to know *you*! Why do you keep chasing after my man? Can't you see that he no longer cares about you? Are you stupid?'

'No, I'm not stupid! *He* is stupid! Because you and your people have bewitched him!'

The two women were now facing each other belligerently, necks stretched out like fighting hens. Dimakatjo laughed sarcastically. 'Bewitched or not, Fanie is in love with *me*!'

'So you are proud that you grabbed him out of my arms?'

'For your information, *he* came running to *me*! Listen woman, this man will be parting with *lobola* for me within a week!'

Gerda flinched at that but quickly recovered and flashed back a mocking smile: 'It must be nice to fall in love with a white man, nê?'

'*Ja!* But it's paradise for a white man to fall in love with a black woman!'

Now it was Fanie's turn to be discomforted. It was a new experience for him to witness something like this: two hens jumping at each other's throats, scratching and tearing each other over a cock.

'*Dames! Asseblief . . . nee, nee, wag 'n bietjie!*' ('Ladies! Please . . . no, no, wait a moment!') Fanie waved a helpless finger at both of them.

'George, do something!' he whispered.

'Leave them alone, Fanie,' advised George, having long since abdicated his role as fire extinguisher. 'This is woman-to-woman. Let them sort it out.'

The women were still glaring at each other belligerently, as if ready to break into violence at any moment.

'You are in demand, lover-boy!' teased George, his ready humour breaking through. 'Why don't you just marry both of them?'

'George!' Fanie shouted. 'You are not helping! You are now fanning the fire!'

There were more tense minutes of silence during which nobody said anything. The opponents appeared to have suddenly run out of steam.

Gerda's shoulders slumped and she looked, teary-eyed, at Fanie.

'At least tell me what it is that this woman is giving you that I cannot?' she said pitifully.

It was Dimakatjo who answered her: 'I give him,' she said, 'a nice *vetkoek*!'

She smacked her buttock rudely to illustrate.

Gerda grimaced.

'And he is,' added Dimakatjo bitchily, 'from the top of his head to the tips of his toes, *nna-wee*!' ('mine only!')

She again leaned possessively on Fanie's shoulder, while Gerda stared defiantly with bloodshot eyes.

'Come Gerda,' said George kindly, 'I will walk you out.'

George was, truth to tell, a little shocked by the spectacle he had just witnessed. He felt that Gerda was not behaving with the proper decorum to be expected of white women who, in his limited experience, did not as a rule create scenes; he believed that Gerda should have displayed more dignity. He felt that she was behaving like the tough type of black woman known as *bitch-never-die* – the stubborn type who does not lose a drop of hope when her man has been 'eaten by a harlot'. She is the kind of a woman who, no matter what, remains obstinately in one spot, immoveable as a boulder that will never be worn down, come rain, hail or fire.

But now all the fight seemed to have gone out of Gerda. Fanie and Dimakatjo watched silently as she was meekly led out by George. They saw George put his arm around her, guiding her towards the stairs. There, she turned her face and sobbed into his shoulder like a child.

23

That Saturday Fanie's car slowed down and stopped in front of Dimakatjo's home in the village of Ga-Mabitsela. Although the people of Ga-Mabitsela were used to seeing cars coming in and out of their village, the sight of a white man delivering a 'daughter of the soil' to her door was unusual enough to attract attention.

Everyone stopped what they were doing and stood watching from the doorways of their huts, or the smokey interiors of their small rondavels that served as kitchens, or looked on from neighbouring yards. Those on their way back from the communal water-pump also feasted their eyes, wondering who the white man was, driving the fancy white car, and why he was there. Most could guess the reason, however, for it was no secret that daughter of Bakone was getting married to a white man.

A few months earlier when Dimakatjo had come home to break the good news to her people about her man's intention to part with *lobola*, tongues had wagged and walked kilometres: *Have you heard this? Have you heard that?* The busybodies had done their work well – so well, in fact, that if theirs was a profession they would have been rewarded with performance bonuses! As a result, only a few of the curious onlookers were not up to date with the juicy news. These few most likely concluded that the white man was Dimakatjo's employer, since many people in the rural areas still held the old beliefs that a white man was always a black person's job provider.

Having checked to see that there was no one in the house, Dimakatjo returned to the car and invited Fanie to enter her home. She had just 'put the guest's buttock down', as the villagers were fond of saying, when they heard a knock at the door.

'*Tsena,*' responded Dimakatjo.

But whoever it was did not enter as bidden. Dimakatjo opened the door and found her Aunt Mashadi waiting on the doorstep, wearing the smile that Dimakatjo had not set eyes on for some time. Leaving Fanie in the main house, the two women went across to the small, thatched-roofed rondavel that served as a separate kitchen. There they chatted excitedly as they prepared the tea and laid out crockery and utensils.

Aunt Mashadi was not Dimakatjo's real aunt, but the aunt of Lukas's divorced wife, Matshidiso. Although the marriage between Lukas and *ausi* Matshidiso had died like a shattered earthenware pot, the friendship between Dimakatjo and *mmane* – Aunt Mashadi – survived and continued to thrive. What bonded the two women together was the fact that Aunt Mashadi was only five years older than Dimakatjo. A widow who supported herself with a small but promising hairdressing business that operated in the grounds of the local store, she stayed about five houses away from Dimakatjo's home. It was a certainty that on the big day of *lobola*, she would play an important role.

'Where are the people of the house?' enquired Dimakatjo, as if she herself were a stranger there.

'Your brother Lukas has gone to look for an ox to be slaughtered for your *lobola* day. Your mother has gone to your Uncle Phari's place, and your cousin Matsobane has gone to fetch some cooldrinks and liquor.'

'Cooldrinks and liquor? Is there a party?'

'No,' Mashadi smiled. 'Your people are preparing for your day of *lobola*!'

'But they did not tell me that this would be happening today!'

'It's not your business! Your *lobola* is *our* business!' Aunt Mashadi flashed her cheeky grin. 'We appreciate the arrival of our prospective . . . *mokgonyana-baas* . . . although we won't meet him today.'

'Should I tell him to go away?' asked Dimakatjo.

'No, don't worry Maki, your people will stay away while he is here. They will wait until the car of the son-in-law goes away. We don't want . . . ' Aunt Mashadi lowered her voice, ' . . . to scare the fowl before it is snared!'

'The bird has been snared already, Aunt Mashadi!' retorted Dimakatjo.

The two women burst into loud, unbridled laughter.

'Anyway, we prefer to hold our meeting after sunset.'

Dimakatjo nodded. She knew the reason why. Her people, like most villagers, had a penchant for discretion. In the culture of the village, it was said that *'he who eats must be discreet, and not behave like a child who does not wipe off the fat of his parents' slaughtered pig'*. This was in keeping with the belief that it was better not to court the jealousy of witches and other ill-doers by flaunting your good fortune in the faces of others.

'Do not be surprised, Maki,' continued Aunt Mashadi, 'when you hear people singing at my house today; they are members of my burial and wedding society, and they will be rehearsing the wedding songs for the big day.'

Modest Dimakatjo wanted to protest that she did not want a big affair, but she knew it would be wasted breath, for her aunt would insist: *'It's not your business!'*

Aunt Mashadi downed a quick cup of steaming tea and then went off to her own place, leaving Dimakatjo to attend to Fanie.

Sitting relaxed in the lounge of the main house, Fanie listened to the people singing a few houses away, in the rich harmony so typical of African choral music. He stood up and went to the window so as to be afforded a better view of the singers. In the yard of Aunt Mashadi's house, young men and women were lined up in two parallel rows, moving rhythmically sideways, backwards and forwards, kicking up the dust as they sang. The song was the well-known wedding song, 'The bride's mother':

Mma-mosetsana . . .
Šala o di bona tša lapa la gago
Se ile sponono!

(Girl's [bride's] mother . . .
Look after your family affairs
The beautiful one is gone!)

Fanie watched, completely absorbed, as the villagers performed their energetic classic. He was so taken with what he saw that he started making a clumsy attempt to imitate the dance sequence, much to the amusement of Dimakatjo, who had come into the room unnoticed carrying the tea tray and who stood laughing at his efforts.

'Why are you laughing, Maki?'

'It's true what they say – white men can't dance!'

At that, Fanie swooped towards Dimakatjo, grabbed her by the waist and spun her round dizzily, tea tray and all.

'Let me show you how this white man can dance!' he challenged.

At Fanie's insistence, Dimakatjo then patiently taught him the sequence he had been watching. A short time later he had mastered it; the student of African dance kissed his instructor triumphantly. She soon cued him to stop, however, and he was forced to conclude resignedly that kissing in these circumstances could be construed as 'culturally incorrect'.

Glancing out the window, Dimakatjo caught sight of her mother and uncle driving into Aunt Mashadi's yard.

Dimakatjo told Fanie it was time for him to leave the house and, without argument, he obliged.

The sun was just setting as Fanie's BMW, with its lone occupant at the wheel, bumped slowly along the uneven road that led out of the village. As if on cue, Mayibuye's old Toyota, carrying Uncle Phari (also known as the Great Porcupine), Aunt Mashadi and Mma-Dimakatjo as passengers, drove out of Aunt Mashadi's yard and bumped along the short distance to enter the gate of Dimakatjo's home. As the passengers disembarked, Mayibuye opened the boot and off-loaded two large cartons, one containing quart bottles of beer, together with brandy, whisky and red wine, and the other filled with a variety of cooldrinks and fruit juices.

The tired choristers, who had exercised their vocal chords and leg muscles virtually all day long, dispersed to their various homes. Mma-Dimakatjo and Uncle Phari entered the *lapa*, where Dimakatjo stood waiting. Uncle Phari greeted his niece with an avuncular bear-hug and kiss, his face full of genuine affection. Tall and hefty in build, clean-shaven and bald-headed under his peaked South African Police Service cap, Uncle Phari made an imposing figure for his sixty-something years. Fondly, he patted the shoulder blade of his niece, who was leaning against his chest. Holding her at arm's length so that he could inspect her properly, Uncle Phari commented that his sister's daughter looked very well. Dimakatjo, in turn, admired her uncle's imposing figure in his police captain's uniform, with its medals of commendation and other decorations and his officer's baton; she felt reassured that her life's plans would continue to unfold well, so long as her favourite uncle was still eating *pap* on this earth.

Uncle Phari, who was her mother's elder brother, had been like a father to her and Lukas, especially during the years since their father's death. Whenever Lukas was being particularly problematic, Mma-Dimakatjo would caution him: 'I'm going to tell your uncle!' – something that Lukas knew to be no empty threat. It might take busy Uncle Phari months to come, but he would sooner or later arrive to interrogate the culprit and demand answers, explanations and apologies for his misbehaviour; he would raise his voice where appropriate, contort his face into a frown and wag a stern finger at the recalcitrant. Lukas would emerge from the interrogation room looking as pitiful as a cockerel drenched by rain. Lukas so much feared his uncle that even when drunk and aggressive, if his uncle should appear in front of him, he would instantly grow as sober as a priest.

Lukas used to amuse his relatives by referring to his uncle in his absence as 'Stop Nonsense!' This was a popular term among urban residents for a cement-block wall erected between properties in order to avoid having to set eyes on troublesome next-door neighbours.

On this particular day, however, the much-feared Uncle 'Stop Nonsense!' was in a relaxed and tolerant mood. Even Lukas felt cheered by his uncle's genial presence.

While Dimakatjo prepared the tea, all those who were to be involved in the *lobola*-day preparations entered the lounge and took their seats. These kinsfolk were referred to as *bakgatha-tema* – 'plough-holders' – since they worked as a co-operative team to ensure that whatever business needed to be done at the various homesteads was completed. Now they whiled away the idle moments until tea came with chat about the late rains and what they would have done, or how life might be different, had the rains kissed their parched earth on time and in sufficient quantity.

The male relatives, Uncle Phari, Lukas, Mayibuye and his younger brother, Thomas, sat on the sofas and chairs, while the women, Mma-Dimakatjo, Aunt Mashadi, and Dimakatjo's elder aunt who was a *sangoma*, seated themselves on grass floor-mats, wrapping light blankets around their buttocks and covering their bare legs with shawls.

At last daughter of Bakone entered the spacious lounge, carrying a huge tray weighed down by a blackened five-litre tea-kettle, cups and saucers, sugar basin, milkpowder and large, unevenly shaped home-baked cakes the size of pieces of cow-dung. These were known colloquially as *kafferkoeke* – 'kaffircakes' – by the villagers, many of whom were still stuck firmly in the past. Since Dimakatjo had already exchanged greetings with all these relatives while she was preparing the tea, she put the tray down on the coffee table close to Aunt Mashadi and, after bending torso and knees respectfully, announced: 'Here is a little water.'

Then she disappeared from the room, as was required of her, to watch television at Aunt Mashadi's house.

The assembled relatives drank their tea and made small talk, building their strength for the hard work of the discussions to come. Those who had not been able to make it to these final preparations were Dimakatjo's cousin, Geelbooi, and Uncle Sepanere, as well as Mma-Dimakatjo's uncle who, because of his great age and wisdom, was addressed by young and old as 'Grandpa'. There was, however, no doubt that these absent relatives would, on the important day, arrive – *palakata*!

Many hands and hungry mouths attacked and made short work of the cakes and contents of the tea-kettle and soon everything was finished. Lukas and Mayibuye had graciously partaken with the rest of the company, though they would have far preferred to break open the beers and brandy, which they considered more appropriate to a celebration of their sister's forthcoming *lobola*. They accepted, however, that it was not yet the right time for such libations; that time would come once they had discussed and concluded the important matters on the agenda.

Aunt Mashadi carried the tray back to the kitchen and returned to her seat. The decisive moment had arrived. All eyes were fixed on Uncle Phari, who would lead the discussion and also chair the meeting, which had no scribe. Uncle Phari's masterful presence pervaded the room and his commanding tone was impossible to ignore. As he stated the purpose of the meeting in a rich, idiomatic speech that never bored his listeners, Mma-Dimakatjo kept repeating at well-timed intervals: 'We are listening, children's uncle!' while other relatives nodded emphatically when his gaze fell on them.

Lukas informed the Bakone gathering that a bull for slaughter had been bought and that it was tied under the *morula* tree in the yard. Mayibuye, assisted by his younger brother Thomas, reported that a fattened horned ram was grazing in the fields together with the flock of the family that was tended by Lukas's nephew, Sefako. According to Aunt Mashadi, malt for brewing *mabele*-corn beer would, within three days, be fermented in several twenty-litre earthenware containers.

When Lukas told the gathering that 'the white man's liquor' had been ordered from the local bottle store, *sangoma*-aunt warned that a lot of money should not be wasted on 'liquor that disfigures people into monkey faces'. Lukas and Mayibuye found this remark amusing. About ten chickens were already cackling in the yard outside, happily ignorant of the moment to come when their necks would be guillotined.

Mma-Dimakatjo reminded Lukas not to forget to buy a turkey, whose size she indicated with her right hand, for a few of the very important guests. Vegetables, too, had been ordered, and come next weekend, they would be efficiently sliced, cut and shredded by the members of the local women's club, popularly known as Women of Society – a community self-help group that traditionally assisted at the organisation of events such as these.

The next item on the agenda was to delegate the tasks. Aunt Mashadi was requested to make her house available as a place where the prospective son-in-law would wait and be looked after while the *lobola* negotiations were in progress. She was also designated to be Dimakatjo's attendant. Thomas would be responsible for collecting the 'go-betweens' – the negotiators representing the groom's family, known as *bo-mmaditsela*. It was suggested that the son-in-law's party should be met at the local trading store and guided from there to the homestead.

Thomas, as the more educated brother who was known for his level head, was appointed chief *mmaditsela* of the bride's family and would be assisted by Mayibuye, who was also tasked with supervising the stocks of 'white man's beer' and other booze. Lukas would be in charge of serving up the *mabele*-corn beer. Regarding the slaughter and skinning of the bull, Lukas and Mayibuye would be the joint supervisors.

With that, the business of the day was satisfactorily concluded. Nothing had been left to chance, and there being no other matters for chewing over, the mini-celebration that Lukas and Mayibuye had been patiently waiting for could now get underway. The eager pair, assisted by Aunt Mashadi, brought out ten quart bottles of beer; a few canned cooldrinks; a two-litre plastic bottle of orange juice; two 750 ml bottles of whiskey and brandy and another of red wine; and three large paper plates containing a variety of snacks. These were set out on the side tables.

Lukas poured a quarter glassful of neat whiskey and handed it to Uncle Phari, who emptied it into his mouth in two quick gulps. As empty glasses were filled and refilled, elbows raised and contents swallowed, the vocal volumes of those who imbibed became ever louder. The teetotallers – Thomas, Mma-Dimakatjo and *sangoma*-aunt – helped themselves to juice, while Aunt Mashadi sipped red wine. Children's uncle held up his empty glass, smiling pointedly at Lukas: '*Motlogolo*,' ('nephew') '*a warrior is not killed by one spear!*' Knowing what the metaphor meant, Bakone all laughed appreciatively. Lukas poured a generous double tot of whiskey and handed it to his genial uncle.

'*A sleeping lion is resting with sleeping teeth!*' Now it was Mayibuye who waxed idiomatic. He was referring to the relatives who weren't there, his implication being that because they were absent, they had missed sharing in the feast.

'Young people,' cautioned Uncle Phari, his gaze fixed on Lukas, 'don't drink too much and be snared by *babalase*. And next weekend, don't mix the affairs of your sister with liquor!'

'*Aowaa, aowaa* uncle!' protested Lukas. 'When I take liquor I drink into my stomach, and not here!' He pointed at his head.

Everybody laughed at this, for they knew too well that Lukas had the tendency to misbehave when his Dutch courage rose with his liquor intake.

Uncle Phari, who was a stern observer of protocol and known not to be fond of drinking excessively in the company of young people, asked permission from Mma-Dimakatjo to take his leave; but on the point of doing so, he remembered something else that he wanted to say. 'Another important thing: time! My people, let us remember that our in-laws are white people; let us therefore keep time. We cannot afford to become their laughing stock. Agreed?'

'*Hao*, uncle, are you still treating white people as gods? Are you still afraid of them, even now that we are long in new South Africa?' said Mayibuye scornfully.

Silence descended heavily into the room, creating a tension that reminded one of the heavy, threatening atmosphere before storm-clouds burst into rain. The threat was so palpable that no one even ventured to breathe. The eyes of all were glued to children's uncle, whose frown-wrinkled forehead and glaring gaze expressed volumes. Uncle Phari drew in a wrathful breath and fired a baleful look at his target. He raised a warning finger; but as he opened his mouth to speak, the words jammed, for *sangoma*-aunt interrupted him: 'Matsobane! How dare you talk to your uncle like that? Your uncle is no ordinary man! Have you forgotten that he is the head of policemen?'

The clanspeople, shocked that Mayibuye had had the nerve to '*grab the tiger by its tail*', wondered in what he had invested his trust. They concluded that it had been drunkenness talking, proving beyond doubt the truth of the saying, '*liquor does not give birth to a weak-kneed coward*'.

Mma-Dimakatjo, being a pacifist by nature, was moved to intervene; she bowed towards children's uncle and performed the conciliatory ritual that villagers called *phophotha*, clapping her palms together three times in slow and soft applause, her eyes pleading sincerely for mercy.

'Children's uncle, Great Porcupine, please do not unleash your sharp quills . . . !'

'Forgive him, children's uncle!' *sangoma*-aunt interrupted Mma-Dimakatjo.

The now-repentant Mayibuye got down from the sofa and unexpectedly knelt in front of Uncle Phari, as he, too, earnestly engaged in the *phophotha* ritual.

Uncle Phari gazed at the offending one for a long moment without speaking.

'*Pasop!*' Children's uncle waved his finger warningly at the repentant Mayibuye. Then his stern face relaxed: 'Because there is too much fermented mud in your head, and not your usual clear brains, I have forgiven you!'

Mayibuye returned humbly to his seat on the sofa. Smiles of relief flashed on everybody's faces. Uncle Phari again waved his finger at Mayibuye, then unexpectedly burst into laughter.

At that, all the people in the room, including the erstwhile culprit, also laughed.

Children's uncle took up his police cap and stood to his feet, ready to be on his way back to his home in the neighbouring village. Because Mma-Dimakatjo knew the Great Porcupine loved whiskey, she asked Lukas to wrap up the half-full whiskey bottle and give it to him as a parting gift.

'There are now enough spears to kill the warrior!' remarked Thomas, evoking much appreciative laughter for his wit.

Mma-Dimakatjo, Thomas and *sangoma*-aunt accompanied Uncle Phari out to his car, still parked in Aunt Mashadi's yard. She herself remained behind, sipping her red wine, while Lukas and Mayibuye downed more bottles of beers. It had been a good and fruitful gathering and 'the plough-holders' were in a cheerful mood, appreciative of the fact that Dimakatjo had given them the excuse to enjoy themselves; they were all looking forward to the real celebrations that would get underway the following Saturday – the day of Dimakatjo's greatest joy, that was just one short week away.

24

For Fanie and Dimakatjo the intervening week seemed to crawl along at chameleon speed. They wished that the remaining days ahead could race by like a fleeing hare chased by determined hounds, so that the great day of their dreams, when they would be pronounced husband and wife according to African custom, should simply arrive – *palakata*!

That Wednesday, as Dimakatjo attended to the last patient before lunch, her thoughts were far away. She was pondering the question of finding a reputable hair salon where she would be able to get a special hairdo for her historic day.

'I always see famous people going into Ola's Hair Boutique on Walter Sisulu Street,' advised Nthabiseng helpfully when Dimakatjo consulted her. 'Let me look up the number for you in the directory.'

Dimakatjo recalled how she had often gazed admiringly at the captivating hairstyles of actresses, singing stars and other celebrities and wondered enviously where they had had their hair done.

Nthabiseng browsed through the directory until she found the page she was looking for. Her moving finger stopped at a particular entry: 'Here it is! I'll write the number down for you,' she told her colleague.

During lunchtime Dimakatjo reminded Dr Makgabo that she would be taking a few days leave, starting from the following day, which she planned to use for preparation for her Big Day.

At knock-off time, daughter of Bakone bid her colleague farewell. Tearful Nthabiseng gave her a hearty hug and a kiss, then handed her a small gift, which was a slim volume about marriage called *Making Love Last*, and a congratulations card. Nthabiseng would not be able to make it to Dimakatjo's *lobola* day since Jack the repentant philanderer was taking her away on another five-star romantic weekend. This was in order to try and heal what he had damaged, after Nthabiseng had told him she was breaking up with him.

As the two young women were about to step out of the surgery on their way to catch their transport home, Dr Makgabo called Dimakatjo back to give her his wedding gift. This proved to be an expensive all-purpose make-up kit that was 'recommended by internationally acclaimed models', according to the accompanying pamphlet, and a huge, A4-size congratulations card done on quality, cream-white paper, specially designed and illustrated by a famous black artist from Mamelodi. The message in Sepedi was inscribed in cursive gold lettering and read: 'A *lethabo la tšatši la lenyalo le tlale bjale ka metse a lewatle!* May the joy of your wedding day be as plentiful as sea-waters!' The illustration comprised a drawing of a calabash, traditionally a symbol for asking for a wife through *lobola*.

Dimakatjo was stunned by her employer's generosity, so much so that for a few seconds she remained speechless. She was overwhelmed by the trouble he had gone to in choosing both present and card; aside from its message and illustration, the white colour of the card was, in itself, significant, for it could be interpreted as standing for *tsela-tšhweu* – 'a white path', one blessed by the gods of her ancestors, whose hearts were believed to be snow white.

With tearful eyes, Dimakatjo hugged and kissed Dr Makgabo: 'It's so very kind of you, doctor! Thank you – *kudu kudu* – for the wonderful gift.'

Dr Makgabo patted her shoulder with a fond smile. Mindful of the fact that *lobola* was more important in African culture than even a white wedding, he generously suggested that she should extend her leave and take the whole of the following week off as well; to this she agreed with alacrity.

On Thursday morning Dimakatjo 'kicked the blankets' with a feeling of anticipation. Today was a special day – the last day before the eve of her greatest day, when she would become a 'real woman' in the eyes of her people.

Her plan was to go shopping for an outfit and then get her hair done. She chose Dinaledi, the woman's boutique in Kgoši Tshwane Street that was frequented by women of status and style and which specialised in African prints in various ethnic designs and colours. Once there, she quickly made up her mind, choosing a gold Sotho *hele* – a knee-length, sleeveless garment immaculately embroidered in the traditional style of the Bapedi of Sekhukhune.

In the fitting room, as Dimakatjo admired her image in the mirror, she thought how perfectly the dress would go with Fanie's Valentine's Day gift – the gift she had not yet used but had been saving for the exact right occasion. She had already decided that it was this beautiful Ndebele necklace that she would hang around her neck on the day of her *lobola*.

From Dinaledi she walked the short distance of a few blocks to Ola's Hair Boutique, one of Central Pretoria's most elegant salons, owned by Nigerian Ola, a much sought-after hairstylist.

In the salon, Ola handed Dimakatjo a glossy catalogue with pictures of black models showing off various complicated hair designs that would leave any customer confused for choice.

'For what occasion do you need this hairstyle?' the guru-stylist enquired, dropping her 'aitches' in the way typical of Nigerian-speakers.

Dimakatjo told her that it was for her *lobola* day. At this, Ola smiled and quickly flipped over a few pages, pointing to a picture of a woman modelling a stunning hairstyle, sculpted from braided plaits twisted into big, complex loops.

Dimakatjo instantly fell in love with what she saw. A three-hour journey of craftsmanship began; Dimakatjo's hair was first of all thoroughly shampoo'd and treated with herbal mixtures, then dried and combed out. Her natural hair was woven into nylon extensions, and beads and shells were fitted with impressive finesse onto the individual strands. These were then woven, twisted and looped firmly together in the centre of her head. Finally, hard-to-please Ola was satisfied and the labour was at an end. The finished result was truly breathtaking to behold, a wonderfully intricate and eye-catching architecture.

Ola held up a large hand-mirror, angling it this way and that in order for Dimakatjo to see the effect from all sides; the glowing and satisfied customer found her image to be that of an unparalleled *sponono* – 'beautiful one'. She couldn't stop smiling at the vision she presented and happily forked out the requested amount. Radiant with happiness, daughter of Bakone emerged at last from Ola's salon.

As she walked to the taxi rank to catch her transport home, heads turned to look at her and several young women stopped her to ask where she had got her phenomenal hairstyle from. Dimakatjo thrived on the compliments and admiring glances that continued to be showered on her all the way to the taxi stop and back to Mamelodi in the taxi.

On Friday morning Dimakatjo woke very early, a little past 4.00 a.m., though she had set the alarm on her cellphone for an hour later. Listening to her favourite Thobela FM Stereo radio station, she boiled up some bathing water for herself and washed in the large basin as usual. Then she made herself a cup of aromatic herbal tea, which she sipped from her favourite white chinaware mug, while she picked and chose among her belongings for the items to pack and take with her on her journey to Ga-Mabitsela. She did not forget to pack her treasured make-up kit, Dr Makgabo's special gift to her; and she also slipped into her luggage the small green paper packet, in which was stored Fanie's Valentine gifts: a meticulously crafted copper bangle, and a necklace made from bright, multicoloured Ndebele beads.

At six o'clock the metered taxi, for which she had arranged the previous day, hooted outside her shack. She wheeled her small, beige suitcase out onto the *stoep* for the driver to lift into the boot. The taxi took her to the Polokwane taxi rank, from where she would board a second taxi for the three-hour trip to Ga-Mabitsela.

25

Fanie drove to work as usual on Friday, notwithstanding the fact that he, too, needed time to prepare for this most important weekend of his life. His plan, for which he had obtained George's permission, was to knock off around 2.00 p.m. He felt a duty to be at work for the morning at least in order to finish up any outstanding business, since he, too, would be on leave for the whole of the following week, enjoying his honeymoon with Dimakatjo.

By 1.30 he had cleared his desk and was ready to be on his way. George was out of the office, off at a managers' lunch, so Fanie scribbled a quick note for him on the message pad: 'I'm gone. You can call me on my cell. C U 2morrow morning! FF.'

From the Welding Company, Fanie drove to one of the hairdressing salons in central Pretoria, where he had his hair cut and treated with special conditioning products. Unlike Dimakatjo at Ola's, he was done in less than an hour. He then went into one of the men's clothing shops, where he bought a smart cream-white suit and matching pair of socks that he intended wearing on the day. Since he was in the car, he decided to pay a visit to Moreletta Straat to see his mother and sister. He was still hoping, even at this late hour, that he could receive his mother's blessings, and that even if she had not changed her attitude to his union, she would at least find it in her heart to wish him well. On his way to the house, he stopped off to buy some sesame-seed health bread, a take-away Greek salad, and some fruit salad for his supper, for he was intending to have a light meal and an early night.

When he arrived at his mother's house his sister Anna-Marie, who had newly arrived home herself, was boiling water for tea. She was thrilled to see him and greeted him with affection, for although they kept in regular phone contact, it was the first time in months that he had paid a visit to his mother's house.

'How is your beautiful bride doing?' Anna-Marie asked him.

'Maki is fine. At least she was the last time I laid eyes on her! She's already at her mother's house.'

'And are you getting good use out of that pre-wedding gift I gave you?' Anna-Marie asked him impishly.

'Absolutely! Riekie, that fly-whisk is doing a terrific job! It's fanning the fires of love like you wouldn't believe!'

As he spoke, Fanie unconsciously lowered his voice.

Anna-Marie was very amused by this. 'Why are you whispering?' she asked. 'You don't have to worry *boet*, *ma* is not around.'

'Where is she?'

'I have no idea. She doesn't tell me anything these days. She's so strange and secretive. Sometimes I get really worried about her.'

Selina came in, carrying a tea tray with rusks and tea – herbal for Fanie and the usual brand for Anna-Marie. Selina greeted Fanie with a chesty cackle and wished him a successful *lobola* day for the morrow. Fanie thanked her with sincerity, for he genuinely appreciated the goodwill with which she viewed his coming union.

'Do you think *ma* will be back soon?' he asked his sister as they drank their tea. Again Anna-Marie replied that she had no idea.

Guilt began to gnaw at Fanie's heart; he felt he should have been less neglectful of his mother over the past few months. He felt that he could, perhaps, have been more diplomatic on his previous visit home, when his mother had vented her feelings on the subject of interracial marriage and spewed vitriolic flames out of her acid mouth: '*Jou kaffer-skoonma het jou getoor!*' He remembered how he had bluntly told her without mincing his words: '*You are my mother and I cannot wish you away. But if you make me choose between you and my love, then it is Maki I will choose.*'

It had caused a rift between them that had yet to be healed. But Fanie also felt that he had had no choice. For to keep silent would have been to betray Maki; and that, he couldn't have done.

When they had finished their tea, Anna-Marie asked Fanie if he was feeling nervous about the coming *lobola* day; he replied that he was a little anxious because he did not know Dimakatjo's culture and therefore had no idea what would be expected of him.

As he spoke, Fanie remembered *Mafuth'ebhubesi*, the special herb ointment fortified with a lion's fat that George had given him, with the assurance that the ointment would empower him with dignity and ensure that the *lobola* negotiations ran smoothly. He wanted to share this with Anna-Marie but something held him back; he was not sure whether it would be 'culturally okay' to tell her. He was beginning to learn that there was a lot of sensitive business in his new culture, much that was better not shared.

Earlier that day, which was her half-day at the bank, Fanie's mother Louise drove to Menlyn shopping centre in the east of Pretoria, where she had an appointment with a therapist named Dr P. Rous. This was her third consultation, and she was not sure whether she was going to continue.

It was now three months since she had developed stomach ulcers and her condition was showing no improvement; if anything, it was getting worse. She had been referred to the therapist by her family doctor as a last resort. He had, over the months, prescribed tablets of various kinds, colours, and quantities, but to no avail. Louise had also swallowed syrups, milky tinctures and other sweet and bitter mixtures recommended by her doctor and various pharmacists, without any success at all. Her bedroom now had so many bottles in it that it looked like a *spaza* chemist.

Her doctor was an old German physician who had a thriving practice and was known for his excellent diagnostic skills and holistic methods. He was baffled that Louise was responding to neither the orthodox drugs nor alternative remedies that he had prescribed. It was for this reason that he had referred her to Dr Rous, a therapist in whom he had great trust; for he was increasingly convinced that her ulcers had a psychological cause.

Louise had resisted the idea at first. 'I don't need a psychologist,' she said, 'there's nothing wrong with my mind.'

'He's not a conventional psychologist,' her doctor told her. 'He uses unorthodox methods. I think you will find him on your wavelength. Why don't you just give him a try?' he urged.

Against her will, Louise allowed herself to be persuaded.

On her first visit, the therapist asked why she had come to see him.

'I'm here because Dr Kopf said I should come and see you,' she told him. 'I don't need a therapist. There's nothing wrong with me except my ulcers.'

They spent the rest of that session and the next one talking about Louise's ulcers and the misery they were causing in her life, and the various treatments she had undergone for them without success. The therapist didn't say much, merely listened attentively as Louise talked. Sometimes they sat in silence for long periods when she ran out of things to say. Each time he tried to probe into what she thought the root causes of her stubborn ulcers might be, she dodged the question, quickly changing the subject. Once, she claimed that her daughter Anna-Marie was the problem in her life, an obstinate girl who was very difficult to live with. The therapist gave her some practical suggestions that might help her to manage her stress better.

When Louise entered the consulting room for her third visit, her eyes were immediately attracted by a big, leather-bound book on the therapist's desk. She recognised immediately that it was the Holy Bible. The therapist saw where her eyes went but he didn't comment. He asked her if there had been any improvement since their last session, and she replied that there was none. After that, he sat in silence, looking at her intently as if waiting for her to speak.

Louise found herself squirming in discomfort. The tension in her mounted until she felt she could hardly stay sitting in her seat. Desperate to avoid eye contact with the doctor, she picked up the Bible from the desk between them; it fell open on the passage, 'Love thy neighbour as thyself'.

As she read it, tears gushed out of Louise's eyes. She broke into heaving sobs, and cried as though her heart would break.

The therapist handed her a tissue from the box on his desk.

'Would you like to talk about it?' he asked her gently.

That day the therapist succeeded in breaking through the granite wall around Louise's heart. She found herself pouring out everything into the counsellor's attentive ears. She told him the whole story about Fanie's romance and coming marriage to Dimakatjo, and her reaction to it. She admitted she was so bitter about her son's liaison with a black woman that she used swearwords such as '*kak*' and '*kaffer*' to curse it. The doctor nodded sympathetically but said little, allowing her to speak without interruption. His silence seemed to encourage her without judgement. Her tears flowed freely as she talked, and it was as if the poison in her heart flowed out with them. Finally, Louise was able to face the truth that her opposition to Fanie's imminent marriage to Dimakatjo stemmed only from her strong racial hang-ups.

'What am I going to do?' she wept. 'I love my son, but now I've lost him! He doesn't even come and visit me any more!'

'There seems to be only one sure way to solve this,' the therapist said, 'and that is to leave this matter in the competent hands of the Almighty. Why don't we pray together?' he suggested.

He laid his right hand on Louise's left hand and his left hand on her right hand. As he prayed, she seemed to feel some hot current transferred from his hands to hers. When he said 'Amen!' she did not raise her bowed head; it was as if guilt and shame weighed it down. She put her face in her palms and sobbed heartrendingly.

The therapist rested his hand on her head comfortingly, as if she were a child. 'Tears are offerings to God. He will hear your heart,' he said.

'Thank you, doctor,' Louise said softly.

She wiped her tears and blew her nose with the fresh tissue he handed her. It was still not easy for her to raise her head, but she finally summoned up the courage to look him in the eyes. The therapist nodded and smiled.

'You will be all right now,' he said, rising to escort her to the door.

She managed a trembling smile in return.

'Goodbye, doctor. How can I thank you?'

'Go in peace, Mrs Fourie.'

It was after sunset when Louise finally arrived home. From the therapist's rooms she had driven to a park in the west of Pretoria, where she spent some time alone, sitting on a bench and reflecting on what had happened during the session.

She had time to watch the black and white toddlers playing together, their mothers sitting on separate benches and never communicating with one other, except to flash occasional smiles. She watched lovers lying on their bellies on the grass, sharing ice-cream, while the ice-cream vendor rode to and fro on his tricycle, ringing his little bell. Doves drank from the water fountain, fluttering their wings and mating each other. And so much else was going on . . .

By the time Louise got home, Fanie had gone. Selina told her that Anna-Marie was out and had said not to wait for her for supper, as she had gone with some friends to a pizzeria not far from their house. That suited Louise, because she did not want to see Anna-Marie at that juncture. She was, in fact, not in a mood to talk to anyone. Tonight was a night of renewal, and she wanted no reminders about what had been in the past. She felt she was a new person, and therefore wanted to write on a clean slate; to write new things, beautiful things. No more ugly swearwords, such as '*kak*' and '*kaffer*'! It was a beautiful relief to feel this way. She could think of Anna-Marie's gift of a fly-whisk fanning the fires of Fanie's love, and not feel bitter or angry. She was now a much better person, who had decided to be Fanie's blessing and no longer a curse.

She needed to be alone tonight to talk to her Creator; to confess her sins to Him and hand over the burden of her prejudice and hatred – this burden that had nearly cost her her health and life.

She removed her shoes and lay down on the bed. Taking up her Afrikaans Bible, she opened it and read through it at random in search of words of comfort and encouragement. After a while, she felt very peaceful. The Bible slipped to her chest and she dropped into a deep, refreshing sleep.

26

At Strydomhuis that afternoon Nicholas Molwantwa stood knocking at the door of Fanie's empty flat until the index finger on his right hand said: *I have had enough!* In his left hand was a gift for *baas* Fanie. It was the third time that Nicholas had walked to Fanie's flat, each time returning with the gift that had yet to touch the hand for which it was intended. Nicholas was dressed in the khaki uniform of the Zion Christian Church; his feet were shod in impeccably polished white *manyanyatha* half-boots, whose soles were made of truck-tyre rubber. It was evident from Nicholas's attire that he was on his way to one of the periodic pilgrimages held by his church. He stood there undecidedly, gazing at his wristwatch and watching the second hand doing its circle of the face. He did not want to send anyone else to hand over the gift on his behalf. *Aowaa!* He wanted to give this gift to Fanie in the flesh. The thought flashed into his mind to write a note for Fanie, requesting him on his return to come down to the one-roomed tool-shack-cum-servant's-room that served as Nicholas's quarters. He took out a pen and scrap of paper from his pocket and started to write the message. He had got as far as, 'To Mr Fourie', when he heard the lift doors squeaking open and Fanie appeared around the corner, whistling chirpily.

Fanie and Nicholas exchanged amiable greetings in Sepedi, and African handshakes.

'Nik, you are smartly dressed today; where are you off to?' Fanie asked as he unlocked the door of his flat.

'I'm going to Moria to see the Prophet,' replied Nicholas, his smile indicating that the compliment was well received.

As they entered the flat, Nicholas enquired about the health of Dimakatjo, whom he, like Nthabiseng, had dubbed 'daughter-in-law of the *boere*'. He nodded approvingly at Fanie's answer that she was 'exceedingly well'. Nicholas then opened the small plastic packet he was carrying and took out something carefully wrapped in gift-wrap paper.

'This is for you,' he said, thrusting the parcel at Fanie.

Fanie ripped it open and found inside a bottle of aftershave lotion.

'Oh, thanks a million, Nik!' he responded, giving Nicholas a powerful bear-hug. Nicholas beamed; it was the first time that he had ever hugged a white man in his life.

'I must go,' he said. 'The bus is waiting at Marabastad.'

'Go very well, Nik. When I see you again I will be a married man!'

Nicholas nodded and beamed again. He took a few steps towards the door, then turned back to say: '*Baas* Fanie, you have made a good choice of a woman!'

'Thank you, Nik. When you said to me, "*This one you must marry*", that was the confirmation for me!'

Nicholas laughed appreciatively.

'Travel safely, Nik.'

'Thank you *baas* Fanie.'

'I wish you could be there tomorrow.'

'Yes, I would represent you very well. And when it's the time to celebrate, I would do like this . . .' He suddenly broke into song, belting out one of the Zionist men's league songs in a strong and ringing baritone. His feet kicked the concrete corridor in a stamping circle dance, while his hands clapped a staccatto rhythm in accompaniment. He leapt energetically into the air with both feet bent up under him, landed with a heavy thud and leapt upwards again. Not for nothing was Nicholas a leading *Mokhukhu* dancer and well-respected member of the ZCC!

Fanie was considerably impressed by this impromptu display. He complimented the beaming Nicholas on being an excellent dancer.

Again they said their goodbyes.

'Don't you worry, son of Fourie. God and the ancestors will be with you tomorrow!' were Nicholas's parting words.

Just before Fanie climbed into bed that night he took his cellphone and set the alarm for 5.00 a.m. He inserted himself between the sheets, lay down and settled himself into a sleeping position; then he pushed the covers away and got out of bed again. Opening the cupboard, he took out Anna-Marie's gift, the oxtail fly-whisk, and waved it in a circle around his head, to ensure that 'the fires of love' were well fanned.

After this, he rummaged in his cupboard for the pocket-knife that he had bought on George's instructions – the knife for 'slaughtering the sheep for the in-laws' that would be needed during the following day's negotiations. He transferred this to the pocket of his new cream-white suit that he intended wearing on this most important of all days. Next, he remembered *Mafuth'ebhubesi* – the mixture-of-herbs ointment fortified with a lion's fat, which George had promised would strengthen him and make him impervious to the machinations of wicked witches and wizards of the village. This, too, he stowed safely in a pocket of the cream-white suit.

These important tasks now done, he got back into bed. His hand reached for the switch to turn off the bedside lamp; but, tired as he was, there was still one more important thing that he recalled must be done before he could sleep. Anna-Marie had encouraged him to involve the Creator in his *lobola* event. So Fanie got up once more, went to his bookshelf and pulled out a leather-bound Afrikaans Bible, from which he blew away a thin film of dust. He paged through it to the Psalms. His searching index finger at last found what it was looking for: Psalm 23, which he had memorised and read and presented to his teachers, parents, church elders and the *dominee* as a schoolboy in Potgietersrus, over twenty years ago. To this day, he could recite those verses by heart:

The Lord is my shepherd, I shall not want.
He makes me lie down in green pastures;
He leads me beside the still waters . . .

He sat down on the chair next to his wardrobe and let his finger guide his eyes through the rest of the verses. As he said the familiar words aloud, he seemed to hear a church organ playing softly in the background. He read the psalm through twice, then shut the Bible, closed his tearful eyes and, clasping his palms together and bowing his head, prayed aloud in Afrikaans: '*Liewe Here, laat die* lobola *dag asseblief glad verloop . . .* ' ('Dear Father, please let the *lobola* day go smoothly . . . ')

Before he could even say 'Amen!' drowsiness overcame him; the Bible slipped out of his lax hands and landed *bhamm!* on the floor. He climbed back into bed and said with a tired voice: 'Father, you have heard me, Amen!'

Then he lay down finally and slept a deep, deep sleep – like someone under anaesthetic for an operation.

27

It was a hot Friday afternoon at Ga-Mabitsela. Within a few hours the hard-working sun would prepare its bedding of coloured cloud, ready to take a well-deserved rest. For the people of the village, this was a special sunset; for the following day, Saturday the 29th of November, promised to be a day as sweet as honey.

At the Machabaphala homestead, in the yard outside the *lapa*, a group of men were busy setting up an old, weather-beaten army tent, hired from an enterprising migrant worker, now retired. Hired plastic chairs would be delivered early the next morning. Umpteen things waited to be done and Dimakatjo's people, with Lukas, Mayibuye, Thomas and their cousin Geelbooi to supervise, offered willing pairs of hands to fetch and carry this, that and the other thing.

Just before sunset the men of the village slaughtered and skinned the festive ox and the smell of the cooking innards, simmering away in a three-legged cast-iron pot, permeated the homestead with mouth-watering aromas. Two young men had been assigned to this important task, for this was the portion for the men. In another pot, steaming stiff porridge was being turned from the bottom of the pot to the top. All the men present, even those who had not lent a hand in the slaughtering and skinning, were given a piece of half-done roasted liver, while the children were given pieces of lung and assured that these were, indeed, from the genuine liver.

The next important task was to chop the slaughtered beast into small pieces that would be boiled the following morning. This, too, would be attended to by the men; the women would be busy with umpteen other duties, such as preparing tea, coffee and cakes for the early visitors, and serving people with porridge and cooked tripe. In the big marquee in the yard, piles of cabbages, carrots, pumpkins, green beans, potatoes and sweet potatoes awaited their attention. Singing and humming as they worked, they peeled, cut, chopped and shredded the vegetables, which they then heaped in large basins and dishes. Not for nothing was it said in the village that '*a woman is a baboon whose hands are eaten*'.

Dimakatjo was one of these indefatigable women. She had ignored advice that she should passively fold her arms because tomorrow was her special day, and had joined in the preparations with the rest of the women.

At 8.00 p.m. solicitous Aunt Mashadi called Dimakatjo to have a bath; hot water had been boiled on a coal-fire and poured into a large, oblong zinc bath that was used for washing the family's clothes, blankets and other household items. When Dimakatjo had finished she dried herself with a towel, then reverently opened the make-up kit that Dr Makgabo had given her and applied a generous dollop of moisturiser to her face. She dressed herself warmly in a tracksuit and wrapped a light blanket around her waist to cover her buttocks. Then she returned to the marquee to lend a hand to the other hardworking and singing 'baboons'.

By nine o'clock that night most of the relatives had arrived, including Dimakatjo's married elder sisters, who had come without their husbands, and her younger aunt who worked as a domestic in Polokwane and had managed to get the weekend off from her employers. But one very important relative, Uncle Phari, was conspicuous by his absence. The reason was that several hours earlier, he had been unexpectedly assigned to a special operations task force to deal with a critical matter of a criminal nature, involving a cash-in-transit heist gang that had been plaguing the region for some time. It wasn't until late into the evening that he found a moment to refuel himself with a cup of coffee and took up his cellphone to call his people.

Dialling through to Dimakatjo's phone, which was answered by Aunt Mashadi, he relayed the message that he had been unavoidably delayed. Disappointment was great among the Bakone clan. There was nothing they could do, however, for Uncle Phari was a 'bulldog of the government', and when *kgoromente* demanded its dog, no one dared point an accusing finger, saying: '*kgoromente, kgoromente*, you are not fair!' Bakone, after all, benefitted greatly from this 'bulldog' that barked '*hau-hau-hau!*' Because it was part of their family, they earned respect and dignity and felt secure. They could only hope that Uncle Phari would be there by midnight, as he had intimated. No one was more hopeful than Dimakatjo.

Meanwhile, Grandpa and the other elders relaxed over a gourd of corn-beer in the lounge of the main house; there were many things to talk and reminisce about, the starting and finishing point of all conversation being Dimakatjo's *lobola*.

These people of Bakone never grew bored with commenting about their white son-in-law, whom they would see eyeball to eyeball the very next day; they, indeed, milked this item until it was as dry as dust. After taking his turn to sip from the crooked, j-shaped gourd that was passed around from mouth to mouth, one septuagenarian enthused: 'We Africans who have seen many days full of troubles used to be fond of saying, "the black man's tonic is a white man"; but today the white man's tonic is a black woman, our own daughter! *Ruri*, times have changed!'

As he expected, his listeners laughed in loud and prolonged amusement, to the extent that they attracted attention from people in other rooms. As they laughed, one could see teeth dyed brown by snuff and stained with the remnants of whatever had been eaten for lunch; for in these parts, toothpaste and toothbrushes were, for many, unheard-of luxuries.

The hired generator went on, stuttering '*kara-kara-kara-kara*', as it nibbled away at the hours; and still the labours of the industrious ones did not end. Just after 10.00 p.m. Aunt Mashadi entered the marquee and walked purposefully towards Dimakatjo.

'Women, they say a woman is a baboon whose hands are never still; but this baboon . . . ' she patted Dimakatjo's shoulder, 'I am now releasing!'

The other women laughed as Aunt Mashadi firmly pushed her protesting charge towards the house. Once inside Dimakatjo's bedroom, Aunt Mashadi commanded: 'Come, daughter-in-law of the *boere*, it's time to sleep. You must wake up feeling fresh tomorrow. We don't want the Fouries to meet a bloodshot-eyed bride with a *phuza* face!' ('drinker's face!')

Obediently Dimakatjo undressed and put on her knee-length, sky-blue satin nightdress. She was concerned that her uncle had still not yet arrived. She had tried calling him to check on progress, but his phone was on voicemail. She did not lose hope, however, believing that God and her African gods were in control of the situation. Peace filled her heart and she fell asleep like an infant whose tummy was round and tight with mother's milk.

In deep, sweet slumber she had a dream.

Dimakatjo dreamed about her white wedding: she and Fanie were standing in front of the onlookers at a church hall in an unknown village. She wore a frost-white wedding dress with five-metre-long train that was held up by four small flower girls, two black and two white. Dimakatjo's feet were in snow-white, sharp-pointed high-heeled shoes. Fanie, sporting a sparkling ponytail, wore a purple silk suit with white shoes.

On either side of the couple stood five well-dressed black best-men, wearing dark suits, and five white bridesmaids dressed in peach. *Mmalo* – what a wedding! The Women of Society were there, all dressed up in their colourful uniforms – smiling, cheering and waving hand-made grass brooms, woven grass bowls, calabashes and wooden porridge spoons.

In the church, the seated audience consisted of men and women in traditional African attire. Some of the men carried shields and knobkieries, while the women waved straw winnowing bowls, gourds and decorated earthenware pots. The audience and Women of Society members sang wedding songs, starting with the popular '*Dikgomo*' – 'The Cattle'. The bride and groom, bridesmaids, bestmen and Women of Society marched to the beat of the song, while the audience cheered, beat drums and whistled . . .

In the midst of all the joyful furore, a white Catholic priest appeared in front of Fanie and Dimakatjo, holding in his left hand an open black book, from which he was about to read. Smiling, the priest raised his holy hand, signalling to the choristers to stop singing. Silence descended; the priest paused to adjust his gold-rimmed spectacles. Looking straight at Fanie, he asked in European-accented Sepedi: 'A e gona pala-monwana?' ('Is the wedding ring available?')

Fanie hurriedly searched his shirt pocket, then anxiously went through his trouser pockets, including the back pockets; anxiety mounted in Dimakatjo as his increasingly frantic efforts did not seem to be showing any success. At last he found the ring in an inner pocket of his jacket – to the audible relief of the onlookers. The priest held up the glittering ring to show the audience, then gave it back to Fanie, who was about to slip it on Dimakatjo's finger.

'Wait a minute!' the priest instructed. He paused, coughed and adjusted his spectacles again before saying: 'If anyone can show any lawful and just reason why these two should not be joined in holy matrimony, let him or her say it now, or else forever hereafter hold their peace . . . '

There was a breathless silence. The priest looked around; nothing happened. There was no movement from the crowd, no one stirred from their seats.

The suspense intensified. Suddenly, there was commotion, movement from the back of the hall; something was happening at last! Heads turned in amazement as a woman appeared, rushing forward from the back of the crowd; a white woman who was quickly recognised by Fanie and Dimakatjo. It was Gerda, Fanie's erstwhile girlfriend and Dimakatjo's bitter rival; Gerda the tireless *bitch-never-die*, grimly bent on disrupting Dimakatjo's greatest moment.

The audience hissed in disapproval.

Dimakatjo began to pant, her heart racing faster and adrenalin pouring through her veins; she was at that moment ready for an all out 'bitch-to-bitch' fist-fight.

'*Hei wena s'febe!*' ('Hey you harlot!') 'What do you want here?' she confronted her enemy heatedly.

She broke away from Fanie and took off one of her high-heeled shoes, intending to use it as a weapon.

'Hold on my daughter! Please!' The Man of God raised his hand earnestly, then his scrutinising gaze shifted to Gerda.

'She is not out of order,' he said to Dimakatjo. 'Remember that I have said: "*If anyone can show any lawful and just reason why these two should not be joined in holy matrimony, let him or her say it now . . .*"'

The congregation mumbled in agreement.

'So give her a chance to speak!'

His eyes moved back to Gerda, standing before him with bowed head. 'Speak freely my child . . . ' he encouraged her.

'Father, I am against this matrimony!'

'Why?'

'This man promised to marry *me*!'

'Have you any proof?'

'Like what?'

'A love-letter, a gift . . . or any form of written promise?'

Gerda confidently searched her pockets; then her searching grew more frantic. Her face crumpled pathetically, and she lifted her empty hands pleadingly; all could see that they were dry as bone.

'If you can't produce your proof, will you please step aside and forever hereafter hold your peace,' the solemn priest told Gerda.

Stony-faced, Gerda stood her ground, refusing to budge.

'Take this woman out! Away to the outer darkness, where there is weeping and gnashing of teeth!'

The priest raised his right palm towards the audience and, suddenly, four stout deacons came marching to the front and carried the kicking and screaming Gerda away. Relief filled the hall like gentle rain. The priest smiled; Fanie and Dimakatjo smiled; everybody smiled.

'Fanie Johannes Fourie, will you have this woman . . . '

'I will!' replied Fanie.

'Dimakatjo Mothepana Evelina Machabaphala, will you have this man . . . '

'I will!' responded short-of-breath Dimakatjo.

The priest gestured towards Dimakatjo's left hand and Fanie matter-of-factly slipped the diamond and ivory ring on her third finger.

'As God's messenger it affords me great pleasure to now pronounce you husband and wife!'

The congregation applauded deafeningly, a sound like pouring rain – known as *matla-ka-dibe* – when it pounds mercilessly on a corrugated-iron roof. As the applause subsided, Dimakatjo and Fanie kissed, at first hesitantly and then amorously and generously, evoking a further burst of enthusiastic applause. The happy couple waved their raised hands to left and right in the manner of celebrities.

The next instant, they were in a huge, six-wheeled limousine convertible. On both sides of the car was inscribed 'Just Married' in large gold cursive. Everywhere were crowds of villagers stomping, cheering, and shouting: '*Lu-iu-iu! . . . Šatee . . . Šatee-weee!*' as they did for weddings. Snuggled like a king and queen on the back seat of the cruising limo, the happy couple stretched their hands through the windows and bestowed a lucky touch on some of the well-wishers.

Suddenly, they were overtaken by a noisy cloud of dust; a hovering helicopter swiftly descended about a hundred metres in front of the car; the door opened, and *bitch-never-die* Gerda leapt down and sprinted towards the limousine. She wrenched the door open and karate-chopped the couple apart, then shoved Dimakatjo out of the way and dragged Fanie off to the helicopter.

The flying machine was soon airborne again; humiliated and angry Dimakatjo, supported by the crowd, screamed frantically and beckoned at the helicopter to return. Surprisingly, it obeyed. When the iron bird landed once again and opened its doors, Fanie was revealed in the doorway alone. Smiling tearfully, Dimakatjo raised her hand towards him, imploring: 'Please take me with you!'

'Come, my sweetheart, woman more precious than mountain-heaps of gold and diamonds!' Fanie said.

He stretched his hand down to take hers and pull her up into the helicopter, but because she was as heavy as ten bags of coal, she fell down again on her disproportionately huge buttocks, crying: '*Hee-hee-joo-nna-joo-nna!*'

There the dream ended abruptly. Someone knocked insistently at the door of Dimakatjo's bedroom.

'Maki, Maki!' called Aunt Mashadi's voice, 'Wake up! Wake up, daughter-in-law of the *boere!*'

Upset and drowsy, Dimakatjo staggered out of bed and unlocked the door. She stood yawning and rubbing her eyes, still half in the realm of the dream. Her smiling aunt handed her a steaming mug of strong herbal tea and left the room again.

Dimakatjo sat on the bed and slowly sipped her tea. She gazed at the empty space on her ring finger, and the missing diamond and ivory treasure seemed to say: *where have you put me?*

She still felt upset by the dream, blaming the unknown witch who had cursed her and caused her buttocks to become so huge and heavy; but when she touched her bottom, she was very relieved to find it back to its normal size again.

28

Fanie had no dreams that he could remember. Sleep for the son of Fourie was of the *šwaa-phapharaa* – interrupted 'stop-and-go' – variety. He awoke twice in the night, at midnight and 2.00 a.m., each time staring in disbelief at the bedside clock, certain that it must have stopped; yet he could see the longer arm ticking its way around the clock-face, patiently piling up the minutes to make another hour. It seemed that he had only just fallen into a proper sleep when, at 5.00 a.m., the alarm on his cellphone woke him.

Groggily, he wrapped his gown around himself without bothering to insert his arms in the sleeves, thrust his feet into his comfortable slippers and shuffled off to the bathroom. He shaved the soft, brown growth that had sprouted on his chin while he slept and slapped on a generous handful of the spicy aftershave lotion that Nicholas Molwantwa had given him.

As he was about to step into the shower, his cellphone rang. It was George, wanting to check on the arrangements for the day. George had not slept at his own home in Soshanguve but had spent the night in Silverton at the house of his cousin Lesetja, who was accompanying him to Fanie's *lobola*. They agreed to meet at Fanie's place and go from there to fetch Uncle Pieter in Wonderboom, a suburb to the north not far from the Polokwane highway, on which they would then travel to Dimakatjo's home. Relieved to find that all was on track so far, Fanie returned to his interrupted ablutions.

At Ga-Mabitsela, 'the dawn for men' was just breaking on the horizon. This was the term still given by the older villagers to the first grey lightness of the sky – the hour when, historically, the men were expected to rise and ensure that everything was secure in the village. This presently gave way to the deep red 'dawn for women', and before long, the sun was ascending over the faded blue mountains to the east of the village, unleashing its sharp little spears into the world.

At the Machabaphala homestead it was evident to all that there was going to be 'big work' ahead. Word of mouth had conveyed news of the event from every tongue to every ear in the village, and as many as 500 people or more could be expected to attend.

Women of all ages congregated at the grease-hungry manual water-pump, chatting and gossiping as usual as they filled their twenty-litre tins and plastic drums, then walking in small groups back to their homes with the heavy water containers balanced on their heads. The item under discussion was, inevitably, Dimakatjo's *lobola*. Men, young and old, had already empowered the information have-nots with news of the '*lobola* of the century' over a bottle of beer, or gourd of home-brewed sorghum-beer, passed from mouth to mouth in the traditional way.

Herdboys, too, acted as efficient agents of the grapevine, dispersing information about Sefako's aunt who had, hands down, broken the village record with regard to a fantastic choice of husband. Some industrious tongues spiced the proceedings with news that even the village chief and some 'big people' from the government would be there to grace the occasion. It was clear to all that this was to be no ordinary *lobola* feast where, at most, between 30 and 50 people might attend. *Aowaa!* Although the number of formally invited guests was small, it was probable that happy gatecrashers would swell the crowds considerably.

The event at the Machabaphala homestead was unique; because *lekgowa* – a white man – was parting with *lobola*! A white man would be the son-in-law of the whole village! Almost every villager shared in the pride of the Machabaphalas and took ownership of the occasion.

Long before the rooster crowed and birds began to chirp in the tree branches, Women of Society members, dressed in their brightly patterned uniforms, began to demonstrate their industriousness in attending to the million and one tasks waiting to be done. Some of the men were involved, too, lending a hand here and there as requested.

By 7.00 a.m. throngs of people were already milling about the Machabaphala homestead, inside the *lapa*, in the yard at the front of the homestead, behind the main house and the smaller huts around it, and in the marquee. Numerous vehicles, comprising cars and vans of varying styles, condition and engine-power, were parked in front of the homestead. More cars continued to arrive, overloaded with relatives and their next-door neighbours, colleagues and friends – as well as their friends' friends and neighbours. Thick smoke billowed skywards from the busy cooking fires and permeated the whole place.

A small truck loaded with 50 plastic chairs duly arrived and with the help of numerous willing hands, these were unpacked and taken to the marquee and the *lapa*. Lukas and his cousins, Thomas and Mayibuye, could be seen here, there and everywhere, conferring among themselves, gesturing orders and giving instructions about what to put where, when and how. Women of Society and some of the female relatives carried round trays filled with the odd-shaped but tasty traditional cakes made from white flour, milk and condensed milk, while tin and chinaware mugs, brimful with steaming hot black tea, were served to the men and older women.

Mma-Dimakatjo, *sangoma*-aunt, Grandpa, Aunt Mashadi and other close older relatives sat in the main house, eating soft sorghum porridge and boiled *mateng* – tripe – consisting of pieces of sliced intestines, *mogodu* (the stomach), lungs and heart – served up with watery gravy in wooden bowls.

That very important relative, Uncle Phari, had still not arrived, for national duty had overridden domestic matters.

As for daughter-in-law of the *boere*, she was alone in her bedroom, pensively chewing the last spoonfuls of fruit salad and yoghurt. Her attendant, Aunt Mashadi, entered the bedroom with an indulgent smile, as if she could read the romantic thoughts in Dimakatjo's mind. Inserting an inspirational gospel CD into the player Mashadi, who had fortuitously once worked as a beauty-parlour assistant, took up Dimakatjo's new make-up kit and skilfully began to apply the cosmetics that would suit the colours of the clothes her charge would be wearing. Fortunately, the magnificent hairdo created by Ola's expert hands was still intact, needing only a little adjustment from Aunt Mashadi here and there; to ensure its durability, Dimakatjo had wrapped her head in a protective *doek* overnight.

Aunt Mashadi finished her work with the cosmetics and excused herself to go about her business elsewhere. Returning at intervals, she would display her charming smile and enquire solicitously: 'Are you okay, daughter-in-law of the *boere*?'

Dimakatjo was glad of the chance to have some time to herself, so that she could relax and daydream and prepare herself for the momentous day that lay ahead of her.

Fanie opened his wardrobe and picked out the creamy-white light cotton suit with three silver-grey buttons that he had bought specially for this occasion; he chose a black floral shirt to go with it, and shiny black shoes. Walking over to the mirror, he examined himself carefully. His eyes liked what they saw, but they also found the man in the mirror a little strange without his trademark ponytail. Fanie had had his hair cut short in order to look respectable for his important day; he was afraid that Dimakatjo's people would associate the ponytail with negative things and form a prejudiced picture of him.

He smiled at himself reassuringly and did a quick rehearsal of the dance steps that he and Dimakatjo had practised a week before at her home; as he moved, he hummed the tune of the wedding song that he had heard the choir practising outside Aunt Mashadi's home.

When he had finished his rehearsal, he sipped some fruit juice to calm himself; nerves were fluttering in his stomach. He remembered the little tin containing *Mafuth'ebhubesi* that George had given him. Fanie searched the inner pocket of his jacket, took out the magical container and opened it carefully.

He put his index finger into the ointment, turned it clockwise and anti-clockwise as instructed, and moved his finger towards his eyelashes; but then he paused and scraped the fingerful of ointment back onto the container. *Maybe I should rather apply this when I am at Dimakatjo's home*, he said to himself. *If I use it now, it may have lost its power by the time I really need it.* He thought about checking with George, then shook his head decisively: *No, I'm right; I must rather wait.*

Replacing the lid on the tin, he wiped the remnants of ointment from his finger with a tissue, threw it into the toilet and washed his finger with soap for good measure. He put the small tin back into the inner pocket of his cream-white suit. From the outer pocket, he then took the pocket-knife that George had advised him to buy; he pulled out the blade, examined it closely, then closed the knife and returned it to the same pocket.

There was a firm 'rat-tat-tat' on the door. Fanie hurried to open it and George stepped briskly into the flat, followed by his cousin, Lesetja. The two men exchanged spirited handshakes with Fanie; they were so impressed with the impeccably dressed son-in-law of Bapedi that they even wolf whistled.

'*Khazi*, can you see that *mokgonyana* is dressed to kill?' Lesetja said, grinning, to George.

'Yes, *khazi*, but I think he is overdressed!'

'*Khazi*, please don't be jealous!' Lesetja flashed a smile.

'No, no, no – I'm not jealous! The truth must be told that Fanie is overdressed, and I just want to give him some advice.'

'What advice?' asked Fanie suspiciously.

'Fanie, this white suit of yours you can keep for a white wedding,' George told him. 'Today we are going to part with *lobola*.'

Fanie glanced questioningly at Lesetja who nodded his agreement.

While George and Lesetja made themselves comfortable on the sofa, Fanie hurried to his bedroom to change. He emerged wearing a smart, well-fitting green suit that produced more wolf whistles from the two *bo-mmaditsela*. Lesetja broke spontaneously into a wedding song, while George held Fanie by the hand, prompting him to dance along. So elated were George and Lesetja that they hoisted Fanie onto their shoulders and, still singing, circled twice around the lounge with Fanie's considerable weight borne aloft. They continued to belt out the song as they left the flat and walked towards Fanie's car. Their noisy exhuberance drew many disapproving glares from the group of *tannies* huddled, as usual, on the first-floor balcony.

Fanie moved his car out and George brought his car in from outside and parked it in Fanie's bay. He then suggested that Lesetja should take the wheel of the BMW so Fanie could relax during the long journey and save his strength; to this Lesetja agreed with alacrity. George then took the passenger seat in front while Fanie, from the back seat, directed Lesetja to Uncle Pieter's place in Wonderboom.

At the robots, they saw a newspaper vendor waving copies of the four morning newspapers in his hands; George called him over as they waited for the lights to change and bought a copy of *Tshwane News*. While he was busy with this, Fanie was doing his own 'one stop shop' out of the other window; from a passing flower-seller he bought a bouquet of brilliant red carnations for Dimakatjo. He also persuaded the obliging hawker to sell him the bucket of water in which the flowers had been resting, telling him they were for his fiancée on their wedding day.

They drove on towards Wonderboom along the recently renamed Oliver Tambo Drive. Fanie idly scanned the front page headlines of the paper, which George had passed to him. He turned over a page and then another: his eyes landed on a picture of a woman and man who looked vaguely familiar to him. He scrutinised the picture more closely and was stunned to recognise Dimakatjo and himself! It was the picture taken of them at their table during their Roodevallei outing, the night Fanie had proposed to Dimakatjo. They were smiling into the camera, heads together, love written all over their glowing faces.

'*Afrikaner Romeo parts with lobola for black Juliet*,' was the caption. The page was headed 'Wedding Bells', and Fanie and Dimakatjo's picture featured with those of three other couples who intended to tie the marriage knot. But how did it happen? How had their photograph landed in the *Tshwane News*?

Wordlessly Fanie passed the newspaper forward to George.

'*Hee-banna!*' exclaimed the grinning George. 'When did you go to the newspapers, Fanie? I don't remember you telling me!'

Fanie made no answer, still recovering from the surprise himself. Lesetja pulled over so he could see the photo, too. He laughed and gave Fanie a congratulatory handshake: 'Hey *monna* – you are now famous!' he said.

'I wonder how it got in there,' said Fanie, still amazed. He caught George's naughty grin in the side mirror.

'George? Did you have something to do with it?'

'Me?' said George, trying to look innocent and failing. 'Okay,' he admitted, 'yes, it was me.'

'Where did you get the photo from?'

'I borrowed it from your photo album and scanned it into the computer when you weren't looking. It was a good choice, *nê?*' he laughed.

Uncle Pieter was sitting at the table reading a verse from his Bible, as was his daily custom. He was wearing a dignified brown suit with thin black stripes, and in honour of the *lobola* occasion had paved a path on the left-hand side of his grey head, symbolising the actual path and journey to Dimakatjo's home that he and Fanie would soon be taking. He had just finished praying and was about to say 'Amen!' when he heard the doorbell crying '*tweng-tweng!*' His nephew and friends had arrived.

Fanie did the introductions and the three negotiators shook hands and exchanged pleasantries; then they all climbed into Fanie's car and headed off north. As the tyres of the white BMW licked the hot tar of the Polokwane highway, Uncle Pieter relaxed at the back with his nephew, speaking to him softly in Afrikaans, while the two men in the front conversed in Sepedi.

Lesetja and George were impressed by Uncle Pieter's forthright manner and felt assured that, in him, Fanie had a source of strength and wisdom. Fanie showed his uncle the photo of him and Dimakatjo in the paper. Uncle Pieter's face beamed proudly when he saw it. His eyes landed on the caption and he chuckled richly and patted his nephew's shoulder.

They travelled through the first tollgate to the second, third and fourth ones. Their well-serviced car with its powerful engine overtook slower-moving vehicles with ease, as if it were an eagle cruising over *mmammati* – a wingless grasshopper. George played Philip Tabane's, *'Rotwane e lebile lapeng la'bo kgarebe!'* on the car's CD-player, and he and Fanie hummed along with enjoyment.

Fortunately, they went through no speed-traps on the way, for Lesetja, carried away by the effortless horse-power of the BMW, was not observant of speed limits. Nor did they interrupt their journey for *'thunda* station' – emergency roadside stops, when men stood in the bushes in order to 'blind mice with urine'.

They had been travelling for close on three hours when Lesetja, at Fanie's instruction, indicated right and swung the car onto a narrow dirt road, stirring up a little dust-cloud in their wake. It was 10.20; they had arrived in good time at the village of Kgoši Mabitsela's people.

The car proceeded with care along the potholed road towards the old trading store, capped by a rusted corrugated-iron roof. The scratches on the veranda, dirt marks on the walls, children's graffiti and peeling paint all indicated that Sekgobela Native Shop, as the sign proclaimed, had 'eaten' many many Christmases in its time. Throngs of shoppers, young, old and aged, walked in and out of the store carrying their various items of purchase. Some customers cycled, while others who had bought heavy items, such as bags of coal or mealie-meal, drove their donkey-carts.

Thomas, who had been at the meeting point since 10.00, was waiting in Mayibuye's old blue Toyota next to the gate of the shop. He recognised the important guests at once as their car slowed down and turned in, for two white men in the back of a BMW being driven by a black man, with another black man as passenger, was not a common sight in these parts. They all got out to greet each other, exchanging vigorous handshakes, smiles and laughter. Thomas addressed Fanie and Uncle Pieter in Afrikaans, switching to Sepedi when he conversed with George and Lesetja. When Fanie talked back to him in Sepedi, his eyes widened in surprise.

They climbed back into their cars and Thomas led Fanie and his people straight to Aunt Mashadi's house. Their appointed host was Joyce Mabotja, Aunt Mashadi's bosom friend and next-door neighbour. Aunt Mashadi had delegated this important task of looking after the son-in-law of Machabaphalas to Joyce since Mashadi herself had to remain with Dimakatjo, as the official attendant of daughter-in-law of the *boere*.

As Thomas's car, followed by that of the newcomers, drove in through the gate of Aunt Mashadi's yard, Joyce saw them from the window. All around Aunt Mashadi's house, front, back and sides, stood groups of villagers, awaiting the arrival of the important guests. Some of the women carried babies wrapped securely on their backs, while others stood suckling their infants. Everyone watched in fascination as Thomas and the Fourie party walked towards the house.

'*Makgowaa! Makgowaa!*' ('White people! White people!') came the shouts, as excited children pointed towards Fanie and Uncle Pieter. Embarrassed adults hushed them.

Wearing a grin as big as her heart, Joyce stood in the doorway.

'*Hayi-yai-yai-yai!* They have arrived at last! The ones we have been waiting for!' Joyce couldn't restrain her joy.

The hostess welcomed the guests into the lounge of Mashadi's house. Enthusiastically she shook hands with each of them, holding their hands with both of hers and respectfully bowing while she mumbled, 'Joyce Mabotja' to each in turn.

Thomas told Joyce that the guests would not be putting their buttocks down as they were heading straight on to Dimakatjo's home. Only Fanie would be remaining here. Joyce then informed Thomas that Dimakatjo had asked for Fanie's car to be left parked in Aunt Mashadi's yard, under the big *morula* tree.

'Son of Fourie,' said Thomas formally, glancing at his watch, 'we are leaving you here. Please relax and feel at home.'

'You can be sure he will be well looked after!' Joyce assured him.

'*Šala gabotse* – stay well, Fanie my friend; I will be seeing you presently to update you on the progress,' George promised, patting Fanie's hairy hand.

Thomas led Uncle Pieter and Lesetja out of the house to Mayibuye's Toyota, while George parked Fanie's car, as instructed, under the tall and thick-stemmed *morula* tree. It was conveniently leafy and cast a thick shade which, on hot days such as this one, was a blessing. Locking the car, George walked back to the house to give Fanie the keys.

'I agree with Maki's thinking,' he remarked, 'that your car is better parked out of sight at this place. Because, who knows? If Maki's relatives see that you are driving a BM, they could perhaps ask for a higher amount of *lobola*.'

Both men laughed uneasily at this joke.

29

Time did not sit down on its buttocks.

At Machabaphala's homestead, several huge three-legged cast-iron pots towered over a fuming coal-fire. Pots filled with beef, stiff white mealie-meal porridge, and sorghum-*ting* – sour fermented porridge – simmered on the embers, the delicious smells tantalising everyone's tastebuds.

In the Machabaphala house, the room for the Fouries was ready, chairs waiting patiently to be warmed by the rear-ends of the guests. In one of the other rooms, Dimakatjo's *lobola* negotiators were seated, surrounded by an air of peace.

Suddenly, from the direction of Mashadi's house, came the sound of a car hooting: '*Pepepeee!*' Those milling around outside could see Mayibuye's Toyota approaching in a cloud of dust. It came to a halt in front of the *lapa* entrance and Thomas climbed out and hurried round to open the passenger door for Fanie's Uncle Pieter. George, at the back, opened his own door and stepped out, followed by Lesetja. Two female relatives standing nearby cheered loudly and broke into shrill ululations of '*Iiu-iuu-iuu!*', prancing ahead of Thomas as he led Fanie's people through the *lapa* entrance. Other bystanders responded by chanting: '*Howaa! Howaa!*' The escort of female relatives continued to prance in the *phepela* style, surging forward with bent knees in short, erratic bursts of movement, leaping into the air at intervals and swinging abruptly to the left and right, as the onlookers continued to cheer. Some of the women formed a guard of honour. This celebratory hullabaloo could not leave Dimakatjo untouched. Daughter-in-law of the *boere* stood peering through the lace curtain at her bedroom window, her face glowing with delight.

Thomas and the guests entered the room that had been set aside for the Fourie people. Thomas made sure that the guests were comfortably seated on the sofas and then went out again. Entering the Machabaphala room, he seated himself on one of the chairs and announced: 'Bakone, our friends have arrived!'

Thomas addressed his announcement to the person closest to him, who was *sangoma*-aunt; she relayed the message to Lukas, who relayed it to the person on his other side. In this way the message passed from person to person until at last it arrived at Grandpa, who responded: '*Aowaa!* That is cream!' By this he meant that it was good news.

The clanspeople of Bakone exchanged glances of delight. But one very important relative who should have been there to savour the rich news with them had not yet arrived; this was, of course, the children's Uncle Phari, also known as Uncle 'Stop Nonsense!'

The question that begged an answer was: should the discussions continue in the absence of Uncle Phari? It was not easy for anyone to answer this, for it posed a serious dilemma. The Bakone people were caught between a snake and a lion, as it is said. Their heads heavy with this gnawing problem, the clanspeople continued to ponder over the matter.

Following a long and uneasy silence, wise Grandpa reminded them of the well-known fable about a princess who was pricked by a thorn. The man who removed the thorn from her foot would incur blame for touching and defiling royal flesh; if, however, the man avoided touching the princess, he would still be blamed for neglecting his patriotic duty.

The Bakone people could continue the proceedings without Uncle Phari, but if things should go haywire, the children's uncle, or some of the other relatives, would point accusing fingers at them; yet, if they waited for Uncle Phari to arrive, precious negotiating time could be wasted.

In the silence, Lukas and Mayibuye exchanged glances.

'I think we must continue, Grandpa,' said Mayibuye, *throwing a piece of wood at the python.*

'Yes, let us remember that "*Moleta-ngwedi o leta leswiswi*" – "he who awaits the moonlight may only find a more starlessly dark night!"' Lukas agreed, tossing a bigger piece of wood at the snake.

'We should remember that our son-in-law and his people are whites who have no respect for African time,' added Mayibuye.

Another troubled pause ensued, in which the older and wiser people, Grandpa and *sangoma*-aunt, continued to 'eat the bones' of their greying heads. Thomas had not yet said anything. However, Lukas and Mayibuye knew that if they had to put the issue to the vote, Thomas would most likely not support them. In their heart of hearts these two dedicated drinkers, who spent much time in each other's company downing beers or brandy, were secretly scornful of teetotaller Thomas.

'Beware, young people, walking is better than hurrying!' cautioned Grandpa.

Sangoma-aunt added that *nonyana phaku-phaku* – 'the scurrying and anxious bird' – lays only one egg. Thomas finally 'broke the peace of his lips' in support of Grandpa and *sangoma*-aunt, saying that, in his view, they should not continue without Uncle Phari; he suggested that they should take a 30-minute break.

Lukas and Mayibuye were not impressed with the idea of a break. They wanted the negotiations to begin immediately and be concluded in the absence of Uncle Phari, since that would enable them to dominate the discussions. They knew that if their uncle were present, they would have no chance of getting the upper hand. Notwithstanding the vehement protests from Lukas and Mayibuye, the Bakone elders and Thomas decided to wait another 30 minutes before beginning the proceedings.

Half an hour went by and Uncle Phari still did not arrive. To make matters worse, it was no longer possible to contact him; for Dimakatjo's cellphone, the only one in which Phari's current number was stored, had inconveniently jammed. It was impossible to figure out how to unjam it since the cellphone manual was sitting in her shack in Mamelodi.

The reason it had jammed was that some hours previously, when Dimakatjo was having a bath, her nephew, the naughty Sefako, had furtively helped himself to her cellphone and recklessly pressed all the buttons simultaneously, while at the same time speaking into it animatedly, in order to impress on on his friends that he was unquestionably part of the cyber-literate generation. Dimakatjo's heart was heavy indeed. She knew that giving Sefako a good hiding would not yield any useful result, but she was sorely tempted all the same!

Dimakatjo guessed, correctly, that her uncle would be trying to contact her. He had dialled her number on more than one occasion, but each time all he got was her voicemail: *'Hi, this is Maki Machabaphala. I'm presently not available. Please leave your name and number and I will call you as soon as possible.'*

Meanwhile, time did not sit down on its buttocks. At an occasion such as this one there were no idle moments; relatives were still pouring in, accompanied by uninvited friends, next-door neighbours, friends of friends and other hangers-on. No one complained about the extra guests because, traditionally, Africans were hospitable people. They did not insist on invitations for weddings as whites and some stingy educated black people would have done, but welcomed those who were strangers to their door.

And besides, this was no ordinary *lobola* feast but a very special event for the village. Because *lekgowa* was parting with *lobola*! A white man would be the son-in-law of the clanspeople and of the whole village! The relatives all came with good wishes for their delectable niece who had grown up before their very eyes; they wanted to see her good fortune for themselves – with their own living eyes – before the gods took them away to the land where the longest stick would not reach.

Time was needed to welcome the good-hearted kinspeople, to shake their hands, enquire about their health and families and give them food – referred to in these parts as 'dirt for the teeth'. The uninvited guests, including the chief's advisor, also arrived and went to sit with their peers; soon, a huge gourd half filled with corn-beer would be passed from one pair of hands to the next, to be sipped from and passed on – a process that would be conducted with dignity, restraint, and no tinge of greed.

Twenty-five more minutes went by; the children's uncle had not yet appeared to put his buttock down where it belonged.

Dimakatjo's hope began to wane; she wondered what could have happened to delay her uncle so substantially. Her heart was heavy, for she feared greatly that her poison might be her brother Lukas's meat. She recalled the *lobola* negotiations of their eldest sister, when Lukas had replaced their uncle who was ill. Lukas had insisted that a higher amount of *lobola* should be parted with than that which had been offered; he appointed himself caretaker of the money received, promising that it would be used for a small 'send-off' to cement the wedding ties. Several months later, it was discovered that he was using the money to buy parts for his broken-down wreck of a car. It also became evident that part of the money had been used to 'grease' the palm of corrupt traffic officials with *tjotjo* – a bribe.

If Dimakatjo had her way, Lukas would never have been included in the *lobola* team to begin with, for she had feared from the first that her greedy brother would be a piece of stone among the cooked mung beans. More than once she had begged her mother to have Lukas excluded, but Mma-Dimakatjo had put her foot down, insisting that Lukas had to be part of the talks. After all, in years to come, he would be the 'children's uncle' of Dimakatjo's children.

Fanie sat on the sofa, alone in the lounge of Aunt Mashadi's house where he had been left. He examined the room in all directions, starting with the tiled floor, shifting his gaze to the white-plastered walls and then the ceiling and back to the walls again. It was a nice room, simple but comfortable. In the kitchen across the way Joyce boiled a pot of water on a gas stove in order to prepare tea for the important guest, who was creating an unprecedented stir in the vicinity. Crowds of curious children gathered outside the house, continually bobbing their heads through the doorway to peep at him, exclaiming: '*Lekgowa! Lekgowa!*' From the hut across the way, Fanie could hear the busy clinking of crockery and cutlery as the tea things were transferred onto a tray that had waited for hours to carry the good things for *lekgowa la* Dimakatjo ('Dimakatjo's white man').

Left to himself, Fanie reflected on the development of his love relationship from its inception until the present – this very moment of sitting here on this sofa, awaiting the progress of his *lobola* negotiations. He also thought about his mother, whom he believed would never change and find it in her heart to chant '*Hallelujah!*' to the fact of his being there, in what she would consider the '*kaffer* place'.

His hostess at last re-entered the room, carrying the special tray with the picture of red roses on a gold background, that was used only once or twice a year on very special occasions. On it was arranged the tea-kettle and snow-white china tea-set: cups and saucers, matching sugar basin, milk jug and silver teaspoons – all of them, like the tray, reserved for special use.

'How is life in Pretoria, *baas* Fanie?' Joyce asked him, venturing to break the ice.

'Please don't call me *baas*! Just Fanie, okay?' Fanie flashed her a smile to soften the criticism. 'Life is great in Pretoria, Joyce. How's life here?'

'It's very nice *baas* F . . . *askies tog* – I'm very sorry . . . *bathong!*' ('Oh people!')

Fanie laughed gently and this helped Joyce to relax.

They continued to sip their tea and nibble at the cakes that Joyce had baked.

'You know Fan . . . *aowaa!* . . . *ag*, please let me rather call you Mr Fourie . . . '

'No, please call me Fanie,' he said, this time in Sepedi.

Joyce laughed in surprise.

'Okay . . . Fanie . . . you see, I am not used to addressing whites by their first names . . . '

'It's okay, Joyce, I understand!'

'We are happy, Fanie . . . ' Joyce paused to take a sip of tea and put her cup back on the saucer, '. . . that you are our son-in-law.'

Fanie beamed at her and nodded.

They drank more of their tea and ate a few biscuits.

Fanie told Joyce something of his background, and about his

experiences at work, where some of his more conservative white colleagues had taken to calling him 'Mandela's Rainbow' when news of his relationship with Dimakatjo got out. Joyce was very tickled by that. When they had finished their tea, Joyce took the tea things through to the kitchen to wash up. She was busy at the sink when she heard a light knock and Dimakatjo entered. Joyce hugged her and complimented *ngwetši ya maburu* – 'daughter-in-law of the *boere*' on her '*s'kwerekwere*' dress. With Dimakatjo lending a hand, she prepared some snacks for her special guest.

'And how's my man, *sis* Joyce?'

'*Baas* Fanie is okay. *Hei wena*, what have I said? Your man doesn't like to be addressed as "*baas*"!'

Dimakatjo laughed at that.

'I'm telling you, Maki, your man . . . he is sô . . . !' ('like this') Joyce raised her thumb to indicate that Fanie was stunning. 'You have really hit a jackpot, Maki!'

'*Aowaa*, *sis* Joyce! I'm Fanie's jackpot!'

The two women laughed uninhibitedly. Joyce gave Dimakatjo the laden tray to carry and re-entered the lounge where Fanie was still seated. Smiling broadly, she waved her hand towards the grinning Dimakatjo, as if to say: *See what I have brought you!*

Acting the part of the traditional woman, Dimakatjo curtseyed meekly. Bending her knees until they touched the floor, she put the tray down on the coffee table, and clapped her palms together softly twice, like an ultra-submissive woman. Fanie and Joyce laughed appreciatively. Then Joyce went out of the room, leaving the lovers to themselves.

Hungrily Fanie embraced Dimakatjo, unleashing a series of torrid kisses, known as *tladi-molomo* – 'lightning from the mouth'. He would have followed up with more, but Dimakatjo restrained him.

There she was in front of him at last, her smile brighter than *letopa-nta* – the ultra-bright moonshine. *Mmalo!* The dimples that the gods of Afrika had blessed her with and which had so stunned Fanie when he saw her for the first time at the surgery, now charmed him anew. She wore a Ghanaian-print dress embroidered with black.

The dark-purple eye shadow that Aunt Mashadi had so skilfully applied made her look truly West African. In no time at all, Fanie's passionate blood was roaring with beastly desire; his wild heart cried: *'mêê! mêê!'* like a goat, and he felt like making love to her right there and then. He had no choice but to restrain himself, however.

The lovebirds chatted contentedly as they nibbled at the snacks that Joyce had prepared and sipped fruit juice; their sentences began and ended with endearments such as 'my sweetie-pie', 'my apple-tart', 'my chocolate'.

Fanie handed his copy of *Tshwane News* to Dimakatjo, who took it reluctantly, for she was not in the mood for reading anything. Her reluctance changed to elation, however, when her wandering eyes landed on the photo of her and Fanie. She burst into joyous laughter, read the caption, and laughed again.

'It's the photo of us at Roodevallei, the night when I proposed marriage to you!' Fanie reminded her. The couple exchanged adoring smiles at the memory.

Fanie told her how the photo had come to be in the paper, through George's machinations. He then went through to the bathroom and brought out the bouquet of red carnations he had been hiding there.

'Close your eyes!' he commanded Dimakatjo, hiding the flowers behind his back.

'Why?' she wanted to know.

'Just do what I tell you . . . pretend you are one of those doormat women you were pretending to be earlier!' instructed Fanie.

Dimakatjo quivered with delicious laughter and did as he said.

Fanie shielded Dimakatjo's eyes with one hand while with the other he inserted the big bunch of carnations between her knees.

'Now open your eyes!'

Dimakatjo obeyed and roared with laughter, exceedingly tickled by the sight of the brilliant red flowers between her knees. She leapt up in order to cling onto Fanie's shoulders and bestow on him *tladi-molomo* – the flaming kiss. In her enthusiasm, she landed with her thighs wrapped around his waist, and her body pressed tightly to his. Joyce, watching from the doorway, viewed the goings-on with a wide, delighted grin on her face.

Time did not sit down on its buttocks.

Dimakatjo's people put their heads together and again chewed over the matter of whether to start the proceedings or keep waiting for Uncle Phari to arrive. Grandpa was still reminding them of *nonyana phaku-phaku* – the scurrying, anxious bird that would lay only one egg; this time, however, *sangoma*-aunt and Thomas did not support him, much to the satisfaction of Lukas and Mayibuye. As a result, it was decided that Uncle Phari or no Uncle Phari, discussions must now get underway; they would pour the news of the proceedings into his ear when he arrived.

Lukas and Mayibuye relished the thought that in their uncle's absence they would be the bosses: two bulls in the kraal. They would be the ones in charge and wielding power the way they had so much desired to. Mayibuye puffed at his crooked smoking pipe with an air of self-importance.

When Dimakatjo's people had finished engaging in the preliminary discussions, they sent *mmaditsela* Thomas as the messenger to apprise the Fouries of their decision. The Fourie's *mmaditsela*, George, responded that the news was *'like a milk-pail facing a cow's tits'*; in other words, things were in perfect order. George surprised himself considerably by speaking in this way, as though he were a wise old traditional man.

Dimakatjo's people sent Thomas back again with the instruction: 'Go and tell the Fouries that the Machabaphalas say, we are waiting, we are listening! We are like dogs waiting for a meaty bone!'

Within a few minutes the Fouries sent George with a new message: 'We are asking for a calabash to draw water for our son.'

The Machabaphalas sent back their message through faithful *mmaditsela* Thomas: 'The Machabaphalas say we have heard you, we have received the news sweeter than honey. But they say: before you can ask for a calabash you should please knock at the door, and we shall say, "Enter!" And before you speak we shall expect an amount for *pula-molomo*, which is for opening the mouth in greeting.'

The Fouries spoke through the lips of George: 'We have heard you, people of Machabaphala. We are still chewing the matter over; we are tanning the hide that you have given us.'

These preliminary discussions had begun to be time-consuming, because George and Lesetja had to translate everything into English for Oom Pieter. As soon as the amounts for *knocking at the door*, *greetings* and *pula-molomo* had been agreed upon, the Fouries tasked George with the duty of updating Fanie about the progress thus far.

30

At Aunt Mashadi's house Fanie was sitting alone with the woman he craved with every cell of his body. Love-struck Fanie lightly touched Dimakatjo's dimples, his hand moving around to her lips, chin, neck, the lobes of her ears and, finally, her chest. Dimakatjo removed Fanie's fondling hand, but the hand was irrepressible. What was wrong with son of Fourie? Had he not been warned? That a fine might be imposed on him for 'misbehaving'? Truth be told, even though he had been warned, the fire in him was just too hot to put out.

Dimakatjo continued trying to chase away Fanie's naughty hand, which had now reached her thighs.

'Stop it Fanie, stop!' she warned.

At that moment there was a '*koko!*' at the door.

Fanie called: '*Tsena!*' and George entered. Dimakatjo immediately stood up and walked out of the room without greeting him. She was not being rude to him, however, and George understood the reason for her behaviour; on this day, he wore the *mmaditsela*'s hat.

As Dimakatjo walked outside to the kitchen, George exclaimed in appreciation: '*Hai sukha madoda! Dudlu! Sponono sa Afrika kgarebe ya ditshegiša-baeng! Aowaa lesogana la ga Fourie, go nyala ga se go lahla dikgomo!*'

Loosely translated, this meant: 'Hey men, behold Afrika's beautiful one, blessed with dimples that evoke appreciative laughter from guests! Son of Fourie, to part with *lobola* for her is not to waste cattle!'

George once again surprised himself with his poetic delivery which seemed, in the celebration of the moment, to come naturally to him.

No sooner had George put his buttock down on the sofa than attentive Joyce came in to serve him and Fanie with more fruit juice. Fanie gazed at his friend expectantly, as if he were a judge who held the key to all future happiness. Son of Fourie was in a hurry to receive the news fresh from the mouth of the Fourie's *mmaditsela*. George, however, was in no hurry, slowly sipping cold and refreshing juice from a tall glass; he swirled the liquid anti-clockwise, making the ice cubes tinkle musically against the glass.

'How's the progress?' Fanie enquired into the pause.

George took another unhurried swig of juice and put his glass back onto its saucer.

Fanie was expecting to hear that perceptible progress had been made with the negotiations. *Hee-banna!* In this case he had *'beaten faeces with a hunting stick!'*

George beamed at him and rubbed his thumb and forefinger across each other to indicate money. 'You are going to pay, *boetie!*'

'But your job is to see to it that I should part with a reasonable amount!'

'No pain, no gain, *my broer!*'

'No George, I'm not here for pain.'

George simply laughed. Fanie took up his glass, shook it in order to loosen the ice-blocks, then returned it to the saucer without having taken a sip. 'Tell me George, how much *lobola* are Maki's people asking for?' he asked anxiously.

'You are in too much of a hurry, Fanie. We are still busy with introductory matters.'

'Do you mean to tell me that you have spent more than an hour dwelling on introductory matters? Are you serious, you don't yet know the amount?'

'*Ka mmago!*' ('I swear by your mother!') 'Before we can discuss the amount, we have three hurdles to jump over.'

'What hurdles?'

'Let me put it this way: there are three steps, each coupled with a corresponding amount.' Here George paused, took up his glass again, sucked at the remaining juice and tipped the ice-blocks into his mouth.

'The first amount is for knocking at the door of the in-laws: R250; greetings: R250; and *pula-molomo*: R200.'

'Tell me the amounts again!'

Fanie took out a pen and piece of paper from his jacket pocket and sat forward expectantly.

George repeated the amounts, while Fanie did some calculations.

'My *magtig*! I can't believe this! You have parted with R700 just for introductory *praatjies*! What a waste of money!'

'You don't understand, Fanie. It's the way things are done here!'

'And what is *pula-molomo* anyway?'

'Have you forgotten? *Pula-molomo* means "opening the lips of your in-laws".'

'Are you telling me that it costs 200 bucks to open the lips of the in-laws? Surely as adults they should know how to speak without being bribed?'

'Fanie, you must appreciate the culture of your in-laws, okay! And you must trust me!'

Dismayed by what he'd heard, Fanie kept quiet. It was evident that George had given the machine in Fanie's head some hard corn to grind.

'And . . . er . . . are you going to ask for a cash discount at least?'

George gazed cryptically at Fanie.

'Listen white man, you are marrying a woman . . . an African woman! You are not buying a piece of furniture! Understand?' George flashed him a smile to soften the words. 'Don't stress, *boetie*. I will see to it that everything is okay.'

George smiled again into Fanie's worried-looking face; then he stood up and briskly left the room.

Joyce entered the lounge to remove the tray with the empty glasses.

'You can relax here, Mr Fanie. Please feel at home,' she said. 'You can remove your jacket if you'd like.'

Gratefully Fanie did so, flexing his stiff shoulder muscles and rolling his neck from side to side to relieve the tension.

He asked Joyce where the toilet was. She pointed to the pit-toilet at the far corner of the yard. Fanie was on his way there when Joyce overtook him, a toilet roll in one hand and a wiping cloth in the other. She asked him to wait a few seconds as she wanted to make sure that everything was in order there.

In the tin shack that functioned as the toilet, Joyce replaced the yellow-pages telephone directory, whose sheets generally served as toilet paper, with an authentic, tenderly flowered toilet roll that she hoped would cause even a cossetted white anus to sigh for more. A short while later Fanie entered; as he rested his behind on the crudely carved but hygienically maintained toilet seat, a green-fly buzzed up from between his thighs and landed on the tin ceiling of the shack; the insect must have been surprised indeed to land its eyes on *lekgowa* in such a spot! The fly waited patiently for Fanie to finish relieving himself, confident that on this day it would be certain to get a taste of the white man's delicious *shit!*

Returning from the toilet, Fanie surveyed the surrounding houses. In front of him, opposite a cluster of huts, he saw a group of young girls busy with a game. They were barefoot and wore short, faded dresses that displayed their lean, dust covered legs. They were playing a children's game known among the girls as '*Mabele-a-sekgowa*' – 'The white man's corn'. The girls formed a circle, which they called *lešaka* – 'the cattle-pen'; they held hands and waited for the performance cue. The leader chanted:

Mabele-a-sekgowa!
('The white man's corn!')
The other girls responded:
Ga a ne ditlhoka!
('They have no chaff!')
Lead singer:
Ke re ke a tlhokola!
('I'm trying to winnow!')
Response:
Ga a ne ditlhoka!
('They have no chaff!')

The girls then galloped clockwise in the circle, still holding hands, until the lead singer again chanted:

Tlhokole-Tlhokole!
('Winnowing and winnowing!')
Response:
Wwehh!

The game ended with all the girls stamping into the centre of the circle, chanting '*Wwehh!*' and then stamping back out again.

Fanie stood and watched the game, enjoying the energetic performance. When it ended, the lone white spectator clapped his hands enthusiastically, drawing much self-conscious giggling from the gratified girls.

Fanie walked back to the house, where the ever-hospitable Joyce was waiting with more tea.

'Where are you going to stay after you get married?' she asked him.

'Maki and I have not yet decided.'

'Please don't go and stay in one of those suburbs where the racist whites live, such as Daanville,' she told him.

Fanie was amused when Joyce mentioned Daanville, the very suburb where, in his dream, he and Dimakatjo had been pelted with tomatoes and eggs by hate-filled whites.

'Why? What's wrong with Daanville?' he asked, pretending ignorance.

'It's full of racists! Those poor whites there can be dangerous. Look at this article!'

Joyce paged swiftly through a soiled, crumpled and outdated newspaper until she found the story that Aunt Mashadi had once brought to her attention. She showed Fanie a picture of a white German man and his black wife. The caption underneath read: 'Black and white love can be dangerous: Wolfgang Schule consoles his wife Sibongile, who was attacked yesterday by a group of white racist thugs.'

Joyce related the story to Fanie of the abuse that Wolfgang, Sibongile and their family had suffered at the hands of their racist neighbours, who objected to their relationship: 'These whites really made their lives a misery. They did cruel and stupid things to them, like emptying rubbish bins on their lawn and spray-painting ugly messages on the fence of their house. Their two little girls were taunted by the neighbours' kids who called them *"kaffer"* and *"hotnot"*.'

She went on to recount how one day, while Sibongile was out shopping at the local supermarket with her children, a group of six white men followed her back to her car. They were armed with *sjamboks*, and as she was trying to unlock her car door, with her arms full of parcels, one of the men threatened her, shouting at her: '*Hei-wena kaffer-bitch, voetsak!*' while another spat at her.

'The poor woman was terrified!' Joyce exclaimed. 'The little girls were crying and clinging to their mother's legs. As the man went for her with the *sjambok*, Sibongile screamed and, fortunately, some white shoppers came to help her. She had to be escorted by the police back to her house . . . '

As Joyce finished her story, Fanie saw out of the corner of his eye a dreadlocked head appearing through the doorway, followed by a very large body, attired in traditional *sangoma* outfit. It was *sangoma*-aunt, come to satisfy her curiosity about the new son-in-law.

'Hallo *mamma, dumela!*'

Fanie greeted the herbalist somewhat nervously, for she made an intimidating sight. Her obese torso was squeezed into a sleeveless vest that seemed in danger of bursting apart under pressure of the huge stomach and breasts that strained its seams. Her hair was woven into thin dreads, stained with dark-red ochre and threaded with small black and white beads. She did not respond to Fanie's greeting, but turned her head away and stepped outside again, disappearing towards the kitchen.

She was soon back again, standing in the doorway waving a flywhisk that resembled the one given to Fanie by Anna-Marie.

Smiling gently, *sangoma*-aunt took a few steps towards Fanie, who retreated nervously. The healer suddenly emitted an alarming growling sound. Fanie retreated further, his arms outstretched defensively to ward her off. Astonished, Joyce watched the odd display.

'Don't worry *baas* Fanie . . . *askuus tog* . . . Mr Fourie . . . I mean . . . Fanie she won't hurt you,' Joyce assured him. 'She's just welcoming you in the *sangoma* style.'

Joyce gently smacked the shoulder of *sangoma*-aunt, who was now beaming at Fanie.

'*Amadlozi ayathokoza!*' she pronounced, waving her oxtail implement at Fanie.

'What is she saying?' asked Fanie.

'She says that the ancestors are rejoicing.'

Joyce took *sangoma*-aunt by the hand and led her firmly from the lounge, leaving Fanie to stare after them thoughtfully. *Sangoma*-aunt's antics had reminded him about *Mafuth'ebhubesi*, the special ointment meant to fortify him against the machinations of witches and wizards and help him to stand his ground with dignity and confidence against all terrors; it struck him that he had just missed a golden opportunity to test out the effectiveness of this magical remedy that George had boasted about!

31

At Fanie's parents' home, Anna-Marie and Selina were putting the finishing touches to their *lobola*-day outfits, ready to head off on their journey to Dimakatjo's place to add their presence to the joy of Fanie's great occasion.

They were on the point of departure when Louise summoned her daughter, calling to her from the bedroom. Anna-Marie went in reluctantly, steeling herself for a fight, expecting the vitriol that usually came pouring from her mother's lips whenever the subject of Fanie's detested love relationship was broached. It struck her that Louise had been strangely quiet about Fanie's wedding of late. Anna-Marie concluded that she was working herself up for a final showdown, and that she would try to order her daughter and Selina not to attend.

Entering the bedroom, she was baffled to find her mother dressed up in her best finery, her large frame resplendent in a smart two-piece suit. On her head was a wide-brimmed hat with a flower on it, and she had even put on a string of pearls.

'I am coming with you, Mariekie,' she said. 'Please ask Selina to put my bag in the car.'

Anna-Marie was too astonished to do anything but nod. She picked up her mother's overnight bag from the bed and then, wordlessly, stooped to hug her warmly. Louise's eyes filled with tears. Her decision to attend Fanie's *lobola* day at the place of his bride in what was, to her, 'darkest Afrika' had not been an easy one for her to come to.

After a night of little sleep, spent wrestling with her conscience, Louise had woken at dawn with the conviction that she must attend Fanie's *lobola*; this was what her God required from her. She remembered the words that she had said to the therapist on her last consultation. If she didn't want to lose her son, she would have to make overtures. She would have to atone fully for her earlier opposition and show that she was willing to embrace her black daughter-in-law into the family fold. Besides, she was full of curiosity to meet this 'Maki' who had so bowled her son over and captured his heart.

Anna-Marie went to tell Selina of the new developments, drawing from her amazed headshakes and exclamations of: '*Modimo o phala baloi!*' Selina then handed Anna-Marie a letter that she had found in the postbox, with the news that she had earlier seen Gerda skulking around outside the house. The envelope was addressed to Fanie, but Anna-Marie decided to open it on her brother's behalf, for she wanted to make sure that it contained no message of ill-will that might upset him.

Inside, was a congratulations card written in Afrikaans, wishing Fanie connubial bliss and blessings; it was simply signed, 'Gerda'.

Anna-Marie smiled in relief, touched by Gerda's gesture and wondering what Fanie's response would be when he saw it. She was glad for everyone's sake that Gerda had decided to let bygones be bygones and find it in her heart to wish the happy couple well.

A short while later, with Anna-Marie at the wheel, the family's old but still efficient Ford Cortina was weaving through the Saturday traffic towards the Polokwane highway. A joyful Selina sat in the back, resplendent in a blue pin-striped suit that was one of Louise's hand-me-downs, a stylish wig on her head and wedding songs bursting from her throat; while in the passenger seat sat a silent Louise, her pensive expression hard to read.

Time did not sit down on its buttocks. The wristwatches of Ga-Mabitsela showed a quarter to two; and still Uncle Phari had yet to tread the soil of the Machabaphala homestead.

The *lobola* negotiations plodded forward. At Mayibuye and Lukas's insistence, Dimakatjo's people raised two further issues that should be chewed by the two families. When Thomas, the Machabaphala's *mmaditsela*, re-entered the Fouries's room, the Fouries were expecting that the discussions would now head swiftly towards the chopping-axe for a speedy execution. They were hoping to be informed about the final *lobola* amount that they should part with; they could not know that the journey was still to be a long one, and that the path would climb and wind and zigzag over many rocky hills before it reached its point of completion.

For the next twenty minutes Thomas, George and Lesetja were locked in serious discussion; the tone and volume of their voices and their facial expressions were all that Uncle Pieter had to go on, since he could not understand Sepedi. But even before George translated for him, the old man knew that the Fouries had been given a tough tendon to chew. What George had to say about the fresh delays in the proceedings did not go down well with Uncle Pieter. Truth to tell, he was becoming more than a little irked by the unreasonableness and procrastinating tactics of the other side. He wanted to try and force the issue; but George persuaded him that the delays were part of the proceedings and that the culture of Dimakatjo's people should be respected.

The Fouries agreed that Fanie should again be updated on the developments.

Thoughtfully George entered the lounge where Fanie was once more seated alone, waiting anxiously for news. Even though Fanie's nose could not smell the trouble ahead, he had a gut feeling that there might be some additional cultural 'etceteras' that had cost implications; he had, of course, guessed right!

'Is everything okay, *mokgonyana-baas?*' George teased Fanie, and both men laughed because it was the first time that George had addressed him in this fashion. Their laughter released some of the tension.

'Let's just say, this *lobola* is an 'exciting' cultural experience!'

George nodded with a reassuring smile.

'How far are the discussions now?' Fanie wanted to know.

'They are progressing well. But there is still a lot of work to be done.'

'A lot of work to be done? You mean you still don't know the amount of *lobola*?'

'Don't be in a hurry,' chided George. 'That's not the way things are done here. Relax and enjoy this "exciting cultural experience"!'

'But what are you discussing for such a long time?'

George paused, then said: 'The people here don't rush things; they don't just do things *chwap-chwap*; they believe in the saying: *"Better to walk than run and fall down on your belly and be laughed at."*' He helped himself to a biscuit from Fanie's tea tray. 'There are two issues that have been raised by Maki's people.'

'Tell me! I am at your mercy. My fate is in your hands,' said Fanie with heavy irony.

George smiled at him serenely.

'What are the issues now, George? And how much do THEY want from me?'

'Relax Fanie, relax!' George touched Fanie's hand. 'It's the culture, and we cannot wish it away. When my uncle was parting with *lobola* – he married a Swazi woman – his people were left at the gate for two hours before someone walked up to them and said: "What are you looking for?" They were not being rude; it was their culture.'

George was pleased with himself for thinking of that example; it seemed that he had convinced Fanie.

'So what is the first issue?'

'It's about a calabash. Asking for a calabash. Do you still remember what "calabash" stands for?'

'Yes! A calabash is a symbol for a wife.'

'Bright white boy! Excellent! A wife is a calabash to carry water for her husband. To slake the husband's thirst.'

'And how much do they want for this?'

'R300.'

'R300!'

George nodded.

'That's R300 plus R700 . . . R1 000 just on introductory issues?'

'Yes, *sebara*!'

Fanie sighed resignedly. He recalled what his mother had once said to him: '*My boy, you are going to sell your car, your flat and the cockroaches to pay lobola. These people are making a business out of lobola!*'

'You promised me that you would see to it that everything is "okay as a milk-pail facing a cow's tits,"' Fanie reminded George reproachfully.

'I'm trying, Fanie! Things are presently going uphill. All I can say to you is, take it easy! We shall arrive at the top of the hill presently. We *will* get there!' George patted Fanie's shoulder soothingly. 'This is a trial, but I say be strong, be patient; you are going to win in the end. Believe me!'

Fanie remained quiet. He knew there was little he could do. Although the negotiation process seemed beset by elaborate cultural landmines, he could not change his mind at this stage. His mind, body and soul screamed to have Dimakatjo as his wife, his life's treasure. Nor could he fire George as his *mmaditsela*; for although he, son of Fourie, had a God-given mouth with which to eat and speak, he could not speak for himself regarding *lobola*. It did not matter whether George messed up or conducted things well, Fanie's response had to be the same – a spirited 'Hallelujah!' George was his only hope at this stage, the one person who could roll back the sleeves of his shirt and dislodge the wheel of the wagon out of the sticky mud.

'And the last issue is . . . ?' Fanie enquired.

George smiled and took his time to answer, deliberately keeping Fanie in suspense.

'This one is a very important issue . . . '

'What? Tell me!'

'It concerns the knife, the pocket-knife that I told you to buy. They need it to slaughter the son-in-law's sheep. Where is that knife?'

'It must be in one of my pockets.'

'Give it to me!'

Fanie hunted through the pockets of his trousers, and then through the pockets of his jacket; but his search did not produce the knife. He searched a second time, more frantically, but with the same result.

'*You* must have it, George,' he said at last, 'it must be in one of your pockets!'

'Why would it be in my pocket?'

'Because it's not in mine. I must have given it to you!'

'When?'

'Didn't I hand it to you when we left my flat?'

'You are crazy, man!'

'Check! Just in case . . . !'

George did so, while Fanie turned his own pockets inside out for the third time; the knife said: *Where have you put me?*

'Please check your pockets again,' commanded a despairing Fanie.

'No! I don't have it, Fanie! Let's look where you were sitting.'

Fanie and George searched the sofa, between the cushions and on the floor around it, but still the knife could not be found. They even shifted the sofa and looked underneath it. The knife asked again: *Where have you put me?*

'Check in your shoes,' ordered George. 'And your underpants!'

'Don't be crazy, George . . . !'

'Listen, it's your *fokken* responsibility! Check everything again,' barked George in extreme irritation.

'George . . . ' Fanie began heatedly; then: 'Wait –' he said. He looked at George with wide, dismayed eyes.

'Now I remember! The knife is . . . in my cream-white suit!'

'Your . . . you *blerry* fool!' swore George.

'I'm not your fool, George!'

'Produce the knife then, wiseman!'

'It's your fault! You are to blame!'

'Me!'

'Yes! You're the one who persuaded me to change out of my cream-white suit! You said it was too much for the day of *lobola*! Didn't you say that?'

'Yes, I said that. But why didn't *you* remember to check . . . ?'

'Because I was full of nerves, okay! I was relying on *you* to remind me of things . . . !' interrupted Fanie angrily.

'And where is *Mafuth'ebhubesi*? Also in the cream-white suit?'

They looked at each other in dismay; for George was right, of course. *Mafuth'ebhubesi* was sitting snugly in the jacket pocket of Fanie's cream-white suit.

'That's why things are going haywire!' George said. 'No wonder the *lobola* negotiations are not running smoothly! You have left your protection behind.'

Joyce, listening to this loud altercation from the kitchen, now entered the lounge. Her appearance brought both men to their senses. Fanie's smarting ego badly wanted the last word. But, fortunately, sense prevailed as both he and George realised there was no point in trying to score points off each other over what had happened; as the villagers would say, what had been lost had gone irretrievably into an unfathomable hole, where the longest stick could not reach.

'Sis Joyce,' pleaded George, 'can you please help? We are in trouble! We do not have a pocket-knife to slaughter the son-in-law's sheep with. They are going to fine us!'

'Please Joyce, help us!' Fanie added his appeal to George's.

'Okay, don't let worry make you age before your time!' Joyce said with an encouraging smile. 'I'm sure I have seen an old pocket-knife lying somewhere in the kitchen drawers. I will go and look.'

'We will appreciate it, sis Joyce!' George responded gratefully.

'If I remember right, it has a sharp edge and is still in good condition.'

'Thank you!' said George and Fanie simultaneously.

Joyce asked George to accompany her and they walked out together to the kitchen.

Standing alone at the window, trying to recover his spirits, Fanie watched the children playing their games outside. The same group of girls that he had seen earlier performing '*Mabele-a-sekgowa*' had now been joined by some of the boys. They were enacting a singing game that involved a 'groom' and 'bride', who was crying loudly and appeared to be receiving parting words of advice from her 'parents'. Fanie could clearly hear his and Dimakatjo's names being called, woven into the children's wedding song. It would have been highly amusing under other circumstances, but at this moment he was too low in spirits to be able to summon up a smile.

Suddenly, he felt a tender touch on his elbow. Turning, Fanie was met by Dimakatjo's smile. He could not find it in himself to smile back at her.

'How is it going?' she asked him.

'Tough!'

'Tough? Why?'

'Because we never seem to get anywhere,' he said harshly. 'Why do your people keep on adding all sorts of amounts?'

'I'm sorry, I can't discuss those things with you, Fanie. For obvious reasons. I'm sure you understand why.'

'No, I don't understand! All I understand is that I'm being treated like a cow that can be milked for everything it's got!' said Fanie in frustration.

Tears came into Dimakatjo's eyes at his harsh tone. Fanie was instantly contrite.

'I'm sorry, *my skattebol!*' he said, enfolding her into his arms. 'It's not you I'm angry with. I just find it frustrating being so much in the dark. I don't like being taken advantage of.'

'You're not being taken advantage of. George is there to see that you are treated fairly. I know it's difficult Fanie, but please try not to get worked up about it!'

The lovers rested their cheeks against each other's shoulders, gathering strength from their togetherness, as always.

'Okay my sweetie-pie, okay!' said Fanie. 'I will try to see this as an "exciting cultural experience"! As long as we can be together in the end, I will be content.'

32

Restless time did not sit down on its buttocks. The two families continued to chew over what had brought them together. A question issued from the Fourie people's lips: 'When you say "*kgomo kgomo*" – "cow cow" – what is the amount in banknotes? These days very few people who part with *lobola* do so with horned bulls and cows that graze and cry *moo-moo*!'

After due consultation the Machabaphalas replied that a cow in banknotes would be R200.

'How many cows will you want from us?' enquired the Fouries.

Bakone clanspeople once more put their heads together until they were all satisfied.

'You shall wash our hands with only twenty head of cattle,' was the message that landed in the ears of the Fouries, who were impressed that so much progress was suddenly made.

The Fouries counted out twenty R200 banknotes that totalled R4 000. George was all smiles as he confidently handed a bulging white envelope to Dimakatjo's people. The Machabaphalas received the money with their hearts as white as the envelope containing it. Fanie's uncle asked for a receipt, and Dimakatjo's people replied that they would provide one as requested. For fines, they added, a separate statement would be prepared. It was further stressed that the matter would be sealed by the girl's Uncle Phari, who had not yet arrived. The following statement, drafted and handwritten by Thomas, was then read before Dimakatjo's people:

The Machabaphalas have received from the Fouries twenty head of cattle that do not graze nor cry moo-moo! as lobola for their daughter, Dimakatjo Mothepana Evelina. The following people saw mmaditsela when he brought the R4 000 from the Fouries:

1............................ 1............................
2............................ 2............................
3............................ 3............................

Three witnesses, Grandpa, *sangoma*-aunt and Lukas signed in the left-hand column. *Sangoma*-aunt was advised to put a cross since she could not write. On the Fouries's side George, Uncle Pieter and Lesetja signed in the right-hand column. George suggested that they should add the following line at the bottom:

Signed at Ga-Mabitsela village on the 29th day of November.

This important statement, that constituted, in effect, a marriage certificate, was written on a page torn from Sefako's Grade 4 exercise book. The quality of the paper and writing was not something to fuss about. What mattered was the idea and intention of the well-meaning people behind it. The same message then had to be duplicated on another page of exercise book, as the Fouries had requested a receipt. The laborious process on the part of Dimakatjo's people repeated itself; Grandpa's shaking hand signed in a mixture of cursive, small print and capital letters, while *sangoma*-aunt again pressed the pen hard to the paper, almost piercing right through it as she carefully drew a cross in place of a signature.

Thomas was about to take the 'receipt' copy to the Fouries, when a new thought entered Grandpa's head; he waved his hand at Thomas imperiously: 'Wait! Your uncle,' Grandpa fixed his gaze on Lukas, 'must see that piece of paper before we hand it to the boy's *mmaditsela*. We cannot complete everything in the absence of children's uncle. Aowaa! Let him come with an axe to chop the head of the matter to death.'

The Fouries were informed that the statement of *lobola* would be kept by the Machabaphala people until the children's uncle had seen it. It was emphasised that this did not in any way mean that the uncle could reverse the process thus far agreed on, or veto the decisions; it was simply a matter of respecting the principle of consultation, so that no one should subsequently nurse a bitter black heart and say: '*Hee-hee kae-kae mafaseng,*' (Loosely, this meant, 'In one way or another') 'my niece was married without my consultation.' Grandpa carefully folded the two identical statements of *lobola* and stored them safely in the inner pocket of his jacket.

Acting on Lesetja's suggestion, the Fouries conferred and sent their *mmaditsela* with the following request: 'For hours we have stretched our lips and scratched our heads. Where is the person who caused all this trouble? We would like to see her! Yes, we have already parted with the cattle that do not graze nor cry *moo-moo!* But we don't want to buy a pig in a bag; we don't want to think that we have a piglet, only to find a puppy when our bridegroom opens the bag at home.'

The Machabaphalas laughed when they received this message, laden with good humour. Since Thomas was now taking a well-earned rest, the Machabaphalas sent Mayibuye to go and summon Dimakatjo.

Dimakatjo's pink shimmer lipstick accentuated her sensuous 'please-kiss-me' lips; her eyes, framed by flattering purple eyeshadow and mascara-enhanced eyelashes, looked dreamy and romantic, and her pupils, large and mysterious.

Swept away as always by his desire for her, Fanie enfolded the flower of his heart in his yearning arms and kissed her voraciously. It was meant to be a short kiss but, inevitably, it deepened and prolonged itself. At that moment, Mayibuye entered, unnoticed by the lovers, who were thoroughly engrossed in the pleasure of their mutually hungry lips.

They broke apart hurriedly as their eyes belatedly registered Mayibuye's presence. Lipstick fresh on his lips, Fanie was like a thief caught scarlet-handed.

'*Mokgonyana!*' Mayibuye waved an admonishing finger at Fanie. '*Pasop!* You are smelling a fine!'

'*Eina! Ag-nee-wat!*' exclaimed Fanie.

Mayibuye's gaze shifted to Dimakatjo.

'Dimakatjo, let's go. Your in-laws would like to see you.'

Dimakatjo stood up and strutted obediantly towards the door. Returning to her own house she entered her bedroom, where Aunt Mashadi was waiting to put the final touches to her appearance. Mayibuye, meanwhile, hurried back to the negotiating room. There, he made a big issue of the fact that he had found *mokgonyana* kissing Dimakatjo, suggesting that for this a fine should be imposed. Predictably, Lukas supported the motion.

Lukas added that Fanie should also be fined for producing an old, rather than a brand-new pocket-knife. The two cousins and comrades-of-the-bottle were patently determined to extract more money out of *mokgonyana*. This irked Grandpa, who grabbed his walking-stick and stamped the floor with it, emphasising that, since he was the one who should speak, Lukas and Mayibuye were out of order. *Sangoma*-aunt and Thomas also reacted angrily to Lukas and Mayibuye's unreasonable demands. Fortunately for Fanie, the two troublemakers lost that round.

In the course of the negotiations, the troublesome pair Lukas and Mayibuye had, on more than one occasion, excused themselves from the session on the pretext of needing to use the pit-toilet. This fooled no one, since they always coincidentally needed to go at the same time. Their real mission was to take a few quick gulps of whiskey or brandy from the half-jack bottles they had concealed behind the marquee.

Earlier that morning Lukas and Mayibuye had each demolished for breakfast a mountain of stiff *mabele*-corn porridge with delicious, well-boiled tripe. They had therefore 'prepared a strong foundation' – as the two seasoned elbow-raisers liked to put it – for the imbibing to come. Since they had been fortuitously charged with the safe-keeping and dispensing of alcoholic beverages, they had easy access to 'the white man's liquor', poetically described by villagers as '*matutu-a-terebe*' – 'milk extracted from the tits of grapevines'.

This fact provided a lifeline for relatives suffering from throats dry as stone. Whenever Lukas and Mayibuye went outside on the pretext of needing to visit the toilet, one or another thirsty relative, desiring to 'smell like a man', would hail them and ask for a double or triple tot of potent *matutu-a-terebe*.

Among the lucky ones who were privileged to receive the blessing of such libation was Geelbooi, one of the umpteen cousins of Dimakatjo and Lukas. He was easy to spot among the crowd, for he wore a brown chequered jacket and a pair of narrow-legged, tight-fitting trousers of the kind preferred by the *tsotsi*-gangsters of Alexandra township in the 1950s. On his feet were gleaming two-tone, narrow-toed shoes, that regularly received the attentions of an industrious shoe-shine boy; and topping his head was a brown hat sporting a green peacock's feather, while his eyes were protected by dark 'mirror' sunglasses. No one could doubt that Geelbooi was, from head to toe, a first-class dandy.

Geelbooi had armed himself with a tot bottle of brandy that was wrapped in newspaper and hidden in the inner pocket of his jacket. From this, he took several swallows; before long, this little fountain of ecstasy had run dry; so Geelbooi went to plead with Lukas to give him a second ration of *matutu* because, as he said, 'one spear is not enough to finish a warrior'.

Lukas obliged; the *matutu* was duly consumed and raced straight from Geelbooi's stomach to his head. His mouth and tongue became looser and his speech spiced with a concoction of high-sounding English phrases. The villagers took admiring notice of him who emitted through his mouth and nose the fascinating sounds of what they termed the 'King's language' – also known as '*Senkhwethe-nkhwethe*' because of the way it sounded to the unschooled ear. It didn't matter to them that Geelbooi's English was a hotch-potch of muddled tenses, mixed up English and Afrikaans phrases and generally crucified grammar rules; to the mostly illiterate villagers, even this fractured form sounded as impressive as Shakespeare.

Geelbooi had no competition among his audience; he was, in fact, rapidly growing bored with speaking to those who did not understand a word of what he was saying – people who had never gone very far with their 'Bantu Education' before 'jumping out through the schoolroom window'. He wanted more sophisticated company, a worthy companion who would be able to speak *ordentlike* – 'genuine' – *Senkhwethe-nkhwethe* with him. Enquiring as to the whereabouts of son-in-law of Bakone, Geelbooi was told that *mokgonyana* was waiting at Aunt Mashadi's house.

He made up his mind that it was time to pay a visit to *lekgowa la* Dimakatjo.

33

Thoroughly inebriated by this stage, Geelbooi staggered towards Aunt Mashadi's house singing the following wedding song:

Kajeno ke mokete
Kajeno ke mokete
Kajeno ke mokete
mokete wa lenyalo!

(Today it's a feast
a feast of a wedding!)

Fanie wee!
O a nyala . . .
Fanie wee!

(Fanie is getting married!
He is parting with *lobola* . . .)

This was the same song that Fanie had heard the choir members practising on the day he had brought Dimakatjo home. When he heard his name being sung with such loud exuberance, he rose to his feet to peer out of the window for a glimpse of the singer. Fanie saw Geelbooi walking with drunken gait towards the kitchen, the song still boiling from his mouth:

Kajeno ke mokete
Kajeno ke mokete
Kajeno . . . '

Geelbooi hiccuped loudly and entered the kitchen without knocking. He found Joyce packing the crockery into a drying rack and greeted her with exaggerated respect, applauding twice and bending his knees in the way of villagers, especially children, when they greeted adults and high-ranking people.

Joyce was much amused by the drunk man in her kitchen who was trying very hard to behave as if his tongue had not touched a drop of *matutu*. Addressing Joyce in his version of the 'King's language', Geelbooi told her that he wanted to meet *mokgonyana*.

Laughing, Joyce assured him that he had come at the right time to keep company with *mokgonyana-baas*, for it had been a while since Dimakatjo's departure and Fanie had been left sitting by himself.

She took Geelbooi through to the lounge and introduced him to Fanie, who stood up with a smile; the two men clasped hands and shook enthusiastically.

'So how's life in Pretoria, *basie*?' Geelbooi asked him.

'Please don't call me *baas*! Just call me Fanie,' he protested mildly.

'It's okay, *mokgonyana* Fanie ... by the way, what's your surname?'

'Fourie.'

'Oh, Mr Fourie!'

Fanie nodded and smiled: 'Life is fine in Pretoria.'

'*Moja, moja!*' ('It's okay, it's okay!') Geelbooi's tongue slipped back into *tsotsi-taal*, the patois of gangsters, smart alecs, shebeen patrons, socialites and hangers-on.

The two men sized each other up, each, for his own reasons gratified to set eyes on the other. Glad to have someone new to talk to and pass the time with, Fanie told Geelbooi a little about his life and his experiences at work at Jacaranda Welding Company. He mentioned that he got on well with his black colleagues and how, as a result, when he first came to the job, other whites there had derogatorily referred to him as '*kafferboetie*'. Attentive, Geelbooi nodded, repeating, '*Shem, shem!*' ('Shame, shame!') in the manner of one who was genuinely sympathetic. His thoughts, however, were busy with a very different refrain: *Yes, they got you right, those whites! You have reaped from the field of apartheid; now you still want to reap again by taking our women away!*

Geelbooi considered Fanie to be someone who had benefited greatly from the past and who, as a result, owed him something; he schemed in his heart how he might take advantage of the fact that gullible Fanie was in the midst of an alien culture.

'Fanie, have you got a cigarette for me?' asked Geelbooi.

'No. I don't smoke any more.'

'Okay. Liquor? Do you have any . . . ?'

'No.'

'You are just a reverend! But that's okay! You, honourable men . . . ' Geelbooi pressed his palms together, pointing them vertically upwards as if in prayer, ' . . . will help us drunks!'

Fanie was amused by this. Although he had cut down considerably on his drinking, thanks to Dimakatjo's influence, he by no means considered himself a teetotaller.

Geelbooi took out a half-smoked cigarette, the last from his pack, lit it and puffed with satisfaction; he sized Fanie up, inspecting him from his shoes to his shirt.

'Where's your jacket?' asked Geelbooi suddenly.

Fanie pointed to where his jacket was neatly folded over the armrest of the sofa opposite. Fanie knew from George's advice in the past that the wearing of a jacket was culturally correct among Africans during special occasions. But he had taken it off at Joyce's bidding when, being a good hostess, she had told Fanie to relax and be 'completely at home'.

'Put it on!' commanded Geelbooi, crushing his smouldering cigarette butt into the ashtray. Fanie hesitated, checking Geelbooi's face to see if he was serious or simply pulling Fanie's leg.

'Haven't they told you that a son-in-law must put on a jacket?'

'Joyce said I can remove my jacket and feel at home!'

'Don't listen to women! Do you want a fine to be imposed on you?' warned Geelbooi.

Fanie hastily grabbed his jacket and put it on.

'A man about to meet his mother-in-law must appear dignified and not look like a herdboy of goats!'

Geelbooi continued to mash the now smokeless butt into the ashtray, like someone crushing the head of a lifeless snake.

'I'm not fighting with you, *mokgonyana*; it's our culture!' he said, suddenly flashing a disarming smile.

Again his critical gaze inspected Fanie. This time, his eye was attracted by Fanie's black and shining crocodile-leather shoes.

'You have nice shoes,' Geelbooi said, pointing to them.

'Thank you.'

'Remove your shoes!'

'Why?'

'Haven't they told you?'

Fanie shook his head.

Geelbooi saw that suspicious Fanie was resisting doing as he was told.

'In the Bible, God told Moses: "Remove your shoes . . . !" People take me for a drunk but I know the Holy Book, *nna*!' ('myself!') Geelbooi hiccuped, belched and quickly cupped his hand over his mouth. Reluctantly Fanie removed his shoes and his socks as well.

'I'm not fighting with you! It's our culture! How can I fight with someone who came to add cattle to my cow-shed?' Geelbooi beamed.

Looking out through the window, he spotted Fanie's white BMW parked under the *morula* tree. Geelbooi's drunk heart swelled with yearning envy. How he wished he could drive that car! He wished Fanie would send him somewhere, so that he could enjoy the status of a BMW driver. All the eyes of the village would be on him and the children would be running behind the car, cheering: 'BM! BM!'

'You have a nice BM!'

'Thank you.'

Fanie wondered what the catch would be. He hoped Geelbooi would not say: 'Give me your car keys!' This time, he would be ready with an answer: 'Go to hell, man!'

Joyce entered with the special tray loaded with a beer mug and bottle of cold beer for Geelbooi, and half a jug of orange juice and a clean glass for Fanie; she set the tray down in front of them on the coffee table.

'Here is a bit of water,' said the genial hostess, modestly understating the offering in the customary way, before walking out of the lounge. Though she did not comment, Joyce couldn't help but notice that Fanie had put on his jacket again and was without shoes.

The cold juice and beer helped to diffuse the subtle tension between the two men. Geelbooi remarked that the gap between people in urban and rural areas was becoming narrower, citing refrigerated beer as an example. He laughed for no good reason, showing off his tobacco-ravaged teeth. Fanie began to warm to Geelbooi; he felt he could not afford to shout: 'Go to hell, man!' for it would not be a nice thing to be rude to one of Dimakatjo's people.

'*Kokoo!*' called a new voice from outside.

The voice was familiar to Geelbooi. It belonged to Uncle Sepanere, one of Dimakatjo's umpteen uncles, who visited once or twice a year, usually when there was a funeral. He walked into the lounge, smartly dressed in jacket and tie, with his trademark Stetson hat in his hand. It was evident that he, like Geelbooi, had been partaking of 'something manly' to cheer him and stir his spirits to a higher level of elation.

Sepanere was close to 70 years old and his hair was beginning to show patches of white. He took a seat on the sofa next to Fanie and made himself comfortable. As a child, Sepanere had been raised on a farm owned by a white Afrikaans farmer who named him Sepanere, meaning 'Spanner', because he often served as a 'spanner boy' when the *oubaas* and *kleinbaas* were busy repairing a tractor or water-pump. Afrikaans words were brewing in Uncle Sepanere's mouth, ready to be spewed out to impress the son-in-law of Bakone, whom he had so much desired to see with his own two eyes. He was deeply appreciative of the fact that his niece had, this day, made them blood relatives of the *boere*.

'Malome Sepanere, meet our son-in-law, Mr . . . '

'Fourie!' Fanie completed.

Fanie and Uncle Sepanere shook hands while Geelbooi watched, his eyes shining. Their hostess brought in an empty drinking glass and Geelbooi filled it with beer until froth crowned it, then handed it to the newcomer. Uncle Sepanere leaned back on the sofa and inspected Fanie from head to toe as Geelbooi had done. His gaze halted curiously at Fanie's bare feet.

'*Hoekom is my baas kaalvoet?*' ('Why is my master barefoot?') he enquired, addressing the question to Geelbooi.

'*Jou baas* enjoys fresh air!' retorted Geelbooi shamelessly.

Geelbooi and Uncle Sepanere laughed long and loudly at this. Fanie, however, did not enjoy being the object of their mirth.

'Please stop calling me *baas*!' he protested, as the laughter of the two black men roared on.

Still speaking in Afrikaans, Uncle Sepanere asked Fanie to forgive them. He explained that despite the political changes in the country, many blacks, especially in these parts, still continued to address whites as '*baas*'.

'*Ja*, I'm one of these people,' confessed Geelbooi. 'When I need a favour from a white man in authority . . . let's say if a traffic officer is about to write me a ticket, I won't hesitate to take off my hat and compress it between my hands, like so, saying: "*Asseblief my basie, asseblief!*"'

Joyce glided in with a fresh trayload of two more cold beers for Uncle Sepanere and Geelbooi and a refill of fruit juice for Fanie. Uncle Sepanere told Fanie to put his shoes back on.

'Now who's telling me the truth? Is it you?' Fanie stabbed his finger at Geelbooi, 'or you, Uncle Sepanere?'

'Let us respect the white hair of Uncle Sepanere,' said Geelbooi diplomatically, with a mischievous twinkle in his eye.

Resignedly Fanie put his shoes back on, removed his jacket again and tried to look relaxed.

34

Meanwhile, in Dimakatjo's bedroom, Aunt Mashadi had executed the finishing touches to the stunning hairstyle of the Pearl of Bakone. She then sprayed it generously with a choice styling product to hold the shape and add a glint of glamour to the whole effect. She also touched up Dimakatjo's make-up. Daughter of Bakone received confirmation from the mirror in front of her that she did, indeed, look like an undisputed African queen.

Dimakatjo had been much heartened by her summons to the relatives' room 30 minutes earlier. Aunt Mashadi's words that: 'Your in-laws would like to see you. They say they don't want to buy a pig in a sack,' had filled her with hopeful expectation. She was certain that the climactic moment could not be far away now; that any ill intentions on the part of witches had been dealt a death-blow, and that she was soon to see the hour of her ultimate joy as an African woman come to pass.

The Fourie and Machabaphala people waited patiently in the lounge for the object of interest to make her appearance. When Mashadi was completely satisfied that her skilful fingers had done their work, she wrapped Dimakatjo in a colourful blanket that covered her completely. Leading her charge by the hand, Aunt Mashadi entered the lounge, where members of the two families sat in a half-moon circle, the men on the sofas and chairs and the womenfolk seated on mats on the floor. Aunt Mashadi and Dimakatjo squatted down on their haunches and leaned forward attentively.

Aunt Mashadi applauded respectfully twice, her eyes on Fanie's Uncle Pieter. George stood up quickly and fished a R50 note from his wallet; he strutted enthusiastically towards Dimakatjo and Aunt Mashadi, waving the R50 note above his head to signal his interest.

Bending down, he beat the floor in front of Aunt Mashadi with the banknote, then returned buoyantly to his seat, walking as if his heels were fitted with springs.

Aunt Mashadi retrieved the banknote and removed the blanket from Dimakatjo's head, so that members of the two families could see 'what was contained in the bag'.

Dimakatjo felt bashful as several pairs of eyes inspected her minutely, as if she were a cow being exhibited to buyers at an auction. Presently, Aunt Mashadi stood up and gestured towards daughter-in-law of the *boere*, who rose demurely to her feet, took off the blanket and handed it to Aunt Mashadi. She then took a few steps forward, halted, and swung her body to left and right, giving all in the room the chance to fix their eyes on the object of beauty in front of them.

Aunt Mashadi, however, was not satisfied: '*Hoh*, Maki, *hoh!*' she protested, 'This is not good enough! Come baby, show them that our girl is not an old crock suffering from *rumatiki*! *Aowaa!*'

Aunt Mashadi snapped her fingers and Dimakatjo obediently swayed forward across the room. In the style of a well-rehearsed fashion model, she pivoted gracefully to left and right, almost losing her balance at one point but then managing to regain it.

'*Chisa* Maki, *chisa wena!*' ('Turn up the heat!') cheered Aunt Mashadi shrilly. 'Show them that you are still roadworthy! You are not second-hand but brand new from the box! Come on my baby!' she encouraged.

Dimakatjo smiled and strutted forward again on her imaginary catwalk, this time more confidently. She spun effortlessly around on her left foot and stood poised, with her right foot balanced on the ball and her hands on her waist in coquettish model pose. There was enthusiastic applause and even a few admiring wolf whistles. Elated, George leapt up and energetically pranced towards Dimakatjo, waving another R50 note; he knelt close to her feet and dropped the note reverently – a gesture that drew more applause and wolf whistles.

'Now you have seen for yourselves!' pronounced Aunt Mashadi excitedly.

This time it was Thomas who stood up and pranced towards Dimakatjo. Halting jerkily, he mock-chopped with an imaginary axe, then stopped abruptly, laid his palm against his cheek, and launched into an impromptu praise-poem:

Mmalo! If eyes could eat they would be full to bursting!
Behold the flower of Bakone
Captivator of eyes of the boere!
Behold the one whom sunrays fear to hurt
The one with dimples –
Sources of laughter for guests
Captivator of a white heart
Extractor of tears of mmisisi!
Mmulu! People of Fourie,
You have not parted with cattle in vain!

Joyce asked Fanie to give Geelbooi his car keys so that he could quickly drive to the shop and buy her a packet of chocolate pudding. Fanie's immediate reaction was to say 'no'; but Geelbooi's beaming face and Joyce's assurances that he was a reliable driver (even though by this time drunk as a skunk) combined to overpower his scruples. Much against his better judgement, he handed over the keys. Whatever his private reservations, he knew that he couldn't say no; for he understood that he was being tested, and that this was in some way a challenge, a trial of trust and kinship.

Watching his BMW ease carefully out through the gate, a beaming Geelbooi behind the wheel, Fanie said a private prayer for its safe return. Fortunately, Geelbooi was in no hurry. He drove the short distance to the shop at a slow crawl, hooting genially at everyone along the way and stopping to tell all and sundry in the village that the car was his, that he had bought it thanks to 'the luck from his ancestors' who made it possible for him to win a good haul of Lotto money.

A good half hour later, Geelbooi drove back again, still playing the hooter and stopping to repeat his lies to those who had not heard them the first time. As he approached Aunt Mashadi's house, he wished that he could drive back to the shop again, or to some other place, so that more villagers could have the chance to see him, Geelbooi, behind the steering wheel of a fancy BMW.

Cruising past the next-door neighbour's property, Geelbooi saw a group of girls playing the *diketo* game; he called to one of them and sent her to take the packet of chocolate pudding to Joyce and relay the message that 'uncle Geelbooi' was going off to ask for some cigarettes from friends elsewhere in the village and that he would be back shortly.

Twenty minutes went by, and then another twenty. By the time that Joyce had made the chocolate pudding, served it to Fanie, and Fanie had finished it and cleaned the plate with his tongue, Geelbooi had still not returned with the car. Fuming, Fanie told Joyce that he was going to phone the police and lay a charge of theft against Geelbooi.

'Please don't worry, Mr Fourie,' Joyce begged him. 'Your car is in safe hands. Geelbooi will return it without a dent or a scratch, you'll see.'

'Geelbooi is busy showing off the wealth of his brother-in-law, that's why he doesn't come back,' added Uncle Sepanere. 'I know him; he is a cheap boaster, that one!' he added with a chuckle.

At that moment, the 'cheap boaster' in question was once again approaching the homestead of the Machabaphalas, still cheerfully hooting and waving to the bystanders. Those watching expected that the car would turn into Dimakatjo's yard; but instead of slowing down, the white BMW drove jauntily past, leaving dust-trails behind it. It was heading in the direction of Sophiatown Tavern, popularly known as Sof'town Tavern – the only 'two-star' shebeen in the village.

On both sides of the dusty street, adults and children stood and stared in fascination at the sight of Geelbooi behind the wheel, cheerfully singing along to the CD that was loudly blaring from the car's powerful speakers; it was the well-known piece by *malombo* guitar virtuoso, Philip Tabane, titled: *'Rotwane e lebile lapeng la'bo kgarebe!'* The white BMW slowed down and stopped outside the shebeen, five houses away from Dimakatjo's home.

Lukas and Mayibuye, as it happened, were part of the crowds milling about in the yard of Dimakatjo's place. They were busy serving the chosen ones among the relatives and friends with tots of whiskey and brandy, for the kinsfolk had complained that they were tired of imbibing *mabele* corn-beer, which some village snobs derogatorily referred to as 'mud'. Having reached the point of completion, there was now a welcome break in the *lobola* proceedings and the two families were taking things easy as they waited for Uncle Phari to arrive.

As the white BMW cruised past the homestead, Lukas's admiring eyes were instantly drawn to it. He hadn't the faintest idea that the car belonged to Fanie, for Dimakatjo had prudently hidden from him the truth about the type of car that Fanie drove out of fear that if he knew the truth, her brother would conclude that Fanie was a rich *mokgonyana* and push up the *lobola* amount.

Now, on seeing the BMW driving past, Lukas wished he could own it. His own old-model version caused him endless anxiety; he sometimes fantasised about robbing a bank and using the spoils to buy parts so that he could get his BMW properly roadworthy. In the village of donkey-carts, the sole owner of a BMW would be a king indeed!

Lukas's amazement was great when he looked down the road and saw Geelbooi stepping out of the coverted vehicle; before he could recover from this shock, he heard one of the boys saying to his nephew Sefako: 'That car belongs to the white man of your aunt!'

Lukas was, at first, puzzled by the phrase, 'the white man of your aunt'. The boy who was speaking was recalling from his memory the previous weekend, when Fanie had delivered Dimakatjo to her home. Sefako was not able to comment since he had not seen the car on that day.

It took only a few moments for Lukas to solve the puzzle. He snapped his fingers in excitement: *'Eeya-eh!* This car belongs to our son-in-law! Today I have seen it with my own eyes! So, the *mokgonyana* is well-off eh?' Lukas said to himself aloud. He looked around, trying to spot Mayibuye and saw him not far away, chatting to one of the relatives who was pleading for the chance to whet his throat with some 'bitter waters'.

'*Khazi!*' Lukas called.

'*E-ye!*' responded Mayibuye.

'*Zwakala hi!*' ('Come here!')

Lukas laughed to himself, his eyes dancing with excitement.

'*Wil jy my weedie?*' ('Do you want to tell me anything?') enquired Mayibuye. He and Lukas spoke in *tsotsi-taal*, as they often did when together, in order to make it more difficult for others to understand what they were scheming.

Lukas pointed towards Fanie's white BMW parked down the street.

'*Wie se smovana is daai?*' ('Whose car is that?') asked a very curious Mayibuye.

'*Is o-baas-mkhonyana se voom.*' ('It's white son-in-law-boss's car.)

'*Ke nnete?*' ('Is it true?')

'*Ka mmago!*' ('I swear by your mother!')

'*Jehrrr! Dis 'n mnca nanana! 'n BM ok?*' ('Wow! It's a nice car! A BM too?')

'*Ja! Dis a dolly ding!* I'm sure *hy kos* over R200 000!' ('Yes! It's a nice thing! I'm sure it costs over R200 000!')

'*Ja! Die lahnee het phang-phang zak eh?*' ('Yes! This white guy has lots of money hey?')

Lukas was glad that he had been able to plant the seed that he was certain was now germinating in his cousin's fertile mind. The two understood each other very well. Mayibuye sensed there was something interesting still to come from his cousin's mouth. He didn't have long to wait. Lukas suggested baldly that the *lobola* amount that the Machabaphalas had received should be increased.

'You are too late!' Mayibuye pointed out. 'We have already given them the amount. And we have received the money.'

Lukas took out a matchstick from the box in his pocket and bit on it with his front teeth – a habit of his when he was busy 'eating the bones of his head'.

'*Ek het 'n* clever idea *om die* amount *te* double!' ('I have a clever idea to double the amount!') Painstakingly, Lukas explained his plan: they would say to the others that when they had told the Fouries that 'each cow that doesn't graze or cry *moo-moo*' would cost R200, they were, in fact, referring to the old British currency of pounds, or *diponto*, as the old people used to say, that used to equal R2 to a pound; this would therefore mean that 'each cow that doesn't graze or cry *moo-moo*' would now be worth R400, according to the old exchange rate. They could unashamedly take advantage of Grandpa's old age by insisting, should he protest, that his memory was faulty and that he had, in fact, mentioned *diponto* with his own mouth. Lukas added that they should also say that according to this reckoning, the Machabaphalas had received exactly half of what they should have received.

Mayibuye said nothing for a while, thinking over what his crony had said.

'*Khazi, ek het 'n* suspicion *die* mission *gaan nie grand loop nie!*' ('Cousin, I have a suspicion the project is not going to succeed!') he finally said.

'*Smôkkô?*' ('Why?')

'*Die ou-toppie gaan moen-ons gurah!*' ('The old man is going to fight against us!')

'*Monie worry van o'mdala, khazi.*' ('Don't worry about the old man, cousin.')

'*Ons moet* worry! *Die ou-toppie gaan* squeal *ons* charge *baie zak van o mkhonyana-baas!*' ('We must worry! The old man is going to moan that we are asking too much money from white son-in-law-boss!')

'*Wat? Jy* worry *van die lahnee wat phang-phang zak het?*' ('What? You are worrying about a white man who has lots of money?') Lukas's expression relayed his disgust.

Mayibuye felt stupid. He was angry with himself that he, of all people, should pity a white man – a 'settler' who had dispossessed him of his fatherland; he, a fire-spitting Africanist, had acted as a settler's advocate!

'*For 'n lahnee daai zak is niks . . . !*' ('For a white man, that amount is nothing . . . !')

Mayibuye nodded: 'S'true. And why should we pity a white man? These settlers have never pitied us,' he said. 'They have eaten our hands . . . we are all bones! They have finished us!'

'*Ja!* These settlers have exploited us for centuries, *khazi!*'

'*Ja-ja!*'

'*Khazi, moenie* worry *van die o'mdala, nie! Hy's oud* – five to *om die* bucket *te skop. Ons sal sê hy het ponte 'n* mention; *hy het vorscheet!*' ('Cousin, don't worry about the old man! He's old and is five minutes away from kicking the bucket. We will insist he mentioned 'pounds' and that he has forgotten!') Lukas said.

Mayibuye nodded. '*n Mnca* idea, *khazi!*' ('A lovely idea, cousin!') he smiled.

'We must just be bold and believe in what we are saying. If this succeeds, we can get . . . eight thou and share it out among ourselves!'

Mayibuye grinned back at him.

Lukas's mind became busy exploring how he could transform the noisy, sputtering rattle-trap contraption that he called a car – which had been dysfunctional for many months – into a purring darling of a BMW.

'If I could have *daai stak van zak,*' ('that heap of money') continued Lukas, 'then I could buy some parts for old BM and send a final instalment of *lobola* to my girlfriend's people . . . '

Mayibuye nodded with a smile.

' . . . and I'll have a white wedding,' continued Lukas, without even pausing to swallow saliva, 'and you'll be my bestman – looking very *dolly* in a three-piece suit and floscheim shoes!'

Flattered, Mayibuye laughed aloud. Lukas joined in and the two plotters gleefully slapped each other's palms, hugged and jumped about in exhilaration. They were overjoyed at the prospect of the successful conclusion of their clever operation. Lukas's scheming mind was, as usual, already kilometres ahead of its owner.

What they had overlooked was one small, important detail: that the Fouries and Machabaphalas had both already signed that all-important piece of paper which, although still awaiting Uncle Phari's final nod, was virtually a marriage certificate!

35

When Geelbooi parked Fanie's white BMW in the yard of Sof'town Tavern, the shebeen queen, Sophia, was elated. She expected the owner of a BMW to be a patron who would repeatedly and happily fork out R50 notes. A classy car such as this added value to her house, which lost points in the eyes of morally superior and socially conscious villagers who swore that Sodom and Gomorrha were thriving there in front of their very eyes.

Ausi-Sofi was pleased indeed to see Geelbooi ostentatiously waving the car keys as he activated the central-locking system by remote, and then walked like a big shot into the shebeen.

If Ausi-Sofi's big black nose could smell, as the saying went, she would know that Geelbooi could hardly spare R20 from his thin and hungry pocket, and that he had come to her shebeen with the intention of 'selling his mouth'. She was soon to discover that Geelbooi was that type of patron who talked much while he drank and bought little, like the broke teachers who came in and sat talking 'big English' for hours over a single bottle of beer. This loose-mouthed intellectual type irked her very much.

Geelbooi was, in fact, not the only BMW driver in the shebeen that day. He had parked Fanie's white BMW next to a sleek red one. Unlike its counterpart, the red one was brand new, in tip-top condition and boasted the latest horsepower in its high-powered German-made engine. It was fitted with tinted windows and equipped with, among other things, a CD-player with ear-shattering speakers, and a silver steel double exhaust pipe. This red BMW belonged to three valued patrons of Ausi-Sofi, known to the well informed as 'AmaGent'.

All in their early thirties, these maGents were suave customers and natty dressers, displaying gold necklaces in the Vs of their open-necked shirts; their fingers flashed gold dress rings, and very expensive mirror sunglasses shielded their eyes. They puffed at cigars as they sipped their iced whiskeys. Two of the maGents came from Mamelodi – also known as 'Flaka' – while one was from Seshego township near Polokwane, about twelve kilometres from Dimakatjo's village. Ausi-Sofi, who'd once lived in Mamelodi, affectionately addressed the maGents as 'home-boys', and they addressed her as 'home-girl' – although she was, in fact, considerably older than they were. But those who knew too much said maGents were not telling the truth about where they came from, as they were confidence tricksters *par excellence* and knew how to get into a shebeen queen's good books.

What had brought maGents together in Mamelodi in the first place was the secret that kept people guessing. Although maGents were seen in the village selling 'soft goods', such as socks, jerseys and scarves, the tongues of sceptical villagers did a lot of wagging. It was said that these maGents were gold and diamond smugglers, or drug-peddlers, or car-hijack and bank-robbery master-minds. Not all the villagers could agree on the true nature of the business of maGents, but one thing they did agree on was that it was of a criminal nature, and that maGents were not hanging out at Ausi-Sofi's shebeen just because they enjoyed her extensive jazz collection!

It was five years since the death of Ausi-Sofi's husband in a car accident in Pretoria, where he had been a travelling salesman. After the traditional one-year mourning period, Ausi-Sofi had decided it was time to go and stay on her husband's little piece of land, known as *kokotwane*, after the four poles that pegged out the site. At the time, there was nothing there save for a shack that served as a storeroom for building materials and some tools. But with the help of funds accrued from her husband's death – money which some heartless ones termed 'your death makes me alive' – Ausi-Sofi was able to set to work, and within a few months of her arrival, the foundation for an eight-roomed house was in place.

Geelbooi had intended to stick to the company of the women patrons – the educated, frustrated spinsters and 'returned soldiers' – a township term for divorced people – whom he desperately desired to impress with his 'ownership' of the white BMW. He sat down next to one of them; but before he could get going with his lies of how, thanks to a few hundred thousand that he had won from the Lotto millions he'd managed to buy the fancy BMW, he was shocked to hear someone asking him: 'Does that car not belong to the suitor of the daughter of Machabaphalas?'

Geelbooi had no idea that some of the villagers had seen Fanie's car when he had brought Dimakatjo home a week before. These idle ones, who had little or nothing better to do than pass on information, had quickly spread the news about a white man driving a fancy white car, who had been seen in the neighbourhood of the Machabaphala place; a white man who, at the time, they had incorrectly guessed to be Dimakatjo's employer. The inaccuracy had soon been corrected, however, and most of the villagers now knew that the car belonged to Dimakatjo's husband-to-be. Soundly caught out, Geelbooi was left with no choice but to tell the truth, which was that the car did, indeed, belong to Fanie, son of Fourie, who was at this very moment being joined through *lobola* to Dimakatjo, daughter of Machabaphala. All the patrons, including the maGents, complimented Geelbooi on acquiring an affluent white brother-in-law.

Geelbooi was one of the revellers who contributed money in a saucer so that more liquor could be bought. He legitimately took more beers. His tongue became looser and, as a result, reverted to churning out black, black lies: he told his attentive listeners that his rich brother-in-law had parted with a *lobola* amount of R20 000. All the patrons were impressed to hear of so large a *lobola* amount, many times more than they had ever heard given before. One of maGents tapped his mate's foot under the table, communicating a coded message.

At that point, Geelbooi said his goodbyes and was soon on his way, swaying back down the steps towards the car. As he revved the BMW unsteadily out of the yard, he did not look back to see the three maGents now standing outside Ausi-Sofi's house, talking in low tones and pointing in the direction of Dimakatjo's place, their eyes glinting with mischief.

On his way home Geelbooi took the long route, driving into and out of several homestead yards, still belching his black, black lies that he had bought this white BMW *cash* as he was not the type who lived on *sekoloto* – the anxiety-creating credit. Fortunately, in the tank of the car there was enough diesel (known among the knowledgeable ones as 'milk from the Arabs' cow') to fuel his journey home.

Time still did not sit down on its buttocks.

Lukas and Mayibuye were so engrossed in the details of their plot that they did not notice Thomas walking past them while stretching his legs outside. Lukas and Mayibuye's body language, the surreptitious pitch of their voices and their use of the exclusive *tsotsi-taal* were all noted by observant Thomas. Back in the negotiating room, he warned the others that he smelt a rat and that Lukas and Mayibuye were up to something. Other negotiators, who also killed time by walking past the two rogues on their way to the toilet or elsewhere, concurred with Thomas's opinion.

'If only the children's uncle was here this would not happen . . .' lamented *sangoma*-aunt.

'Shh!' Placing his forefinger against his lips, Thomas alerted the others to the approach of Lukas and Mayibuye. As they took their seats it was evident to all that the two troublemakers were, indeed, brewing something. All waited for them to speak, but Lukas and Mayibuye simply sat gazing at each other, their glances clearly conveying: *You speak first!*

All the eyes in the room finally congregated on Mayibuye, who had no choice but to unleash the wind from his mouth: 'Er . . . Grandpa, show us that piece of paper on which we acknowledged that we have received *lobola* from the Fouries.'

'Why?'

'Please just produce it; we want to check something,' insisted Lukas.

'Check what?' asked Thomas with uncharacteristic impatience.

'Just give them the piece of paper so that we can see what they are up to!' *sangoma*-aunt suggested.

But Grandpa said: 'Listen, young people; put your idea on the table so that we can have the chance to consider it . . . '

He was rudely interrupted by Lukas: 'Grandpa, we say produce that paper! Finished *en klaar*!'

Grandpa felt threatened but still hesitated to produce the document that was demanded. Lukas and Mayibuye stretched their open palms towards Grandpa imperiously, almost as if they had rehearsed the gesture. *Sangoma*-aunt glanced pathetically at Grandpa and the old man suddenly searched deep inside the inner pocket of his coat, from where he produced the contested document, the two copies folded together. He shoved them into Lukas's hand.

After scanning through the top copy, Lukas handed them both to Mayibuye, who matter-of-factly shredded the important papers with his tough, bony fingers. He then thrust the shreds into the hand of Lukas who kneaded them like a hungry man would do with stiff porridge. The body language of the two men expressed defiance and contempt. Mayibuye's belligerent posture was typical of *ntwa-dumela* – a man or woman who thrived on fighting, as if he or she was born to wrestle, battle, and break other people's necks. On everybody else's face was written consternation and shock.

'*Hee monna!* Are you mad?' Grandpa exclaimed angrily.

'What are you trying to do, young men?' asked *sangoma*-aunt in bewilderment.

'We will explain!' said Lukas.

The silence stretched tensely. You could almost hear the heart of every person in that room hectically pumping the blood to go roaring through their veins.

'Grandpa, we have torn up the piece of paper because there is a serious mistake on it!' justified Mayibuye.

'What mistake? Why do you tear the paper before you explain?' challenged Thomas.

Mayibuye and Lukas strategically avoided answering him and focused on Grandpa instead.

'Grandpa, do you remember that during the time you were still young your currency was pounds?'

'Yes. Why?'

'And today we have asked the Fouries to give us twenty head of cattle that do not graze nor cry *moo-moo*, in pounds?'

'No! Have we asked the Fouries to give us cattle that do not graze nor cry *moo-moo* in pounds?' enquired Grandpa, scratching his grey beard in confusion.

'Yes! *Khazi* is right!' Lukas supported his crony. 'You, Grandpa, asked for the money in pounds, not rands!'

'No, I don't think we have . . . !'

'You have, Grandpa, you have . . . !' insisted Mayibuye.

'No! It can't be so! No one mentioned pounds! *Aowaa!*'

Thomas, always the clear-headed one, shook his head decisively and added: 'We have asked for money in rands. Who is still speaking in pounds in these modern times?'

'Thomas is right!' agreed *sangoma*-aunt.

'Yes, Thomas is right! We did not . . . !'

'You did, Grandpa! You have forgotten!' Lukas interrupted Grandpa.

'You are an old man! You forget easily,' shouted Mayibuye.

'If you say we have asked for the money in pounds do you mean that the money we received is incomplete?' asked Thomas.

'You have hit the bull's horn, *khazi*!' responded Lukas.

'And how much is left still to get?'

'*Ehr* . . . R4 000,' said Mayibuye, without batting an eyelash.

'No! We can't ask for an additional amount so large! We can't!'

'If we have asked for a cow and we are given a calf, who is to blame?' Lukas rudely interrupted Grandpa again.

'No one is to blame! We have told the Fouries a specific amount and they have given us what we asked for: twenty head of cattle that do not graze or cry *moo-moo*. Period!' emphasised Thomas.

'You are missing the point, Thomas! Our son-in-law can afford what we are now asking for!' said Mayibuye.

'Yes! He is a white guy, and he drives an expensive BM . . . ' added Lukas.

'Black or white, BM or not, truth is truth!' Thomas dug his heels in.

'*Aowaa!* We can't ask for additional money – no! That will mean that we are unreliable and our word means nothing . . . ' said Grandpa.

'I agree with Grandpa! If we increase the *lobola* amount now, the Fouries will think we are crooks – people full of *mathaithai!*'

'There's no *mathaithai* business here. It's our culture!' retorted Mayibuye.

'This is not about culture! This is sheer exploitation!' shouted Thomas.

'Young men, what you are requesting is not possible,' said Grandpa with finality.

'It *is* possible . . . !'

'It's impossible!'

'It's you who makes things impossible!' responded Lukas challengingly.

'You are motivated by nothing but greed!' Thomas retorted heatedly.

'It's not greed! It's our . . . !'

'Listen here *khazi* – don't talk rubbish!' Thomas's patience was reaching the thin end.

'*Khazi, khazi!* You watch your big mouth!' Lukas pointed a threatening finger at Thomas.

'Lukas and Matsobane – please, be reasonable!' appealed *sangoma* aunt.

'Listen here, all of you!' Lukas said vehemently. 'I am the only boy in this family. In my father's absence, I am . . . ' he stamped his right foot on the ground, ' . . . in charge here! *I'm* the boss! You are just relatives who are here as mere witnesses. *Ja man, ek slaan die kataar!*' ('Yes man, I call the tune!')

'That's right!' Mayibuye cut in. 'Since his father has gone to the gods, *he* is now . . . ' he stabbed his index finger in the air for emphasis, ' . . . the boss! And to all of you I say, "*We build a kraal around the king's voice!*" '

Mayibuye had stirred a pot brimful of trouble. The proceedings, as they say in the idiom-rich speech of the village, had ascended up a mountain; the proceedings were now constipated in front of young blood and grey hairs. Dimakatjo's people had to 'chew the bone' tossed to them by Lukas and Mayibuye. The tender clay that was producing an earthernware pot had turned hard as *koromolo* – stone-dry bread.

All tired eyes now rested on Grandpa. The old man was not doing well in exerting his authority; nor was his white hair respected by Lukas and Mayibuye. Dimakatjo, overhearing everything from her room across the way, was inexpressibly dismayed. She felt extremely angry with Lukas and Mayibuye.

Where was Uncle Phari? A lion roaring far away was no better than a dead one! Uncle Phari, the Great Porcupine, the one person in whom Dimakatjo had invested all her hope, was not there in this hour of great need to loosen what had been made constipated by mischievous Lukas and Mayibuye; to heal what was bewitched and make straight what was now crooked. What should be coming out as beautiful as the gods of Afrika could design it was deformed and ugly as *manko-disebene* – the fabled baby monster born with seven noses.

'This is hard to chew, it's as tough as tendon. My teeth are shaky; those with strong teeth,' Grandpa stabbed his finger towards Lukas and Mayibuye, 'let *them* chew it and swallow it!'

There was a very uncomfortable silence. Suddenly the old man grabbed his *rotwane* – walking-stick – and pointed it towards Lukas and Mayibuye.

'Hey, you babies, *ba nkganga mekgato!*' ('still reeking of your mother's breast-milk!') The old man squinted his eyes towards Lukas and Mayibuye, surprising everybody with his quivering anger: 'Have you called us here so that you should play *diketo*, the children's game with us?'

He rose stiffly to his feet, took his hat from a nail in the wall and prepared to stalk from the room.

'No, you are not going anywhere, Grandpa!' commanded *sangoma*-aunt.

'Let him go! Let him go!' barked Lukas.

'We can speak for ourselves! Our mouths are not only for eating *pap* and *morogo*!' boasted Mayibuye.

'Lukas and Matsobane, you are ungrateful! Why are you bent on spoiling your sister's greatest day?' chided *sangoma*-aunt.

'Now I am convinced: a black man's "thank you" is "*voetsek*"!' Thomas said disgustedly.

'Hey, you small boys! Because you have seasoned the mung beans with soil, now you are going to eat and swallow them!' said Grandpa.

To Lukas and Mayibuye, however, Grandpa's words had as little effect as a spear that has hit a stone wall.

Thomas fixed his eyes on the recalcitrant pair: 'I am going to tell the Fouries the news of what you have done; I'm sure it will make your black hearts *twaa*-white!' he said, his voice heavy with sarcasm. 'I hope you are happy that you have brought the family into disrepute!'

'No, Thomas, don't go!' appealed *sangoma*-aunt.

'Let him go! Let him go!' insisted Mayibuye.

Thomas left without another word.

'So goes the idiom,' said Grandpa: '*When a child cries for a mokhure-tree wind-pipe, cut one and give it to him! Soon the sun will be hot, the pipe will shrink and refuse to emit its music. And the frustrated child will be left crying "ngwee-ngwee!"*'

It was left to Thomas to dish up to the Fouries tidings that jammed and hardened their stomachs. George and Lesetja heard that the milk-cow in the Machabaphala kraal had run wild, had kicked away the milk-bucket, and as a result the pail was shattered to pieces. They heard that the bees had stung the seasoned honey-maker. Faithful *mmaditsela* had to deliver the sour news. The path towards the Fouries was paved with the sharp thorns of a mimosa tree, but Thomas had to trample them barefoot.

Although Uncle Pieter could not understand Sepedi, he could read well enough from George and Lesetja's faces and pick up from the tone of their voices that trouble had descended in a mighty way. When they interpreted for him, they only confirmed what he had already detected.

George told Thomas that the Fouries would like to confer among themselves. The state of affairs was so grave that the Fouries decided it would be more efficacious not to communicate through *bo-mmaditsela* but to speak directly with the Machabaphala people. They sent a message back asking the Machabaphalas to come to their room. Grandpa and *sangoma*-aunt felt like telling the Fouries that the stirrers and brewers of the pot of trouble were Lukas and Mayibuye but, strangely, they did not do this. Their attitude seemed to be: *Let things go haywire so that Lukas and Mayibuye should regret it in the end.* But at the same time, they still hoped that the children's Uncle Phari – Uncle 'Stop Nonsense!' – would come just in time to be a fire extinguisher.

'People of Machabaphala – why are you killing us?' implored George, focusing his eyes on Grandpa. 'Why are you castrating an ox with a big axe? Castrating a bull from which you expect some calves to be delivered?'

At that, Grandpa shifted his gaze towards Lukas and Mayibuye, clearly indicating: 'Straighten up what you have made crooked!' He himself kept silent, feeling that those whose mouths were 'not just for eating *pap* and *morogo*' should now speak.

'We hear you, people of Fourie.' It was Mayibuye who spoke, taking the reins of authority from Grandpa. 'We are not killing you. It's our culture. Don't they say in English: "When you are in Rome do as Romans do?"'

'No, this has nothing to do with culture!' protested Lesetja.

'Do these people think that we are a Volkskas Bank?' demanded Uncle Pieter in Afrikaans.

Thomas translated for *sangoma*-aunt and Grandpa.

'We are tired of this bunch of crooks! Blood-suckers! Come, let us go!' Lesetja said, spitting fire.

'*Ja, kom ons loop!*' Uncle Pieter prepared to heave himself up from his chair.

Lesetja was already on his feet, on the point of walking out, but George restrained him.

Humbly George lowered himself to his knees and engaged in the *phophotha* ritual – earnestly clapping his hands gently twice, as any villager would do when wanting to appease the wrathful gods or plead for mercy. He paused and looked straight into the eyes of Grandpa, who again shifted his gaze towards Lukas and Mayibuye.

George then asked the Machabaphala people to leave the room and give them a moment to discuss the matter privately.

Seated in her own room, meanwhile, tearful Dimakatjo heard for herself, because her ear 'had no lid', the wrangling going on between the Fouries and Machabaphalas. Daughter of Bakone had by now lost all hope. She was furiously angry with her brother and Mayibuye; she could not bear to see her dream hitting the dust this way. *Aowaa!* Witches and wizards would celebrate all night long! *Joo-nna-joo!* She wanted to take decisive action but she felt powerless, a victim of circumstance. For her to try to intervene would be like an ant biting an elephant that was not even aware of its pitiful attempt; it would be like a frail and sickly person attempting single-handedly to shift a mountain. It was now up to God and her ancestors to lend a providential helping hand.

Aunt Mashadi entered Dimakatjo's room with the intention of comforting her charge. She assured Dimakatjo that even a heavy cloudburst does stop eventually and before long the sun shines again. Her words could not console, however, and as soon as Aunt Mashadi had exited again, daughter of Bakone shed copious tears. She could not quieten her heart that was as wild as a goat resisting slaughter. Suddenly, a perverse urge came over her to summon Lukas and Mayibuye to her room.

She called her nephew Sefako and asked him to take a message to the two troublemakers, but not to disclose that she was the person summoning them. She felt she had to have it out with her brother and cousin once and for all – these two diabolical wizards who appeared to be doing their best to short-circuit her happiness.

Lukas and Mayibuye followed Sefako back inside the house and were surprised to be led to Dimakatjo's room, instead of to the Fouries as they had expected.

'*Buti* Lukas, and *khazi* – why are you two wrecking the day of my marriage?' demanded Dimakatjo tearfully.

'What do you mean?' Lukas asked.

'If you don't want Fanie to part with *lobola* for me, then I will go and live *vat-en-sit* with him! Without him paying a single cent! Is that what you want? Then why are you making things so difficult? Do you think that Fanie just goes to the toilet and *shits* money like diarrhoea?'

'*Khazi, khazi!* Do you hear what you are saying?' chided Mayibuye, while Lukas sat stunned by his sister's hell-fire words. '*Khazi*, your behaviour is un-African! Where have you seen a girl speaking for herself during *lobola* negotiations?'

'Shame on you!' agreed Lukas, finding his voice.

'Shame on *you*, greedy people!' fired back Dimakatjo.

Their loud, angry voices could be heard by all in the house.

Aunt Mashadi hurried in, in time to witness the children of the same womb eating one another up viciously. She escorted Lukas and Mayibuye back to the room occupied by the Machabaphala party, then returned to comfort Dimakatjo as best she could.

In the Machabaphala room, tension multiplied like an AIDS virus. The hearts of the Machabaphala people were by now so heavy that they could not even muster enough appetite to eat the delicious food that had been placed before them 30 minutes earlier.

Lukas and Mayibuye had made their point and it seemed that they had won this round of the *lobola* wrestling match. In Grandpa's words, *a child had cried for a* mokhure-*tree wind-pipe, and it had been cut and given to him*. Let the child leap sky-high, celebrating that he had managed to twist his father's tough arm to get his desire. For soon, the sun would grow hot, and the pipe would shrink and refuse to emit its music, and the child would certainly be left weeping, '*Ngwee-ngwee!*'

The Machabaphala people sat despondent, wishing with all their hearts that the children's uncle, 'the government's bulldog', would appear to stop the fire and restore the dignity that the occasion deserved.

Grandpa was no longer angry; he seemed in a surprisingly relaxed mood in the midst of the confusion. He reminded the Machabaphalas of the wisdom of an idiom that they might have forgotten in that hour of darkness: *'Obstacles and trials are an old man of a lion.'* By this was meant that problems could appear intimidating, but when you came closer to them and stood your ground, they often turned out to be easily overcome.

Had it not been for George's patience and tenacity, the Fouries would, by now, have given up all hope and gone home empty-handed. George had succeeded in persuading them to see the setback as a challenge rather than an insoluble problem.

'But must we so easily agree to be exploited by these greedy people?' Lesetja dug his heels in.

'Listen, Lesetja! Parting with *lobola* should never be regarded as exploitation,' George admonished. '*Lobola* is a test for a man; if he loves the girl of his dreams, then he must work hard to please his in-laws, no matter how hard-to-please they might be. Why should we cry when these people are not even asking for half the amount that could be parted with in Xhosaland in the Cape, where *lobola* is very high? We have no choice but to pay up; we cannot go home empty-handed. *Aowaa!*'

Uncle Pieter had been nodding his head unconsciously as George spoke, almost as if he could understand what was being said.

The Fouries finally agreed that they should increase the *lobola* amount, even though the new demands were very steep. In relief, George dashed across to Aunt Mashadi's house, where Fanie was tensely waiting for news.

36

Fanie's anxious heart relaxed somewhat when he saw Geelbooi driving his car in through the gate at last. But he was still very annoyed that his trust had been so abused. Geelbooi begged Joyce to plead with Fanie on his behalf. When she had done her part, Geelbooi came shuffling in, his bent knees, stooped shoulders and bowed head clearly demonstrating his contrition. He fell to his knees and applauded gently in the *phophotha* manner to indicate his regret that he had given offence.

Fanie gazed sternly at the offender for a protracted moment, then told Geelbooi coldly that he would have to look at the car to check it was not dented or scratched anywhere. Fanie, Geelbooi and Uncle Sepanere inspected the car together from boot to bonnet. Finally, since Fanie could not detect any damage, he told Geelbooi that he was forgiven.

At that moment George arrived, and Geelbooi and Uncle Sepanere went on their way, heading for Dimakatjo's place.

George filled Fanie in *phaa!* – 'straight to the point' – about the latest developments.

'To be honest with you, the going is not easy, Fanatjie. These people are forcing a limping cow up a steep mountain. At this stage, I'm not even sure if you will get married!'

'You are not even sure that I will get married? Tell me George, why are you here?' asked Fanie in horror.

'I shouldn't have said that!'

For a moment, the two men faced each other like tiger and leopard sizing each other up as a delicious carcass lies between them.

'Speak to me, George,' said Fanie, 'what's the problem? What is the latest trick? What do THEY want now? More money?'

'Yes, more head of cattle.'

'More cattle? Do they take me for a cattle breeder?' Fanie fumed.

'Fanie!' George raised his voice in warning, 'YOU are going to take it easy, okay?'

George explained how it had happened that more money was now wanted by the Machabaphala people. He told Fanie that he had persuaded Uncle Pieter and Lesetja to part with a further amount, because he didn't want the Fouries to go home empty-handed, in the way that he had once witnessed with *lobola* negotiations that had gone awry.

Fanie recalled the words that George had said to him as they sipped chilled beers together at the Democracy Jazz Café several months back: *'You must pray that Maki's people are truthful and fair people; that they should not be people with heads as hard as rocks. If they are a bunch of* tsotsis *full of* mathaithai *then the* lobola *negotiations will go like a limping cow that is forced to walk up a steep mountain.'*

'I want Dimakatjo to be my wife, George. But these people are unreasonable! They are just plain greedy! Do they really imagine that I am made of money . . . ?'

'Shhh!' cautioned George. 'Remember that "these people" are now *your* people, Fanie!'

'My mother was right!' moaned Fanie. 'If she were here today she would say: "Ja, I told you! Those blacks are making money out of *lobola. Nou gaan jy kak en betaal!*"'

'Don't talk nonsense, Fanie! Stop your *nywe-nywe-nywe-nywe*! My mother, my mother! You know what, no one forced you to part with *lobola*; *you* have invited *them*, remember? Now stop complaining and play your part!'

Joyce coughed loudly from the TV room. There was silence between the friends as they realised with embarrassment that their loud bickering was being overheard.

'Now, have you got the extra money in your pocket?' George asked, lowering the pitch of his voice.

'No. It's in my bank account.'

'Give me your bank card.'

Fanie handed it over.

'And give me your PIN number.'

'How much are you going to withdraw?' asked Fanie.

'Four thousand.'

Fanie had finally come to realise that kicking and crying and complaining would not help the situation. If such protestations were, indeed, helpful, then they would have saved the pig when it was being chopped by the merciless axe. So, meekly, he wrote his PIN number down on a piece of paper and handed it to George. The two men looked into each other's eyes for a prolonged moment. George squeezed Fanie's shoulder: 'Son of Fourie, be strong, be patient; you are going to succeed in the end. Think of this experience as being similar to a boy's initiation at a mountain or bush school. I know it's rough; it is painful, but you will come out a man in the end!'

Dimakatjo had once said something similar to Fanie: *'You must be strong, Fanie, you must pass the test. Then my people will respect you as a man.'*

Fanie handed over the keys of his BMW to George who patted Fanie's palm reassuringly and then stepped out of the room.

The going was rough and painful indeed for son of Fourie, but deep inside his guts, Fanie agreed with George. *Yes, this experience is like a mountain school,* he thought. *I did not attend such a school because I am a white boy. But many black boys did go through those tests of manhood, and the experience made them tough and strong. That's why these people have survived the onslaught of apartheid . . . these people who, from this day on, will be my people; they survived because they know how to endure hardship and challenge. Now I must undergo my own test . . .*

He watched his white BMW, with George at the wheel, reverse out of the yard and drive off to the nearest ATM, twenty kilometres away in Polokwane.

An hour or two previously, when Geelbooi drove Fanie's car out of the yard of Sof'town Tavern, the three maGents were standing outside Ausi-Sofi's house talking in lowered tones.

'MaGents, are we going to ignore R20 000?'

One of the three had fired off the question whose answer was obvious. The other two shook their heads. They badly wanted to get their hands on the big *lobola* sum that they had heard Geelbooi claiming his rich brother-in-law was going to part with. There and then, they began to plan 'Operation Lobola', through which they expected to snatch the target money with the greatest of ease.

MaGents had idled their time away in this village for several weeks because they were, out of necessity, lying low here. Their itching hands and bored minds cried out for action – something that was exciting . . . risky . . . and pocket-filling. It was usual for them, once they had successfully executed one of their 'missions' in the city, to disappear for a while and go and take a break in some obscure rural settlement. There, they would pose as clothing salesmen. They had chosen this location because one of the maGents lived in nearby Seshego and he was familiar with the villages in the area.

Executing 'Operation Lobola' looked to be a ridiculously easy task. There would be numerous people milling about at the bride's homestead. Everyone would be in a relaxed mood. There would be umpteen pots on the go, simmering with beef and mutton stews, as well as other dishes that provided excellent fare for the tastebuds. MaGents had mentally ticked off the first item in their criminals' notebook: 'studying thoroughly the target of the intended attack'. They had already worked out their escape plan, deciding that they would disappear to another hide-out far away from this location, perhaps never to set foot in this neighbourhood again.

As the red BMW of maGents reversed out of the shebeen and headed towards the Machabaphala place, Dimakatjo's nephew Sefako and his peers were playing in the dusty street. Armed with his catapult – known among the villagers as *seraga-mabje* – 'the stones-kicker' – Sefako was having a field day shooting missiles at his friends. He was using the hard, home-baked dough cakes known as *kafferkoeke* as his 'bullets'. Sefako unleashed yet another missile from his weapon, but this time it shot wide of his dodging target; the 'bullet' landed with full impact – *thwaaa!* – on the windscreen of the flashy red vehicle belonging to maGents. The vehicle halted sharply and out stormed one furious leGent, ready to beat the living daylights out of the culprit.

Their car had stopped, fortuitously, at a spot directly opposite Dimakatjo's home. An old woman slowly walked towards the angry leGent, clapping her hands gently twice at short intervals, while earnestly pleading that Sefako should be forgiven his sin of naughtiness. LeGent accepted the old woman's plea by nodding haughtily. He and his mates then took this opportunity to study their intended target – the Machabaphala homestead. Their single handgun was loaded, ready to kill if necessary – though as a rule they were not fond of killing, for they were too fastidious for that. Their intention was merely to 'redistribute' whatever they desired from its terrified possessor. Sharp operators, they got more kicks from using trickery than bullets. This was partly the reason why their second weapon was a toy gun.

The car resumed its journey, with the three maGents chuckling inside it, assured that their prey would be easy meat. The one aspect that caused them slight concern was the nuisance posed by cellphones. These gadgets had the potential to wreck the mission by giving the alarm at inopportune moments; this they knew from bitter experience in the past.

Very soon, the red BMW had completed its quick tour of the outer limits of the village and was cruising back again in the direction of Dimakatjo's house, hooting in celebratory style. Curious villagers watched from their hut doorways and *lapas*, all eyes on the hooting red car. At the Machabaphala homestead people looked on with mounting curiosity as the flashy car with tinted windows slowed and came to a stop opposite the entrance gate. They were expecting some important relative to dismount. Scarcely had the wheels stopped rolling, when two of the maGents leapt out, the driver remaining at the wheel. MaGents then made for the *lapa* entrance, energetically engaging in what the villagers appreciated as *phepela* – the particular way of prancing forwards and sideways, then halting abruptly, before resuming again. Drunk with the joy of the occasion, some of the unsuspecting relatives and guests were even prompted to join in the maGents's *phepela*.

The faces of maGents were radiant with smiles, showing many white teeth – *'killers in the midst of laughter'*. With shocking suddenness and almost simultaneously, the two maGents produced a pair of guns; one was the real gun and the other, a realistic-looking toy. LeGent in front, who toted the real killer-weapon, shot into the air, while the one at the back swung his toy version to left and right, gesturing to people to move across to a particular spot.

Pandemonium reigned as people were herded towards one corner of the *lapa*. Frightened children grabbed onto their mothers' dresses or hid, crying, behind their mothers' legs. Those inside the house peered through the windows, their eyes wide with fright. The more timid ones hid in the wardrobes or under the beds; several were packed like sardines in the pit-toilet. Those unfortunates in the thick of things held their breath as they stared into the muzzle of potential death.

The Christians and Catholics in the crowd clawed at their rosaries and crucifixes, quietly mumbling what might be their last prayers in preparation for meeting their Maker; while those who believed in talking to God through their ancestors called to a lengthy list of departed parents, grandparents, and great-grandparents, on both their mothers' and fathers' sides of the family tree.

'All of you in the house, come out!' bellowed real-gun leGent, his voice emanating pure aggression.

'And all hands up!' shot from the mouth of the toy-gun wielder.

Shaking people poured out of the main house; but not the Pride of Bakone, Dimakatjo, or the Lion of the Fouries, Uncle Pieter. A group of Dimakatjo's relatives, including Grandpa and Lukas, remained in the house to protect them. Dimakatjo's people were ready to use their bodies as shields if necessary against the gunmen. Under one of the beds they securely stowed Uncle Pieter, for they feared that he could easily be taken hostage. Dimakatjo's eyes overflowed with despairing torrents.

As for the naughty Sefako, he was safely out of the way of terror. The boy was perched high up on a tough top branch of a leafy peach tree. He had his trusty catapult in his left hand; with his right, he felt for a few stones in his pocket. He had planned to use them to shoot a small bird, just for the fun of it. He did not want to roast and eat the bird, since there was plenty of meat in his house, enough to see the family through many weeks to come.

Sefako was far from terrified by the hold-up drama being played out below him. He was, in fact, very angry; he breathed nothing but brimstone acid.

He was furious that these strangers were wrecking this great day – what was meant to be the greatest day – of his beloved aunt's life. As the anger mounted in him, he again fingered the little stones in his pocket that he had not yet used. A few minutes before, he had been firing *kafferkoeke* at his peers; in a moment he would use a little stone to shoot at a much bigger target. Sefako took out one of the stones, inserted it into the leather piece of the catapult and stretched the rubber sling tautly, aiming it towards leGent holding the real gun. However, he did not release the stone, for he felt he was not ready yet. The adrenalin in his blood was not coursing strongly enough to compel him to do the excellent job required.

'Anyone holding a cellphone bring it here. Or we will shoot!' commanded real-gun leGent.

'And if anyone calls the police, we will shoot all of you, starting with the girl for whom *lobola* is being paid,' added toy-gun leGent.

There was a stir as cellphones were retrieved and passed from one pair of fright-shaken hands to another, to be finally dropped at the feet of real-gun leGent.

The adrenalin level in Sefako's blood was gradually rising. Real-gun leGent waved his killer weapon towards his left and right before bending from the waist to scoop the cellphones into a closer pile. Toy-gun leGent swung his fake weapon from right to left to cover his stooping mate.

'*Ons soek die zak van lobola!*' ('We want the money for *lobola!*') barked real-gun leGent.

'Bring it here! Now!' Toy-gun leGent completed the instruction.

There was a heavy silence, tenser even than the tensest moments of the *lobola* negotiations. Nobody moved, nobody spoke. All stood rooted on shaking feet, wondering if their last moments had come.

At the top of the peach tree Sefako closed one eye, stretched the rubber strings of his catapult as taut as they would go, inhaled deeply, held his breath and aimed at real-gun leGent.

'Didn't you hear me? I said bring that *fucken* money of *lobola* here *now*!' Real-gun leGent fired into the air to emphasise his demand.

In the Machabaphala room, all eyes rested on Grandpa, the bank-that-stood-on-two-legs.

'Old man,' appealed *sangoma*-aunt, 'Give those children of Satan the money and save our lives!'

Hesitating, Grandpa shook his white-haired head.

'Give it here, Grandpa,' Lukas whispered, holding out his hand imperiously.

'No, don't give it, Grandpa!' implored another relative.

At that moment Sefako released the chosen stone, which whizzed determinedly towards its target – the hand of real-gun leGent. *Thwaaaa!* The stone hit its target. Real-gun leGent shouted in pain and the gun fell to the ground. The gangster stooped quickly to retrieve his fallen weapon but a woman standing close by bravely threw a kettle filled with hot tea at him to frustrate his effort. Toy-gun leGent swung his fake weapon to left and right as he sprinted towards the waiting car, plastic pellets popping harmlessly from the barrel of the gun.

'*Is chandies!*' ('Things have gone haywire!') panted toy-gun leGent to his companion in the driver's seat, as he hauled himself into the already moving vehicle. He banged the door closed and the tyres of the high-revving BMW spun crazily and scratched their imprint into the dust. The red car made a squealing U-turn, almost capsizing itself and veered away, enveloped in a dusty whirlwind that trailed it until it was out of sight.

The angry crowd swiftly surrounded the now disarmed leGent; they descended on him like a pack of meat-hungry vultures eager to claw out the most delicious parts from a fat, fallen ox. They kicked, clouted, punched and pinched him, hit him with brooms, wooden spoons, plates, tea-kettles, trays and whatever else was to hand.

Lukas and Mayibuye hurried up armed with pick handles, ready to *moer* the life out of the 'dog'.

'*Hoh-hohh!*' With outstretched hands of peace, Grandpa appealed for mercy and sanity.

'Let the *skelm* shit in his trousers!' Lukas shoved the heavy end of the pick handle against the criminal's ribcage, and the man shouted in pain.

'My people, I beg you!' Grandpa made another impassioned plea. 'This is the day of joy, not blood. Let us not take the law into our hands and play *diketo* games with it!'

Sefako the hero appeared in the midst of the crowd, grinning from ear to ear and waving his effective weapon triumphantly. It was the humble catapult that had rescued the Bakone clanspeople from pain, shame and even possible death. Yes, this nephew of Dimakatjo had saved his people from humiliation that would have given the wizards and witches of Ga-Mabitsela cause to celebrate long into the night.

Some of Dimakatjo's relatives twisted the criminal's hands behind his back and tied them together tightly with a well-tanned thong of cowhide; they did the same with his feet. The captured criminal lay helplessly on the ground, like a chicken awaiting beheading. Vengeful Lukas gave him a last swift kick.

Mayibuye hoisted the grinning Sefako onto his shoulders and *toyi-toyi*'d around the *lapa* with him. There was much celebratory singing and dancing, as others from the crowd took turns in lifting Sefako up and toasting the young hero – the little David who had downed and humiliated the *tsotsi* Goliath. From the window of her bedroom, the Pride of Bakone watched the joyous goings-on and shed more than a few tears of gratitude.

Meanwhile, returning from the ATM in Polokwane, where he had withdrawn the R4 000, George was enjoying himself behind the wheel of Fanie's car. He drove at 180 kms per hour – a reckless speed considering that the speed-limit in those parts was 100 kms per hour.

Once out of Seshego, Fanie's car sped on towards Blood River. Just before driving over the bridge, George's eyes alighted on what appeared to be a traffic officer. It was one, indeed; a black traffic officer standing to attention at the side of the road, his vulture-like eyes shaded by his peaked cap as he peered into the distance, keeping a look-out for offending drivers. A blue-and-white Metro Police car was hidden behind a conveniently thick clump of thorn bush nearby. A few metres away, a white traffic officer sat perched on a picnic chair, officiously inspecting the speed-reader. Suddenly, the black officer stepped into the middle of the road, his hand held up to indicate that George should stop; George reluctantly decelerated, put his indicator on and steered towards the left-hand shoulder of the road. The front and back wheels scratched on gravel; but instead of bringing the car to a halt as expected, George suddenly accelerated again and sped off, drenching the two traffic officers in a billowing dust-cloud. Red-faced, the white officer cocked his firearm and shot at the errant vehicle, but, fortunately, the shot went wide of its target.

'Don't shoot, Koos!' the black officer cautioned his colleague, reminding him that in democratic South Africa police were expected to use their firearms judiciously.

'Write down the registration number!' the black officer commanded the other, who was his junior in age as well as rank.

'How can I see it in all this dust?' the white officer responded, with considerable irritation.

'Okay, then let's chase the offender,' said the black officer.

The two officers hurriedly put their speed-trap gadget in their car and sped after the lawbreaker. The BMW should have been no more than five kilometres ahead of them and easy to spot. They raced along the twisting, narrow road, blue emergency light flashing and loud siren warning other motorists to give way. Behind the steering wheel, the white officer did an excellent job of travelling at speed on the uneven, patched and potholed tarmac surface.

Ten kilometres further, there was still no sign of the offending BMW. The police car sped down towards Mmakgabo High School in the territory of Paramount Chief Kgabo Moloto. At the top of the slope ahead of them they glimpsed, at last, a white rear bumper and were encouraged to accelerate with the intention of overtaking the offender. It surprised the officers somewhat that the vehicle in question was travelling at a relaxed and easy pace, apparently in no hurry to flee the wrath of the law.

A few minutes later, they overtook a laden white stationwagon huffing and puffing under the weight of multiple bags of oranges. The sheepish officers realised they had *'missed the hare and beaten faeces with a hunting stick!'*

The misbehaving BMW, meanwhile, was nowhere to be seen. This was because George had turned off to the right a few kilometres back, heading towards the village of Ga-Maleka, which lay about five kilometres to the south of Ga-Mabitsela. George couldn't stop grinning, certain that he had safely outrun the police. From this point on he was forced, of necessity, to keep his speed down to between 40 and 50 kms per hour in order to avoid the throngs of cattle, goats, chickens and toddlers that beseiged the route from the nearby homesteads.

The traffic officers pulled off the road and sat silently digesting their discouragement. To quarrel or point fingers at each other would not help to catch the offender. White officer took out a 1.5-litre flask full of steaming, aromatic tea and poured it into two cups; the two officers then quietly sipped until the last drops were in their stomachs. Black officer then asked if white officer would mind if they made a detour to visit his widowed mother who lived in a village about five kilometres to the north, since they were about to knock off duty anyway; white officer did not mind. They changed places, with black officer now taking the wheel, since he knew the roads well in that part of the province.

At Dimakatjo's homestead, people were still celebrating Sefako's victory against crime with song, dance and jubilation when their joy-drunk eyes caught sight of a convoy of police cars and vans driving in through the gates.

It was Uncle Phari, arriving – *palakata* – at last! Dimakatjo's people collectively heaved a huge sigh of thankfulness. The long-awaited one, the Great Porcupine, Uncle 'Stop Nonsense!' had finally turned up to set his foot on Bakone soil. No more would the power-hungry pair, Lukas and Mayibuye, be able to lord it over them.

As Uncle Phari strode with his entourage towards the entrance of the *lapa*, joyful pandemonium broke loose. *Sangoma*-aunt leapt and pranced erratically, jerking her torso sideways, backwards and forwards in the popular *phepela*. Other women joined her, improvising their own 'swaggering' display.

Sangoma-aunt's lips parted and her vocal chords let loose a piercing ululation:

Liliililiiii!
Children's uncle has arrived!
Father has come,
hunger has died the death
of an earthenware pot!

Another female relative added to the praises:
Lu-iu-iuuu-u!
The Great Porcupine has arrived!
His sharp quills are our protection!
The sun is shining on
orphans trapped in the deep, dark valley!

A third relative interjected:
Liliililiiii! Šatee-weee!

And throngs of people responded:
Šateee!

Uncle Phari was accompanied by a white colleague and three black sergeants, all of whom had, in keeping with the abundant African *ubuntu* values, been invited by Uncle Phari to come and celebrate his niece's important day. These VIP 'dogs of the state' were given their own spacious room to relax in, where they would be served 'bones' to gnaw at – in the form of a sumptuous meal, washed down by a variety of beverages. Uncle Phari had apologised in advance to his colleagues for the fact that he would not be joining them, since his attention would be on the *lobola* negotiations.

The clanspeople were overjoyed that their own flesh and blood, the faithful 'bulldog of *kgoromente*', was at last in their midst. They wished that he could have been with them from the first, since he was the children's uncle, the one who wielded the axe of finality and authority. As Uncle Phari exchanged greetings with umpteen relatives, Mma-Dimakatjo and a few others brought Sefako to him, recounting the young man's heroic performance in proud detail to their impressed listener.

Uncle Phari was then introduced to the Fouries; with heart as white as an egret he greeted Uncle Pieter and *mmaditsela* Lesetja, for George was still on his way back from Polokwane with the additional *lobola* amount.

'It is good that the young people have made it possible for us to meet today!' Uncle Phari told Uncle Pieter with a broad smile.

On enquiring about Fanie, he was told by *sangoma*-aunt: 'Your son-in-law is here, and he's well looked after.'

For Dimakatjo, the arrival of the children's uncle was a moment of indescribable joy, but for Lukas and Mayibuye it was one of unpleasant reckoning; for they knew that they would be called to account for their domineering tactics.

Mma-Dimakatjo was just beginning to fill Uncle Phari in on the events that had transpired in his absence when Dimakatjo came bursting into the room and hugged her adored uncle tearfully.

'Uncle, where were you when my day turned sour?' she sobbed into his shoulder.

'What has gone wrong, *motlogolo*?' asked Uncle Phari in concern.

'*Buti* Lukas and *khazi* Matsobane have been causing problems! They don't want me to get married! They . . . '

'They don't want you to get married?' echoed Uncle Phari in perplexity, scarcely able to believe what he was hearing.

'*Eng, malome!*' ('Yes, uncle!') Dimakatjo continued to shed more tears.

Aunt Mashadi approached and covered Dimakatjo's head with a shawl, leading her charge to the bedroom, where she tried to calm and console her.

Bakone clan called Uncle Phari to their room of negotiations.

'The children's uncle has arrived and the problem that is hard and stubborn as a tendon will at last be chopped by the axe!' exclaimed an elated Grandpa.

Uncle Phari apologised for arriving so late and the clanspeople assured him that they appreciated that national duty had had to take precedence over domestic matters. Although the children's uncle was burning to hear exactly how Lukas and Mayibuye were bent on derailing the *lobola* negotiations, he restrained his curiosity for the moment.

The well-fed and well-hosted men of the law asked one of the relatives to send word to Uncle Phari that they would now be on their way. The Machabaphala people excused the Great Porcupine once again while he bid his colleagues farewell. On their way out, the 'dogs of *kgoromente*' collected the unfortunate leGent and bundled the criminal, now handcuffed, into the back of the police van, amidst the cheers and applause of the villagers.

As the entourage pulled away, a grinning Sefako waved his catapult cheekily at the captured leGent, who could be seen miserably peering out through the wire grid on the windows.

And so it was that courage, on this occasion, triumphed over crime.

37

Uncle Phari was persuaded by Mma-Dimakatjo to have a quick meal, consisting of the expertly fermented sorghum-corn *ting* porridge, with thick and tangy, deep-brown fried-onion-and-tomato gravy, a fried half a chicken, and cooked vegetables. A chocolate cake with custard accompanied this sumptuous meal. When Uncle Phari had done justice to the business of chewing and swallowing, he emptied a glass of fruit juice into his mouth and took his seat in the negotiating room at last.

All eyes were focused on the Great Porcupine, for his masterful presence pervaded the room instantly.

'What is this I hear, that Lukas and Matsobane are stones among the mung beans?' Uncle Phari demanded.

The elders gave him a detailed account of what had happened in his absence and precisely who had said what, when, why and to whom.

'I reminded them, children's uncle, that walking was better than hurrying but they would not listen,' said Grandpa.

The culprits were glued to their chairs, listening nervously as their 'charge sheet' was presented. They could not claim that what was being said was not the truth. Uncle Phari listened intently to every word.

'As we are sitting here now,' said Grandpa, 'one of the *lobola* negotiators is not with us.'

'Where is he?' demanded Uncle Phari.

'He has gone to fetch the additional money from the machine.'

As the people apprised Uncle Phari further of the progress and stumbling blocks of the negotiations, his eyes flickered more than once towards Lukas and Mayibuye. What he was hearing was so incredible to his ears that he could scarcely believe it. He was amazed that the Machabaphalas had allowed themselves to be browbeaten by the two young jackals.

Children's uncle fired several more questions at his people. They were now beginning to repeat what they had already told him. For a long while Uncle Phari was silent, the machine in his head busy grinding the hard corn it had been given. At last he was ready to respond. He took a deep breath, preparing to pour the wind out of his mouth.

'Young men, what were you trying to do?' he asked the recalcitrants sternly. 'Are you aware that what you have done is pure witchcraft? You have bedevilled this most important day of my niece's life! Because of your greed, you almost derailed the train of this *lobola*! You are crooks! And you have caused the Machabaphala people to go back on their word.'

The Great Porcupine waved his index finger imperiously: 'You should have joined that criminal in the police van! Go on – get out! I don't want to see your faces any more!'

Even the air seemed to freeze under his biting contempt. Lukas lifted one of his buttocks off the sofa, but Mayibuye did not budge an inch.

'Please, children's uncle, do not chase them away!' pleaded *sangoma*-aunt. Kneeling, she engaged in the conciliatory *phophotha* ritual. 'When the bird is angry it does not chase away the young ones! Put your spears down, children's uncle . . . Great Porcupine; who can bear the pain of your angry quills?'

A few moments earlier, Lukas had been drunk, but now he was completely sober. The clanspeople sat quietly, their body language continuing to plead. Not for nothing was Uncle Phari known as Uncle 'Stop Nonsense!' He drew in his breath and all leaned forward in anticipation of his judgement.

Staring coldly, he addressed Lukas and Mayibuye once more: 'Your behaviour has not only been infamous but un-African,' he told them. 'You have stepped over the line and gone against the will of your elders. I will spare you from banishment because of the pleas of your kinsfolk.'

He looked sternly at their sullen faces. '*Pasop* young men! Be thankful that today you have survived the lion's mouth. You must thank your ancestors that I managed to come here just in time to sort out this mess!'

The fight-or-flight chemicals in Lukas's blood were demanding release. Although he did not like the taste of humble-pie, he restrained himself from speaking, for he dared not talk back or shout insults at his uncle the way his temper urged him to. Mayibuye, too, kept quiet; the two young men had no choice but to swallow the scolding, in keeping with the cultural precepts that prescribed that *'a real man is a sheep that cries inwardly when it is slaughtered, unlike a goat that screams "mêh-mêh!"'*

A minute's silence was like a torturing hour to the two partners in crime. Uncle Phari still continued to look at them chidingly, as if he had more words to say.

'Let the matter now face the axe, children's uncle.' It was Grandpa who broke the unnerving silence.

At his words, Uncle Phari's stern manner relaxed.

'How much have the Fouries already given you?' he enquired.

'R4 000 so far. Excluding fines.'

'How much are the fines . . . ?' Uncle Phari's question was interrupted by a knock at the door. Thomas stood up and stepped briskly to open it.

A grinning George stood in the doorway, a white envelope in his hand. Thomas took it from him and stepped back inside the room.

'It appears that our friends have brought something delicious for us. Is it true?' asked Uncle Phari, his eyes fixed on Thomas.

'It's true, uncle.'

'Open the envelope.'

Thomas obediently ripped the envelope open and exposed a pile of red and blue notes in R200 and R100 denominations.

'Count it!'

Assisted by Mayibuye, Thomas began counting the banknotes, only to be interrupted by another knock at the door. Hurriedly Thomas packed the money back into the envelope and hid it in the inner pocket of his jacket. This time Mayibuye opened the door; two of the relatives stood there, their faces registering bewilderment. Behind them was a stern-faced black traffic cop – colloquially known as *sepitikopo* ('speed cop') – accompanied by his white colleague.

'Who is the owner of that white BMW parked outside?' the black officer demanded.

Nobody answered; nobody said a word. All stared in bafflement at the uniformed men in front of them.

The black officer was referring, of course, to Fanie's BMW, now sitting innocently in the open in full view of everyone. As soon as the two officers' eyes alighted on it, they had recognised that this was the same white German-made lawbreaker that had evaded their speed-trap and outrun them a short while before on the road from Polokwane. Now they had him! The long arm of the law had caught up with the offender – this traffic culprit whose luck had now run out, whose gods had this day betrayed him.

The black officer was no stranger to the people in the room, and their faces were all very familiar to him, too. The older Bakone clanspeople had known this officer when he was just a small boy with naked buttocks and mucous trickling out of his nostrils, herding cattle in the village fields. In their minds he was still this small boy, younger even than Lukas; but now he was wearing the cap of authority, the blue uniform of the law.

It was because of this uniform that the black officer had to maintain his sternness; he could not afford to exchange friendly greetings or flash 'toothpaste advert' smiles at anyone, for he was an officer on duty.

There was no way that Dimakatjo's people could cajole him with African familiarity, or bribe him with *tjotjo* – 'shut-up money' – because the white officer was standing there shoulder to shoulder with his colleague; furthermore, the white officer could speak their language, albeit badly and with a poor accent. Under such circumstances there was no chance that the most wanted car of the day could turn out to be without an owner.

Dimakatjo's people were wondering how George, their go-between, had managed to transgress the law of the road. They had no chance to ask him, however, for George had disappeared.

A few minutes earlier, he had been standing idly beside Fanie's car, chatting to some of the genial relatives, when he chanced to look across the way and saw, to his shock, a blue-and-white traffic patrol car parking itself at the next-door neighbour's homestead.

George quickly retreated and dashed towards the pit-toilet at the back of Dimakatjo's property. He was petrified beyond description; the last thing he had expected was that the traffic officers – whom he had felt certain he had outrun by a good stretch of kilometres, thanks to the power of the German-made engine – would track him down and ferret him out.

George had no way of knowing that the black cop happened to live in the very same village as Dimakatjo's family – so close, in fact, that when Dimakatjo's parents' rooster crowed, or their hen cackled, the officer's family could hear them. Because of his employment with the traffic police, the black officer currently stayed in Seshego township and visited his mother on his off-duty weekends once or twice a month.

On this occasion, when the officer and his white colleague had arrived at his home, they could not find a single soul in the house; the black officer was told by a passerby that his mother, sister and niece were at Dimakatjo's home, partaking in *lobola* celebrations. When the officers arrived at Dimakatjo's place a short time later, the first thing their amazed eyes landed on was a white BMW, which they instantly suspected to be the very car that they were searching for. Their suspicions were aggravated when they felt the temperature of the car's bonnet and found it to be still hot.

'I said, who is the owner of that white BM over there?' the black officer asked again, his voice louder and more officious this time.

Again, his question was met with silence. All eyes turned towards the Great Porcupine; since he was a man of law himself, a bulldog of *kgoromente* no less, it was expected of him to intervene.

Uncle Phari put two and two together and made the right amount. Rising from his chair, he beckoned to the traffic officers to follow him and stepped out of the room. In the *lapa*, Uncle Phari quickly whispered to two male relatives, who hurried off towards the pit-toilet where George had last been seen heading at great speed. There he still was, cowering inside with the door firmly closed.

'*Kô-kô-kô-kôôô!*' A harsh knocking came at the corrugated-iron door with its collapsing hinges.

'*Ke sa nyela!*' ('I'm still relieving myself!') responded George in irritated tones.

'*Na o nyela maswika monna? Etšwa!*' ('Are you shitting stones? Come out!') retorted the man waiting on the other side of the door.

A few seconds later a quaking George was escorted towards the *lapa*, where the two traffic officers waited with the Great Porcupine and other concerned relatives. Deep in his heart, the black traffic officer respected and even feared the formidable Great Porcupine; but since on this day the black officer wore the cap of the law, he could not let respect get in the way of him doing his job.

The Great Porcupine did not intervene further in the proceedings but held his jaws closed and let the law take its course.

George stood before the two *sepitikopo* like a sickly chicken drenched by a merciless *matla-ka-dibe* downpour.

'*Hei monna*, are you aware that you have wilfully transgressed the National Road Traffic Act No. 93 of 1996 section 69 sub-section 7 item 7?'

Whatever his feelings on the inside, black officer did a good job of masking them. He exuded nothing but authority as he stood sternly surveying his suspect, looking straight into George's intimidated eyes.

'Have you got R6 000 for a spot fine?' white officer fired at George.

George made a pathetic strangled sound and wagged his head weakly from side to side.

Both officers pulled their caps lower on their foreheads, clearly asserting their unassailable power. Uncle Phari realised it was time to do something.

The Great Porcupine hurried discretely towards the entrance of the *lapa* and whispered to some of the female relatives; two of them hastened to the back of the homestead. They called to an old woman there and beckoned her over, escorting her to the *lapa*, where a very hang-dog George was facing his come-uppance.

'Honourable officers, please forgive me!' pleaded George humbly. 'I don't have the money to pay such a huge fine.'

'In that case, you are going to rot in jail for 24 months!' responded black officer. As he finished his sentence, the old woman who had entered with Uncle Phari walked forward into view; it was the black officer's mother.

'*Kubu, Kubu!*' Black officer clearly heard the voice of his mother addressing him.

To be addressed as '*Kubu*', the hippopotamus, the totem animal of their clan, meant that something had to be taken note of; this word was often used when a special favour was requested, or as a preface to conveying serious tidings or initiating discussions. As a young boy, the black officer used to hear his mother pleading with his angry father, passionately addressing him as '*Kubu!*'

'*Kubu, Kubu!* Beast of the restless waters,' continued the black officer's mother.

Two more old women and two old men came shuffling forward to kneel beside the black traffic officer's mother; the humble, grey-haired people then engaged in the conciliatory *phophotha* ritual, applauding gently and earnestly before the two traffic officers, demonstrating in face, body and bones how sorry they were and requesting pardon for the offence that had been committed.

'*Kubu, Kubu!*' This time the old people swelled the plea into a chorus of pleas. 'Please forgive him, my child!' black officer's mother said, for the final time.

The two officers exchanged rueful glances, then scanned the crowd of villagers surrounding them. It was evident that they had both been touched by the humility of the black officer's mother's plea, as well as the pleading words and supplicating body language of the other old people. As it was said, '*a finger can only touch the chest, but words penetrate through and reach the heart*'.

Again the two officers exchanged glances; then, simultaneously, both smiled and nodded. It was evident to all that George was forgiven. Black officer shook a warning finger at the offender, but his face was smiling. Uncle Phari laughed and led the people in a burst of spontaneous applause.

'*Ke a leboga, Kubu!*' ('Thank you, *Kubu!*') said George, smiling back at the black officer with huge relief written all over his face. He turned to also smile his thanks at the white officer.

'*Kubu, Kubu!*' chanted Uncle Phari.

'*Kubu, Kubu!*' responded appreciative villagers from all corners of the homestead.

As the two officers were escorted out of the *lapa* and across to the marquee to be given refreshments, Lukas and Mayibuye took the opportunity to walk discreetly around the back of the house, where they slugged down a triple tot each of potent whiskey.

The officers were pampered with festive food and softdrinks for, still being in uniform, they could not partake of liquor.

White officer was amused and overwhelmed by the generosity of the villagers.

'Is this what you people call *ubuntu?*' he enquired of his colleague.

Black officer simply grinned, his industrious mouth busy doing justice to a delicious chunk of fried chicken.

Bakone clanspeople sighed in relief and continued where they had left off. Thomas and Mayibuye started afresh to count the banknotes that they had received from George. They totalled R4 000 exactly.

Uncle Phari then beckoned to Grandpa and *sangoma*-aunt and the three went to stand outside the room, where they communicated in whispers and nodded to one another. When they returned and took their seats again, it was clear that Uncle Phari was ready with his axe to chop and finally execute the matter that had remained like a stubborn tendon for the greater part of the day.

'Bakone, let's agree,' said the Great Porcupine, 'that of the additional R4 000 we shall take only R2 000 and return the rest.'

'Return R2 000?' Lukas interrupted Uncle Phari. '*Aowaa, malome!* According to our culture, that which arrives and lands at the chief's court cannot be . . .'

'. . . returned! Lukas is right,' Mayibuye said, rushing to the support of his ally.

'Listen here . . . !'

'*Aowaa, malome* . . . !' Again, Lukas rudely interrupted his uncle.

Dimakatjo's people were astounded that Lukas had the temerity to answer back the venerable Great Porcupine; this same Lukas who used to fear Uncle 'Stop Nonsense!' like a hedgehog scared to death by lightning. *Mmalo!* It was true – the white man's liquor didn't give birth to weak-kneed cowards!

'Listen here, young men,' roared Uncle Phari, 'I'm in charge here! And there is only one bull in this *kraal*! Not two or three! My boys, your time of full adulthood is coming; you will be uncles when your sisters' children get married. That is when words of wisdom will be expected from you.'

Lukas opened his mouth to speak again, but Uncle Phari stared at him challengingly until he subsided. Uncle Phari filled his lungs with ample air before chasing the wind out of his mouth:

'My people, the affairs of the day have at last arrived at the sharpened axe. From this R4 000 we are going to take only R2 000. Of this R500 will cover all fines imposed, while R1 500 shall stand for the following supplementary standard items: father-in-law's coat, mother-in-law's shawl, father-in-law's walking-stick, mother-in-law's headdress and father-in-law's smoking pipe. I, Epaphrus Makgorometša Mashabathakga rest my axe!'

The Bakone clanspeople, with the exception of Lukas and Mayibuye, applauded with wide smiles, joy shining from their eyes. *Ruri*, a momentous task had been achieved, and all the faces were alight with relief and elation.

Aunt Mashadi was there to witness with her own two eyes and listen with her two ears as the children's uncle's axe did a perfect job; her heart, too, was full of joy.

'Now what is going to happen to the remaining R2 000?' asked a patently disgruntled Lukas.

'It must be for washing our hands and whetting our tired lips,' said Mayibuye provocatively.

Mayibuye was referring to the kind of fine known as *mangangahlaga* that was often imposed by the chief and his council during a tribal court hearing. The word meant, literally, 'to stretch the cheeks'.

'We are not in a tribal court now. And you are once again out of order, young men!' warned Uncle Phari. He waited for several moments to let his words sink in and then continued: 'The remaining money will be given to our daughter and son-in-law. They can use it to go on holiday or buy furniture. I, Epaphrus Makgorometša Mashabathakga now rest my axe!'

Bakone once more applauded, some of them – *sangoma*-aunt, Mma-Dimakatjo and Aunt Mashadi – conveying their joy by engaging in the *phepela* swagger as they exited the room.

Deeply disgusted by the outcome, Lukas and Mayibuye headed out for an unscheduled smoke-break. Thomas the go-between was tasked with the duty of pouring the good news into the ears of the Fouries. All the negotiators representing the two families were then requested to meet in the *lapa* for the purpose of getting to know one another, and in order for the whole world to see that the agenda for the day had been successfully concluded. Tears, pain and patience had paid off and obstacles and trials, as Grandpa had wisely advised, had at last been proven to be '*an old man of a lion*'.

George and Thomas were sent to fetch Fanie, whose patient waiting had at last borne fruit. As the two go-betweens headed out of the *lapa* towards Aunt Mashadi's house, they saw a party of new arrivals being escorted into the yard. George's eyes were drawn to a young white woman whose face looked vaguely familiar to him; it was Fanie's sister Anna-Marie, accompanied by her mother Louise and Selina, the family's long-serving domestic. They had at last arrived, having been delayed by a navigation error on the map that Fanie had drawn for Anna-Marie to follow.

These important guests were welcomed like special dignitaries and taken to the marquee, where they were pampered with delicious food and drink and every courtesy was extended to them.

38

Aunt Mashadi performed an energetic and triumphant *phepela* as she entered Dimakatjo's room.

'*Palesa ya* Bakone!' ('Pearl of Bakone!') she enthused, addressing Dimakatjo in this way for the first time. 'Today you are a woman indeed, a woman leaving her home as the cattle from your in-laws bellow "M*muuu!* M*muuu!*"'

Aunt Mashadi embraced and kissed Dimakatjo, whose face was radiant with delight. A single teardrop spilt from her eye and meandered down her cheek, marring the flawless finish of her make-up; this, vigilant Aunt Mashadi instantly restored.

Aunt Mashadi then dressed Dimakatjo in the beautifully embroidered gold *hele*-print garment wrought in the style of the Bapedi of Sekhukhune; it had an undercloth of fine, transparent purple georgette, that served as a petticoat; this was fastened around her waist and reached down to her calves. Her ankles were ringed with *maseka*, the silver African ankle-bangles customarily worn by married women. In keeping with the tradition, she walked barefoot.

A lavishly embroidered *doek* was then put on Dimakatjo's head, while a light-weight shawl covered her shoulders. Aunt Mashadi wound bead-straps around her charge's biceps and slipped onto her arm the familiar copper bangle that was part of Fanie's original Valentine's Day gift to her. Pearl of Bakone then took out the little box in which was stored Fanie's special gift that she had kept hidden away for months – the glamorous multicoloured Ndebele-bead necklace. She hung it in its rightful place around her neck and smiled contentedly. Finally, Dimakatjo's face was covered with a pale-green chiffon cloth that made it possible for her to see out without herself being clearly seen.

From the window of her bedroom she watched the proceedings, delighted to see her relatives and other well-wishers celebrating joyfully in anticipation of the climax of the day. Among those entering and exiting the *lapa* she spotted Fanie's sister Anna-Marie. She was in the company of an older white woman. Dimakatjo studied the stranger curiously, wondering who she could be. She guessed the woman to be Fanie's aunt, or Uncle Pieter's wife; not for a single moment could she envisage the possibility that it might be Fanie's mother. It seemed impossible that that racist old battle-axe would come to grace Dimakatjo's marriage day with her presence and say 'Halleluja!' for her son's *lobola* to a black woman. Sandwiched between the two white women was a beaming black woman who Dimakatjo guessed to be Selina, the family's domestic worker.

Great was Dimakatjo's astonishment when, a short while later, she was informed by Aunt Mashadi that the older white woman was, in fact, Fanie's mother. Dimakatjo was so overwhelmed that for a while she could find nothing to say. She gave a silent prayer of thanks that her mother-in-law had at last accepted her as her son's rightful wife. *Now I am indeed daughter-in-law of the* boere! Dimakatjo thought, and emitted joyous peals of laughter of the kind that might lead any listener to assume that she was *ruri-ruri* – indeed – a person unhinged with joy.

The go-betweens of the two families and scores of Dimakatjo's people presently came together in the *lapa*, where they exchanged African handshakes and smiling greetings, with much laughter and many sighs of relief.

Dimakatjo's people greatly appreciated the presence of Fanie's mother and sister. They were, of course, not aware of the fact that Fanie's mother had been dead against her son's love-affair – so bitterly opposed to it that she had even used words such as '*kak*' and '*kaffer*' in reference to it. As was the custom, the Fouries were addressed as '*bakgotse*' – 'the friends'.

'We are exceedingly pleased that, as from this day, the Fourie and Machabaphala people are one clan through cattle,' announced Uncle Phari, speaking first in Sepedi and then in Afrikaans for the benefit of the special guests. He was loudly applauded by all.

Fluent in Afrikaans, the Great Porcupine communicated very well with the Fouries. Others among Dimakatjo's people also made a spirited attempt to show off their smatterings of '*die taal*' and demonstrate that they were not linguistically deficient in this department; for, after all, some of them had been employed for decades as domestic workers and farmhands of the *boere*.

There was fresh excitement as an indigenous dance troupe, known as Men of *Kiba*, arrived at Dimakatjo's place. About twenty strong, they comprised male dancers who also played steel mouth pipes, and three woman drummers. The troupe had been brought by slow-moving tractor all the way from Ga-Kibi, a village which lay about 80 kilometres to the north of Ga-Mabitsela. The 'whip-cracker' or captain of this troupe was known as *malokwane*. On seeing Mayibuye's mother, he addressed her as 'aunt' – for she was his father's sister.

'*Khazi*, why didn't you tell us that you would be coming with a dance troupe?' Lukas asked him.

Malokwane explained that this wasn't intended but that when he had told the Men of *Kiba* that he would be attending the celebration, they had insisted on accompanying him. This meant that they had volunteered to perform without charge and would, instead, be thanked with food: stiff maize-meal porridge, meat, and a generous quantity of home-brewed *mabele*-corn beer. Lukas conferred with his mother and uncle and they agreed that they had no objection to feeding the dance troupe, who had the reputation of being endowed with devastating appetites.

George and Thomas, accompanied by an escort of two other vehicles, steered Fanie's zigzagging, hooting, dust-kicking BMW towards Aunt Mashadi's house, where the long-suffering bridegroom was waiting. Once there, George and Thomas alighted and strutted forward in the *phepela* swagger towards the house, while the drivers of the two other cars hooted intermittently. They found Fanie and Joyce standing in the doorway with an air of expectancy.

'Mr Fourie, today you are the son-in-law of Bakone clanspeople, *ka patla le jase!*' ('with a stick and a coat!') George announced in the traditional manner; by this he meant that Fanie had been accepted fully and completely into the family. Grinning from ear to ear, he gave Fanie a hearty handshake and a prolonged bear-hug.

'*Magtig! Dank die Here!*' ('Heavens! Thank the Lord!') Fanie exclaimed in relief.

Joyce and Thomas took turns to congratulate Fanie with their own enthusiastic handshakes. George and Thomas then led Fanie to another room. There, they removed his shirt, trousers and shoes and dressed him in a traditional bridegroom's outfit. A hand-tanned heifer's hide was fastened securely around his waist, reaching down to just above his knees. Joyce came in to hang a necklace of coloured beads around Fanie's neck. A sheepskin was draped around his shoulders, and handmade sandals with tyre-rubber soles were strapped onto his feet. Lastly, a fighting-stick and shield were put into his hands.

George stood back and admired his handiwork: 'You look like a real *lesogana!*' ('a full-blooded young man!') he said.

George and Thomas then drove Fanie and Joyce to Dimakatjo's place. As before, the BMW performed its own version of celebratory *phepela*, zigzagging jerkily, hooting noisily and braking sharply every few metres, generally creating lots of dust and causing bystanders to wave excitedly and shout: '*Šatee! Šatee!*' As Fanie's car entered the gate, Dimakatjo's people were standing lined up on both sides of the *lapa* entrance, waiting for the bridegroom to arrive. The industrious Women of Society left their labours and hurried up to form a guard of honour, together with the Fouries and some of Dimakatjo's people.

'*Iiuu-iuuuu!*' ululated *sangoma*-aunt, lifting up a handcrafted grass broom.

'*Aria-ria-ria!*' Aunt Mashadi cried, as she raised a grass bowl high into the air.

Other relatives called out their various contributions, invoking the ancestors' blessing of plenty on the marriage:

'Cream! Cream!'
'Rain of love! Rain of love!'
'*Howaaa! Howaaa!*'
The women burst into song:

Kajeno ke mokete
Kajeno ke mokete
Kajeno ke mokete
Mokete wa lobola!

(Today is a wedding day
It's a feast for *lobola*!)

A soaring soprano voice continued: '*Fanie wee!*' And other voices joined in: '*Wa lobola!*' ('He's parting with *lobola*!') All the singing voices then completed the song together:

Fanie wee
Wa lobola!
O nyala Dimakatjo!

(Fanie is parting with *lobola*
Fanie is marrying Dimakatjo!)

When Fanie's cruising car ultimately halted, the two traffic officers, now well stuffed and full of good humour, began controlling and directing the milling crowds of people, making a buffer zone between the villagers and Fanie and his entourage.

Fanie was led through the entrance of the *lapa*, while the women's voices, joined by male tenors and baritones, continued to belt out the wedding song.

Treated in VIP style, Fanie, along with the go-betweens and other relatives, walked on a path of special handcrafted grass sitting-mats, known as *magogwa*. As Fanie paced towards the centre of the *lapa*, a bare-chested Lukas emerged from the rondavel, his loins covered with a tight-fitting *setsiba* – the traditional lion-skin loin-cloth of the Bapedi tribespeople; from this, several *meswe*, or *meerkat* tails, dangled at front and back. Striding quickly forward waving a shield and brandishing a *knobkierie*, Lukas stopped abruptly in front of Fanie and gestured with his hands, challenging him to a stick-fight. Taking up the challenge Fanie advanced cautiously towards his opponent, beating his shield powerfully with his stick. Fortunately, he had been well prepared by George for this very moment.

Feet firmly planted, Lukas moved his shield forwards and backwards. Suddenly Fanie unleashed several mighty blows with his fighting-stick, which landed heavily on Lukas's shield and stick. Lukas retreated backwards, raising his shield and stick in a sign of surrender.

The people loudly applauded Fanie.

'Because you have defeated me, I am giving you my sister!' pronounced Lukas, to enthusiastic applause.

'You can see for yourselves that our son-in-law is no weakling!' enthused Mayibuye.

At this moment there was a commotion from the Machabaphala place. Murmurs filled the air as Dimakatjo emerged, covered from head to ankles in a colourful blanket of blue, yellow and red that had been put around her. Leading Dimakatjo forward towards her man was, of course, Aunt Mashadi.

Dimakatjo and Fanie were made to kneel a few metres apart, facing towards each other. Whispered instructions were given to them to move forward on their knees, until they were separated by the distance of one arm's length.

Aunt Mashadi then uncovered Dimakatjo from the shoulders up; her breathtaking hairstyle was still intact, as if it had been freshly created. *Morwedi'a* Machabaphala was holding a large, coloured earthenware pot, filled to the brim with home-brewed *mabele* cornbeer.

She carefully handed the calabash to Fanie who sipped from it and put it down.

The people applauded enthusiastically.

Another instruction was whispered to Fanie and Dimakatjo, who rose to their feet. The onlookers again applauded. Grandpa stepped towards the couple, launching into an impromptu praise-poem:

Cattle, cattle break walls
and open mouths of people,
make people mix blood,
and share life from one wooden plate,
cattle, cover people with love!
Iuu-iuu-iuu!

The crowd responded: 'Šatee! Šateee!'

With a beaming smile Uncle Phari walked towards the couple. Though he was, by nature, so dignified that rumours abounded that he regularly applied a lion's-fat ointment, the children's uncle was, on this day, exuberantly joyful.

'Child of Bakone,' Uncle Phari addressed Dimakatjo, 'you have behaved very well; it's good that you were not a "nice-time girl", changing boys like tissues for your nose. Your excellent moral standards have, today, paid huge dividends. Well done, *motlogolo!*'

Once more the people applauded.

'In those days when I was still a young man,' the children's uncle rested his smiling gaze on Fanie, 'when a bicycle was as good as a car, before cars became as common as they are today, naughty boys who had a sense of humour used to remark the following when they saw a young man carrying a girl on his bicycle: "A dog is running away with a meaty bone!"' His audience laughed with enjoyment.

Eyes still fixed on Fanie, Uncle Phari now launched into an impromptu praise-poem:

Hau-hau-hau!
Agee! Behold the bulldog of the boere
running away with the T-bone steak of Bakone!
The bone has been bought
the dog is not a thief.
We, Bakone have rewarded the dog!
Hau-hau-hau!
Šatee! Šateee!

Sections of the crowd responded appreciatively: '*Ii-li-li-li-liiiii! Howaa! Howaa!*'

39

After this, Fanie and Dimakatjo were taken to the marquee, where several tables had been joined together in an oblong-shape. The special couple occupied their allotted seats, two chairs covered with a white sheet and fitted with cushions, which had been placed at the centre of the table facing the crowds. The VIP guests and relatives then seated themselves on the remaining chairs.

The rest of the guests – invited and uninvited – had to be content with standing or sitting on the floor. Facing the couple was a thickset, pot-bellied man sporting a thick, grey-peppered beard: this was the bishop of *Vukani-Ma-Afrika* ('Wake-up-Africans'), one of the many sects of the Zionist church. The bishop was garbed in the green-and-white Zionist robes, decorated with multiple hand-stitched green crosses. As a symbol of his authority, the Man of God held a long, episcopal crook, taller than he was and cross-shaped at the top. Facing him were members of the *Vukani-Ma-Afrika* congregation, dressed like their bishop in the green-and-white church uniform, the men wearing knee-length white overcoats, the women with green headdresses on their heads. As Fanie, Dimakatjo and some of the relatives took their seats at the VIP table, the Zionist choir was led by their charismatic bishop in song. They also performed a dance sequence, similar to the one that Nicholas had demonstrated to Fanie at his flat on their last meeting.

When the bishop was satisfied that the holy dancers had done justice to the occasion with their performance, he waved his hand, signalling to them to stop. In the silence that followed he opened his mouth, which was completely obscured by a thick, grizzled forest of beard and moustache: 'It affords me great pleasure to officiate at this *lobola* occasion. And I have no doubt that in heaven the angels are celebrating this important event; *ameni!*'

'*Aaaamennnii!*' roared the congregation in response.

'I say, in heaven,' repeated the bishop in a louder voice, 'the angels and God are dancing! For God loves *lobola*! *Aamenii!*'

'*Aaaamennnii!*' bellowed the congregation on cue.

'Yes, He . . .' the bishop pointed heavenwards, '. . . created marriage! God is love! But He is not impressed with *vat-en-sit* love relationships of modern times. God loves *lobola*! *Ameni!*'

'*Aaaamennnii!*' responded the congregation as before.

'Dear Bakone, Fouries, guests and Ga-Mabitsela villagers . . .'

Here, the bishop broke off abruptly. His eyes had been attracted by something peculiar: a drunk man, staggering straight towards him across the floor. It was Uncle Sepanere. He halted unsteadily, making a futile attempt to regain his balance.

'Excuse me, *moruti*' ('reverend'); Uncle Sepanere gave a loud belch, belatedly cupping his mouth with his palms to stifle it. 'Listen here! I am the girl's uncle . . . *bhrrrrr!*' Another loud belch shot from his mouth.

Thomas and Lukas stood up and hurried towards the old man, grabbing him by the biceps, ready to march him away.

'*Hohh-hohh!* Wait – let him speak before you remove him,' instructed the bishop. 'Perhaps he has something important to say. Freedom of speech, please!'

'Hey, listen!' said Uncle Sepanere. 'Today apartheid is dead! A white man is our son-in-law. And . . .' Uncle Sepanere hiccuped loudly, emitting a pungent smell of home-brewed beer. At that point Thomas and Lukas led their inebriated relative out of the tent.

The bishop waited for the laughter to die down and resumed his interrupted sermon: 'We shall read the Word of God, from the Book of Genesis, Chapter 24, verse 53. It reads thus: "Then the servant of Abraham brought out jewellery of silver, jewellery of gold, and clothing, and gave them to Rebekah. He also gave precious things to her brother and to her mother . . ."'

There was a pause while he examined his audience, then he continued: 'It's not my intention to preach today. What I would like to emphasise is that God loves *lobola*; He loves marriage. To you, the couple, I just want to say briefly: do not build your marriage on the sand of modern times but on God the indestructible rock! *Ameni!*'

'*Aaaaamenniiiiii!*' responded the congregation enthusiastically.

The hundreds of guests were then served with food. As they ate and drank, they inadvertently reflected their differing class and status levels: there were those at the main table who ate with forks and knives, used napkins and paper serviettes, sipped champagne and wine and peppered their mother-tongue with English phrases. The rest of the company, the majority of the people there, sat on benches or floor-mats, or squatted under the *morula* tree and ate their way through mounds of *pap* and chunks of boiled meat with their bare hands.

Members of the *Kiba* dance group, also known as the *dinaka* dancers, did justice with their teeth and fingers to a mound of steaming stiff porridge and meat, which consisted of roughly hacked pieces from the head of the slaughtered bull, skewered on a two-metre-long iron stake. *Joo* but those people could eat!

After demolishing the delicious mounds of food in record time, many of the satiated ones could be seen using index fingers and thumbnails to prod out the stubborn shreds of meat that had taken refuge between their teeth. This happy and excessive indulgence constituted what the villagers knew to be 'a good feast'.

Having gorged themselves to stomach-bursting proportions, the guests were then served with generous helpings of corn-beer, as well as 'white man's beer'. After half an hour or so of this convivial elbow-raising, Uncle Sepanere, Geelbooi and their comrades-around-the-bottle were seen holding hands, as innocently happy as children. Uncle Sepanere led them in singing:

A bo tle re bo kakate
bo pale
re bo tšholole!

(Let it [liquor] come
we shall gulp it
and pour it away
if we can't finish it!)

In the midst of all this eating and drinking, two hooting *kombis* turned into the yard and jerked to a halt. Each vehicle was bursting at the seams with male passengers, all of them singing, clapping their hands and stamping their feet as they sat.

These were Fanie's fellow workers from the Jacaranda Welding Company. They had turned up to show their solidarity with Fanie on this great occasion. They wore their factory uniforms, comprising blue overalls, boots, welding masks and protective gloves. Alighting from the *kombis*, the men began to chant and *toyi-toyi* forward towards the marquee where Fanie and Dimakatjo were seated. The leader chanted: 'Viva, Fanie . . . !' And others responded: 'Haayi! Haayi-haayi!'

Viva, Fanie . . . !
Haayi! Haayi-haayi!
He's a comrade!
Haayi! Haayi-haayi!'

Still chanting, the men approached Fanie and Dimakatjo, lifted them up, chairs and all and hoisted them shoulder-high, carrying them around the tent, to the amusement of all.

'*uFanie uyalobola!*' ('Fanie is parting with *lobola!*'), the lead singer chanted, while others responded: '*uFanie uyindoda!*' ('Fanie is a real man!')

After executing this comradely performance, the men handed over the gift they had brought for the couple, which was a smart-looking trolley suitcase. Fanie was greatly touched by the thoughtfulness of the gift and the trouble his fellow workers had gone to to bring it to him. The workers were led, still singing, to sit behind the main house, where they were served with generous portions of food.

Suddenly the people heard the sound of *lepatata* – the African bugle that is made from a bull's long, curving horn: '*Hla-bu-bu-bu-bu-buuu!*'

Malokwane, the captain of the dance troupe, cracked the plough-cattle whip, and in an instant the Men of *Kiba* were on their feet, converging around three African drums that had been placed in front of the *lapa*. Not a single dancer ignored the authority of *malokwane*'s call, for fear of a sharp whiplash landing on the tardy one's back. A thickset woman with powerful biceps took her place behind *sekgokolo*, the big, round drum, which she beat effortlessly with a half-metre-long piece of thick rubber hose.

Middle-sized *phoisene*, and the smallest drum, *matikwane*, named for the 'tickey' sound it produced, completed the rhythm section. Kneeling behind their instruments, the beaters of these smaller drums pounded powerfully with their bare hands, known as 'porridge-breakers'. The Men of *Kiba* were dressed in knee-length red-and-green chequered Scottish kilts, worn with sleeveless white vests and snow-white tennis shoes.

'*Shway! Shway!*' blew the leading pipe-blower, and the others followed, emitting notes of varying scales.

'*Kutung-kutung . . . bham! Kutung-kutung . . . bham!*' The drums complemented and guided the pipes.

The dancers waved an assortment of artifacts, such as *knobkieries*, sticks, hammers and even tennis racquets in their left hands, while their right hands firmly pressed the mouthpieces of the pipes to their lips. Some of the dancers had plastic cow-horns perched on their heads, from which the name *dinaka* was derived.

The dancers now began to stamp softly on the ground, gradually adding variations to the movements, until they created a spectacular sequence of stamps, knee-lifts and turns. They converged towards the drum-beaters, then unexpectedly did a swift about-turn in the opposite direction, causing their kilts to swirl up high and briefly expose their undershorts, thus eliciting loud peals of appreciative laughter, especially from the women in the audience. As the drum tempo increased, so did the speed and energy of the *dinaka* dancers, with some of the troupe members becoming totally possessed by their own frenzy.

Between the sweating dancers and the crowd of spectators was a two-metre-wide space that was occupied by two swaggering young village beauties. With energetic grace they glided forward in their white tennis shoes, in a manner characteristically described as '*go sepela godimo ga mae*' – 'walking on top of a chicken's eggs'.

The swaggering girls were glamorously draped in sleeveless *hele* fabrics, their bare arms adorned with coloured strings of beads and their faces painted with red ochre, on which had been drawn black dots in a triangular design, and a thick black line down the centre of the nose, known as *tshumu*. Their shoulders lifted jauntily to the rhythm and their arms moved gracefully this way and that, while their hands held grass winnowing bowls and brooms as props.

From the front of the crowd, Fanie's mother, sister and uncle watched the performance wide-eyed, seeing for the first time in their lives the spectacular intricacies performed by the dancers of *Kiba*. Selina stood with them, her face wreathed in ear-to-ear smiles.

The next dance sequence was even more energetic and riveting than the previous one; the drum-beater pounded the *phoisene* drum with ear-shattering strength while *matikwane* seemed to sing: '*Matopola-ka-pitšeng! Matopola-ka-pitšeng!*' ('Potatoes-in-the-pot! Potatoes-in-the-pot!')

A finger-length pipe of bone known as *letsie*, that had been cut from a sheep or goat's thighbone, punctuated the drum rhythms with a stirring '*Tsie!-Tsie!*' sound.

Dimakatjo stood close to Fanie, watching the proceedings. The lovers had not yet had the chance to exchange any words in private, but it was enough for the moment that they could stand together as a united couple.

Thomas came bounding up to them, joined their hands together and pushed them into the 'swaggering space' between the audience and the Men of *Kiba*, indicating that they should 'make dust for the song'. The couple had no choice but to comply, with Fanie gamely doing his best to copy the moves of Dimakatjo but always moving a little off the beat. This surprised no one, since it was a well-known joke that whites had no rhythm. The viewers laughed indulgently and applauded Fanie for his effort.

'*Tsie!-Tsie!-Tsie!*' The bone pipe added its glamour to the beauty of the rhythmic harmony.

'*Howaa! Howaa!*' roared sections of the audience alternately.

'*Iu-iu-iu-iu-iuuu! Šatee! Šatee-weee!*' responded various others, drunk with exhilaration and more potent things.

Sangoma-aunt leapt towards the Fourie party, grabbed hold of Uncle Pieter's hands and pulled him into the swaggering space. Uncle Phari held out a gallant arm to Fanie's mother. When she hesitated, looking alarmed, he laughed aloud and gently but firmly grabbed her hands: 'Come, there's no apartheid here!' he joked.

All in earshot roared with appreciative laughter, and Louise had no choice but to smile sheepishly and go with him. Thomas and Anna-Marie moved enthusiastically to join the other 'swagger' dancers, while jovial Selina didn't wait to be asked but grabbed hold of George and pulled him with her into the 'show-off' space. For the rest of the number, all concerned had uninhibited fun, shaking their hips, stamping their feet and waggling their shoulders and behinds to the hectic *Kiba* rhythms. Even Fanie's mother lost some of her initial stiffness and seemed to be enjoying herself, her large frame following Uncle Phari's lead with surprising agility.

When the song finally came to an end, the crowd roared appreciatively, applauding the dancers and other participants, especially the new in-laws. Aunt Mashadi then asked Fanie and Dimakatjo to return to the marquee. The couple stood at the entrance with the rest of the Fouries, while Dimakatjo's relatives lined up and came shuffling forward, gliding their feet towards the son-in-law of Bakone. Black hands firmly clasped white ones in the elaborate and prolonged African handshake, accompanied by approving exclamations such as: '*Jo-jo-jo! Mmulu! Šiba! Bonang!*' ('Yo-yo-yo! My gosh! Here they are! Look!') Some bobbed and curtseyed with the respectful courtesy characteristic of Bapedi people, while others spoke to their new son-in-law in an enthusiastic but severely battered Afrikaans that betrayed their woeful lack of schooling. Ever-smiling

Fanie answered them in an equally imprecise Sepedi – to their everlasting delight.

As the indefatigable dancers of *Kiba* continued to blow their pipes, beat their drums and titillate the viewers' eyes with their energetic, dust-kicking dance sequences, Fanie and Dimakatjo found a brief moment to talk to each other out of the crowd.

'How are you doing, my darling bride?' asked Fanie adoringly, enfolding his beloved into his arms.

This endearment caused Dimakatjo to break down into copious tears of joy.

'Why are you crying, my love?' he asked in concern, caressing her tenderly. He waited patiently until she had dried her eyes and was ready to speak.

'I am crying because I am so happy!' she told him tremulously. 'I can't believe that your mother has come after all, Fanie! My joy is now complete!'

Fanie nodded. 'I am also overwhelmed,' he said. 'She was the last person I was expecting to see here. God has answered our prayers!'

They held each other tenderly for several moments.

'My love,' said Fanie, 'seeing that all our relatives are already gathered together, why don't we just do our white wedding ceremony right here and now?'

'You mean right at this moment?' asked Dimakatjo.

'Why not? I'm sure your Uncle Phari could act as a Justice of the Peace?'

'Honey, you have taken me by surprise! I don't know what to say!'

'Just say "yes",' said Fanie, kissing her hungrily.

'But look at how I am dressed – I don't have a white wedding dress!'

'That's okay. You are excellent just the way you are!'

'Thank you, my love! But what about . . . '

'What now?'

'The wedding ring?'

'No problem!' Fanie inserted his hand into his jacket pocket and took it out again, his fist closed tantalisingly around something. He laid his knuckles against Dimakatjo's open and expectant palm, but to her surprise nothing was delivered into it from Fanie's hand. Instead, he mischievously scratched her palm with his fingernail. They burst into loud and carefree laughter.

'Where is my diamond and ivory ring?' she asked him with pretended indignation, remembering the ring from her dream.

'Still at the jewellers, waiting for you to choose it,' he answered wittily.

They laughed again with much mirthful enjoyment.

'I love you Fanie!'

'I love you too, *my skattebol!*'

'It's a nice idea to get married now, but let's not rush it, okay? Let's save the white wedding for another day, when we can do it properly.'

Fanie's response was to kiss her thoroughly, uncaring of the fact that they were providing 'a bioscope' for the gaze of all.

'Where are we going to be spending the night tonight? You still haven't told me,' Dimakatjo said, looking dreamily into Fanie's deep brown eyes.

'You will see!' Fanie smiled. 'I have a big surprise for you, my darling.'

'What? Tell me now!'

But he continued to smile mysteriously and said: 'You'll find out when the time comes!'

With that, Dimakatjo had to be content.

One last hurdle remained. Dimakatjo had yet to meet her mother-in-law face to face for the first time. So much depended on this moment and Dimakatjo was justifiably nervous, for everything she had heard about Fanie's mother led her to anticipate that Louise would not be easily won over. Dimakatjo had heard several stories about black brides who were never accepted by their husband's white families, forcing the couple to live as though orphans, cut off from their relatives.

She became aware that Louise was standing alone off to one side, from where she had been watching her son and daughter-in-law chatting and laughing, holding hands and kissing.

Fanie led Dimakatjo over to introduce them. The two women eyed each other warily, each waiting for the other to speak. It was Louise who broke the silence:

'*Aitsa,* but you are beautiful!' she exclaimed. Tears welled up unexpectedly in her eyes. 'Fanie *my seuntjie . . .* ' she began; but whatever she had been about to say was interrupted.

Loud explosions were heard as the corks were drawn from three magnums of champagne that Lukas and Mayibuye had brought out from their secret stash. A tiny amount was poured into every available glass, with more generous portions reserved for the privileged ones, such as the relatives and other VIPs. Toastmaster Mayibuye commanded everyone to raise their glasses. He sipped appreciatively from his own glass and, grinning, said: 'If witches have laced this champagne with poisonous herbs, then they have wasted their time!'

Everyone took this as the signal to down their own glassfuls.

Mma-Dimakatjo and *sangoma*-aunt stood on either side of their new white mother-in-law, putting her at ease with their friendly smiles. Taking her by the hand they walked her around to show her off to relatives and villagers sitting and imbibing *mabele* corn-beer and cooldrinks, some having tea and chewing cakes in the marquee or the *lapa,* or behind the main house.

Fanie's Uncle Pieter sat next to Uncle Phari on a hand-made bench under the *morula* tree, in the company of about a dozen older relatives. There, *mabele* corn-beer flowed like milk and honey in the land mentioned in the Bible. A drinker would gulp from the gourd, fill his mouth to his satisfaction and swallow audibly, spitting out the malt dregs with a satisfied sigh, exclaiming: 'What a good strong brew!' And so the huge, one-litre gourd was passed from one pair of hands to the next, until it landed in Uncle Pieter's lap.

Fanie's uncle held the quarter-full gourd and glanced obliquely at Uncle Phari, who smiled encouragingly and indicated with a nod that the other should take a good gulp. Uncle Pieter, however, took a small and circumspect sip, as if he were drinking a medicinal mixture. As he passed the gourd into Uncle Phari's hands, the old men nodded and chuckled appreciatively at their new relative, acquired through cattle that do not graze or cry *'moo-moo!'*

40

If anyone thought that the activities of the day had reached a climax and were about to wind down, he or she had mightily *missed the bird to hit faeces with the hunting stick!* Fanie was sitting lost in thought, still digesting the fact that he was now a traditionally married man, when he saw Aunt Mashadi suddenly stand up and launch into the familiar song: '*Rotwane e lebile lapeng la'bo kgarebe!*'

This song sounded like sweet honey to Fanie's ears, for it evoked in him many tender memories. He had first heard it sung by George over nine months previously, as he was on his way to meet Dimakatjo for their first lunch date. Even at that stage it had been evident to George that Fanie had been bitten by a particularly virulent lovebug. Since then the song had become a recurring theme-tune in Fanie's life.

Singing with gusto, Aunt Mashadi gyrated her hips and stamped her feet to the beat of the song, clapping her hands in rhythm. Other voices enthusiastically joined hers. The singers lined up in two rows, with men and women facing each other, leaving between them a space of about twenty metres. The soprano voices of the women sang the first part of the song: '*Rotwane e lebile . . .* ' While the male voices completed: '*. . . lapeng la'bo kgarebe!*'

The song became more and more vibrant each time it was repeated and the rhythmic handclapping, louder and louder. Older men such as Uncle Phari joined in to swell '*Rotwane*' with their deep baritones. There were now about 25 women and 20 men enthusiastically belting out the song and giving their vocal chords a strenuous work-out. The '*Rotwane*' number stirred many romantic memories of the 'good old days', when these older people were teenagers. The younger ones could only look on enviously, feeling that they had missed out on those good times enjoyed by their parents and grandparents. Most of the spectators now sang along and clapped their hands to the catchy beat.

Pacing forward to the timing of the song, Lukas stepped across to the women's row, where he pointed at a woman and drew her arm through his; he then took her back with him to the men's row, where she chose a man of her fancy and took him along to the women's row.

From the women's row, the man now chose Aunt Mashadi and took her along to the men's row, where she chose Fanie and took him to the women's row; there, Fanie, predictably, chose Dimakatjo, drawing approving applause from the exuberant spectators. Among them were the excited girls that he had earlier watched doing 'The white man's corn' game. They waved gaily to Fanie, who reciprocated.

When Fanie arrived back at the men's row, he did not let go of Dimakatjo as expected so that she could choose another man; instead, son-in-law of Bakone gyrated on the same spot, seemingly undecided, then returned with Dimakatjo to the women's row. This evoked loud cheers, applause and peals of laughter from spectators and '*Rotwane*' participants alike.

Lukas, however, leapt to intercept the rebels and returned them to the men's row, where Dimakatjo obediently chose another man.

As the uproarious '*Rotwane*' continued, Aunt Mashadi could be seen whispering to Lukas and handing him a *doek*. Lukas folded the black cloth over double, and headed for Fanie, whom he blindfolded securely, tying a handkerchief over the *doek* to ensure that Fanie couldn't see through it. Smiling goodnaturedly, Fanie went along with the game.

Aunt Mashadi then whispered to Mayibuye who lead Dimakatjo away, hiding her behind one of the cars. Aunt Mashadi sent a young woman to the house to fetch a blanket; with this, she covered the girl completely. '*Rotwane*' continued unflaggingly, without losing a fraction of its flavour or oomph. Acting on Lukas's instructions, a young man led the blanket-covered woman forward and halted her in front of blindfolded Fanie. Lukas then removed the *doek* and handkerchief from Fanie's eyes.

'*Mokgonyana*, is this the woman for whom you have parted with *lobola*?'

Fanie hesitated before answering. Sections of the '*Rotwane*' crowd intensified the fun by shouting: 'Yes! No! Yes! No-o-o!' in an effort to confuse him further.

Fanie seemed to enjoy his moment of confusion. He looked at the blanket-covered woman as if his eyes could see through the covering and accurately identify the person inside. To compound the difficulty, the woman in the blanket was of a similar height and build to Dimakatjo.

'*Mokgonyana*, is this the woman for whom you have parted with *lobola*?' asked Lukas again.

'No! Yes! No! Ye-e-s-s!' shouted the spectators ecstatically.

Fanie finally ventured to answer: 'No!'

Aunt Mashadi then uncovered the young woman and the spectators and '*Rotwane*' participants applauded loudly when they saw that Fanie had guessed right. Again Lukas blindfolded Fanie, while this time Aunt Mashadi covered Dimakatjo with the blanket. She was then brought in front of Fanie. His blindfold was taken off and he was again asked: '*Mokgonyana*, is this the woman for whom you have parted with *lobola*?'

Without hesitation Fanie nodded. Aunt Mashadi then removed the blanket from Dimakatjo and Fanie embraced and kissed the woman of his dreams, while again the crowd loudly cheered and applauded.

And, finally, it was time for the newly-weds to depart.

Aunt Mashadi came to fetch them from Dimakatjo's bedroom where they had been left alone for a short while to gather themselves for the journey ahead; to smile into each other's eyes, hug, kiss and share their joy at the fact that they were now man and wife.

'We are waiting for you two lovebirds. Come!' a beaming Aunt Mashadi said as she escorted them outside, where the crowds waited to say their farewells.

Elaborately crafted grass sitting-mats had been laid down from the house to the entrance of the *lapa*. The good-humoured traffic officers had arranged the people to form a guard of honour from there up to the gate. It was announced through the police bullhorn that the couple were now leaving for their honeymoon at the five-star Skukuza Inn in Mpumalanga Province. This was Fanie's surprise wedding present to his bride, for which he had been saving up for many months. There was jubilation and celebration from the crowd at the news, fresh cries of: '*Iu-iu-iu-iu-iuuu! Šatee! Šatee-weee! Howaa! Howaa!*' from various well-wishers drunk with exhilaration and other things.

Dimakatjo was so overwhelmed by the news that she could hardly find a word to say.

'But how will we get there, Fanie?' she asked. 'Are we driving all that way tonight?'

'Patience, my sweetie-pie,' Fanie said. 'All will be revealed!'

Hardly were the words out of his mouth when a distant vibration of '*thwaa-thwaa-thwaa-thwaa!*' attracted the attention of all.

The singers stopped singing and the cheering people stopped cheering and everybody remained still, gazing open-mouthed at the whirring object descending from the sky towards them. It was a helicopter, very similar to the one of Dimakatjo's dream. It caused much marvel and consternation among the crowd, for most of these rural villagers were seeing the iron bird for the first time in their lives.

Dimakatjo could only stare, dumbfounded, at the flying machine while Fanie stood beaming proudly beside her.

'Do you like your surprise?' he asked her.

'It can't be real! I must be dreaming again!'

'Don't you remember what I said to you that day when I was drunk with love? The day we first spoke about *lobola?*'

'You said a lot of things!'

'And one of them was: "I'll buy you a helicopter and we can fly to the moon for our honeymoon!"'

'But you were only joking!' stammered Dimakatjo. 'How did you manage this, Fanie . . . it must have cost a fortune!'

'No, it cost me nothing,' he laughed. 'Uncle Pieter arranged it all. It's his wedding present to us. The pilot is his son, Johan. He works for a private helicopter company and has done us a special favour.'

The helicopter swung low towards the *morula* tree, then made a sharp turn to the left, gradually descending lower and lower as it approached a soccer field about 100 metres away from the Machabaphala homestead. The village boys playing soccer there forgot about their game and ran for their lives.

The iron bird created a spectacular dust-cloud as it came to land in the centre of the field; it was instantly surrounded by throngs of curious people, catapulted out of their huts from all directions like *dintlhwa* – the fat, brown edible flying ants that emerge from the ground after a heavy rainfall.

Fanie, Dimakatjo and Aunt Mashadi climbed into the traffic cops' car and were whisked off to the soccer field in style, while the rest of the crowd made their way there by whatever means they could, walking, running or riding, according to their age and available mode of transport. Leading the singers, Aunt Mashadi broke into another well-known wedding song:

Mmamosetsana . . .
Šala o di bona
Tša lapa la gago
Se ile sponono!
Se ile sponono!
Agee se ile sponono!

(Girl's [bride's] mother,
Look after your family affairs
The beautiful one is gone!)

Lukas, Mayibuye and Thomas loaded the couple's luggage into the helicopter. As they were about to board, Fanie and Dimakatjo turned to wave enthusiastically at the jubilant crowd. The people waved back, cheering, ululating and singing with all the energy they could muster.

Fanie and Dimakatjo climbed into the helicopter and went to sit close to the window, from where they could look out on the crowd. The traffic officers used their bullhorn again to command the people to move away so that the helicopter could take off safely.

The rotor on the roof of the helicopter began to turn, whizzing round faster and faster, as the engine whined loudly. In no time at all the iron bird was airborne, rising steadily upwards, stirring up whirlwinds of dust to drench the awestruck spectators.

Dimakatjo's eyes panned from left to right over the multitudes of well-wishers, who were now shrinking rapidly into the distance: MmaDimakatjo, Lukas, *sangoma*-aunt, Uncle Phari, Aunt Mashadi, Grandpa, her cousins Mayibuye and Thomas, her mother-in-law Louise, sister-in-law Anna-Marie, Uncle Pieter, Selina, Women of Society in their colourful uniforms, and umpteen relatives and villagers; she waved at all of them, saving a special wave for her ten-year-old nephew, Sefako, whose tiny figure she could just make out, standing with his head craned up in wonder and his trusty catapult dangling from his neck.

Fanie's final wave was directed especially to George, who had saved the day with his wise tenacity and whose naughty advice Fanie would not forget: that when he made love to Dimakatjo he should remember to put on a cap if he wanted a baby boy, and a *doek* if he desired a girl.

High above the clouds, Fanie and Dimakatjo were able to relax at last and stretch out their tired leg muscles. The couple turned to each other, squeezed hands and exchanged smiles. They burst into carefree laughter, relishing the fact that they were alone at last. Love-struck son of Fourie leaned across his seat to lightly caress the Pearl of Bakone – the woman he craved with every muscle in his body, with his heart, liver, kidneys and pancreas gland, and the surge and groan of all his male hormones.

In just a few short hours the couple will be alone in their Skukuza Inn hotel room. There, Dimakatjo will not dream of saying to Fanie: 'Not tonight, darling!' *Aowaa!* Her body will surely be yelling: *Here I am; touch, taste and enjoy me until you crave no more – and I will do the same with you!*

Inhibition-free between *twaa*-white sheets, she is going to deliver herself up, body and soul, to the hands and mouth of Fanie. She is going to take to heart the words that her horoscope once advised: '*Plan to be more adventurous and energetic with regard to sexual intimacy.*'

This time, she will not try to resist or fight down her enraptured erotic feelings; she will not feel the need to bridle her love-making murmurs, or suppress the tender words that well up to indicate that she has totally and with every corner of her being surrendered to Fanie. *Aowaa!* Her *kuku* will be ready for his penetration. And she won't mind if he boasts in his heart that he has conquered her entirely. She won't care that he now possesses her, soul, body and bones. For she is his, and he is hers.

Let it be openly said: '*Agee!* The bulldog of the *boere* is running away with the T-bone steak of Bakone!'

Tonight, they will celebrate their union with their lusty, eager bodies – veins, livers, kidneys, pancreas glands and miscellaneous other organs and juices all roaring towards a thunderous satisfaction. The final minute will at last arrive – *palakataaa!*

And Fanie will have the joy of hearing Dimakatjo blissfully crying: '*Joo-mma-weeeee!*'

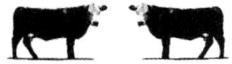

Nape 'a Motana

Glossary

Abuti Elder brother (Sepedi). Derives from Afrikaans 'ou-boetie'.

Afrika Alternate spelling of 'Africa', common to most indigenous languages in South Africa.

Agee Behold! (Sepedi)

Ag nee wat An interjection of dismay, similar to 'oh no!' (Afrikaans)

Aitsa Exclamation, equivalent to 'my word!'

AmaGent (singular, LeGent) Trendy and streetwise young gangsters who live off the proceeds of criminal activities and have a penchant for showing off with fast cars, fashionable clothes, and other flashy accessories (tsotsi-taal).

Ancestors Deceased elders, believed to be still living on in a spirit realm, who are venerated as a source of guidance, blessings and prosperity. They continue to intervene in the affairs of the living and must be regularly honoured and placated through, among other things, ceremonial slaughter.

Aowaa No; usually uttered as an emphatic exclamation (Sepedi).

Askuus tog Excuse me; please forgive me. Corruption of 'eskuus tog' (Afrikaans).

Asseblief — Please (Afrikaans).

Ausi — Contraction of 'ou sis' – 'old sister'; denotes affectionate respect (Sepedi).

Azania — Alternative name for South Africa, widely promoted during the political struggle as the real and valid name. In some circles, this is still regarded as the authentic name for South Africa.

Baas — Afrikaans for 'boss'; a respectful and servile manner of address still widely in use among many older Africans when addressing a white man, especially in Afrikaans-speaking areas.

Basie — Little or young boss (Afrikaans).

Babalase — Hangover; a corruption of the Afrikaans word 'babbelas' or 'babelaas'.

Bakkie — A small pick-up truck (SA English).

Bantu Education — A chronically inferior system of education imposed on black South Africans under apartheid.

Bapedi — The Northern Sotho people, concentrated mainly in Limpopo Province.

Bathong — Exclamation of dismay; literally, 'Oh people!' (Sepedi)

Bioscope — Cinema (SA English).

Blerry	An Afrikaans profanity, equivalent to the English 'bladdy'.
Boer	Farmer; often used disparagingly to refer to all Afrikaners (Afrikaans).
Boerewors	Traditional Afrikaans sausage.
Bo-mmaditsela	Go-betweens (Sepedi).
Broer	Brother (Afrikaans).
Burial and wedding society	(See Women of Society).
Buti	(See Abuti).
Chisa	Turn up the heat; go for it. Derived from 'chesa' (Sesotho) and 'shisa' (isiZulu) meaning 'to burn'.
Dagga	Marijuana (SA English).
Dankie	Thank you (Afrikaans).
Die taal	Literally, 'the language'; refers specifically to Afrikaans.
Di-voetsek	Colloquial name for the shoes worn by the Mokhukhu dancers of the Zion Christian Church. The term is a corruption of the Afrikaans 'voetsak' – a crude and threatening way of telling someone to go away or 'get lost'. Di-voetsek is a humourous co-option of this word, denoting the fancy footwork of the Mokhukhu dancers. (See also Manyanyatha).

Die volk	Literally, 'the people'; signifies the Afrikaans nation (Afrikaans).
Diketo	A traditional game played with small stones by young rural girls (Sepedi).
Doek	A headscarf (SA English).
Dominee	Minister of religion (Afrikaans).
Dudlu	An exclamation that shows strong appreciation for a chubby woman (isiZulu).
Dumela	Hello (Sepedi).
Eina	Ouch! (Afrikaans)
En klaar	And finished (Afrikaans).
Flaka	Colloquial name for Mamelodi, taken from 'Vlakfontein', the name of the original farm that was bought by the Pretoria municipality and on which Mamelodi was started.
Floscheim shoes	A popular brand of narrow-toed, two-tone shoes worn by township dandies and other fashionable ones.
Foie tog	Exclamation of disgust (Afrikaans).
Fokken	Fucking (Afrikaans).
Fokol	Literally, 'fuck all'; nothing (Afrikaans).
Ganya/Ganja	(See Dagga).

Gauteng Province	Formerly the PWV area (Pretoria, Witwatersrand and Vereeniging).
Hao	Exclamation of surprise, shock or disgust (Sepedi).
Hee-banna	Emphatic exclamation, equivalent to the English 'my goodness!' (Sepedi).
Hei-wena kaffir-bitch, voetsak	Literally, 'Hey you kaffer-bitch, get away' (Afrikaans).
Hoermeid	Tart or whore (Afrikaans).
Home-boy/girl	Someone who hails from the same town or region as yourself.
Hotnot	Contraction of 'Hottentot', the original colonial term for the Khoi-khoi people; a derogatory term for those of non-European origin, particularly Coloured people (Afrikaans).
Ias cap	Floppy cap made of soft, usually chequered material, favoured by gangsters; also worn as a symbol of acquired manhood by boys returning from mountain or initiation school.
isiXhosa	The language of the amaXhosa people, spoken mainly in the Eastern and Western Cape provinces.
Iu-iu-iu	Sound of ululation; similarly, 'liiuu', 'uiwui' and so on.
Ja	Yes (Afrikaans).

Jah-man	A play on the Rastafarian speech mannerisms and habit of calling on 'Jah', the Rasta God.
Jislaaik	My gosh! (Afrikaans)
Jol	A good time; also implies to sleep around (slang).
Joo-mma-wee!	Literally, 'Oh my mother!' An exclamation of pain, delight or other emotion (Sepedi).
Jou	Your (Afrikaans).
Kaffer	Kaffir; a derogatory word for people of African descent, at one time in widespread use in South Africa (Afrikaans).
Kafferboetie	Literally, 'kaffirbrother'; derogatory term assigned to those perceived to be on friendly terms with black people during apartheid (Afrikaans).
Kafferkoeke	Literally, 'kaffircakes'; a particular kind of traditional cake made from flour, water and condensed milk and baked in a coal or electric oven (Afrikaans).
Kaffermeid	Literally, 'kaffirmaid'. The derogatory term widely used for African and Coloured women during apartheid (Afrikaans).
Kak	Profanity; literally, 'crap' or 'faeces' (Afrikaans).

Kaput	Finished; exhausted (German origin).
Karateka	One who is expert at karate.
Ke mang a boditseng	A well-known number sung by Mahotella Queens and other popular choral groups during the 1960s and 70s.
Kettle drum	A large, bowl-shaped drum that produces a deep, booming sound when struck.
Kgoromente	Corruption of 'government'.
Kgoši	Chief; king (Sepedi).
Kleinbaas	Little boss (Afrikaans).
Kleinmiesies	Little missus (Afrikaans).
Kombi	A ten or fourteen-seater minibus van, often used as a licensed taxi (SA English).
Kom binne	Enter; come in! (Afrikaans)
Knobkierie	A short stick with a knobbed head, often used as a traditional weapon (SA English).
Kosher	Authentic, permissible (Yiddish).
Kraal	An enclosure for cattle, sheep and so on; a cattle pen (SA English).
Kudu	Large antelope with striped markings and majestic spiralling horns.
Kudu kudu	Very, very much (Sepedi).

Kuku	Vagina; in colloquial use mainly in Gauteng province; probably originates from the Afrikaans 'koek' meaning 'cake'.
Kwerekwere	Derogatory name given to foreigners, especially those from other parts of Afrika.
Lapa	Large cleared area of stamped earth in front of or at the centre of rural homesteads, where gatherings can take place (Sepedi).
LeGent	(See AmaGent).
Lekgowa (plural, Makgowa)	A white man (Sepedi).
Legwara-gwara	Smooth-talking conman; a heartless trickster (Sepedi).
Limpopo province	Incorporates the northern part of the former Northern Transvaal and what used to be the 'homelands' of Lebowa (Bapedi people), Gazankulu (vaTsonga), and Venda (vhaVenda).
Lobola	Traditional bride-price; formerly paid in cattle, but nowadays given as a cash payment. The lobola agreement constitutes an authentic marriage certificate in traditional culture and can be used to register the union formally at the Department of Home Affairs.
Luister	Listen (Afrikaans).
Ma	Mother (Afrikaans).

MaGents	(See AmaGent).
Magtig	An exclamation of surprise, relief or disbelief; equivalent to 'Heavens!' or 'My gosh!' (Afrikaans).
Magwinya	Fatcakes, also called 'vetkoek' in Afrikaans (Sepedi).
Mahlwa-a-di-bona	Literally, 'the one who has seen or experienced many challenging things'. In the context of love-making it refers to a sexually experienced partner (Sepedi).
Makgowa	(See Lekgowa).
Malombo	A particular South African music style introduced by acclaimed guitarist Philip Tabane in the 1960s; said to be inspired by the spirits, called 'malombo' in tshiVenda, hence the name.
Malome	Uncle (Sepedi).
Mamelodi	Township on the outskirts of Pretoria. (See Flaka).
Manyanyatha	The impeccably polished hand-stitched white leather shoes with tyre-rubber soles worn by the Mokhukhu dancers of the Zion Christian Church. (See also Di-voetsek).
Mathaithai	Trickery (Sepedi).
Matric	Now Grade 12, the final school-leaving qualification.

Matutu	Extract of; literally refers to a mother's breast milk (Sepedi).
Matutu a mabele	African beer; extract from sorghum corn (Sepedi).
Mealie	Maize; corn-on-the-cob (SA English).
Meerkat	Small Southern African mammal similar to a mongoose in appearance.
Meisie	Girl (Afrikaans).
Mevrou	Mrs; madam (Afrikaans).
Miesies	Variation of 'missus' or 'mistress'; a respectful and servile term of address for white women, still in automatic and widespread use in many areas of the country.
Mma	Mother (Sepedi).
Mmaditsela (plural, bo-mmaditsela)	A go-between (Sepedi).
Mmalo	My gosh! (Sepedi)
Mmane	Younger aunt (Sepedi).
Mmamogolo	Elder aunt (Sepedi).
Mmisisi	Sepedi version of 'miesies' or 'missus'; a white woman.
Mmulu	(See Mmalo).

Modimo o phala baloi	'God is more powerful than witches' (Sepedi proverb).
Moenie nonsens praat nie	'Don't talk nonsense' (Afrikaans).
Moer	Murder (Afrikaans).
Moerkoffie	Traditional Afrikaans ground coffee.
Mokgalo-berry	A tree with small red, edible berries, one of the Acacia species; known in Afrikaans as 'wag-'n-bietjie bos' – 'wait-a-bit tree', because of its habit of hooking you with its strong, curving thorns and delaying you while you extricate yourself.
Mokgonyana-baas	Son-in-law who is a boss (Sepedi).
Mokhukhu (plural, Mekhukhu)	a) A dance performed by some of the male members of the Zion Christian Church. b) A shack. Because of the housing backlog and the waiting list for affordable housing, many black people are still forced to live in shack settlements even though they may have jobs and be earning salaries (Sepedi).
Monna	Man (Sepedi).
Morogo	Wild spinach (Sepedi).
Morula	Also known as 'Marula'; a tree with yellow fruits which, when fermented, produce a potent alcoholic beverage.

Moruti	Reverend (Sepedi).
Morwedi'a	Daughter of (Sepedi).
Motlogolo	Niece or nephew (Sepedi).
Mountain school	Also known as 'Bush school'; a ceremonial period of seclusion on a mountain top or other remote area where young men undergo various tests of manhood, including circumcision, to mark their passage into adulthood.
Mpimpi	Informer (isiZulu).
Mpumalanga	Formerly the Eastern Transvaal.
Mullah	Money (tsotsi-taal).
Mung beans	Small, hard, dried green beans.
Muti	Medicines; herbs and concoctions used by traditional doctors and diviners for their healing power or other properties.
Nê	Not so? (Afrikaans)
Nee	No (Afrikaans).
Ngaka (plural, dingaka)	Doctor or medicine-man (Sepedi).
Ngamola	A well-off, well-to-do man, especially a business man (Sepedi).
Ngwan'a	Child of (Sepedi).

Ngwetši	Daughter-in-law (Sepedi).
Oom	Uncle (Afrikaans).
Oubaas	Literally, 'old boss' (see Baas); often used respectfully, but can also be used to refer to an old man of any race (Afrikaans).
Ouma	Grandmother (Afrikaans).
Ou maat	Old friend (Afrikaans).
Oxtail fly-whisk	Used for practical purposes to chase flies away, but also used by dingaka or traditional doctors as part of Ancestor ceremonies, rituals and so on.
Palakata	Physically, in the flesh; appearing 'just like that!' (Sepedi)
Pan African Congress	The radical political party started by Robert Sobukwe in the 1950s which subsequently became known for its uncompromising Africanist stance and anti-white sentiments.
Pap	Stiff porridge made from mealie-meal (Afrikaans).
Pasela	For free (Sepedi).
Pasop	Be careful! (Afrikaans)
Phophotha	Traditional humble clapping ritual enacted in an appeal for clemency (Sepedi).

Pinched the tail of a black mamba	Committed a fatal mistake (Sepedi proverb).
Pirate taxi	One that operates unlawfully, without being registered.
Plaas	A farm (Afrikaans).
Poepdronk	Very drunk; literally, 'fart drunk' (Afrikaans).
Poor whites	Those of a particularly low socio-economic designation; often has derogatory connotations.
Potjiekos	Traditional Afrikaans stew made in a large cast-iron pot (SA English).
Praaitjies	Corruption of 'praatjies' – 'little talks' (Afrikaans).
Rakgadi	Paternal aunt (Sepedi).
Rotwane e lebile lapeng la'bo kgarebe	'The suitor's walking-stick is pointing towards the girl's home' (Sepedi).
Rumatiki	Corruption of 'Rheumatism'.
Ruri!	Indeed! (Sepedi)
Sakkie	Little bag (Afrikaans).
Sangoma	African spirit-medium; diviner.
Šatee	Hooray! (Sepedi)

Sebara	Brother-in-law (derives from the Afrikaans 'swaer').
Sepedi	The language spoken by the Bapedi people, mainly in the Limpopo province; also called Northern Sotho, it is one of the eleven official South African languages.
Seuntjie	Little son; the diminutive form is often used affectionately in Afrikaans.
Shebeen	Tavern (Irish origin).
Sis	Short for sister.
Sjambok	A raw-hide whip (SA English).
Skattebol	Sweetheart (Afrikaans).
Skeberesh	Harlot (Sepedi).
Skelm	Rogue or thief; someone who gets up to mischief (Afrikaans).
Skinder	Gossip or slander (Afrikaans).
Skinderbekke	Those who gossip; literally, 'gossip-mouths' (Afrikaans).
S'kwerekwere	(See Kwerekwere).
Sodom and Gomorrah	Two morally degenerate cities mentioned in Genesis in the Bible, said to have been destroyed by God with fire because 'their sin was very great'.

Spaza	A small, informal backyard shop, operating from a home or portable container, generally found in townships and informal settlement areas.
Speak speaker, speak!	An encouraging interjection called out at gatherings to those who have the floor, to indicate that they are perceived to be talking sense and should continue.
Stoep	Veranda (Afrikaans).
Takkies	Tennis shoes (SA English).
Tannies	Aunties (Afrikaans).
Tata ma-millions	Literally, 'Take the millions'; one of the Lotto slogans.
Throw a piece of wood at the python	To say something meaningful during a discussion or meeting (Sepedi idiom).
Tiekie-lines	Prostitutes. Originates from the low denomination 'tiekie' or 'tickey' coins used to pay for a prostitute's services by those lining up to wait their turn with her. In the days preceeding South Africa's conversion to a Republic, the currency was British pounds, shillings and pence.
Townships	Segregated residential areas on the outskirts of cities and towns that were designated as black living areas during apartheid.

Toyi-toyi	A rhythmic chant with synchronised dance step, often accompanied by the clenched fist salute and singing of freedom songs, that was part of the anti-apartheid protest culture, especially during the 1980s.
Tsena	Enter; come in (Sepedi).
Tsotsi	Gangster or criminal (SA English).
Tsotsi-taal	Literally, 'gangster speech'; a street-wise patois comprising mainly Afrikaans, with English and some vernacular words and phrases thrown in. It has a particular 'in-group' status among young urban black males, particularly in Gauteng, and is associated with being 'city-wise'.
Tukkies	Affectionate name for University of Pretoria.
Twaa-white	Something so bright it shines.
Twak	Rubbish (Afrikaans).
Ubuntu	The isiZulu word for the culture of African humanism, that is also known as 'Botho' in Sepedi, Sesotho and Setswana.
Vat-en-sit	Slang for living together without marriage (Afrikaans).
Veldskoene	Comfortable soft shoes made from untanned leather, originally worn and popularised by Afrikaners (SA English).

Vetkoek	(See Magwinya).
Voetsek	(See Di-voetsek).
Volkstaat	Literally, 'People's state'; specifically, a state for the Afrikaner people.
Vostaan	Corruption of 'verstaan', meaning 'understand' (Afrikaans).
Wena	You (Sotho and Nguni languages).
White wedding	The term given to Western-style weddings, in which a white wedding dress is worn by the bride, as distinct from traditional marriage ceremonies involving lobola.
Women of Society	Self-help women's groups in rural and urban communities that provide financial, practical and emotional support in times of need or celebration, such as at burials, weddings, christenings and other such events.
Xhosaland	Old colonial term for territory occupied by amaXhosa people of the Eastern and Western Cape; it is still colloquially in use among certain groups today.
ZCC	Zion Christian Church; one of the oldest and largest hybrid African spiritual churches that blend traditional African forms with Christianity.